*In memory of all the helpless children
who became Eternal Angels
because a parent broke a sacred trust.
Not all victims receive right justice in our courtrooms.*

"No guilt is forgotten so long as the conscience still knows it."

Stefan Zweig,
Beware of Pity

Chapter One

Verdict Day–Early Evening

Palpable tension filled the conference room at the Newton Police Headquarters. Out of twelve jurors, eight anxiously waited for a family member or friend to come and pick them up. "What's the big deal with having our cell phones off now!" someone complained testily. Being sequestered for seven weeks had smothered any remaining sparks of excitement of being a juror on a high profile trial.

Earlier, in Trenton, NJ, extensive media presence and a sizable crowd had gathered in front of the Trenton Court House. After the verdict was announced, angry chants rose up in protest. When the trial judge debriefed them, he'd said, "I'm concerned for your safety. I've issued an order for you to be transported and released from the Sussex County Seat in Newton. I know Belvidere is closer to your homes, but we've got the same situation there."

Now, their jury liaison, Officer Edwards, entered the conference room. He glanced down at the paper in his hand. "Juror 1389."

Dorsie Renninger quickly rose from her seat. "That's me," she said. She handed him her Court ID card.

He quickly checked her details against the Jury Release Form. Satisfied they matched, he asked, "Security Name?"

"Harold Raines, brother."

"Thank you ma'am," he said. He walked over and picked up her bags. "Now, if you'll come with me."

Dorsie said nothing to the remaining jurors. She offered no warm goodbyes or the social nicety of we'll-keep-in-touch. The ordeal was over. The jury's verdict announced and officially entered into the State of New Jersey Criminal Justice Database to be retrieved at any time but never to be changed. Behind her, she heard the conference room door click shut. One thought, and one thought only, ran through her mind.

God forgive each of us for what we've done.

Left alone at the door leading to the station's vehicle bay, Dorsie reviewed what was known about her in relationship to the Tracy Ann Maddox trial. She was Juror 1389 in the court system but designated as Juror Four to the media and public. Now, she was within minutes of being officially released and able to assume her own identity and to go about her day-to-day life. She stood at the bay door counting the minutes as they went by. She glanced down the hallway. It was empty, devoid of any activity one would expect to find in a police headquarters. She concluded it was for security reasons. It eliminated the possibility of any personnel recognizing a juror and minimized the risk of a juror's name finding its way to any media source. Their names were ordered sealed by Judge Howard. Now, she was deeply grateful for that order. The interior door to the bay swung open and she quickly backed away.

"Sorry Ma'am," said Officer Edwards. "Didn't mean to startle you. You're cleared. Good to go. Bags are in the car."

Dorsie entered the vehicle bay then climbed into the passenger side of her silver Honda and thanked Officer Edwards before he closed the door.

Seconds later, Dorsie turned to her brother. "Harold, thank you. And thank God!" She slumped back in the seat with a deep exhausted sigh. "As far as I'm concerned I should never have to do jury duty again. Being hustled about, guarded and hidden makes you feel like a prisoner. Like you've done something wrong. Seven weeks!" She rummaged in her handbag and withdrew a small, well-worn maroon leather organizer then flipped it open. "Gawd, how am I ever going to catch up on things? This list…umm…I'm going to have to call Rose and thank her for helping you mind Diva and Pavarotti. Oh! What's today?" Her fingertips brushed along her forehead. "Yes…yes, of course, of course. Labor Day. Damn, I'm going to miss another Habitat Board Meeting. It's tomorrow! And I'm sure my clients have been satisfied with Brandon stepping in but I'm going to have to touch base with them anyway. Then there's . . ." She rattled on and on in an agitated stream of chatter.

Harold wasn't listening as he gave his twin sister a quick once-over. He noted her silver mane was haphazardly pinned up, her clothes were a bit rumpled and she'd lost some weight but otherwise she still appeared to be the same sister he loved dearly. She wasn't going to like it when she found out the media described her as Juror Four, an elderly, not-yet-retired businesswoman. He turned his eyes back to the road getting more and more uneasy with her non-stop recitation of things that could be labeled unimportant in lieu of what she'd just done in the last seven weeks.

He glanced over at Dorsie again. With force, or it seemed that way to him, she was scratching out items on her list. Dorsie and her lists, he thought, knowing firsthand how, to her, these were not frivolous things. In the beginning, they were the roadmaps that built their family business. How many lists had she made during the duration of the trial? He glanced over at her again. With jerking, impatient movements, she flipped back and forth between pages in her organizer. He could count on his hand the number of times he'd seen her in a state of agitation. Dorsie usually was the cool cucumber type, always in control even in the most trying circumstances. *Stay true to form, Ole Gal,* he telegraphed silently. He was absolutely certain she was going to need the protection of that cool exterior just as a law enforcement officer needed a bulletproof vest. When she reached out to turn on the radio, he brushed away her hand, "Dorsie, I don't think that's such a good idea right now."

Dorsie struggled, fighting the seat belt in order to face her brother. She could tell from his profile that his brows were furrowed, a sure sign he was worried or upset. "Harold?"

"You just don't know the whole of it. It's…its bad. The verdict, well…What can I say? Don't listen." His mouth settled into a grim, tight line.

"Judge Howard warned us. He ordered for our names not to be released for…." She waved her hand helplessly. "Right now, I just I can't remember for how long, but I'm sure it's in the juror packet they've sent us home with." She reached for the radio button again. "I saw some CNN and the Fox News reports while I was packing my stuff. After weeks of having our TV viewing monitored…" She snapped her fingers in the air. "…just like that we could watch anything we wanted. I have to hear and see it all. I have to!" She fiddled with the station seeker until she found a station at the start of a special announcement.

"Jack Roberts for NPR News reporting live from Trenton, New Jersey. It's quiet here in front of the courthouse now. Earlier in the day, in a rare judicial occurrence, a jury elected to deliberate on a holiday. Today, Labor Day, at 10: 35 a.m., the jury in the Maddox trial rendered their verdict. Tracy Ann Maddox, the young mother charged with murdering her two

year old daughter, Jenna Maddox, was found not guilty. Jenna was last seen on June 17th in 2008 with her mother. Her remains were found on November 12th in a wooded stretch of land not far from the Maddox family home. Maddox failed to report her daughter missing for 30 days and created a tangle of lies to cover up the absence. Deliberations began mid-afternoon yesterday with the jury breaking at 10 p.m. They resumed their deliberations at 8:00 a.m. on this Labor Day. Even though it's a holiday people began to gather in front of the courthouse as early as 4:00 a.m. Many had remained here throughout the night. By 7:00 a.m., the crowd had swelled to well over 300. Stunned silence followed in the initial seconds after the verdict was announced. Once the crowd grasped what had happened, outrage exploded and chants filled the air. "They Got It Wrong! Twelve Stupid People!" reverberated non-stop. The jury, in the second unanimous decision of the day, declined to meet with the news media. However, Maddox's defense attorney, Alberto Diaz, addressed..."

Dorsie kept flipping between stations. It was all the same. Public outcry. Comparison to the OJ Simpson trial. Disbelief of how justice could fail an innocent victim. Doubts that the jury hadn't taken enough time. Questions about the jury's IQ. She shut the radio off. The cold, hard reality of the public's outrage struck like an electrical jolt of a Taser gun. She struggled to breathe. Her heart began to pound rapidly. She crumpled forward, head to knees. "What have *I* done? What have *I* done!"

Alarmed, Harold pulled off the highway to the side of the road. Gently he pushed her upright. "Dorsie?" He waited for her to say something. Now, he could see she was extremely pale. He took her hands in his. They were sweaty. "Do we need to turn around and head for the E R?"

"No...no...just drive."

He pulled back onto the highway and continued on, glancing over at his sister often. Just as reported in every news clip she heard, he himself was in disbelief, had questions on how and why his sister cast a not guilty vote on all the major counts brought against Tracy Maddox. He knew his sister just as well as she knew him, the good, the bad and the ugly. Each knew the complex and bruising details of each other's lives and shared the same moral values. They both possessed abilities to be analytical; both skilled at viewing scattered information and putting it together into a cohesive whole. She had another skill, one he lacked. Dorsie was very, very good with people. She connected. That's what made her an exceptional interior designer. She listened to clients with sincere interest and paid attention to small details in their conversations then catalogued them for further use. Without a doubt, she would have listened just as intently throughout the Maddox trial. For Dorsie to vote not guilty did not fit with how her thought processes worked. He mulled it over for long minutes then concluded something major had to have happened. She seemed fine at the last family visitation day less than two days before the trial's closing arguments began. But for now, he decided he wouldn't press, wouldn't bombard her with questions or ask for explanations. He'd wait, knowing eventually she'd tell him. He reached over and took her hand in his, holding tightly, just as he always did when he knew she was scared, hurting or in need of support "'Ole Gal, you'll make it through this. It's a bump in the road."

They both remained silent for the rest of the drive home to Blairstown, a small township within Warren County. After granting Maddox's attorneys' request to have jurors picked from outside the Trenton, East-West Windsor and Princeton areas, Warren County was selected to pool the jury from. According to census information Warren County had similar education, income, age and race balances as those in Mercer County where the State vs Tracy Maddox trial was held. Blairstown was a quiet place and often referred to as "God's Country" by those who came to escape the crush of city life. Rolling hills, elite estates, up-scale housing enclaves and farmland all were within driving distance to the Delaware Water Gap and skiing venues in the Poconos. It's other notable locations included Blair Academy, a prestigious prep school, Alina Lodge, a long term drug and alcohol addiction rehab facility. And, most famous and of high interest to horror film fans, on the outskirts of town was Camp No-Be-Bo-Sco, the actual location for the first of the Friday the 13th motion pictures. Blairstown was full of good people, decent people with short-comings, quirks, opinions, worries, disappointments and joys who held fast to strong family values and community pride. Ask any of its residents and they'd tell you it was a great place to start a family, raise a family and even take your last breath, in a place with good, clean air.

"You're almost home," Harold said as they passed the Blairstown Diner and turned onto Stillwater Road. "Things will look different in the morning once you get some rest. Rose has been helping out at the shop. Everything's under con…"

Whoop. Whoop. Whoop.

"What the hell?" Harold glanced in the review mirror and saw the flashing red and blue lights of a police cruiser then immediately pulled over to the side of the road.

Dorsie twisted in her seat and looked out the back. "That's Bud Eckley. Something's wrong. I can feel it. You weren't speeding. Nothing to stop you for a traffic violation." Flustered, she ran her hand over her forehead. "Inspection sticker. Damn. I can't remember the expiration date. I shouldn't have told you to bring the Honda. I just thought it needed to be driven after sitting." She pounded her fists on her thighs. "How stupid! How stupid!"

Harold rolled down the window as Bud approached.

"Evening, Harold." He touched the brim of his cap. "Dorsie," then turned his attention back to Harold. "Mind steppin' out for a sec?"

"What's wrong?" Dorsie asked.

"Just gotta' talk with Harold, Dorsie. Won't take long."

She watched as Bud and Harold stood near the cruiser. The flashing lights had an eerie effect. Every muscle in her body tightened with tension as she saw her brother repeatedly run his hand over his bald head then quickly glance back at the van. "For Gawd sakes!" She climbed out of the van and approached them while muttering under her breath. "Tell me!" she said testily. "I know you, Harold, as well as I know myself. All that rubbing and glancing. Big signals that something's not kosher."

Bud Eckley answered for Harold. "Dorsie, I'm gonna' be goin' up before you on Stillwater and then down Ward Road," he said. "Edwards is a buddy. Gave me a heads up when you left and I've been waitin' for ya since. Now, Dorsie, this ain't gonna' be pretty. Vince Di Paolo tipped us off. At first he thought there was somethin' goin' on down at the dry-out lodge. But when them news vans stopped at your house, Vince's nose for trouble kicked in. He guessed what happened. Somehow those news vultures got ahold of your name. Cars are parked up and down the street. There's a sizable crowd and they ain't just neighbors."

Unnerved by what she'd just heard she felt as if all the air rushed from her lungs. She swayed slightly. "What? How? Judge Howard said…"

Bud took hold of her arm. "Let's get you back in the van." He gave her a minute to get settled in the seat. "Di Paolo made the suggestin' that you stop at his house. Stay until things look a little better. Since his house is the first after the turn, them news people won't be lookin' there. And I just keep goin' up Ward Road as if I'm doin' a patrol sweep." He looked to Harold. "Sounds like a mighty good plan to me, don't ya think?"

"No," Dorsie said forcefully then continued on in a weary tone, "I want to go home. I want to sleep in my own bed. Eat a meal I've made." She leaned her head against the backrest and closed her eyes. Long seconds passed as she felt burning anger rise up from her stomach into her throat. *Damn you, Tracy Maddox. How many more lives are you going to impact?* She swallowed hard. Her eyes snapped open and she stared straight ahead. "I don't have to talk to anyone. They can shout questions. Push mikes in my face. Take my picture. Do whatever they want. I don't have to talk to them," she said vehemently.

"I understand," said Bud. He threw Harold a questioning glance and when Harold responded with a nod, he said, "Ok, Dorsie. Harold, just follow me."

The drive down Ward Road seemed to happen in slow motion, all a continuous blur of colors, people, cars and sound. Dorsie sat straight in her seat, eyes focused forward with her chin slightly raised while intense tension coursed through her entire body. She never glanced right or left. Gave no indication she heard the rude shouts being directed at her. When Bud's cruiser approached her house then slowly passed it, she had a clear view of her driveway. The tension wire within snapped and unexpected hysterical laughter burst from her lips. Her hands flew to her mouth in order to squelch it. There blocking the bottom of her driveway sat Di Paolo's beefy sons. All three were sitting in lawn chairs with coolers at their sides and handing out bottles of water and sodas. A makeshift sign displayed the price – $1.75. When they spotted the Honda approaching, they swung into action, clearing the way like traffic cops, waving in Harold, giving him a non-stop route straight into the garage.

"Do you believe that?" Harold exclaimed as the garage door closed blocking out the scene outside.

"Believe what? Everything? The sight of the Di Paolos? Oh-my-Gawd, it feels sooo good to just laugh!" Dorsie gasped still trying to gain some control.

The door leading into the house from the garage swung open before Dorsie and Harold were out of the van. Vince Di Paolo stepped into the garage and opened the van's door for Dorsie. "My boys sure are somethin', aren't they?" In spite of his wide smile, his heavy drooping eyelids gave his face a sinister expression. "It was all part of da plan," he said continuing on non-stop, his Brooklyn accent getting stronger and stronger. "You needed to get in withoutta hitch. Got ya spare key from the Wilson's next door and came in by way of Norton's pasture on the ATV. Brought in supplies. Coffee, bread, eggs, milk, bottle of scotch, bottles of wine, cheese, crackers, etc., etc. Marilyn knew you'd wanna sleep in your own bed after being in lock-down in a hotel for seven weeks."

Once inside the kitchen, Dorsie turned to Vince Di Paolo and touched his arm lightly. "Thank Marilyn..."

"Jesus Christ, Dorsie. What the hell happened? Where you guys nuts? It was a slam-dunk. She did it and you guys let her go free. Why's that?" He stared hard at her, the kind of in-your-face glare.

Stunned, Dorsie took an involuntary step backwards.

"Whoa! Whoa! Take it easy, Vince,' said Harold.

"Nothing! Everything!" Dorsie shouted back. "The jury foreman . . . he . . . the others . . . they wouldn't. Diaz, he . . ." She sank into a chair. "Gawd damn it, Vince. I can't talk about it. I can't talk about it!"

Vince Di Paolo held up his hands in a backing off motion. "Sorry...sorry, Dorsie." He turned to Harold and said in an apologetic, self-effacing tone, "The wife, she's always tellin' me I violate what she calls . . ." He made quotation marks in the air. "Social etiquette."

Dorsie put her arms on the table and rested her head against them. Vince Di Paolo's questions, asked with such brutal bluntness, made her heart turn over in a sudden and sickening way. For a moment she felt as if her heart was going to stop beating. But as seconds ticked by its, rhythm remained steady, she could hear it. Tha-thump. Tha-thump. Tha-thump. Suddenly, her inner voice rose above the sound.

Not Guilty. Not Guilty. Not Guilty. Too late. Too late. Your fault. Your fault.

"What a fuckin' mess!" Harold said. "The whole town's out there."

The phone began to ring.

"Don't answer it!" Vince Di Paolo ordered. "Don't answer the phone. Don't answer the door. Or your cell. You both got caller ID, right? Christ, Harold. The whole damn town knows Dorsie was on that jury. Everyone watchin' the trial. A lot of them together down at the Inn. Not just the regulars either. Hell, the recluse Elma came outta' hiding. All of them, hangin' on every word the talkin' heads were spittin' out. Not missin' one minute of that HLN bitch." He snapped his fingers rapidly. "Nancy somethin' or other had to say. Shit, nobody believed the story -- Dorsie off in Europe. Antiques buying trip. They asked ya nothin' 'cause they knew."

Harold sat down heavily across the table from Dorsie. "I know! Old Wilbur came into the shop. Gave me a wink-wink-nudge-nudge while holding up four fingers." He glanced over at Dorsie. She still had her head buried in her arms. "Every day he came in asking for you. Didn't trust me to pick out something his wife had her eye on. Said you would know what it was but I didn't want to bother you with it. You had enough to…"

The phone began to ring again and when the answering machine picked up a reporter's urgent-sounding voice leaped from the speaker. Di Paolo yanked the phone cord and disconnected it. Harold's and Dorsie's cell phones rang simultaneously. Di Paolo shook his head and finger, warning them not to answer.

"Shut the damned things off." A progressive sound of chimes rang out from the doorbell. Harold started to rise from his chair. "Didn't ya hear me?" Di Paolo barked. He waved his hands in a sit down motion. The chimes kept sounding and sounding, repeating and repeating. Di Paolo marched to the door, unlocked it and flung it open. A hand reached out with a mike as camera lights blazed into the dark foyer. He batted the mike away. "Get the hell offa' this property. You creeps have rules," he sneered. "Follow 'em. If not, I'm gonna' kick your asses all the way down the driveway." He slammed the door shut and came back into the kitchen. He glared at Harold. "Either of ya got a gun? For protection?"

Harold glanced up at him and shook his head.

Di Paolo pulled a small semi-automatic from his windbreaker pocket then laid it on the table. "Unloaded. Point it. Scare the shit outta anybody bein' a nuisance. Got it?"

Harold closed his eyes and rubbed his hand across his mouth. "Damn it! Get that thing out of this house! This is Blairstown. Not the City."

"Get this straight in your F'in head," Di Paolo said. He picked up the gun from the table. "Blairstown shmerstown." He waved the gun with each word for emphasis. "Dorsie's name is out there. Get it? Out there! Lots of crazy people." He stopped in mid-sentence and glanced over at

Dorsie. "Dorsie, ya ok?" She was staring at the gun in his hand, shaking, arms wrapped around herself as if to hold herself together.

Dorsie felt nausea rise up and collect at the back of her throat. She rose from the chair unsteadily and lurched towards the granite counter top. She felt hot. Her vision blurred. She gripped the edge of the counter to keep herself from falling. *Deep breaths. Deep breaths,* her inner voice commanded. She took them and slowly her vision cleared but her stomach revolted. She pitched herself forward, lowered her head then vomited into the shiny stainless steel sink.

Chapter Two

Day One Post-Trial, Early Morning

The next morning Dorsie woke feeling as if someone were shaking her awake, telling her she was late. Late for what she didn't know. It took her seconds to realize she was in her own bedroom not in a room in the Westin Hotel. She lay staring at the ceiling, knowing what time it was, 5:30 a.m., give or take a minute or two. For seven weeks, six days a week, she snapped awake around the same time. In those days, she'd felt the full weight of the kind of wired-tiredness that resulted from being in a highly charged atmosphere like that of the courtroom. So, she'd relished the silence in the hotel room. The hum of the air conditioner had acted as white noise, creating an atmosphere for her to dig deep and recall the previous day's witnesses' testimonies. Never before had she given much thought, or much credit, to her ability to catalogue subtle details found in events, conversations and even body language. But, every morning when she woke at 5:30 a.m., she knew what happened in the courtroom would be another supreme test of those abilities. By eight, she was dressed, ready and waiting for the guard to rap three times on the door, letting her know it was time to gather with the other jurors in the hallway and go down as a group to the vans waiting to transport them to the Trenton Court House.

Now, there was no need to meet a schedule. She stretched her body then let out an audible groan. I feel as if I've run the New York Marathon, she thought, acutely aware of how every muscle in her sixty-two year old body ached. How are the others faring? she wondered. Did any of their names go public? Were they confronted with the same chaos she faced last night? Her thoughts ran rampant. How was her name discovered? Who would do such a thing? A court clerk? Some reporter who knew someone who knew someone in the court system? She was certain she ran every scrap of paper, envelopes, magazine covers with address labels through the shredder in the hotel room. Prescription label, she thought. No. No. She'd made sure the label was shredded to bits before she threw the empty bottle in the trash. Did she forget and throw something in the trash? No, she thought discarding the likelihood. The court guard had collected their trash, and there had to be a protocol for disposing of it. Her thoughts leaped to her fellow jurors. They never used their last names with each other no matter where they were. A family member? Had a juror slipped and mentioned names to anyone cleared for family visitation times? How? How had this happened? She had to call Judge Howard immediately. Did he know? Of course, he must know. Surely someone from the Blairstown police would have notified him. Oh Gawd, would they have known to do that? She reached for her cell while frantically thinking, did I put the number given to us in my contact list. A search on her cell showed nothing. Damn, damn. The information packet is in the kitchen or maybe still in the van. The word kitchen triggered a flash of Vince Di Paolo placing a gun on the table. She shook her head as if to dislodge the image. "Did that really happen?" she ask aloud clutching the cell phone as if it were the only real thing she was sure of at that moment.

Her thoughts continued to go on unbridled. How did I even end up on that jury? At the time when the notice arrived in the mail to appear for jury duty, it seemed like an annoyance, like a chink thrown into a schedule packed with things to be done for two big clients. Almost as if she had a photogenic memory, an image of the Jury Voir Dire Questionnaire appeared but she couldn't read it, couldn't see what was checked and what wasn't. Next she saw herself looking at Judge Howard. In her mind she was right there again listening to his instructions.

"Ladies and gentlemen, my name is Judge Marvin Howard and I will be presiding over all aspects of this trial. I'll start by giving you a brief description of what this trial is about." He went on to give the details of the charges brought by the State of New Jersey against the defendant, Ms. Tracy Ann Maddox. First Degree Murder, Second Degree Murder, Voluntary Manslaughter, Abuse, Abandonment, Cruelty and Neglect of a Child, Four Counts of Lying to Law Enforcement and Four Counts of Obstructing Justice. These charges will be explained to you fully again at the end of the trial," Judge Howard said then continued to address the jury pool. "The attorneys for the State are Mr. Gregory Ashcroft,

Ms. Susan Tyler-Burke and Mr. George Sullivan. Mr. Alberto Diaz is Ms. Maddox's lead defense attorney with Mr. Grayson Felding assisting. These are the primary men and women you will see taking center stage during the proceedings."

Absolute stillness filled the room as she and the other jurors looked towards the table where Tracy Maddox and her legal team sat.

Judge Howard continued, "You're being handed a list of potential witnesses. Please review it. I'll give you a few moments." The courtroom remained hushed except for the normal sounds found anywhere where people were trying to be quiet, a clearing of the throat, a seat creaking under the shifting of weight, the rattle of papers, and the hum of the air conditioning. "Now," said Judge Howard after minutes had passed. "I will ask by a show of hands if your answer is Yes to the following. Do you know Ms. Tracy Maddox? Do you know any of the lawyers?" He paused and looked over the potential jurors. Satisfied no hands were raised he continued, "Do you know any of the potential witnesses? Look at your fellow jurors. Do you know any of them? Two hands were raised. Sir, Ma'am you are excused. Please follow the court clerk."

All eyes followed their exit from the courtroom then turned back to Judge Howard.

"The attorneys are going to be asking you a series of questions, answer them to the best of your abilities," he instructed. "At the end of the questioning I'm going to ask you to tell me a little about yourself, what kind of employment you've had. General things." He shook his head slightly and a small smile spread across his face. "I'm even going to ask you what kind of bumper sticker you have on your car. Political ones are excluded. Also, I'm going to ask what you do in your spare time. I always like that part. Gives me ideas of what do with my spare time." he said with a hearty chuckle. He saw potential jurors expressions relax. Satisfied his tried and true statement lowered the tension level in the courtroom he said, "Mr. Diaz, we'll begin with you."

Dorsie listened intently as ten potential jurors were questioned paying very, very close attention to Alberto Diaz more than the potential juror he was questioning. During a pause in questioning of the fifth juror, she thought she heard someone whisper *Con Man* and turned in her chair to scan the faces of the others then turned back around again. *Con Man*. She heard the whisper again only this time she recognized her own inner voice, the one that surfaced every now and then from the deep recesses of her subconscious. She took note then turned her attention back to what was happening in the courtroom.

Six jurors were dismissed after three or four questions from either the defense or prosecution. Every juror was asked a different set of questions. What are they going to ask me? she wondered then heard the court clerk call "Juror Number 1389." She stood and walked to the podium.

"Good afternoon," Alberto Diaz said with Old World politeness just as he had with each potential juror. "Thank you for your time especially since it's a beautiful day outside." He paused to review his notes, lifted his head then scrutinized her for a few moments.

"Ma'am, I beg your pardon for my first question. I'm not asking because of the color of your hair. Are you retired?"

"No. I'm an active partner in a small interior design business."

"You must have to pay special attention to detail. And be flexible . . . um . . . like if someone wants a round table but you think a square one would be better . . . more in line with design theory."

"I juggle and keep track of many things when working with clients. As far as what's right or wrong from a design point, in the end it really doesn't matter. Design theory isn't meant to be fixed. It's meant to be flexible. When all furniture, fabric, wall coloring and accessories come together only one-thing matters. The homeowner will find it all comfortable. Be able to live with it day-in and day-out."

Alberto Diaz glanced toward the table where his defense team was seated. Seconds passed before he turned back to her and asked the next questions.

"Do you have a daughter? How old? And if she works, what does she do?"

"I have a daughter. She's 40 and she's a nurse. I also have a son four years older than she is."

Again Diaz glanced at his defense team.

"As a mother, I'm sure you still remember their early years. Did either of them have any problems in school or with law enforcement?"

Dorsie was taken aback by the question but answered in a firm voice. "The worse thing my son ever did was throw snowballs in the mailbox in Candlewood Lake in Connecticut. He was ten. I found out by accident when I overheard him and his buddy laughing about their prank. They got a lecture on how if anyone had caught them they could have gone to jail. I had the local Deputy Sheriff sit the boys down and explain why. After that, he was grounded for a week or two."

"I see," he said with a grin. "Boys will be boys. That kind of thing. I remember doing some crazy things myself."

Judge Marvin Howard cleared his throat loudly from the bench.

"No charges were filed?"

"No."

Abruptly Diaz changed the direction of his questioning. "Tell us what magazines you read regularly."

"Mostly ones concerning antiques, architecture and interior design," she replied then added "Handyman, National Geographic, Discovery and lots of crossword puzzle books. The skinny ones like magazines."

He followed with, "Do you read crime or detective/who-dunit novels?"

"No."

"Do you work with or do volunteer work for any organization focusing on domestic violence, rape or victims of crimes?"

"No," she answered then added, "But I am on the board of the Warren County Habitat for Humanity."

He nodded then asked several more questions that seemed inconsequential to her then said, "Thank you. I have nothing further."

George Sullivan, one of the prosecution attorneys, stood, glanced at his notes then faced Dorsie.

"We all thank you for your time," he said matter-of-factly then launched into his first and second questions. "Have you ever been exposed to the scent of dead animals or rotting flesh? Have you ever had the opportunity to take a tour of a crime laboratory?"

"No and no," she answered.

In rapid fire he continued asking multiple questions. "Do you have grandchildren? Have you known anyone you could say abused their child or neglected their child? Would you report child abuse to the proper authorities?"

"No grandchildren. I don't know any abused children. Neglect covers a broad range of circumstances. Based on life experiences, what one-person sees as neglect another may not. If I suspected child abuse, yes, I would call the proper authorities."

From the bench, Judge Howard said, "Tell us about yourself."

Now, she remembered she stated she was a widow who lived with two Bengal cats, Diva and Pavarotti, who were more demanding than any husband. From the bench, Judge Howard had let out a hearty belly laugh breaking the heavy mood in the room. "Bengal cats. Just how big are these cats?" he had asked leaning forward in his seat. After describing the breed as tabby striped cats with leopard spots, he leaned back, thought for long moments as if he had to render a decision then said, "Little cats with big egos. I've seen quite a few of those from the bench over the years."

That was when she heard Alberto Diaz give a small laugh so she glanced towards him. It was then that Tracy Maddox locked eyes with her and flashed a dazzling smile. She would forever remember it because she never saw Tracy Maddox smile like that again. She only saw that smile in pictures, the ones shown at the very end of Susan Tyler-Burke's closing argument when she emphatically pointed to the video screen in the courtroom. Images of Tracy Maddox being young, sexy and having a good time while her daughter had been missing for 30 days appeared on that large screen one after another with a brief pause between them. "Ask yourself," Susan Tyler-Burke had said. "Who would have benefitted most from Jenna's death? We believe you can see the answer there."

Now, vivid images of small, adorable, innocent Jenna Maddox asserted themselves. She gave a deep sigh and rubbed a hand over her face to blot out all the images cascading in her mind. Her cell phone vibrated in her other hand. She flipped it open and saw it was her daughter, Megan, calling. During jury questioning had she mentioned Megan was a nurse at North Carolina Children's Hospital? A nurse yes. But not that Megs was a care coordinator in the Newborn Critical Care Unit. Would that have made a difference in her being selected?

She hit the call receive button. "Megs, you're calling early or maybe I've just lost track of what shifts you're working. I know we talked every day, but my mind was elsewhere. I wasn't retaining much other than what was said or going on in the courtroom."

"It's okay," Megs said. "How are you doing? Did you sleep at all? Uncle Harold said things were pretty rough when you got home yesterday. Dave's worried. He wants to fly up there."

"No. No, Megs. There's no need. Honey, I'll let you know if I need help. I promise." She heard Megan sigh on the other end.

"Mom, I've got to ask you a question. I know it may be too soon, but Dave and I want to know. We can't stand it anymore. We have to know!"

With dread, Dorsie knew pretty much what the question was going to be. "What is it, Megs?"

"Mom! What about the cadaver dogs' alerts in the car. In the yard? You don't know this, but Dave knows those dogs. He certified them."

"Megs, I can't . . . Oh, honey, please. I just can't talk about this yet. I need time. I promise I'll sit down with all of you and explain," she said, brushing away the tears streaming down her cheeks. .

Megan heard the catch in her mother's voice. "Mom. I'm sorry. Sorry. How insensitive of me to even ask right now. You know how passionate Dave is about K-9s and their abilities. He has questions, that's all."

"I know, honey. I suppose everyone's got questions." She grabbed a tissue from the nightstand and wiped her nose. "Can we talk about this another time? It's not good for me right now."

"Sure. Sure, Mom. Please take care of yourself. Rest as much as you can. Eat healthy. Get out in the sun. You need sunlight after being cooped up inside all that time. I'll talk to you tomorrow. Remember, we can be on the next plane out."

Dorsie murmured," I know honey. I love you," then closed the cell phone and returned it to the bedside table.

She closed her eyes and burrowed her head deeper into her pillow. Talk about it. Talk about it, she thought with rising anger. *Tell us. Not guilty. What made you do that?* Over and over and over the question bombarded her mind. And Dave, her son-in-law, a K-9 trainer and partner of K-9 WD Training, what was she going to say to him? She'd gripped the arms of her chair in the jury box to keep from reacting during the entire testimony regarding the cadaver dogs used to search Tracy Maddox's car and the Maddox's backyard. When Sgt. Gussard testified to his and his dog's training and certifications, specifying K-9 WD Training, she immediately knew the possibility existed that her son-in-law might have evaluated and certified one of the two dogs. Should she have said something? Would she have been dismissed as a juror? It didn't matter now, she thought. The trial was over. Nothing mattered now. She glanced at the clock on the bedside table then stretched her arms slowing towards the ceiling trying to ease the tension in the center of her shoulder blades. As she lowered her arms, she discovered bruises on the inside of the fleshy part of her left upper arm. She sat up in the middle of the bed, turning her arm so she could see the outer portion. More bruises were there, evenly spaced in a four finger spread. She rubbed and rubbed at them as if she could rub them away as menacing images of the jury foreperson's face rushed to the forefront of her mind. To stop it she threw back the covers and swung her feet to the floor grounding herself in the now. Don't think about it, she told herself. Don't go there. Ever!

Chapter Three

Day One Post-Trial, Mid-Morning

Outside the sounds of car doors slamming caught her attention. She walked to the bedroom window and peeked through the blind slats. Several media vans were still parked across the street. Had they been there all night? she wondered with disgust. Below on the street, cameramen and reporters ran along a limo with blackout windows as it slowly pulled into the driveway and stopped. The door swung open and her son, Brandon, stepped out. He stood still for a moment then looked back towards the house. She felt as if he were gazing up at her bedroom window from behind his aviator sunglasses. Microphones were immediately thrust at him. She could see his lips moving as he waved off the reporters and strode towards the garage door. She heard it rumble open then close. She darted into the bathroom and hastily took care of necessities, pulled her long silver hair up into an old-fashioned ponytail then headed for the kitchen.

"Mom," Brandon said, spreading his arms wide waiting for Dorsie to walk into them. "You look like a ragamuffin. Tough night, uh?"

Dorsie walked into his gigantic hug, then pulled away and held her son at arm's length. "I'm sooo glad to see you. I was watching from the window. Those vans. Those reporters."

"Don't worry. We're going to take care of it. Aren't we Uncle Harold?" he said when his uncle entered the kitchen with a big yawn.

Harold nodded while rubbing his eyes and yawning. He stood before the automatic timed coffee pot, yawned again then poured three cups and handed them around.

"Rick and I mapped out a plan last night." Brandon said, referring to his longtime partner, an assistant producer for HLN in NY. "You say nothing. I'll make a statement with Uncle Harold. Rick scripted it out. He's also pulling in his markers from his contacts, trying to find out how your name got to the media." From the table Brandon picked up the press packet given to all the jurors at the end of the trial. He glanced at the answering machine. "There's probably a request already on there from Lynda Del Myra's assistant or one of the other anchors' assistants." He walked over, plugged in the phone, hit the answering machine and started deleting messages. Over his shoulder, he said, "Rick's also going to pull all the clips aired on Lynda's show regarding the entire Tracy Maddox saga. He thought you'd want to review them. Sometimes I think he knows you better than I do."

"Bless his heart," Dorsie said. "I knew so very little going into this. Just the Maddox name and something about how much a trial was going to cost NJ taxpayers."

Brandon turned around and faced his mother. "Mom, give yourself a day or two. Even a week. Rick wants me to confiscate your laptop." He imitated Rick, 'Mama D doesn't need to read all that shit. Blogs. Twitter. None of it.'"

Harold nodded his head in agreement. "So how are we going to get those media people off the street?"

"After we make a statement today, it's no comment. No comment. No comment," Brandon answered, looking over to his uncle. "I called Rose and had her meet me at your place before I came here." He nodded to the clothes draped over a chair. "Picked up your standard Brooks Brothers fare. Figured you'd want fresh duds when the cameras turn the lights on us." His tone turned serious. "Rick said you need to know there's a big downside to all this. Beyond the trial."

"And that's exactly what?" Harold ask then added, "Thanks for those," glancing towards his clothes.

"Well . . . Reporters are nosey creatures. They have our names. One of them is going to start digging around, gathering facts on all of us. Who knows what one of them will latch onto? Try to turn it into a different angle of coverage."

Dorsie groaned. "We have nothing to hide."

Harold ran his hand over his bald head. "So, they find out we're not exactly paupers. That as a family we own real estate in Tribeca. That we give to certain charities. That we built the business through hard work. That Megan and Dave are in Fuquay-Varina, NC." He paused for a breath. "That Megan is a nurse and Dave trains K-9s. That you're openly gay. That at my age, Rose is my live-in partner. That your mother doesn't live extravagantly." Harold stood and patted his nephew hard on the shoulder. "Unlike, someone I know."

"Uncle Gino," Rick said before he flipped open his cell to take a call.

"What's Gino have to do with this?" Dorsie asked in exasperation.

Harold rubbed his bald head and looked at his sister. "Shit. We know the rumors around town about Vince Di Paolo. Speculations about big connections up in North Jersey and across the river. Speculations about a Soprano-type character. Gino fits the bill. Or they'll talk to somebody in town who'll tell them who that man was that was berating reporters. That'll lead them to discovering Vince Di Paolo is married to one of Gino Carapelli's nieces. They'll wonder about his connection to us. It won't be hard for them to uncover how Gino's been a client of yours for years."

Brandon's rising voice caught their attention as he spoke to Mandy, an assistant in the NYC studio. They both looked towards him.

"I figured they'd be there too. Don't say anything," Brandon advised. "Reply, no comment. No comment. Ask them to leave the store. If they don't, call the cops." He sat down across from his mother. "Reporters. Wouldn't be surprised if a couple of them are sitting outside the shop here waiting for it to open or for you or Harold to appear." He slipped a piece of paper across the table. "Read this over. I just need to make sure you agree."

Dorsie whispered, "I'm sooo sorry." Tears brimmed at her eyelids, threatening to spill down her checks. "Sooo sorry. I had no idea how being on that jury would affect all of us."

"Mom, you have nothing to be sorry for." Brandon reached out and covered his mother's hands, wishing somehow he could make everything better, just as she had with a kiss on the top of his head when he was little. He studied her face. At sixty-two, she was still attractive. Not a line, not a crinkle on her smooth skin that hadn't been there for as long as he could remember. Her eyes, always reflecting her moods, were gray and troubled. Without the benefit of makeup, the dark, dark circles beneath them were harsh indicators of the stress she was under. "You did your civic duty. If the rest of the world doesn't agree with the verdict . . . fuck em'. Like everyone else, I have questions. But they can wait. When you're ready you'll tell us." He squeezed her hands tightly. "We love you. We'll help get you through this. Whatever it takes, we'll get it done." He held her-tear filled gaze. "We love you."

"Megs and Dave . . . the cadaver dogs . . ."

"I know, Mom. I know." Brandon let go of her hands and tapped the paper on the table. "Read. We can make any changes you want."

Two hours later, behind half-closed blinds at an upstairs window, Dorsie watched her son and her brother face reporters, microphones and cameras. She knew what their answer to reporters would be. Rick had done a thorough job of anticipating just about every conceivable question that could be asked. Later, she'd catch the news clips. She sighed as she watched Brandon. She was so proud of him. There he was standing tall, looking every bit the consummate, successful, upscale New Yorker, perfectly dressed in fashionable black, hair stylishly groomed and his signature gold chain bracelet flashing in the sunlight. Genetics gave him the same physical appearance as his father. But his father had been more comfortable in hardhat, jeans, work shirts and boots with a well-worn tool belt around his waist.

What about Ann and Nick Maddox? she wondered. Were they proud parents once? Now, today, what were they feeling? When the verdict was announced, a natural reaction would have been for them to collapse into each other's arms in relief. But they didn't. And what about Tommy Maddox, what had he felt? How heartbreaking it had been to see him breakdown on the witness stand telling how his sister was a habitual liar. How he had tried to tell his mother his sister needed professional help only to be told to mind his own business. How wrong of Ann Maddox to do that. Was the portrait of her family in her mind so perfect, so immune to life's erratic happenings that she couldn't see the picture-perfect-life was only a false image? Other members of the jury had been put off by Nick Maddox. But she had been put off by Ann Maddox in spite of the emotionally draining testimony on the stand regarding the 911 call. Oh, she felt for Ann Maddox. But how could she so brazenly lie on the stand even when evidence presented clearly showed she was committing perjury? Would she lie for Megs or Brandon if their life depended on it? For long, long, moments she pondered the question trying to place herself in scenarios where her children had done a horrendous wrong and were about to be punished severely for it. If one of them had caused an accident where a death occurred, would she want to see them put in prison?

Or if one of Dave's dogs went rogue and killed a child, would she want Dave to be locked away?

Her thoughts remained locked on Ann Maddox. Surely, Tracy Maddox's brazen, elaborate fabrications didn't just start overnight. Tracy was an individual who had honed lying to a craft, a lifestyle choice. But still, what kind of parenting skills did Ann Maddox lack? What caused her never to seek help for her daughter in spite of the warning signs that would have sent another parent into a something's-definitely-wrong-mode? Could Ann Maddox even conceive that her daughter was responsible for her granddaughter's death? How could Ann Maddox agree to let Diaz throw her husband and son under the bus with such dramatic, salacious allegations? Oh yes! Diaz had zeroed in on the mother lode of emotional hot buttons, she thought. Mention molestation of a daughter by a father and the mind reacts with revulsion in both women and men. That was the beginning of the con. More politely called legal strategy to throw doubt into everyone's minds.

Dorsie heaved a heavy sigh, exhausted from the way her runaway thoughts kept intruding into the here and now. She gave a slight unconscious shake of her head in an effort to dislodge them but they remained dominant. Suddenly hot, searing anger engulfed her. Diaz's con worked! Tracy Maddox was free to strut, flash her dazzling smile and live the good life. It was wrong, wrong, wrong. We all should be damned, she thought bitterly. We're all guilty. Ann Maddox. Nick Maddox. She, Dorsie Raines-Renninger, was guilty too. We'll all have to atone, she thought. Karma will see to it.

Pounding on the back kitchen door jarred her out of thoughts. She started for the kitchen then heard Vince Di Paolo's voice mixed in with Brandon's and Harold's.

"Feelin' better?" Di Paolo asked when Dorsie entered the kitchen. He motioned towards the table. "Ziti, lasagna, Italian wedding soup. Marilyn said to freeze it." He tapped an aluminum-foiled dish. "Christ, she was up all night cookin' as if the whole family was comin' for Sunday supper. She does that when she's upset."

"I'll call and thank her," Dorsie said reaching for the phone.

"No. Don't do that," Di Paolo commanded, placing his hand on Dorsie's. "Let her be . . . for now."

Dorsie raised her eyebrows in question. It went unanswered.

23

"Look, I went out this morning to do a little intel. Get a feel for things." He glanced from Brandon to Harold then faced Dorsie head-on. "Dorsie, ya gotta' lay low. Town's not in a forgivin' mood right now. At the Inn last night and this morning down at the diner everyone's speculatin'." He spread his hands in a helpless almost apologetic gesture. "Wantin' to know how one of their own could let a baby killer go free. Stay outta sight. Things will cool down."

Dorsie started to pace back and forth from kitchen to hallway then back. Di Paolo stopped her on the third round. He pressed a business card in her hand. "Friend of mine owes me," he said. "He'll be over to install a security system tomorrow morning."

"What?" Dorsie sputtered. "Gawd, Vince, I've never felt unsafe here."

He gave a half smile in wry amusement. "Things go on in small towns you wouldn't believe. We have gossipy old maids. Police scanner listeners. Heavy whiskey-drinkin' hunters with guns. Some riffraff." He paused and the amused smile vanished. "Better to be safe than sorry. Your situation. It's changed. Your name. Address. It's out there for any wacko to get a hold of."

"You're scaring me, Vince."

Di Paolo put his arm around Dorsie and pulled her close in a friend-to-friend way. "Let my guy install the security system. Ain't gonna' cost ya nothin'. No harm in that. Am I right? Or am I right," he said glancing over at Brandon and Harold. They both nodded in agreement. "Now, got another suggestion you ain't gonna' like. Havin' had experience with such and such, my advice – get out of Jersey. Go someplace. Let all this Maddox trial craziness cool down. I gotta' place down in Florida. Nothin' fancy. Quiet. Someplace where nobody's gonna' recognize your name. Think about it. You look like you need some sun."

She shook her head several times. "I want to be in my own comfortable house. I want to relax in my own chair. Listen to soothing music. Hear the cats purring or meowing." She put her hand on her forehead. "Oh! I haven't even thought about them. They probably won't know who I am now. They're ok, aren't they?" She turned to Harold seeking an answer. He nodded his head slowly several times. "Could you and Brandon go get Diva and Pavarotti and bring them home?" She walked out of the kitchen into the living room and stood before the large window. She peered through the blind's louvers. The media vans were gone. "It looks safe now," she said returning to the kitchen.

Di Paolo nodded at Brandon and Harold. "Stayin' 'til ya get back." He turned to Dorise and handed her a business card. "My private cell. Call it anytime." He turned it over to show her a number written on the back. "Gino Jr.'s emergency number. If ya can't get me right away. Call Gino Jr. Anything outta' place or hinky around the house call 911. Then me. I can get here faster than the police. If anybody threatens you, call me."

Dorsie stared at the card then met Di Paolo's eyes. "Vince, now you're really scaring me. It can't be that bad."

"Dorsie, you ain't got it yet. The Maddox trial went nationwide. Global. Look when the old man," he said then checked himself. "When Uncle Gino tells me make sure nothin' happens to you, I take it serious. I do what Uncle Gino says." He spread his hands. "You know how it is. He's always had a soft spot for you, Brandon and Megan. Considers you family."

She sighed and patted Vince Di Paolo on the arm knowing the loyalty Gino Carapelli commanded.

Minutes went by as the past intruded on the present. She found herself remembering how she came to know Gino Carapelli. Back in the seventies when she, Harold and her new husband, Steve, were first starting out they knew the wasteland of empty commercial space in Tribeca was opportunity knocking. Somehow between inheritances and loans they had cobbled enough money together to buy a small building and set about renovating it with their own sweat. Dorsie's Design and Renninger's Renovations came into being in those gutted spaces. Word on the street got around. As soon as one loft was finished, it was snapped up before a listing appeared in the real estate section of any paper. A young, full of himself, Gino Carapelli was among their first buyers. He still owned the space and through the years sons, daughters, nieces and nephews, any number of extended family members inhabited it for short or long periods of time. Every few years or so, Uncle Gino would hire her to redo and update the whole place. When Gino Jr. finally decided to tie the knot, as a wedding gift, Uncle Gino had her gut a more than modest property he owned in Westchester County. She was to bring it up to his new daughter-in-law's New Millennium standards. In many ways, she too owed Uncle Gino a sense of loyalty. Way back, when she'd been strug-gling after Steve's unexpected death, Gino Carapelli, through his quiet influence, had helped launch her into the cutthroat NYC interior design scene.

She patted Vince Di Paolo's arm again. "Ok. I'll take your advice about the security system. Thank you. But I'm staying right here. Thank Uncle Gino for being concerned. "Just tell him . . ." She paused then said with a catch in her voice. "Tell him to take care of himself instead of worrying about me."

"Uncle Gino's no old fool." Di Paolo said quietly then added, "If he's worried, you pay attention."

Di Paolo's cell rang. He glanced down at the caller ID. "Gotta' take this." He walked out of earshot of Dorsie. He listened intently then growled, "Son-of-a bitch! I'll be right there. No . . . No I agree. At least for right now," he said turning to look at Dorsie who was staring out the kitchen window." He flipped the phone shut, approached Dorsie, put his large hands on her shoulders in a friendly manner and turned her around. "Dorsie, I gotta' leave. Don't answer the door. Phone. Only if it's Bran-don, Harold or me. Stay inside."

"But I need to get out there." She pointed out the kitchen window. "Look at my garden. It needs attention. It seems as if the landscapers did a good job while I was away. But oh, those sunflowers are drooping too much. And the zinnias. I thought I'd . . ."

"Just listen, will ya. Stay inside. Wait 'til Brandon's back." He gave her a little shake. "You gotta' promise me. Swear it on Uncle Gino's name."

"Why? What's happened?"

"Trust me," Vince Di Paolo said then left by the back kitchen door.

Chapter Four

Day One Post-Trial, Mid-Afternoon

Vince Di Paolo ignored the speed limits as he drove down CR 521 then onto Route 94 heading for *Dorsie's Antiques and Design*. It took him fifteen minutes to get there. The shop was in the center of a semicircle of upscale boutiques. Each shop was connected to the next. The Coffee Bin was at one end. It was a bistro in the true sense and a gathering spot that served steaming strong coffee, café au laits, croissants and baked-on-the-premises pastries. Everyone in town knew to come early because by twelve noon very little was left except the gourmet cheeses and bins of coffee beans. At the opposite end was Creative Hands, a pottery shop that featured handcrafted pottery and hosted classes for country weekend packages offered by the B&B across the highway. Butting up against *Dorsie's Antiques and Design* on each side were Gram's Quilts and Chasing The Seasons, an eclectic boutique known for its gift-for-anyone-for-any-occasion merchandise.

Now, in front of *Dorsie's Antiques and Design*, patrol cars and vans were parked with doors open, radios sqawking and lights flashing. A small band of people had gathered in front of The Coffee Bin taking in all the activity. Vince bounded up the steps, got stopped by an officer but managed to crane his neck over the crime scene tape at the door and get a look inside the shop. "Jesus Christ," he gasped turning one way then the other taking in the graffiti on the walls. Antique chairs were overturned their cushion slit open. Small tables toppled. Their aged wood patinas were smeared with neon paint. Smashed crystal, plates and vases littered the floor. Old mirrors in old frames had been shattered. Every painting in the shop had been old slit from corner to corner. Doors were ripped off a large breakfront and its gleaming wood gouged and splintered.

Inside, Harold turned from the detective on the scene and hurried toward Di Paolo. "I must have forgotten to set the alarm." He rubbed his hand over his bald head. "Too much in a hurry to go over to New-ton to get Dorsie yesterday." He glanced towards the shop's large front window. "At least they left that intact. They didn't get to the office upstairs."

Blairstown's Criminal Investigative Division was already processing the scene for evidence and taking photos. Detective Eugene Farino motioned Harold toward where he and Brandon were standing but Di Paolo mistook the cue and followed as well.

"Vince," he said giving Di Paolo a less than welcoming nod, not pleased to see him there. He glanced at Brandon and Harold.

"You can talk in front of Vince. He's like family."

Farino raised a surprised eyebrow. "As I said earlier, based on pri-mary findings this was no random act of vandalism. I'd say it was specifically targeted based on experience and gut instincts. Especially since Dorsie's name hit the media. Headquarters notified Trenton and Howard's office last night about the media frenzy. Someone's updating his office on this newest development as we speak. He may decide to get the top cops in on it too," he added, referring to the New Jersey State Police. "Have you told Dorsie yet?" Harold shook his head. "We're going to need to fingerprint her. Her prints, like yours, Harold, are probably all over this place. I doubt we're going to pick up on anything since the public is in and out of here. Busy Labor Day weekend busi-ness? Lots of guests over at the B&B?

"Relatively busy here," Harold replied. "Can't say how many guests are over there." He paused and glanced around the wrecked shop. "I just can't remember about the alarm."

Detective Farino grasped Harold's shoulder firmly. "Harold, don't beat yourself up. Whoever did this was determined. We'll be patrolling Dorsie's street with a frequency the neighbors are bound to notice. Your's too. But now, you can help us out by starting to look over the place, see what's missing."

Harold turned to Brandon. "Maybe you should go back to the house. I hate to leave it up to you to break this to your mother, but right now I think my place is here." His shoulders slumped. "Brandon, it goes without saying, make sure the NY store is on high alert. Maybe we need to talk to Dave about getting a dog. He sighed. "How could two cats have stopped this? Go. Take Diva and Pavarotti home."

"Sure . . . Sure. Uncle Harold." Brandon put his arm affectionately around his uncle. "I'm a phone call away. Don't worry. I'll take care of mom. You want Rose to come out here?"

Harold shook his head. "Nope. Let's keep this in the family. No sense frightening her too. I'm glad Vince convinced your mother to let him put in that alarm." He glanced around the many moving bodies in the shop and not finding Vince Di Paolo, he looked out of the still intact window to the parking lot. Di Paolo was there, phone to ear, gesturing with his arm like a madman.

Brandon carried the cats' carriers to his mother's Honda and settled them in the back seat. Vince walked over to him and pointed to the sky. "See that. Vultures. News choppers. Here too quick." He patted Brandon on the back as they walked to the driver's side door of the Honda. "Tell you mother I'm on this. Not to worry. You too. Got the shop in Tribeca covered. Gino Jr. will reach out to the precinct. Call in favors. Extra police drive-bys otta' do it." He closed the door after Brandon got in and glanced in the back. "Good thing nothin' happened to those cats. Would've broken your mother's heart."

"Amen," Brandon said then started the Honda. "Take care Vince. And thanks. Appreciate what you're doing."

Brandon drove onto Route 94 almost as if he were on autopilot, mentally blocking out Diva and Pavarotti's mewing coming from the back seat. He felt heartsick for his uncle. Hell, he thought, uncle didn't describe what Harold meant to him. Father would be a better word. After his dad's accidental death, he had clung to Harold as if his uncle could save him from emotions he had no words for. Uncle Harold was his rock, his go-to person, tell-him-anything person. At twenty he came out-of-the-closet to Uncle Harold before anyone else. His uncle hadn't blinked an eye or flinched. He'd just encircled him in a hug filled with nothing but love then made sure he had exposure to successful gay men to serve as role models – colleagues of his at Sotheby, men who worked in or supported the cultural arts in NYC and men who had helped build and bring Tribeca into what it was today. Uncle Harold's unconditional love, along with his mother's and sister's, were the cornerstones of what made him who he was today.

Now, a big blow had been delivered to his uncle. Most thought *Dorsie's Antiques and Design* were his mother's love. Not so. Once he'd ask why "*Dorsie's Antiques*" and Uncle Harold had replied, "Name recognition. Dorsie you remember. Harold is a name you forget." Harold was the brains behind the name, the antiques man with expertise taken from a love of all things old and his career at Sotheby as an antiques appraiser. Brandon could remember spending many behind-the-scene hours with his uncle at Sotheby absorbing it all, the smells, learning about how pieces were researched then authenticated for sale at auction. His uncle's love of antiques and his mother's talent for using them in design were in his genes. Ten years ago, Uncle Harold turned over the management of the Tribeca studio and appraisal consultancy to him. Now, Harold only ventured into the city when absolutely needed, unlike his mother, who still was in demand as an interior designer.

His mother, Brandon thought. This turn of events, the trashing of the shop, would it push her over the edge? He knew being alone in the house would drive her straight to the TV. She was probably already surfing through news channels, TV tell-alls and talk shows, searching out every bit of information she could on the Tracy Maddox trial. He didn't know if he himself could stand up to the criticism being aimed at the jury. He now wished Rick wouldn't send her HLN's pre-trial clips. Once she saw and digested all the coverage leading up to the trial, along with each day's analysis of the courtroom proceedings, what she thought had happened to Jenna Maddox would be forever altered. He knew his mother well. She was strong. Was known for facing all kinds of problems with calm resilience. But he wasn't sure about this current situation because he knew she had a conscience. With certainty he knew his mother would be facing a formidable battle with that very same conscience once she had benefit of many facts never aired in the courtroom due to legal rules of law. He gave a deep sigh. Whatever had possessed her to cast a not guilty vote? He turned into the driveway. Punched the garage door opener then pulled in. He retrieved Diva and Pavarotti from the back seat then stood before the door leading into the kitchen, bracing himself for what he was about to tell his mother.

Inside, in the family room Dorsie sat on the edge of sofa leaning towards the TV listening intently to Channel 6 news.

"In yet another shocking twist surrounding the Tracy Maddox trial. Fox News has just learned through an unnamed source the name of one juror. The juror designated as Juror Four to the public is Dorsie Renninger, a Board Member of Habitat of Humanity in Warren County . . ."

Dorsie gasped when her picture was flashed up on the screen. She recognized it as the one in the Habitat's current brochure.

"Earlier, our reporter had a chance to speak with her son, Brandon Renninger, and her brother, Harold Raines. Both Raines and the Renningers are well known in Tribeca with an antique and design studio on Franklin Street and a shop in Blairstown, New Jersey.

Dorsie watched the clip run of Brandon's statement.

"Tell us how your mother is doing? What are her thoughts on the public outcry over the verdict? Did she tell either of you what went on in the Jury Room? How did they arrive at a decision in such a limited amount of time? What were the deciding factors?

She watched Brandon ignore the questions then give a nod to Harold before turning towards the cameras and microphones.

"It's unfortunate that my mother's name has been released to the media. Judge Marvin Howard, in Trenton, has been advised and will be making inquiries as to how this occurred. We ask your cooperation in respecting her privacy as well as the privacy of her neighbors. She has the press packet that was given to all jurors. If she chooses to make a statement, she will use the contact names and numbers given there. Right now she wishes not to speak with any media outlet. After being away from home for seven weeks, she needs time to regroup but importantly she needs rest. Again, we ask that you respect her privacy. At this time we have no further comments."

A report's voice shouted out. *"How's it feel to have such a stupid mother and sister?"*

Harold glared at the pack of reporters *"I'll answer the question directly to the person who asked it? Please raise your hand and move forward."*

The cameras turned on a skinny, scruffy reporter with jumble of cameras hanging from his neck. He jockeyed his way to the front of the group as the other reporters fell silent with microphones thrust forward waiting for Harold to answer.

"Sir, I do not have a stupid sister. What I have before me is a reporter lacking in manners as well as a limited vocabulary. Good luck with your career."

The clip ended showing Brandon and Harold walking up the driveway.

Dorsie flipped to another channel, MSNBC, airing a montage of clips showing reactions to the verdict in Times Square, the gasps of people clustered around TVs in an upscale eatery in San Francisco, the disbelief on faces in a pub in London and a close-up of tears streaming down the face of a mother with a toddler on her hip standing before TVs in Best Buys in Columbus, Ohio.

She switched to CNN's Headline News channel.

"We have Marcia Clark, the prosecuting attorney on the O.J. Simpson trial. Marcia, give us your thoughts on the verdict.

"Well, Vinnie, when jurors are forced to spend day and night with each other, they become a tribe unto themselves. Because they have only each other for company, and because most people prefer harmony to discord, there's a natural desire to cooperate with each other. Psychological studies bear this out. A group kept together for any length of time becomes more and more alike, in sync. They avoid contentiousness and seek harmony. Serious, thoughtful, careful deliberation produces contentiousness and conflict. Also, since it's a group decision, some jury members may not feel that responsible their duties. They just go along with the others. These jurors were inclined to acquit from the very first vote . . ."

Dorsie changed to yet another channel.

"The court of public opinion made up its mind about the guilt or inno-cence of Tracy Maddox long ago. The closing arguments took eleven and a half hours. The jury rendered a not guilty verdict after less than 12 hours of deliberations. They had no questions for the judge and did not request testimony transcripts for review. We have a panel to help us understand what went wrong . . ."

Brandon stood in the doorway to the family room studying his mother. The TVs light cast an eerie glow on the shiny wetness on her face as violent sobs wracked her body. She was on an emotional razor's edge. He felt helpless and the only thing he could think of to do was to release Diva and Pavarotti from their carriers. He bent down and opened the doors. The cats made a beeline for his mother, mewing and mewing, snaking around her ankles before jumping up on the sofa. As he watched the scene unfold, he doubted that even her two beloved cats could pro-vide the level of comfort she needed. He walked into the room, sat next to her, removed the remote from her hand and clicked the off button. He held his mother in his arms. She buried her head in his shoulder while

Diva and Pavarotti mewed and showered her with love-rubs. He waited patiently for the sobs to stop. He had no idea how his mother was going to react when he told her about *Dorsie's Antiques and Design* getting trashed. His stomach churned. He took a deep breath.

"Mom, brace yourself." She lifted her head and looked into his face. He wiped her tears away. From somewhere she produced tissues and did a more thorough job. He took another deep breath and just spit it out, told it like was. "The shop has been vandalized. Uncle Harold's there with the police and a detective. They don't think it was random but targeted. They'll want you to go down to the station to be finger printed so they can catalogue them as prints belonging to known people."

Dorsie stared at Brandon uncomprehending for a moment. "What!" she gasped. Blood drained from her face turning it deathly pale. Pent up emotions spilled out. "It's my fault," she choked. "Damn. Damn. Damn Tracy Maddox to hell." Her voice rose to a high pitch. "Damn the rest of the jury for being seduced into Diaz's con. Damn whoever released my name. Damn Eric . . . I should have . . ."

Brandon grasped his mother by her arms and shook her. "Look at me," he said sternly. "You are not responsible for other people's actions. Isn't that what you always taught us? You have no control over what others do, only yourself. None of this is your fault." He stared into her eyes. He didn't like what he saw. "I think we need to call Megs and Dave. We need a family conference call. I also think Megs should come up and stay with you for a while. Sound like a plan?" he coaxed. "I've got to get back to the city tomorrow. Uncle Harold's going to be busy. Police Reports. Inventory. Inventory Values, Insurance Claims. Clean up . . ."

Dorsie slumped back against the cushions, closed her eyes and fought for control of her emotions. When she felt she had them in her grip, she said "Maybe Harold needs us there now. Oh, poor, poor Harold. How he loves that shop. I never understood why, but he loves it. He calls the Franklin St. studio Chic-ville and the one here Simplicity. He hates to part with anything in there. It's like he's losing a friend when a piece gets sold. How bad is it?"

Brandon glanced over at his mother's profile unsettled by the calmness of her voice. Since they were sitting so close their arms touched and he could feel her trembling. Pavarotti jumped up into his mother's lap purring loudly and he hoped it would have a soothing effect on her. "Total loss from what I could see," he finally said.

She continued on totally unaware she was shaking uncontrollably. "Harold's world just fell apart, you know that don't you? I'm a prisoner in my own house. Hated by people I don't even know. Karma . . . for what I didn't . . ." she said as her voice trailed off not finishing the sentence.

The garage door rumbled open then rumbled shut. Neither she nor Brandon moved from the sofa knowing Harold was the only other person with an opener. Seconds later he appeared in the doorway. "I forgot to give you the cat food and litter. I've sent Rose over to Stroudsburg to stay with her sister until things settle down." He sat down heavily next to Dorsie on the sofa. "Brandon, how 'bout pouring us a couple of stiff drinks." Harold reached over and took his sister's hand in his. "Don't you go thinking this is your fault, Ole Gal."

"Hard not to."

Harold leaned his head back against the sofa cushions silently vowing he would never tell Dorsie of the note found in the shop with its crudely cut out words from newspaper headlines – *Juror #1389. Dorsie Renninger. Stupid bitch. You're going to get yours. Watch your back.* Even after all this was over, he would never tell her what the note said. At the shop, Detective Farino had asked him to keep the note's content to himself, pointing out the significance of the words "Juror 1389". Farino had explained how only a limited number of people would have had access to or knew that particular piece of information. He squeezed Dorsie's hand and felt her grip on his tighten.

Brandon paused in the doorway with a tray of drinks. His mother and his uncle seemed to be asleep, heads resting back on the sofa's soft cushions, their hands clasped together. Their chests rose and fell in unison with each breath. As he studied them he realized he'd never given much thought to the fact they were twins. But now, viewing them, their profiles seemed as one. Age had not erased their almost identical features. And, it always amazed him that the contrasting feature between them was Harold's baldness and his mother's flowing hair now turned beautiful silver. He stood in the doorway hesitating, wondering whether he was going to break the spell of one twin comforting the other in some deeply symbiotic way.

Chapter Five

Day Two Post-Trial

The next day, mid-morning, Dorsie, Brandon and Harold sat at the kitchen table waiting to place a call to Megan at a pre-arranged time. Once connected with Megan, Brandon conferenced in her husband Dave.

"Megs, Mom and Uncle Harold are here with me. We've got a bit of a crisis going on. As you probably know from Dave, the shop has been vandalized and Mom's name is out there pinned directly to the Maddox trial."

"I saw the clip of you and Uncle Harold. They're running it on HLN and oh, boy, you don't want to know what Nancy Grace's comments were." Megs said. "What a mess. Mom, how are you holding up?"

"I've had better days," Dorsie answered. "Brandon wants you to come up and stay with me. I've protested. I know how busy you are. Frankly, I don't need babysitting."

Megs interrupted. "It's not babysitting, Mom. We just want to be cautious. Dave and I discussed it last night." She paused and cleared her throat. "Mom, you know I'd come if I could. It's just that right now I'm the care coordinator for the team taking care of preemie quads born a few days ago."

Dave's baritone voice with it heavy Southern drawl came through the speaker. "Arrangements are bein' made. Will be there early evenin' if the weather is cooperatin'. Dorsie, hush what's 'bout to come from ya lips. Don't wanna' hear a word. It's all settled. We've got a trainin' session comin' up in Montgomeryville over in Pennsylvania. That's as the crow flies from you. Can do the upfront prep work right now. Me and Thor are comin'. Better warn those pansy cats of yours. Thor's comin' to take over their territory."

"Megs, honey, you worry about those babies, not me," Dorsie said. "Dave, Thor. That's quite a name."

"Yep. He's just 'bout ready to be certified for protection detail. Will be goin' to D.C. To a foreign diplomat with a gaggle of 'lil ones. Bein' up there with you will give him some transitionin' time. Act as a deterrent to any hostile . . ."

"So, now you all think I need a protection dog. Don't you think we're getting a little overdramatized here?"

"No ma'am. It's an opportunity. Thor's attuned . . . aw . . . attached to me, his trainer and Megs. Had him since he was a pup. He needs a transition phase. He's also gotta' complete another educational program with kids. Already talked with Warren Regional High School. They're a go. Just some school policy details to work out."

"Excellent!" Harold chimed in. "The last exhibition you did for the middle school was a hit. Town talked about it for weeks. The students. They just ate it up. Wanted to start a fund-raising drive to buy a K-9 for our police department."

"Dave, what airport, so I can arrange a car." Brandon interjected to keep the conversation on point.

"Aw shucks, Brandon, cars are for city boys," Dave drawled in his best Southern accent. "Coming into ABE. Private plane. Thor's no stranger to limos. Jeeps and pick-ups are more to his likin'."

"Okay. Good. Now, we've got Mom covered," Brandon said, glancing over at her. "Megs, Mom's here frowning big-time. Any last words?" he asked.

"Mom. We understand why you want to be home. We really do," Megs said in a tone she used with frightened, distraught new parents. "But you have to be realistic. Now is not the time to be fiercely independent and alone. We all love you. Maybe we're overreacting but we want you to be safe." She paused for a breath then concluded. "Besides, with Dave and Thor there, you'll be able to get out of the house. Thor's very energetic. Needs lots of exercise and walking. You'll be a good transition person for Thor before he moves on to his assignment in D.C."

Dorsie dropped her chin to her chest in resignation. "Well, I certainly can tell I've been out-voted. And of all things, I'm now being sequestered by my own family. As if being holed up in a hotel room for seven weeks wasn't enough along with guards, bailiffs, escorts keeping a watchful eye. So here I am again being assigned to another guard detail," she grumbled then added with sincerity, "Dave, you and Thor can be here for as long as you want."

The front door chimes sounded.

"Alarm guy is here. Dave, I've got to get back to the City, so I'll miss seeing you. I'm leaving mom in your good care. Megs, love ya. Talk with you in a day or so."

From that point on the house was full of activity. Vince Di Paolo ushered in and introduced the security alarm technician who went from room to room doing his assessment. Brandon, Harold and Di Paolo huddled in the backyard deep in conversation as if they were avoiding eavesdropping technology. Much later, the technician gave them instructions on how to operate the alarm system, leaving a detailed instruction booklet then climbed in his van and drove off. At four in the afternoon the house fell silent. Di Paolo departed. Brandon and Harold made a list of things needed to be stocked in the house and headed for the hardware store, A&P and liquor store.

Dorsie sat in her favorite winged back chair in the living room and took a deep breath. Behind her eyes she could feel a monstrous headache building but felt too exhausted to get up and take something for it. Peace and quiet, she thought. That's all I want. Quiet. To be alone. After seven weeks of being in close proximity to the other jurors in the jury box, not to mention the packed courtroom, all she wanted was private space and to be outside in sunshine and fresh air or walk down the road and thank Marilyn Di Paolo for the wonderful food she'd sent over. She wanted time to relax in her own way. Get up when she wanted. Eat when hungry not on some pre-arranged schedule. She didn't want to get dressed or put on makeup. Or worse, be polite because that's what you do when you're among strangers. Damn, she thought, I just want to be grumpy. I deserve to be grumpy. I need to decompress in my own time in my own way. Watch what I want on TV and catch up with all the news.

Dorsie sighed in resignation. Now, Dave would be here. Not that she didn't love him; adore him for his brawn and down-home Southern Boy characteristics. But he wasn't coming alone. She certainly would have preferred Megs at his side not a German Shepherd. Oh, my, she thought, Diva and Pavarotti definitely weren't going to like this unexpected invasion any more than she did. Her son-in-law was high energy, and at times could be military spit and polish. He'd be filling the house with his overflowing energy. She wanted couch-potato laziness.

Dave and Megs, she thought, two people with surpluses of energy. When she first met Dave, she immediately saw his resemblance to Garth Brooks but not with country music stage presence. On closer inspection she found the telltale signs of a military man. Her impression was on target; Dave trained and handled working dogs in preparation for their Department of Army Certification. During his service then after his marriage to Megs, as a civilian contractor, he'd been deployed to Iran and Afghanistan as well as missions involving top U.S. leaders and foreign dignitaries. In spite of his go-where-needed attitude, she'd always cast him as a father of a large brood. But that didn't seem to be the case. After traveling down the roads of various infertility options, Megs and Dave stopped and accepted their circumstances. She would never be a grandmother, not unless Megs and Dave decided to adopt. The preemies in the NICU were the ones who received all of Megs's motherly care. Dave released fatherly instincts with firm but gentle handling of all the dogs he trained.

Suddenly, she felt deep, deep sadness. Not for herself but for Ann, Nick and Tommy Maddox. To have the adorable Jenna in their lives then have her taken from them in such a brutal way. Disgust rose like bile in her throat. Didn't Tracy Maddox know there were people out there with such deep longing for a child that could never be? Tracy just threw Jenna away in a trash bag in a place where . . .

Dorsie stopped her thoughts from going further, not wanting to think about a small skull, tiny bones moved by animals and left to the elements. During the trial she had forced herself to be dispassionate, thinking through what was being presented as evidence and listening like a student to expert witness testimonies. But now, released from the Juror's Oath, her emotions were seething, bubbling below the surface ready to explode like a volcanic eruption.

I'm sooo tired, she thought, feeling the ache of every muscle in her body. The pulsing behind her left eye increased and she recognized the symptoms of migraine waiting to inflict its excruciating pain. For long minutes she massaged her temples then used a Chinese technique of acupressure on her hand. She counted to ten, released the pressure then took deep breaths. She repeated the process again and again until the pounding pain began to recede. She rose slowly then made her way to the kitchen, located a bottle of aspirin, rattled four tablets out and washed them down with a Diet Coke. I need to sleep, she told herself remembering how a dark room and sleep helped her to get migraines under control.

She closed the bedroom blinds completely and lay on the bed in the darkened room. Vaguely, she felt the thump of Diva and Pavarotti jumping onto the bed then settling down along her side. Within minutes she was asleep. But her mind was not in a restful state. Images clicked behind her closed eyelids one after another. Tracy Maddox sitting stone faced at the defense table. Alberto Diaz fumbling with a flip chart. Nick Maddox in the witness box. Judge Howard leaning forward asking if all his admonitions had been heeded. Admonitions. Admonitions. Admonitions a disembodied voice repeated and repeated.

Suddenly, she was thrust into the unconscious terrain of her brain's dreamland.

Vivid colors exploded on her dream screen – glorious colors of intensities not found on the earth – blues bluer than the sky and oceans. Yellows from the golden of gold to the palest of pale of an unknown spectrum of sun light. All the colors of the rainbow were there magnified by 100 times before changing to a sublime vapor of mist.

Jenna Maddox stepped out of the wondrous light. She blinked rapidly for several seconds before her beautiful brown eyes focused on a fixed point. In her sweet, sweet innocent voice she began to sing. "Pleez don't take my sunshine away." Her ponytail bobbed. It swayed. Her little pink tutu glimmered like gossamer angel wings. She pranced making an invisible outline of a circle then pranced some more shrinking the circle with every one of her little steps. "Pleez don't take my sunshine away," she sang in a sweet, sweet, voice then periodically stopped and gazed toward the center of her imaginary ring. There, in the middle sat a beautiful, impressive German Shepherd bathed in radiant light. He did not move. His dark, dark eyes were bright. Patient. Waiting. Jenna tiptoed toward him then threw her arms around his massive neck. She rubbed her cheek against his. Her little pink lips bestowed a loving, little girl kiss on his snout. She leaned her small head against his magnificent one. Together they stared outward toward some distant place.

Dorsie jolted into a wakeful state, heart thumping. "Jenna!" she called out loudly then covered her mouth with her hand as the last remnants of the dream faded away. For long, long minutes she culled her memory banks for what she might know about dreams just as she had every time this dream surfaced. Jenna and the German Shepherd's first visit came long before forensic evidence on the smell of human decomposition or the cadaver dogs' alerts began in the witness testimonies. Their nighttime visits were random but continued throughout the trial. The dream never changed. It never morphed into anything else. Always it was vivid, intense, and emotional.

I wanted to talk with someone about it, she told herself silently while thinking of Millie, Juror Nine, and Millie's revelations from the Lord. What weight had the other jurors placed in Millie's guidance from the Lord because of their deeply seated Christian values? Was it really humanly possible to cast aside lifelong values and opinions? Everything they heard in the courtroom was tainted by their own personal point of view or who they were at their very core. Millie believed the Lord spoke to her. She had Jenna and the German Shepard. In the reality of the courtroom, forensic facts had been recorded and not the voice of the Lord. But what if she'd had been able to talk to Millie about the Jenna dream before deliberations began? Could Mille have taken Jenna as the Lord's guidance too? But no discussion happened because they were bound by admonitions. She pounded her fists against the bed's coverlet. "Damn. Damn. I should have tried harder. I could have . . ." she said aloud.

A soft knock stopped her in mid-sentence. "Are you okay in there?" Brandon asked from the other side of the bedroom door then opened it. "Come on Mom, you've got to eat. Marilyn Di Paolo's wonderful baked ziti is almost heated through. Uncle Harold made his specialty – Caesar Salad. We've got good crusty bread. The best Chianti we could find. Afterwards, we got freshly ground Hawaiian Kona coffee and you can add a healthy shot of whatever you want on the side." He walked to the bed and extended his hand to help his mother rise. He put his arm around her and pulled her close. "Everything's going to work out. You'll see. This is just another one of those bumps in the road."

"You sound like Harold," she said with a deep sigh. "I hope you're both right."

———

In town, Vince Di Paolo pulled into the Blairstown Diner next to Bud Eckley's police cruiser. He found Eckley with the usual now-off-duty-before-going-home fare – pie and coffee. He slid into the stool next to him. "Whatcha' find out?"

"Reached out to Newton," Eckley replied. The procedure there for security of the jurors was to have anyone picking them up go to the front desk, identify themselves with two forms of ID. Their names were checked against the one given by the juror. No one in the station knew names, just the official juror record number. It's possible someone recognized one of the jurors then tried to match them with a number. But Newton's a tight ship. Doubt that any leaks came from there. How 'bout you? Any headway?"

"Old man Gino, made some calls to his old crony judges who in turn called their cronies in Trenton. Seems Judge Howard runs a tight ship, too. Word is he's stompin' and cussin'. They're afraid he's gonna' send himself right into a heart attack."

Eckley shoveled a forkful of pie into his mouth and chewed thoughtfully. "Farino thinks the bit at the shop was done by a local. Didn't share why he thought that. Asked an odd question too. Wanted to know whether Dorsie or Harold mentioned anything about Blair Academy. Know anything about that, Vince?"

Di Paolo shook his head. "Maybe he thinks some of those richie-rich kids got lose and went on a spree."

"Doubtful," Eckley said. "Never had a problem with anyone from Blair as long as I've been on the force. Although we've had our suspicions on a couple of things – mostly drugs. Never could gain a foothold in that direction. Blair's tight lipped and tight assed. They handle their own problems."

Di Paolo rapped his knuckles on the countertop then stood. "Keep your ear to the ground. Catch ya later." Once in his car, he sat for a moment before starting the ignition. Blair Academy, he thought. Was someone else in town on the jury? Someone from up at Blair? Hell. Dorsie was tellin' nobody nothin'. Gotta' get it out of her. Like in casual conversation. "Shit," he grunted while thinking how hard it was for him to be soft shoed in any conversation.

Chapter Six

Day Three Post-Trial

Early Thursday morning the Blairstown Diner's doorbell jangled when Dorsie and Harold entered. Out of curiosity, heads turned to catch a look at who was coming in. Immediately, the noise level inside the diner lowered in pitch. Conversations ended abruptly, the clatter of silverware against plates or coffee cups dropped by several decibels. Very few offered a word of greeting as Dorsie and Harold made their way to an empty booth even though most counter seats and booths were occupied by tried and true regulars.

After sliding into the booth, Dorsie looked across the table at Harold. "That certainly was uncomfortable. I wasn't quite expecting that. For Gawd sakes, we know these people. They know us!"

"Shake it off, Ole Gal," he said then handed her a menu.

Shelly, the waitress, came and stood before them with a scowl on her face but with her pencil poised to take their order. "What can I getcha' today? The usual Dorsie?" Dorsie nodded and Harold raised two fingers in the air, indicating he'd have the same. Shelly left and seconds later returned with a pot of coffee and filled their mugs. She glanced at Dorsie. "Can I ask ya something?"

"You can. But, first tell me how Andy's first day at school went? Was it better than last year?"

"Ya. He did ok," Shelly answered then blurted out, "How could you let that girl walk? What kind of mother doesn't report her child missing? What kind of mother goes out in a dress-cut-down-to-the-boobs and enters a hot body contest? After . . . after," Shelly sputtered, "her child was dead? Supposedly drowning in the swimming pool. Just tell me Dorsie, what kind of mother does that?" She waved her hand in a swiping gesture towards the diner's counter. "No. Tell us all. Every damn one of us got it that you were on the jury when you didn't show up like regular.

None of us bought Harold's story of 'she's-on-an-antique-buying-trip.' You ain't never gone to Europe before and if ya was now, ya would have mentioned it 'cause you would have been excited."

The atmosphere in the diner turned still again. People in other booths craned their necks, staring back towards Shelly. Folks on bar stools at the counter passed glances from one face to another. Shelly's questions hung in the air like tangible things.

Dorsie froze. Her throat threatened to close shut. She opened her mouth to speak but nothing came out. Finally, after what seemed like unending seconds, she pulled her thoughts together and forced herself to speak calmly. "Shelly, I really don't want to talk about this. All I can tell you is the jury did its job."

"Job, my ass," Shelly retorted, "What happened to you Dorsie Renninger," she scolded like an old, disappointed, elementary school teacher would to a former student. "Your mind turn to mush? We all know you ain't no dummy." She turned on her heel and left their booth. Minutes later she returned with their breakfast plates then served them without saying a word.

Dorsie studied her food. Her stomach crawled with disgust at herself for uttering such a pat statement – the jury did its job. All those expectant glances, she knew what they were about. Every one of them wanted a blow-by-blow instant rerun of what happened during the hours of deliberation. She wasn't going there even though Judge Howard had told them they had no restrictions; that they were released from civic service duty and private citizens once again. He only offered them his wisdom – *Be prudent in your discussions with others. Respect each other's privacy. Refrain from using others' names.*

Dorsie glanced over at Harold. He was drinking his coffee and she could see, like her, he'd barely touched his food with the exception of his toast. She picked up hers telling herself she needed to eat something. She took one bite then put the piece down.

Did your job? You didn't! You did wrong!

—

Outside in the bright sunshine of the day, Crystal Yates parked her car in the diner's lot. For long minutes she remained listening to an expert on jury selection being interviewed on NPR radio.

"... *both the defense and the prosecution in the Maddox trial wanted smart, skeptical, independent and self-aware jurors,*" he said. "*They wanted jurors who could ask hard questions and resist the pull to give weight to anything put forth during their deliberations that was clouded with emotions . . .*"

Crystal switched off the radio as Dorsie Renninger and Harold Raines crossed in front of her car on the way to theirs. She gave consideration to the jury expert's opinion then quickly acknowledged that Dorsie filled the being smart and independent criteria. So did her Eric. What a surprise it had been when he was selected to be on the jury for the Tracy Maddox trial and then ended up as jury foreperson. Yes, she concluded, Dorsie Renninger and Eric Van Zant met all the characteristics both lawyers wanted in a juror for *that* trial. She felt her stomach rumble then climbed out of the car, heading for the diner and a much-needed fortifying breakfast. It'd been a long night. It was her first night of a month's duty on the graveyard shift at Warren County's 911 Communications Center. As a Public Safety Call-Taker, it was part of her job to review the incoming calls and actions taken and summarize them in the Daily Briefing Bulletin. She'd been stunned when she'd read the extent of vandalism at *Dorsie's Antiques and Design*. Things that bad just didn't happen in Blairstown.

Once inside the diner's door, Shelly, the waitress came rushing towards her. "Did you talk to them? What'd they say?"

"Shelly, stuff it. Those two have had a lot dumped on them. Now, be the nice person that you are," Crystal said, patting Shelly on the shoulder kindly, "and don't go adding any kind of fuel to the fire. Keep your trap shut."

After settling into a booth, Crystal was sorry for being so curt with Shelly but in high school Shelly had been dubbed "Blabber Queen." Her thoughts turned back to Dorsie Renninger and Harold Raines. She could honestly say she knew them more beyond seeing them around town. Harold because of the antiques and Dorsie because they both worked together at Habitat for Humanity. Dorsie was on the board and relentless at pitching in on every new project. Dorsie also used her interior design contacts to get donations of furniture, rugs, lamps, and household goods or anything she could for the new home they'd just built. for some deserving family.

Crystal thought about Harold. She liked Harold Raines because he always took the time to share his knowledge of what made an antique an antique. After many visits to the shop, she discovered that it was Harold who ran the business there and not Dorsie. Harold started her on the hunt to find and build a nice collection of antiques to furnish the fixer-upper cottage she'd bought and restored. She smiled thinking of how lovely it had all turned out and how fantastic it was going to be to have Eric there too.

She glanced out the window towards the hill that hid the grounds of Blair Academy. Never could she have imaged falling in love with a blond, blue-eyed, smart and lots of fun Phys Ed Instructor for a prep school with a reputation like Blair's. Most of the faculty at Blair lived on campus and didn't exactly socialize with anyone in town. Meeting Eric was just one of those in-the-right-place-at-the-right-time kind of things. After a particularly stressful month at work, she'd gone over to Columbia, to the Lakota Wolf Preserve, to take a walk along the observation paths. She loved those wolves. They were beautiful and just looking at them helped her to jettison all the stress and details of frantic 911 calls. One day Eric Van Zant had also been walking the paths. They talked, met for pizza then one thing led to another and in mid-May at the end of Blair's school term, they decided they would live together. But as luck would have it, they'd spent only a few weeks together before Eric was selected to be on the jury of the Tracy Maddox trial then sequestered somewhere near Trenton. Most of his things were still in boxes in her garage. But now, she thought, with the trial over she and Eric would have cozy, cuddly, love nest nights. When the winter winds howled and heavy snow prevented them from getting out, they would be in their own little private heaven.

She cupped her coffee mug in her hands while continuing to gaze out the window at the bright sunshine day. Her thoughts swung back to Dorsie Renninger and she tried to recall if she'd ever mentioned anything about Eric to Dorsie. Well, certainly they knew each other now after being sequestered together for seven weeks. Her brows furrowed. How odd Eric had reacted when they'd watched news clip of Dorsie's son and brother making a statement. She was taken aback by his response. "That holier-than-thou bitch deserves anything she gets," he'd said with unusual anger. It was so unlike him. If fact, she had to admit his personality seemed to have done a flip-flop from before the trial to after the trial. It was freaky. Sweet, calm Eric had disappeared only to be replaced by an Eric who would get angry over nothing only to then be replaced by a morphed Eric-the-Energizer-Bunny, inspecting windows, doors, gutters then making duplicate, triplicate lists of tools he'd have to get at Home Depot over in Stroudsburg. He couldn't seem to relax. For two nights now, when she reached to the other side of the bed she found it empty. She'd found him pacing on the deck one night and then the next night down at the pond skipping stones at two in the morning. Post-trial stress, she told herself. That's why she'd held off asking what made him say such a thing about Dorsie Renninger. Like everyone else, she wanted to know just how that jury came up with a not guilty verdict. How in the world had her smart Eric not put together the circumstantial evidence, points A to B to C leading to one person – Tracy Maddox. But she could wait. Winter was coming and while under warm covers with his body pressed against hers, he'd tell her just how and why he'd voted not guilty.

—

Eric Van Zant sat in his car in the long-term parking at Philadelphia International Airport. He'd just come from taping a segment at WTXF-FOX 29 and they'd told him the interview would air on the evening news. Nailed it! he thought. They didn't even ask the hard questions. Was he good or was he good? He liked his little spin using and emphasizing the phrase "forced by the law." What more would anyone want? People of America. The verdict has been explained! End of story. The other jurors? Naw. Moron lemmings! They wouldn't be pouring their hearts out now with all the backlash circulating out there. Wimps. All of them. But they'd keep quiet for another reason. In those good Christian souls greed had reared its ugly head. He'd convinced them he had contacts at St. Martin's Press. Would be able to negotiate a book deal for them all. He made clear that there was one condition – no talking to the press after the trial. "No interviews. Zip the lips," he'd said. "It'll up the ante on any book deal offered." Incompetents! he thought. Stupid deputies and guard watchdogs. He'd done all that persuading right under their noses. But now, he wasn't exactly sure about Kate Krieger. Chances were she might talk but he had her in the palm of his hand from the start. Spoon-fed her what to say and what not to say. She'd be telling the same story. The others. Has beens. Weaklings. Morons. Except for that Dorsie bitch. He'd shut her up real fast. If she'd been appointed as jury foreperson, Christ they would've been there for another two weeks and singing a different tune. But now, they were private citizens again. Thanks to him. Free to do what they wanted. Go where they wanted. Shit, he had places to go. People to see. He was "The Man who saved Tracy, the Hot Bod Mom".

Eric flipped open his cell, checked his voicemail then deleted all messages from Dr. Zucker's office. He deleted Zucker from his contact list. He noted the time – one twenty-five p.m. Crystal will be zonked out, her cell off, he thought then pressed the call button. When voicemail kicked in he said, "Hey, it's me. I'll be gone for a couple of days. Don't worry. I'll call. Just don't touch the stuff I left in the garage. I'll take care of it when I get back." He flipped his cell shut, locked the car, grabbed his carry-on from the trunk then walked to the Terminal Transport kiosk. He raised his face to the sun while he waited for the mini bus. He felt the sun's power pouring into him. Fuck Blair Academy. Fuck Dr. Zucker. He reached in his carryall and pulled out an empty prescription bottle. He glanced at the label – Lithium 900 mg. Take one tablet in a.m. Take one tablet in p.m. Refills: 0 – Prescribing Physician: Irwin Zucker, M.D. "Fuck you Zucker," he mumbled aloud. "Haven't needed this shit," he said then tossed the bottle in the kiosk's trash can. He stood rocking back and forth on his heels repeating The Man. The Man. The Man. Hot Bod Mom knew he was The Man too! Every day he'd sent her Mind Messages. She'd gotten them. Definitely had been tuned into the same awesome telepathic wavelength. Otherwise, why had she kept staring at him and sending him Mind Messages back?

Chapter Seven

Day Four Post-Trial

At noon Dorsie watched a Town Car pull out of the driveway and onto Ward Road. "Bye Brandon," she whispered, throwing a kiss then shut the front door and set the alarm. Blessed peace and quiet, she thought. The house was finally quiet. She picked up the FedEx box from the foyer table and took it into the family room. In it she found neatly labeled DVDs in chronological order, thick file folders and flash drives along with a note from Rick.

Mama D – These pretty much cover HLN's coverage from the time Jenna Maddox was reported missing to the events leading up to the trial. I'll send the entire live trial coverage later but you may not want to watch them since you were there right in the middle of the action. I thought you'd want them anyway. I had one of the researchers gather all the material appearing in print from various media outlets including those on the Internet. Remember, the media is a huge monster feeding on "freedom of the press". It will say anything, do anything to get ratings. It will sensationalize the smallest of irrelevant material. Every talking head on any program has their own approach to feeding viewers information in a shocking, mind-numbing or confrontational point of view.

Mama D, you know I'm not one to interfere, but maybe you shouldn't go through these right now. Don't watch/read any post-trial analysis. Stay away from blogs. Settle back into your own skin first. I'm always here for you. Love you, Mama D – Rick.

Bless you, Rick, she thought then leaned her head back against the sofa cushion. She was tired, more accurately drained of all energy reserves. Earlier, she and Harold had their fingerprints taken at the police station and afterwards she had insisted on going to the shop to see for herself what condition it was in. Her knees almost buckled under her when she saw the devastation inside. Even the vintage hardwood floors had been smeared with neon paint. Everything appeared to be beyond recovery. Harold's prized, priceless piece, the old Victorian breakfront, had deep, deep gouges in it and the mirror was shattered. Inside, her heart had ballooned with unbearable sorrow. The brutal attack on all the things in the shop was equal to an assault on a group of defenseless children. Antiques were Harold's children. Her name was on the window by calculated marketing reasons but what was inside belonged to Harold's astuteness and gentle care.

Your fault! Your fault!

Now, she reviewed once again the questions Detective Farino had asked both her and Harold earlier at the police station. "Can you think of anyone who might have a reason to do this?" They'd both answered no. You fool, she thought in retrospect.

Why not say Eric Van Zant?

Because Judge Howard asked us to respect other the juror's privacy, she countered to that nagging inner voice.

Different than just babbling names.

No it's not.

Look at the bruises.

He was under stress, she continued in countering the badgering voice.

Note to Judge. Why not?

Stop! Just stop!

Dorsie leaned her head back against the comfortable sofa cushion mentally exhausted from the tug-of-war going on in her head. Intent on only resting her eyes she drifted further and further into sleep to the place where dreams and recall waited to be unleashed. The Jury Room Door opened and she stepped back into its hallowed space.

"We have eight for Not Guilty and four for Guilty on the major charge of First Degree Murder," Eric Van Zant, the Jury Foreperson announced after counting the first secret ballot. "Does anyone have anything to say?" he asked, pausing and giving a daring glare to each of the jurors seated at the long, shiny table.

Dorsie glanced down at the bullet points she'd listed on her legal pad then studied Eric Van Zant for a minute or two unsettled by his demeanor. She took a deep breath and ignored his bully-like glare and said, "I'd like to open a discussion regarding the smell of human decomposition. I'd like to look at the testimony of . . ."

"Naw. Naw. Naw." Eric interrupted, gesturing with his arm, slashing it through the air. "We're not going to go through that junk science stuff. The body farm. That chromate gas spec . . . whatever the hell that thing is." He looked at the others for confirmation. "It'll take us too long. We all want to get out of here, right? Look at Burton. He can't even sit any longer. And Millie, there. She's got that 50th Anniversary Cruise coming up real fast. Lisa's got her oldest starting first grade this year. She's probably already missed his first day of school."

"That's not what I'd like all of you to look at," Dorsie continued. "I'd like to talk about what the cadaver dog alerts mean. Specifically, on the trunk of the car. The tow yard manager's experience with the smell of decomposition. He has no vested interest in the case whatsoever. Also, the crime scene investigator who processed the car has had experience with the smell of decomposition." She glanced at Rodney; the juror who was a veteran of the Gulf War, hoping for support. He remained silent, drawing furious doodles on his legal pad.

Eric leaned forward in his chair at the head of the table, his face darkening then he laughed. "You want to talk about DOGS!"

"Yes. Let's ask for Sgt. Gussard's testimony regarding his and his dog's training and certifications. I'd like to explain something to all of you."

"Oh, so you're an expert on DOGS," Eric fired at her.

"No, I'm not. But my son-in-law is. He's a police K-9 trainer. I've seen the rigorous training K-9s go through."

"So, your son-in-law LIKES dogs," Eric sneered.

"No. Eric," she countered holding his gaze. "He TRAINS police K-9s. If we take a look at the cadaver dogs' training and certifications, I believe we'll see they have an extremely high level of correct alerts. They establish credibility. A fact we can't ignore. A substantial fact that there was human decomposition in the trunk of Tracy Maddox's car."

"Garbage. Garbage. It was garbage," Eric countered and hurtled on, pointing an accusing finger at her. "You're biased. You're not impartial on this." He turned to the other jurors. "We have to discard what she's saying and move on."

"No, Eric. I'm not biased. I'm stating well known facts and the testimony will bear that out." She glanced around the table then decided to take a chance, risky because she didn't know what the answers would be. "Did any of you lose someone or know someone who lost someone on 9/11? Just raise your hand."

Four hands shot up in the air and she sought out the eyes of those four fellow jurors. "Who do you think helped find an overwhelming amount of human remains at Ground Zero? Cadaver dogs. Search and Rescue Dogs. They were instrumental in bringing closure to many, many families. Trained cadaver dogs do not alert on garbage. We can't discount their alerts in the trunk of the car. Let's go over the tapes of the dog searching the car and the tape of the dog in Maddox's backyard."

"No!" Eric shouted, "We will not be asking for testimony or tapes. We will not be reviewing any of that shit over there," he decreed pointing to the evidence table. "We will not be doing that Ladies and Gentlemen of The Jury, will we?" he asked, glaring, making sure he made eye contact with each of them. "This is the way it's going to be. We will wrap this up quickly because I . . ." He stopped took a deep breath for control. In his most persuasive tone he said, ". . . because I know each of you in your good Christian hearts knows a mother would *never* kill her child. I can see it in your eyes. In your expressions." His voice grew louder. "It's been there all along. From the very beginning. Hell, who needed all those expert witnesses," He banged his fist against the table to emphasize his next words. "NOT GUILTY! SHE IS NOT GUILTY OF MURDER!"

No one moved. No one uttered a word.

Dorsie glanced at the others. Shock registered on some faces, others stared down at their legal pads, and two buried their heads in their hands. Damn it, she thought. I will not be bullied. She stood and faced Eric. "We can ask for any witness testimony we want. You were appointed Jury Foreman by Judge Howard. However, according to New Jersey law . . ." She grabbed a Juror's Instruction Packet from the center of the table then flipped though pages and pulled one out. "The jury foreperson's duty is to communicate with the court on the jury's behalf and to facilitate discussions between jurors," she read. "The foreperson does not carry any more weight in the deliberation than any other juror." She glanced around the table then brought herself to her full height, made sure Eric was in eye contact with her then said, "You do not have the right to tell us what we can or can't ask for. Or what we can or can't look at. Or how we should vote."

Eric shoved back his chair from the table so violently it hit the white board easel behind him sending it crashing loudly into the credenza. Bottles of water flew to the floor from the impact. "You bitch," he snarled while rounding the end of the table then reached out and grabbed her arm then shook her. "You think you can take control from me? YOUR take on the trial is WAY off. SHE IS NOT GUILTY OF ANY MURDER."

Shocked silence filled the room again.

Shaking and stunned beyond words, it took a few seconds for her to break free of his grasp. "Don't ever touch me again," she said, mustering as much of a forceful voice as she could. "You're not the decision maker for the rest of us. I'd like to send a note to Judge Howard. Please, perform your duty as Jury Foreperson."

"You fuckin' bitch," growled Eric Van Zant. "No note is going to The Honorable Judge! Not from you! Not from anyone!" He reached towards her again. "Not if you know what's . . ."

The Jury Room door vibrated with rapid-fire pounding. All eyes turned toward it.

Now, the pounding continued to reverberate through the house. Her eyes flew open and frantically searched the room. She sat forward and realized she was in her home, in the family room. Her cell was vibrating on the coffee table and she snatched it up. Oh my Gawd, that's Dave. He's pounding at the front door. She rushed to let him in.

"Well, 'bout time Dorsie. I was about to break it down," he drawled. He walked in, dog following and closed the door shut before the alarm could kick in. He motioned with his hand and the dog sat. "You weren't answering your cell. The house was dark. No one answerin' the door. I gotta' tell ya, definitely pushed me into big time worry mode."

"Oh Dave, I'm so sorry," she said reaching out to give him a hug. "I fell asleep. Lost track of time. Don't even know what time it is." She turned on the table lamp in the foyer then walked to the kitchen flicking on lights as she went. "You must be hungry. Let me get you something."

"Nope. Grabbed a bite on my way here."

Dorsie turned towards him and got her first look at the black German Shepherd at his side. The Shepherd's muscular body was pressed tightly against Dave's leg.

"Dorsie, meet Thor. You and he are gonna' be real pals. Now, just stand there and don't move. I'm gonna' let Thor get a good healthy sniff of you.

We gotta' get off on the right foot, right from the start. Don't be embarrassed if his snout sniffs your crotch." Dave grabbed Thor's collar and gave a gentle pull. Thor's front paws lifted slightly off the floor. Dave released his hold on the collar. "Meet. Go." Thor sniffed the perimeter of the kitchen, paused at the cats' food and water bowl then quickly moved on to sniff Dorsie's shoes, ankles, calves of her legs, thighs then a quick pass across her crotch. He returned to Dave's side and sat down. "Good boy," Dave praised while bending down to pat him heartily on his side. "Come on over now Dorsie. Put out your hands, palms flat and let him sniff again."

She followed Dave's instructions. Thor's cold nose passed over the center of her fingers and palms. He looked up at her, began wagging his tail and gave a short, clipped bark.

Dave whispered. "Say his name. Then Good Dog."

"Thor. Good Dog." She smiled when his tail immediately began to swish rapidly back and forth across the floor. He got up, circled around her twice then came to a stop in front of her then sat down tail still wagging.

"Woof. Woof."

Dave handed her a treat. She placed it in the palm of her hand and let Thor lap it up then gave him a pat on the head. "Good boy."

"That went very, very well," Dave said congratulating them both. "Basically all this sniffin' is his way of learnin' his territory. His people." He gave Thor substantial rubs along his rib cage then signaled by hand again. Thor moved away and laid down in the kitchen doorway, resting his head on his paws, his bright, dark eyes watching every move being made.

"Dorsie, you're gonna' to be his people for a while. Right now, I'm the alpha male in Thor's world. I'm gonna' turn over the role to you. You will be alpha even though he looks like he's the alpha dog. Ain't gonna' be hard." He walked over to Dorsie and put his arms around her in a bear hug then pulled away and gave her a wide smile. "'Cause you already have ninety percent alpha traits runnin' through your veins. You just keep it under wraps. I "got it" the minute Megs introduced me to you. You eyed me up and down. Said a couple of things very quietly that signaled you were top dog in the Raines-Renninger world."

Dorsie gave Dave a playful swat against his well-muscled arm. "We should drink to a good beginning. I'll drink to being glad to have you here," she said. Within minutes they had neat glasses of Scotch in their hands. They clinked glasses. Dave sat next to her at the kitchen island with his stool pulled so close to hers that he could drape an arm across her shoulders. They sat sipping slowing in a comfortable silence. "Gotta' get some stuff from the van," Dave said, setting down his empty glass then looked towards the alarm box near the door leading to the garage. "What's the security code for the alarm?"

"It's on a piece of masking tape, below."

"Jeeze, Dorsie. Ya think that's . . ."

"I know. I know. But Dave, I just can't keep anything straight in my head right now." She made a swirling motion in the air. "Lots of stuff just ping-ponging around in there."

"Right," he said giving her a hard once over inspection, noting loss of weight, lines of strain on her face, dark bluish smudges beneath her eyes. "Right," he repeated. "But we're here now. Gonna' help you. Get you out in the sunshine and fresh air. Gets your blood circulating." He tapped his temple. "Good for the mental constitution too." He glanced over at Thor. "Stay," he said and went through the door leading to the garage. Minutes later, he returned carrying a duffel bag and pulling a small soft stadium cooler behind him. He quickly and efficiently set up an area for Thor's water and food bowls. "Come," he commanded Thor.

"You tired?" he asked Dorsie after Thor finished his food routine then returned to his lay-down spot. She shook her head. "Me either. Slept on the plane. Megs sends her love along with instructions for me to see that you're eating well. Resting. Getting exercise." He paused and raised a finger in the air. "Wait, there's more," he added with a grin. "I've also got to make sure ya get your Alone Time. Those orders came from Brandon." He glanced over at Thor. "Okay, Dorsie. Out we go for DDD, as commonly known as Dog-Do Detail. Better get a sweater. A little nippy out there now."

They walked out though the garage where Dorsie grabbed a light windbreaker off a hook while Thor industriously sniffed around Diva and Pavarotti's litter pans. When he finished, Dave clipped a leash to his collar and they walked down the driveway.

The night was clear and the air carried the cool scent of fall. Dorsie linked her arm though Dave's as they walked.

"Tough seven week tour?" Dave asked. He reached down to unleash Thor.

Dorsie gripped his arm tighter. "Yes, it was. It took some getting used to being observed all the time. Deputies outside our hotel room doors. Guards within earshot when we made calls. We had to log them. Guards or deputies around us all the time. Watching. Listening. I imagine that's how a prisoner feels." She paused. "Don't get me wrong, they were nice. Doing their job. Making sure none of us talked about the trial to each other or to anyone we spoke with on the phone. If we had any request, they filled it if it was possible." She paused again. "We had a choice of eating dinner in the private dining room or ordering room service. Most evenings three or four seats were empty. The newspapers we got were pretty well cut up. All references to the trial removed. TV viewing was limited too." She paused for a breath. "Of course, having Harold or Brandon come during family visit periods helped. You know how Brandon is. He brought me delicious, gourmet foodstuffs from the city, industry magazines and proposals to review for upcoming projects. Harold just exuded moral support."

"Did you like the other jurors?" Dave asked.

"Oh, we did the usual get-to-know-each-other social thing. Chit chats about family. The guys focused on sports with each other. But mostly, by the end of the court day, we were pretty well wiped out. So many details to keep in your head. We could take notes but our notebooks stayed behind on our chairs in the courtroom. We couldn't even take them with us when we deliberated. Hard to see what the point was of giving us notebooks if we couldn't use them for reference. Judge Howard told us they'd be destroyed along with anything we used in the Jury Room."

"You go through List Withdrawal?" Dave asked with dead seriousness. He gave a soft grunt of satisfaction to himself. Whenever an opportunity came up to tease Dorsie about her lists, he took it.

Dorsie glanced at him and saw a small smile form on his lips. "Stop it! Anyway, Judge Howard really tried to keep us on schedule, although there were a few unexpected turns. Like the day Tracy Maddox got ill. I barely could hold it together seeing the duct tape superimposed over Jenna's mouth." She turned towards Dave. "Did they show that during the coverage?"

He shrugged. "Wait a sec," he said. He walked over to where Thor sat near the edge of the road and picked up Thor's droppings in a plastic bag.

"Am I going to have to do that?"

"It's all part of the package. Sort of like diapers are with babies. Don't you scoop the litter pans? No difference."

"Oh, I should think so. We talking mountains of poop compared to little, dried out turds."

Dave's hearty laugh carried through the night air as they turned in the road and started walking back towards the house.

"Dave, when you're on protection detail, how do you know when something isn't right? What stands out to you?"

"Odd question, Dorsie. Got a reason for asking?" When she didn't answer, he thought for a moment then said, "Well it's sort of an accumulation of knowing human behavior and experience. If someone looks nervous, there's a reason. If he's going onstage to make a speech, its reasonable nervousness. If he's in a crowd and looks nervous, I do what's called a body scan. Pay attention to arms and hands. Where his eyes are focused. Sometimes the dogs will pick something up even at a distance. Their sixth sense is far better than ours is."

"You think we humans are capable of picking up on it too?"

"Sure. Haven't you ever had the hair stand up on the back of your neck without knowing why? We all have an energy field around us. That feeling you get is your sixth sense reacting to energy every one of us emits. There's an Alpha field, more or less an electromagnetic one. Then there's the Beta field. That comes from our core. Reveals who we are. An aura, to use a pseudoscience or metaphysical term. Science has proven an electromagnetic one. The other, they're still out on." He paused, cleared his throat giving her arm linked through his a reassuring pat. "But I believe it's the Beta field we react to. We pick up bad vibes. Sixth sense goes on high alert. Animals instinctively probe the Beta field. Law enforcement, fireman, combat soldiers and FBI agents all learn to rely on their gut. Con men and bullies can ferret out their marks with a quick once-over look." He glanced over at his mother-in-law. "I know you got reasons for asking, care to share?"

Dorsie inhaled a deep breath as Eric Van Zant's face flashed in her mind's eye followed by Alberto Diaz's. She shook her head. "Just something I'm trying to work out." They walked halfway up the driveway. She stopped and faced her son-in-law. "I believed the cadaver dog's alerts. I want you to know that. I tried to convince the others the dog was right." She brushed her hand across her forehead. "I tried, but . . ."

"Hey . . . hey," Dave seeing she was visibly shaken and not just from the chill in the night air. "Come on. Let's get you inside. Another belt of Scotch is what you need." Once inside he poured two more generous glasses of Scotch and set them on the kitchen island. "Dorsie, you're one of the most level-headed people I know. Must've been somethin' in testimonies or evidence aside from the cadaver dogs that made you go the way you did. I'm not gonna' probe. From experience, in some situations there's more than meets the eye." He paused. "I wasn't hangin' on to every bit of crap the media was feeding to Joe Public. So, settin' aside my bias for well-trained K-9s, I'm not gonna' second guess your decision."

"Thank you. You're a good man," Dorsie said with heartfelt fondness.

"Drink up. We've got one more detail to do yet." He motioned to Thor. Thor sat up on his haunches, alert and ready. "We're going to make him go through all the rooms. Get him acquainted with his new territory. Won't take him long. Not unless those pansy cats of yours kick up a fuss." He pulled up on Thor's collar. Thor's paws lifted slightly from the floor. Dave released his grip on the collar. "Search. Go."

Thor sniffed his way through every room in the house stopping only to sit and whine at the side of the bed in Dorsie's room. "Don't panic," Dave said. "That's Thor's cat whine. He does that at home when he goes in search of Jacko, our cat, his big-time-buddy." Minutes later they were in the family room. Dave brushed aside the FedEx box on the sofa and sat down. He intently studied the coffee table's top scattered with DVDs, file folders and flash drives. "This the stuff Rick sent?"

"The research assistants at HLN are certainly thorough."

"This is not a good idea," Dave said picking up a couple of DVDs and examining their labels. "Don't second guess yourself. *What Ifs* will get you nowhere. *What Ifs* are enemies. I've had good buddies destroyed by *What Ifs*. Don't go here," he said waving a DVD. "Leave it be."

Dorsie heard the sincerity in her son-in-law's voice, saw it in his eyes.

I can't let it be, she thought. Somewhere in all that material is a single detail powerful enough . . .

Powerful enough. To what? Redeem you? her inner voice chided.

Chapter Eight

Day Five Post-Trial, Morning

At 5:45 a.m. Dorsie entered into the last REM stage of her sleep cycle. Her body lay still beneath the covers but behind closed eyelids her eyes moved rapidly back and forth as if she were watching a vivid, intense play or a movie in which she herself was a participant. Once again she found herself back in the sanctity of the jury room.

"... Please, perform your duty as Jury Foreperson," she said to Eric Van Zant. She heard the rapid pounding coming from the Jury Room door but she stood her ground not backing away from Eric.

The deputy assigned to guard them swung open the door. "Everything ok in here?" he asked craning his neck forward in an effort to scan the room.

Burton, who had been pacing the room, blocked his view. Before Dorsie could turn towards the assigned deputy, she heard Burton say, "Easel just got knocked over. We're fine. Thank you." She heard the heavy door close.

Rodney, the Gulf War Veteran, was now standing between her and Eric Van Zant. "Let it go. We're all tired," he said to her in a terse, low whisper then turned and used his body to make Eric back-step away from her, making him move towards his seat.

"You fuckin' bitch," Eric growled over Rodney's shoulder. "No note is going anywhere. Not from you. Not from anyone. Not if you all know what's good for you. I'll make sure . . ."

"Calm down. Shut up!" Rodney said. He he placed both hands on Eric's chest and pushed him back into his seat.

Dorsie sank into her chair shaking from adrenaline rushing through her body.

Kate, the juror who just graduated from nursing school, rushed to Eric Van Zant's side. She whispered in calming tones, rubbed his arm in a soothing gesture as if she might be attending to a patient. She threw Dorsie a fury-filled glare. "I'm not going to send someone as young as Tracy Maddox to prison for life based on a dog's nose. Dogs make mistakes. That's enough reasonable doubt for me. I don't give a crap what dogs did at Ground Zero. Drowning seems like the most logical explanation, not duct tape and chloroform."

"It was an accident. Just like Diaz said. Nick Maddox, the father, helped cover it up," said Sara the juror with the voice of a lifetime smoker. Her words spewed forth released from the admonitions not to discuss anything with her fellow jurors until deliberations began. "I don't trust anything Nick Maddox said. Having an affair with that woman. Goes to show you what kind of man he is. Him trying to commit suicide sums up just how guilty he is of something."

Still shaken Dorsie fired back in anger, "The detectives never considered Nick Maddox a suspect or even a person of interest. Let's . . ." Sara's expression stopped her from going further because Sara's eyes kept darting back and forth towards Eric.

Another juror's voice erupted, "Ashcroft. How many times did he have us trotting back and forth out of the courtroom? Did you see him laughing at Diaz? That really pissed me off! Who the hell did he think he was? Thought he had a slam dunk with us, well let me tell you . . .."

"He ignored us," another juror said. "Diaz showed respect. Said good morning to us every day. Smiled at us."

Dorsie heard the comment, wasn't sure who said it, because her focus was on Sara who kept glancing over at Van Zant then back to her. She remained focused on Sara trying to decipher the meaning in her glances.

"Didn't care for Ashcroft myself," said another male juror. "Who did he think he was smirking and laughing behind his hand while Diaz was showing us that chart."

Dorsie turned her attention to the juror speaking.

"But getting back to it being an accident. Hell, the kid could open the sliding glass door. Climb up the pool steps. My boy, at that age, was climbing on everything, always getting himself into predicaments. That little girl climbed the steps to the pool, jumped in and drowned. An accident. No doubt about it."

"There's no evidence of that," Dorsie said, her anger turning into frustration. "Just a picture showing Jenna standing at a sliding glass door, not actually opening it. You're assuming she could open the door. Let's examine that picture close up before we jump to any conclusion."

"The Grandmother left the ladder up. Just forgot she did," said Lisa, the youngest juror among them who was also a mother of a six year old. She kept looking nervously at Eric Van Zant. "It had to be an accident. Mothers don't murder their children. No one said Tracy was a bad mom. No one said she abused Jenna or neglected her. They said she was an awesome mother. She took her to the beach. To Great Adventure. She made sure she was with a babysitter when she went out with all those guys. Being a slut doesn't mean she killed her baby."

"Lisa, the babysitter didn't exist!" Dorsie said. "It was a lie. She lied to her mother about all those places she and Jenna were. If you believe Jenna drowned in the pool then Jenna was already dead. Tracy couldn't have taken her to those places. There was no babysitter. The police investigations proved that. It was a lie."

"Oh!" Lisa mouthed then looked downward. "Well, being a liar and a slut doesn't mean you're a killer," she said without looking up. "It's just like Diaz said. Tracy Maddox has issues 'cause her Dad did . . . well you know . . ."

"Lisa," Dorsie said patiently, "molestation was not part of his closing argument because there was no proof of it. He just said that in his opening statement for shock value. There's no evidence confirming Tracy Maddox was molested by anybody."

The semi-retired juror whose mother was a stroke victim being attended to by a round-the-clock caregiver stood. "Look here," Walter said. "I appreciate what you're trying to do. I listened to all that fancy forensic evidence. Didn't understand the half of it. I'm not ashamed to admit it. Seems that Diaz's expert witnesses cancelled out the prosecution's expert witnesses." He sat down, leaned back in his chair and clicked his pen open and shut as he continued outlining his logic. "I don't need to hear or see any more testimony. I'd still be left with not knowing which expert is the expert. I'll give you the cadaver dog's nose. The tow yard manager's nose. Also the nose of the guy that processed the car. But that ain't enough for me to send a very pretty young woman like Tracy Maddox to prison for the rest of her life. Prison life isn't for someone like her."

"Right," someone murmured in agreement.

Millie, the juror anticipating her 50th Anniversary Cruise, quietly added, "Lord forgive me 'cause I just ain't smart enough to understand those fancy words them experts used." She placed her hand on the Jury Instructions Booklet beside her legal pad. "I don't really understand all this stuff either. Been prayin' every night for guidance. Last night the Lord spoke to me. Told me that lovely girl didn't kill her baby."

For several seconds, Dorsie remained standing, stunned and in disbelief of what she was hearing. She grabbed her Jury Instruction Booklet then rapidly searched for the explanation of the charges being brought against Tracy Maddox. Her gaze made a sweeping scan around the table. "Are you all trying to say she's also not guilty of . . ." She paused, put on her reading glasses, then read directly from the page describing the charges against Tracy Maddox. "...Abuse, Abandonment, Cruelty and Neglect of a Child shall consist in any of the following acts by anyone having the custody or control of the child: (a) willfully forsaking a child; (b) failing to care for and keep the control and custody of a child so that the child shall be exposed to physical or moral risk without proper and sufficient protection . . ." She glanced at each juror. "There is no evidence of drowning. Tracy Maddox was the last person seen with Jenna. There was no babysitter to kidnap Jenna. Nick Maddox was never a person of interest to the investigators. The only person last seen with Jenna that day was her mother. If you truly believe she drowned then her mother, Tracy Maddox, wasn't paying attention to her. Not watching her. Neglecting her." She glanced at the booklet in her hand again and shook it in the air. "Failing to care and keep the control and custody of a child."

At the head of the table Eric stood and shouted. "Don't YOU get it, you fuckin' know-it-all? Nick Maddox was the only one who SAID the kid was with Tracy on the day she went missing. The kid drowned. The SOB, friggin' molesting grandfather covered it up. End of story. We all want to get the fuck out of here. Don't you get THAT?"

Dorsie followed Eric's gaze as he tried to make eye contact with each juror. Some jurors scribbled on their legal pads and did not look up. Others distracted themselves with something else.

"Mzzzz. Dorsie, sit down," Eric said with scathing politeness. "You've heard what the others are thinking. Since I'm not the only decision maker here, Ladies and Gentlemen of the Jury, wrap this. Cast your ballots." Minutes later he announced, eleven – Not Guilty – One Guilty.

What happened to the other three Guilty votes? Dorsie frantically wondered then stood again and said, "Please, please we need to really look at evidence, testimony."

"My mind's made up," someone said.

"Mine too," another juror added. "It's late. I need to rest."

Another added nastily, "Maybe *she'll* feel differently in the morning."

Minutes later, they broke off deliberations and the left the sanctity of the jury room.

—

Dorsie ascended up out of REM sleep shouting, "Wait! Please! We need to . . ." She glanced over at the bedside clock while remnants of the dream bled into her now awake state. Now, she still desperately wanted to go back to that jury room and make it all happen differently.

MEOW! MEOW!

Okay. Okay. I'm up," she grumbled at Diva and Pavarotti. She heard the garage door rumble up and concluded Dave was taking Thor out for his morning Duty Detail. "I see you got past Thor. Come on. It's safe." She gave Diva then Pavarotti a long stroke on each of their backs. She wiggled her feet into slippers as they scampered out of the bedroom down the hallway towards the kitchen knowing food was seconds away. After filling Diva and Pavarotti's dishes, she glanced at the automatic coffee maker. The carafe was half-full. "Bless that man," she said, and then poured herself a cup of coffee. She went into the family room, picked up the TV remote, clicked On and found a local TV station.

" . . . *Alternate Juror Speaks On Maddox Verdict. Stay tuned for Action News 6* crawled across the lower headline banner. She waited and waited through commercials then other news until the anchor finally said. "Now, Action News' interview with John Hudak, an alternate juror in the Tracy Maddox trial. Dorsie watched as the clip began.

John Hudak stepped from his front door onto a small portico. "Can you comment on the verdict?" an off-camera voice asked "Did you agree with the verdict and could you tell us why?"

Hudak leaned towards the mike thrust at him. "Um . . . well, to me, there just didn't seem to be enough hard evidence. No smoking gun, so to speak. If I had been in jury room, I probably would have voted not guilty."

"When you say hard evidence, is it possible you wanted a nice, neat package like the popular *CSI* TV series gives every week?"

John Hudak blinked rapidly for seconds then wiped his hand across his mouth. "Um . . . nooo, that's not what I'm saying. Circumstantial evidence isn't enough to convict."

"There have been many convictions of this type on circumstantial evidence, for one, the Scott Peterson case."

"I'm not familiar with it."

"Jenna's hair was found in the trunk and FBI forensic analysis showed it was consistent with decomposition. Isn't that hard *CSI* type evidence? If Tracy Maddox didn't dump Jenna in a trash bag where she was found, who did?"

Hudak blinked rapidly again. "Um . . . I don't know for sure, um . . . I suspected Nick Maddox had something to do with covering it up."

"So you believed Alberto Diaz's outrageous opening and closing statements?"

"Um . . . I think that's what started me thinking down the road of reasonable doubt."

"Right from opening statements you had reasonable doubt in your mind?"

"Um . . . not sure what you're getting at."

"There was no viable evidence presented pointing to Diaz's speculative scenario. Why do you think he waited three years to say it was an accident? If Jenna drowned, why let hundreds of people search for what they believed to be a missing child?"

Hudak shrugged.

"Mr. Hudak, do you have children? Grandchildren? Could you cover up?

Hudak's face took on the expression of a frightened deer in headlights. He turned and reached to open the door to his home. "If you'll excuse me, that's all I have to say."

Dorsie shook her head in disbelief then clicked over to ABC's Good Morning America show. Laura Spencer was interviewing Kate Krieger, the nursing student juror.

". . . I didn't think it was my job as a juror to connect all the dots. That's the prosecution's job," Kate Krieger said. "To show us how they're connected and they didn't do it. No one could tell us HOW Jenna died. Having boyfriends and a tattoo doesn't make for a crime."

"Did you fully understand what circumstantial evidence means and how to draw reasonable inferences? Wouldn't you agree using circumstantial evidence is a way of reasoning, to draw probable conclusions from facts that are known?"

Kate Krieger sat up straighter in her chair. Her chin lifted slightly. "I would say I did. After all, I just graduated from nursing school, so I couldn't be labeled as stupid, as the public would like to believe. The jury foreperson was very good in helping each of us understand the charges, jury instructions and information. He was an excellent facilitator."

"Did the jurors examine any of the evidence presented in the trial or review transcripts of witness and expert testimonies?"

"No. Why would we? It was an accidental drowning. Once we were in agreement on that, nothing else mattered."

"Who do you think put Jenna Maddox in the trash bag? One mile away from the Maddox home?"

"To speculate or come up with scenarios as to who might have done that . . . well, that wasn't part of my job as a juror. It was up to the police and prosecution to figure it out. They didn't. It was a terrible accident, a drowning and Tracy Maddox just couldn't deal with it. Lying doesn't make someone a murderer."

The camera returned to Laura Spencer and Dorsie realized she'd been viewing a previously recorded clip.

"There you have it. My interview yesterday with Kate Krieger on the verdict in the Tracy Maddox trial," said Laura Spencer. The camera zoomed in for a close-up. "Being a juror is difficult and even more so when the issues are as upsetting as those in the Maddox trial. The jurors deserve our respect and thanks even if we agree or don't agree with their decision. We'll be back after this commercial break with our live interview with Greg Ashcroft on his reactions to the verdict."

Dorsie waited through the commercials again. Good Morning America returned showing Greg Ashcroft sitting in a chair across from Laura Spencer looking quite relaxed.

"We've just heard what juror number three, Kate Krieger, had to say on the jury's verdict. Did you expect it to be not guilty on all charges?" Laura Spencer asked.

"I was stunned," answered Ashcroft. He shook his head slightly."I believe our team did our very best to present the most comprehensive evidence to the jury. We focused on the thirty days leading up to Jenna not being reported missing and Tracy's lying to law enforcement. The jailhouse tapes showed her lying to her parents. If Jenna drowned, then Jenna was never missing and Tracy knew that fact. She lied to her parents and her brother. We see her lying on those tapes. It's possible she even lied to Diaz in the beginning. When Diaz found out from Tracy . . ." He paused. "Let me emphasize this. ONLY TRACY said Jenna drowned. We have no way of knowing when she told Diaz that. As to the verdict, I can only assume the jury did not put much weight on the smell of death as testified to by credible individuals who know that smell. Or maybe because they don't like dogs in general some of them found it hard to believe in cadaver dogs. Or . . ." Ashcroft shrugged. "You never know about juries. We presented pictures of Jenna's remains and what story those remains told us. Obviously, the jury didn't see what we saw. I'd like to add a clarification. Nick Maddox was never a person of interest in the investigation of Jenna Maddox's death. Nor will he be."

"Do you think anyone will ever know what happened to Jenna Maddox?"

"Tracy Maddox is the only one who knows what happened to her daughter. The rest of us? Well, knowing why or how doesn't seem plausible at this point in time. My assumption is this – Tracy Maddox will never tell anyone. If she does, it will be because extraordinary monetary gains can be had. But how would we know if she was telling the truth?"

"Do you think your amusement at Diaz during closing statements angered the jury?"

Greg Ashcroft smiled broadly. "Alberto Diaz is known to be somewhat flamboyant and he definitely was on a roll during closing arguments. It amused me from that perspective. I just wasn't able to contain it. But no, I don't think it affected the jury. I would hope juries make decisions based on evidence and not based on whether Diaz and I liked each other or not."

Dorsie punched the mute button on the remote and buried her head in her hands. Oh, if you only knew, she mouthed silently. She got up from the sofa and marched to the kitchen with purpose. She picked up the media packet given to all jurors and grabbed the cordless phone. She marched back into the family room and stood in front of the TV and shouted at Laura Spencer's and Greg Ashcroft's images on the screen. "Maybe I should let you interview me. Would you be shocked to know the jury just wanted to go home? Or that the majority of the jury didn't give a crap about expert testimonies? And yes, Greg Ashcroft, your amusement did have an impact on some jurors. Diaz's over-the-top opening statement stuck in almost all the jurors' minds. Nothing seemed to dislodge it. Even common sense. They believed it. When you laughed at Diaz, it was like you were laughing at them too."

Dorsie sat down on the edge of the sofa and rubbed her temples. "I wish I never heard of or saw Tracy Maddox. I wish I could go back and do it over again," she muttered.

Her inner voice sprung up. *But you can't. Juror 1389 voted Not Guilty. On all charges. Proud of yourself?*

The garage door rumbled closed. A minute later she heard footsteps in the kitchen. Diva and Pavarotti jumped off the sofa and went into hiding beneath it. Click. Click. Click sounded on the kitchen floor. A second later Thor entered the family room and sat down in front of the coffee table and faced her.

"Woof. Woof." His ears pricked up and his tale wagged before his head dropped to sniff beneath the sofa. Suddenly, Diva slithered out. She jumped up on the coffee table, sat down, licked her paw and cleaned her face, totally ignoring Thor. He tilted his head sideways and watched. When she finished, she stood, tail high in the air and delicately navigated around the edge of the table, passing inches from Thor's snout. On the second pass she stopped and stretched out right in front him. "Meeeeoooow". Thor gave what sounded like a whimper and pushed his snout closer to sniff. Diva turned her head and ignored him.

"Well, I'll be damned," Dave chuckled from the doorway. "That sure in the hell is not a pansy cat." He came in, pushed aside the FedEx box next to her and sat down.

"How 'bout goin' for breakfast at the diner. My treat."

"Dave, I don't think . . ."

"No thinkin'. You're a regular there, so I hear. Besides, we are goin' to do some subtle intimidation. My style. An in your face kind of intimidation without anyone knowin' its happenin'. Once the locals get a look at me and Thor, you bet word will travel and nobody will be botherin' you. After breakfast we're gonna' do some more trainin'. Not for Thor but for you. Thor knows what's expected of him. But you, you need to learn key commands and practice them." He glanced at the coffee table and saw Pavarotti had joined Diva. Thor sat before them quietly, seemingly fascinated by each move of their cleaning ritual. Dave faced Dorsie again and gave her a wink. "I think all of you are gonna' do just fine. Come on Ole Gal, get your bootie movin'," he said in his finest Southern drawl.

"There's a conspiracy going on here," Dorsie said. "Everyone wants me busy, busy, busy. Give me fifteen minutes to make myself presentable."

At the Blairstown Diner, Thor's official K-9 Training bib along with Dave's K-9 trainer ball cap and vest commanded everyone's' attention. All watched in fascination as Dave commanded Thor to Search. No one moved a muscle if Thor paused to sniff them more thoroughly. All clapped when Thor finished then obediently went to his lay-down position next to Dave. Dave's breakfast was interrupted as a few customers came to ask questions about Thor and his training. When finished answering Dave added, "Thor's goin' be with Dorsie for a while. 'Cause by now ya all know what happened up at the shop. Y'all know there's folks out there not happy 'bout the outcome of the trial," he drawled. "This good, law abidin' town wouldn't want anythin' happen' to Dorsie now, would it?"

Afterwards, they went to the pharmacy where Dorsie got her prescriptions and they stopped at the A&P where Dave spoke with the manager and gained permission for Thor to enter. Once inside they made their way up and down the aisles with a grocery cart holding only a few items. Heads turned. Questions were asked. Some asked permission to give Thor a pat. To everyone who stopped to speak with them Dave made a point to interject, "Thor's goin' be with Dorsie for a while." They repeated the same routine at Blairstown Feed and Supply under the guise of Dorsie purchasing heavy duty construction trash bags for the clean-up going on in the shop. The next two hours were spent down at the Warren Regional High School football field where Dorsie learned to take Thor under her total control by learning leash skills, hand signals and verbal commands. Dave knew eyes were on them when Dorsie gave the attack command and Thor charged him, clamping his jaws on his arm which was outfitted with protective gear.

"Mission accomplished," Dave said as they turned down Ward road heading home.

"Pull in that driveway there," Dorsie pointed. "I'll just be a minute." She climbed out of the van, headed for the front door and rang the bell. One of Vince Di Paolo's brawny boys answered then yelled over his shoulder, "Ma, its Dorsie." He glanced over her shoulder. "Awesome. Big Thor," he said then rushed out to the van leaving Dorsie standing in front of the opened door.

Marilyn Di Paolo appeared. "Vince isn't here," she said coolly.

"Oh no, I don't want to see Vince. I just wanted to thank you for the food you've sent over." Dorsie pushed back a stray strand of hair from her face. "Things have been kind of out of the ordinary."

"I imagine they have. Would've you expected anything different after such a verdict," Marilyn said with icy sarcasm. "You should be ashamed of yourself, Dorsie," she said then slammed the door shut.

Dorsie stood staring at the closed door dumbfounded. She and Marilyn had worked together on several projects together for Habitat for Humanity; had gone into NYC shopping together when Marilyn redid her family room; had more than once caught a "chick flick" at the movies over in Stroudsburg. She considered Marilyn a friend, not a bosom-buddy-tell-all-to-friend, but still a friend. She turned away from the closed door and headed for the van. Once inside she quietly said, "Let's go."

Chapter Nine

Day Five Post-Trial, Evening

Back at the house Dorsie begged off going with Dave to check on Harold's progress photographing all the damage done in the shop. Glad to be alone, with the exception of Thor and the cats, Dorsie poured herself a healthy scotch on the rocks and settled on the sofa in the family room. She sipped her drink slowly savoring the taste of Johnnie Walker Black. She switched on a lamp as daylight began to fade from the room then picked up the remote and clicked into HLN's program *Consider This* . . . with Lynda Del Myra then realized she'd missed the first few minutes.

". . . Shocking revelations from the jury foreperson on the Tracy Maddox trial," announced Lynda Del Myra. "Just minutes ago, Philadelphia's Fox News channel was kind enough to share their interview with us. You'll only see the jury foreperson in outline. Wait until you hear this! Let's run the clip."

The Fox News anchor appeared on the screen. "As jury foreperson can you tell us what charges you decided to deliberate on first?" asked the anchor.

In shadowy light a silhouette appeared in profile. "The lesser charges of Lying to Law Enforcement and Obstruction of Justice. Those were pretty clear-cut. There was hardly any discussion about those. Lying, we gave forgiveness to. The major charges took more time. We wanted to work through the night, but some of the older jurors were fading fast. I decided they needed their rest. But before we adjourned, I proposed they think deeply about a Not Guilty verdict because Not Guilty was the only way to go. No one saw Tracy Maddox put her daughter in the Tangle-Wangles. Every juror had reasonable doubt about one thing or another which bolstered a Not Guilty decision. But Diaz gave the answers I needed and I reminded the jurors of Diaz's statements. Jenna was never missing. She drowned in the family swimming pool. I was forced by the absolute letter of the law to lead them into achieving this verdict."

"How did the four initial votes for Guilty change to Not Guilty?"

"Intense, fast, overwhelming discussions. Once I pointed out the errors in their thinking, those who felt a Guilty verdict was appropriate had no choice but to change their votes. They finally realized just how shoddy the prosecution's evidence was and how it meant absolutely nothing or had no bearing on the charges."

Dorsie stood up. Weeks of frustration and stress erupted. "You son of bitch. You're lying." She forcefully hurled the remote at the screen. It hit a lamp instead. Glass shattered. Sparks flew. Thor jumped to his feet, barking ferociously. His barks blotted out Dave, Harold and Di Paolo coming in the kitchen from the garage.

"What the hell?" Dave, Harold and Di Paolo shouted simultaneously.

Shaking from head to foot, Dorsie pointed to the TV.

". . . I was forced by the letter of the law to bring this jury to a unanimous vote of Not Guilty. Tracy Maddox needed to go free. It was my duty to see she did. As a juror, you understand."

"There you have it," Lynda Del Myra said. "They were forced. Shoddy evidence. Error in their thinking. No choice. Stay with us. On the other side we're going to our expert panel to see what they think of this! Shoddy evidence. Unbelievable. Tangle-Wangles?"

Dave unplugged the lamp. Harold found the remote and clicked the TV off.

"Turn it back on," Dorsie commanded. "I want to hear. He's lying. There were no overwhelming discussions." She faced Harold and Di Paolo. "You know he's from Blairstown too. Eric Van Zant."

Di Paolo's face registered surprise. "You mean that arrogant, Aryan looking dude from Blair?" *He* was the foreman?"

Lynda Del Myra's voice came from the TV. "We go to Joe Fields, our law enforcement analyst. " Joe, shoddy evidence?" she asked with raised eyebrows.

From his little square block lined up beside the other experts on the panel, Joe Fields shrugged his shoulders. "Must have picked that up from Dr. Spitz. Remember during the trial Spitz used shoddy to criticize the medical examiner's findings. Something just doesn't smell right to me here, Lynda. Can't tell you why, but years of law enforcement experience and my gut is sounding alarms." He shook his head. "I just don't know WHAT to think of this interview. Or the jury for that matter, based on these comments."

"Neil Getz, Defense Attorney" Lynda said. "What's your take?"

"Look Lynda, it was a circumstantial evidence case. The forensic evidence along with experts' testimonies was extremely technical in nature. I have to admit what really bothers me is this juror's communication style. Error in their thinking. The tone of voice in which it was said. No choice but to change their votes. The use of "I" so often. Sounds to me like something a grandiose, disciplinary, authority figure would use."

"Erin O'Shea, our trial analyst from *Unlikely Confessions*, you were in court the entire time, and had a chance to observe the jurors. Give us your thoughts."

"Lynda, I could see the jury box very clearly from where I sat. By body outline, I think this is Juror Eleven. The physical education teacher, blond, blue-eyed. I didn't pay a whole lot of attention to him at first. His use of Tangle-Wangles brought me up short. Let me explain why."

"Hold it, Erin," Lynda Del Myra said. "On the other side, we'll come back to this."

Commercials began to run one after the other.

"See. See. Somebody's picking up on it," Dorsie said gesturing towards the screen, taking the remote from Harold and hitting the mute button. She turned to Di Paolo, "What do you know about Van Zant?"

"Not much," Di Paolo said. "Van Zant is hooked-up with Crystal Yates. You know Crystal. Works down at the County 911 Center. You and Marilyn worked with her down at the Habitat. Also, Van Zant hasn't been seen around town. Kinda' odd since Blair is already into the Fall term. Kids started arriving mid-August."

"Vince, how do you know all this?"

Di Paolo spread his hands. "Come on Dorsie. You know I got sources. Not much goes on that I don't know about." He glanced at the TV then motioned to the remote in Dorsie's hand. She clicked off the mute button.

"We're back," Lynda said. "Erin explain – Tangle-Wangles."

"Well, I'll have to verify this from my notes. But I believe the area where Jenna Maddox was found was referred to by the kids in the neighborhood as the Tangle-Wangles because it was overrun by trees, weeds and prickly brushes. I believe this term wasn't used in testimony or any verbal discourse during the entire trial. If my memory serves me right, it was only mentioned in the local newsprint coverage. I don't see how this juror would know this term if he had no media exposure leading up to the trial."

Joe Fields interrupted. "Stealth Juror?"

Erin continued on, "Throughout the trial I did notice how at times, Juror #11 would focus intensely on Tracy Maddox. There was an odd moment or two when I thought the two of them were locked in a staring battle, like two predators. Gave me chills, then Tracy's expression went to its blank slate look."

"Neil Getz," Lynda said. "Stealth Juror. Explain to the viewers."

Getz replied, "A stealth juror is one motivated by a hidden agenda in reference to a legal case. They try to get seated on the jury so they can influence the outcome." He shook his head. "I just don't see this getting by Greg Ashcroft. He's very experienced. Or Judge Marvin Howard. Judge Howard is one sharp, savvy, seen-it-all guy."

Joe Fields piped in. "Could have turned into a stealth juror as the trial progressed."

Lynda added, "Possible. You know what they say about juries. You can never really be sure what a juror or juries as a whole will do. Given Neil's concerns about the language used by this jury foreperson, it does give pause for thought. Stay with us. I've got the producers cueing up the interviews from Kate Krieger and John Hudak. One present during deliberations, the other an alternate dismissed once deliberations began. Plus we've gotten verification on the vandalism of a family owned business of Juror Four whose name somehow got released in spite of the judge's orders. Out of respect for this juror's privacy, or what's left of it, we won't be broadcasting the name. Stay with us. There's a lot more to come."

Dorsie sat down abruptly then slumped back against the sofa's cushions. "This is all too much. Too much." Anger rose with a vengeance within her. She lifted her head and she sought out Di Paolo's eyes. "Vince, I've never asked you to do anything outside of the box for me, right?" He nodded. "But now I'm going to. Find out anything you can about Eric Van Zant." She glanced at Harold, Dave then back at Di Paolo. "Use all your sources."

"Done."

"I'll go get something to clean this up," Harold said then motioned with a shake of his head for Dave to follow. Once in the kitchen he said "I don't like it," while pulling a small clean-up broom, dust pan and trash bag from a cabinet near the garage door. "You have no idea what sources Di Paolo has available to him. If he goes to Gino Jr. or Gino himself, who knows what'll happen. We don't need anymore . . ."

Dave considered Harold intently. "Look," he said. "You two are wired to the max right now. Let Di Paolo poke around. Whatever he digs up just might be enough to help Dorsie put this Maddox thing behind her. You too, for that matter."

"Dave, you just don't understand," Harold said wearily. "Gino Carapelli has always had a real soft spot for Dorsie. Believe me, Uncle Gino's contacts are far reaching."

Dave took the cleanup tools from Harold and drawled, "Ain't it a good thing Dorsie missed that beautiful 52 inch screen?" He paused and flashed a wicked grin at Harold. "Uncle Gino and Dorsie? Really?"

"No! No! I didn't mean it that way," Harold sputtered.

"Didn't think so. Just checkin'," Dave said with a laugh then headed for the family room.

An hour later Vince Di Paolo left. Harold decided to stay the night and joined Dave for Thor's DDD detail. Dorsie scooped up and dumped all the files, DVDs and thumb drives scattered on the coffee table into a beach tote and headed for her bedroom. Once there she sat down heavily on her bed and placed the beach tote beside her. She unleashed her silver hair from its haphazard up do and let it spill down. From the nightstand she grabbed a hairbrush and brushed vigorously. After finishing she emptied the contents of the beach tote onto the bed and began sorting chronologically labeled file folders then laid out a row of DVDs in front of the bedroom TV. From behind her came a tap on the door.

Harold walked in and sat in the wing-backed chair. "I have a confession to make," he said bluntly.

In front of the TV, Dorsie sat back on her haunches and raised her eyebrows in question.

Harold leaned forward, arms resting on his thighs, hands clasped together. "I keep thinking about the alarm in the shop. How I could have forgotten to set it. I couldn't have . . ." He lowered his head and took a deep breath. "I wasn't at the shop. I was picking you up. Rose said she'd close up. She must have forgotten."

"Look at me Harold," Dorsie said firmly. "Remember what Detective Farino said. Whether the alarm was set or not set, whoever wanted to trash the shop would have found a way in." She gazed at the top of her brother's bent head. "Don't ever voice this to Rose, you hear? She's already going over and over it in her head trying to remember if she took care of the alarm. She's probably already filled with guilt. So let it just be. What happened to the shop was beyond anyone's control."

Harold leaned back in the chair. "It's nice having Rose in my life. I'm not like you, content to be alone. I like the companionship." He paused again then cleared his throat. "Do you think it's wise to have Di Paolo look into this Eric Van Zant? He's liable to go off half-cocked."

Dorsie stood, walked to the window and peeked through the louvered blind. A patrol car slowly passed the house on its way toward the end of Ward Road. "Vince won't go off half-cocked. He's not a thug, Harold. You know that. He'll just get Gino Jr. to use his information-gathering network. Probably all that will happen is one of them will call in a favor from a private investigator. That's all I want. Basic info."

"Why? The harm is done. The child is dead. Nothing will bring her back. Even if you all decided Guilty. What's the point?"

"Eric was appointed jury foreperson by Judge Howard. In the beginning he was very nice to everyone. For some reason I stayed my distance from him. I had this vague sense there was something "off" about him. Don't ask me what because I don't know. As the weeks went by, this feeling I had got stronger and stronger. One night I even had one of the guards check on him to see if he was alright. Don't know what that entailed but one of the guards came back and told me everything was fine."

"Well, you've always had good instincts, quick insights into people and I've seen your gut feelings turn out to be true many times. But I'm having a hard time understanding what you hope to accomplish by knowing this Van Zant's background."

"Damn it, Harold! Listen to me! I just have to know. Why he . . . what caused him to . . . I HAVE TO UNDERSTAND!" She saw Harold's stunned expression. "Sorry. Sorry. Didn't mean to sound like a shrew."

Harold stood and gave his sister a brotherly hug. "It's okay. Dave's got it right. We're wired to the max right now. And exhausted. So let's try and get a good night's sleep." He headed for the bedroom doorway then stopped and turned. "We'll get through this. We've been through worse."

"Yes we have," Dorsie said wearily. "Now go. I need a long hot soak in the tub. Probably an attitude readjustment too. I'm sorry I snapped."

Harold waved his hand in dismissal then glanced at the file folders neatly lined up on Dorsie's bed. "Ole Gal, placate me. Put that stuff away," he said then left.

Dorsie went back to the window and raised the blind. Ward Road was empty. The lights were on in neighboring houses and it looked as if all was well on Ward Road. But not with me, she thought. She thought of Harold and Rose and how the widening aftermath of the trial was affecting them. She thought of Megs and Dave, not being together because of the backlash from the trial. How many of the other jurors were facing the same post-trial impact? Would anyone else talk to the press? How were the detectives and investigators who worked the case feeling? Would Tracy Maddox still be friends with those who took the stand? Maybe Harold was right. Why did she have to know about Van Zant? Exactly what would it accomplish?

Nothing. There is no "Do Over". You did wrong.

She flung herself into the wingback chair Harold had just occupied. Tears of anger and frustration spilled down her cheeks. She sat there for a long, long time struggling with her emotions and going over what if she had said this . . . what if she had done that . . . what if she had . . ..

———

In the parking lot of Warren County 911 Communications Center, Crystal Yates wiped away tears and blew her nose. Eric where the hell are you? she asked silently. Why haven't you called? She hit the redial button on her cell. Eric Van Zant's number rang and rang and rang with no automatic voicemail pick-up. Stupid. Stupid, she silently scolded herself. Why didn't you find out more about his family and friends? She couldn't remember a single name he ever mentioned. Maybe someone up at Blair who knew Eric could help her, she thought, and began to plan when and how she'd contact Blair Academy. She got out of the car, closed the door, groped around in her purse and hunting for the pack of Salem's and lighter she'd bought earlier. She shook a cigarette out of the pack. After flicking the lighter at the end, she took a long drag; exhaled smoke up into the night sky then took another drag. She squinted at the burning end of the cigarette, tossed it and ground it out. Jesus, she thought. Smoke free for five years and here I am sucking the crap back into my lungs. She came to a decision while walking across the parking lot towards the Center's Employee Entrance door. Before she contacted anyone at Blair, she'd go through Eric's stuff that was in the garage. Maybe in one of those boxes was something to help her track Eric down.

Chapter Ten

Day Six and Seven Post-Trial

At 2:00 a.m. Dorsie left her bedroom and padded down the hallway to the kitchen. TV sounds still came from the family room and she poked her head in to see who was still awake. The man really does sleep, she thought while gazing at Dave lying on the sofa in a position most often found in the mummified remains of royalty. Thor was stretched out on his side, back pressed against the sofa. He lifted his head slightly, eyed her then laid his head back down. Curled up against Thor's exposed stomach were Diva and Pavarotti. She tiptoed into the room and shut off the TV. Back in the kitchen she stood still and listened to the quiet house. On a paper towel she wrote a note for Harold and Dave – Let me sleep in. Go about your business. I'll be OK. She draped it across the coffee pot. Making a plate of cheese, crackers and grapes to go with a glass of wine she headed back to her bedroom. From the floor she picked up the fat HLN reference folders, placed them on the bed and crawled back under the covers. She took a sip of wine then opened the first file and read a copy of a newsprint clipping.

Princeton-Windsor Gazette
West Windsor Toddler Still Missing – Mother Arrested
By Roland Miller
July 10, 2008
 Scores of volunteers from surrounding communities, students from Princeton and Ryder University, Trenton State and Mercer Community College still continue to search for the two-year-old missing toddler, Jenna Maddox, who was reported missing on June 15 by her grandmother, Ann Maddox. After confronting her daughter, Tracy Maddox, revealed the toddler had been missing for thirty days, stating she was taken by a baby-sitter, Jodi Smith, a part time Mercer County Community College student.

Sources close to the investigation now say there are no student records, covering a five-year period, for a Jodi Smith. There are also no resident records for a Jodi Smith at the address furnished by Tracy Maddox where she stated the babysitter lived. The same sources stated there were also no employment records for Tracy Maddox at Jackson Great Adventure where Tracy claimed to have worked for the past two years as a Customer Service and Planning Coordinator.

Tracy Maddox was taken into custody on June 16th, charged with Child Neglect, Making False Statements to Law Enforcement and Obstruction of Justice. She remains in custody at the Mercer County Correctional Center in Maximum Security. Her family was unable to procure the bond amount.

The Help Find Me Foundation has donated office space for the volunteer effort and local business owners combined their efforts to offer a $200,000 reward for information leading to finding Jenna. The offer will be withdrawn in ninety days. Investigators are asking for anyone with information to call the Tip Line at 800-279-3190.

Dorsie ploughed through folder after folder reading some material and passing over others. Another newsprint headline caught her attention.

Trenton Times
July 29, 2011
FBI Profiler Classifies Tracy Maddox
By Michele Sherman

FBI profiler, Dr. Irina Stoltz, a renowned criminal profiler with over 15 years of experience in profiling serial murders to aberrant sex crimes, tells us Tracy Maddox's behavior and deception tactics place her close to the borderline of being a sociopath with predatory characteristics. According to statistics, female offenders of this type are very good at generating false statements with just enough truth in them to appear real. She also points out these particular female offenders are very, very skilled at manipulating men and she feels Alberto Diaz has too much machismo to be immune to this. "Many men have no defenses when it comes to women who are masters at deception coupled with seduction," Dr. Stoltz says. "I don't mean outright sexual seduction with regard to Diaz, but if you take a look at the eye and brow movements of Tracy while talking to Diaz, you'll see the

*element of seductive playfulness there. She'll use that to get whatever she
wants or get him to believe whatever she wants." According to Dr. Stoltz,
Tracy Maddox needs male attention. "Watch her glance at the camera in
her arrest tape," she says. "You'll see a seductive arrogance being played
out there."*

*Dr. Stoltz also notes that Tracy Maddox showing indifference about
her missing child is also a hallmark sign of sociopathic traits or predatory
behavior. Dr. Stoltz offered this insight: "From the beginning when this
sad, sad event became known, it was doubtful Jenna Maddox would be
found alive. I thought in a very, very short time period her body would be
found."*

Dorsie removed her glasses and rubbed her eyes then leaned her head
back against the stacked pillows supporting her shoulders and head. She
tried to bring up and recall images of interactions between Tracy and
Diaz. Not much was in her memory bank. Nothing was there because her
focus had been on the witness box, the attorneys and their interactions
with Judge Howard. Suddenly, in an instant flashback to the jury selection process, the image of Tracy Maddox with her dazzling smile
appeared. She shook her head as if to banish it, picked up the sheaf of
articles again and rifled through them. Another headline caught her attention. She yanked it out and read.

*Princeton – Windsor Gazette
Maddox Pleads Guilty to Check Forgery
By Roland Miller
January 23, 2010*

*Tracy Maddox is now a convicted felon. Before Judge Ronald Bevard,
Maddox pleaded guilty on the charges of one count of petty theft, four
counts of check forgery, and wrongful impersonation. Maddox was
charged with stealing hundreds of dollars from a friend, Becky Hertzog, in
July 2008. Investigators said Maddox used Hertzog's checks to buy more
than $400 worth of clothes and groceries at area Wal-Mart and Shop Rite
stores. Afterward, her attorney Alberto Diaz said, "She will plead to what
she's guilty of and nothing more. That has been her approach all along."*

*Judge Ronald Bevard sentenced Maddox to twelve months with time
served on the petty theft charge and ordered her to pay court costs, a fine*

of $1,000.00 dollars and restitution to the victim. Under the Forgery Laws of New Jersey, a Fourth Degree Offense, he sentenced her to eighteen months and a $10,000 fine and two years' probation. He ordered the sentence of eighteen months to be calculated after the twelve months sentence is served, beginning with the first day of Maddox's incarceration. On the Wrongful Impersonation, Fourth Degree he sentenced her to eighteen months, another $10,000 fine and two years' probation.

The disposition of these cases leaves just one case left for Maddox to fight, the charge that she murdered her two-year-old daughter, Jenna, in 2008. She pleaded not guilty and is still being held with no bail in the Mercer County Correctional Center.

Dorsie's head was spinning trying to calculate how long Tracy Maddox would remain in jail. Undoubtedly, she thought, Diaz and Judge Howard were still in the process of figuring out a potential release date. Why weren't these check forgery charges revealed during the trial? She was sure it wasn't. What else did Tracy Maddox do that the jury didn't know about? Dorsie squeezed her nose between her brows and desperately tried to recall the testimony of Becky Hertzog. Could I find the court transcript online, she wondered then got out of bed and headed down the hallway to get her laptop in one of the guest bedrooms. "Damn," she muttered when she found herself facing a closed door, remembering Harold had decided to stay the night. Back in her own bedroom she gathered up the news clippings and put them back in the file folders. Bending down, getting on her hands and knees, she sorted through the DVDs stacked in front of the TV. Deciding to watch them in chronological order, she popped in the DVD labeled September 15, 2008. She pulled the wingback chair into a better position to view the TV screen then clicked the TV and DVD player to on. HLN's Lynda Del Myra appeared on the screen introducing the 911 tape from Ann Maddox. She fast-forwarded not wanting to hear the wrenching emotion in Ann Maddox's voice or see the many photos of the adorable Jenna Maddox. Fast Forward-Stop-View.

Fast Forward-Stop-View. Some clips she listened to entirely; others only a minute or two. On and on until early morning Dorsie sat red-eyed and riveted to the TV screen clicking and viewing, clicking and viewing. She paid close attention to the chaotic clips of Tracy Maddox being released from jail where Diaz had a protective arm wrapped around her while running interference through reporters and cameras. The more she watched and listened the more bizarre the coverage became – clips of an HLN anchor and private investigators hired by Ann Maddox showing them retracing the steps taken in searching a wooded area behind a small office park, supposedly at the direction of a psychic. Clips of interviews with the township surveyor who found Jenna's remains ran several times. On and on the clips went. Arguments back and forth between talk show panel experts. There were interviews with Tracy Maddox's boyfriends. From those she learned how Tracy told Rod Alessio he was the father of Jenna then told her parents she didn't know who the father was. The Alessio family interviews revealed hostility towards the entire Maddox family.

By six a.m. after watching an angry crowd outside the Trenton Court House chanting "Justice for Jenna. Justice for Jenna" she lowered her head and took deep breaths one after the other. Her recall of the actual trial and what she just viewed on the tapes became blurred. She moaned feeling ferocious pounding within her skull. A cold sweat enveloped her body as her stomach did flip-flops. She stood, feeling faint but made to it the bathroom. There, after vomiting, she grabbed towels and lay down on the cool tile of the bathroom too weak to stand. Suddenly, deep in her chest her heart skipped beats then went into overdrive. She tried to take deep breaths but the tightness in her chest and throat prevented strong gulps of air. Cough hard, she told herself. Cough. The runaway heartbeats continued. Tense the muscles, she commanded herself. She could barely make any part of her body function in the right way. Cold water, she told herself but was too weak to get to either the sink or shower faucet. Two minutes passed before blackness descended on her.

In the family room Thor scrambled to his feet sending cats flying. He raced down the hallway pushed hard against Dorsie's bedroom door then raced into the bathroom. He sniffed and licked Dorsie's face then whined. When she didn't respond, he filled the quiet house with ear piercing barks.

Dave's eyes flew open and his body swung into high alert as if he were in a combat zone. He raced towards the area of the house Thor's barking was coming from. When he located Thor and found Dorsie on the bathroom floor, he knelt down. "No. No. No. This can't be." He felt Dorsie's carotid artery for a pulse. He held his fingers there counting beats while looking at his watch. Two hundred beats per minute. Quickly, he filled the sink with cold water, lifted Dorsie and plunged her head into it until she came to, sputtering.

Harold appeared in the doorway.

"Clear the bed," Dave commanded like an officer.

Harold flung all the file folders off. Dave laid Dorsie down and slapped her cheeks. "Come on Dorsie, snap to."

Dorsie took a deep breath and coughed. She gazed at Dave disoriented.

"Where are you?" he asked loudly.

"At home. What happened?"

"I'm calling 911!" Harold shouted reaching for Dorsie's cell on the bed stand.

"No! No!" Dorsie sputtered. "Harold, it's the SVT thing."

Dave placed his fingers on her carotid artery and counted beats again. Eighty five beats per minute. Satisfied her heart rate was no longer in supra ventricular tachycardia and well within normal range, he asked, "You feeling better?"

Dorsie nodded. "Haven't had one of these episodes in years. It's controlled with medication now. I know how to do the vagal maneuvers. Mine didn't work but you plunging my head in cold water did." She gave a sweeping glance at his drenched sweatshirt.

"Maybe you still should go to the ER," Harold said.

Dave checked Dorsie's pulse again. She shook her head a Harold then grabbed Dave's arm. "Don't tell Megs about this. Please. I know what caused this. Too much scotch, a glass of wine, no sleep and stress." She glanced over at Harold. "I'll make an appointment with Dr. Berman tomorrow. I promise."

"You better. I'm going to make sure you do because I'm going to drive you over to Stroudsburg myself!" Harold said. He walked over to Thor who was patiently in a lay-down position at the doorway. He squatted and ruffled Thor's coat. "Good Dog. Good Dog. I think Dorsie should keep you around. Permanently!" He glanced at his sister. "Get out of those wet clothes. You need food. A steaming hot cup of chicken noodle soup cures everything."

With Harold gone, Dorsie got up to a sitting position. "Really, Dave. I'm ok. I've had all the necessary tests. This is not related to heart disease. It's just the common garden variety of SVT. Faulty electrical connections in the ticker. Over the last couple of days, I've probably hit every one of the triggers that brings this on."

"I know," said Dave. "Megs gave me a full medical briefing. Things to watch out for. Migraines. SVT. Unusual fatigue. Inability to sleep. Nightmares. Poor appetite. Increased consumption of alcohol." He arched an eyebrow. "Mood swings? Can't say I've seen any of that yet. Wait a minute, or have I?" He paused. "You know Megs, she covers all the bases. Also, Megs carefully counted off the important markers of post-traumatic stress syndrome. For a second, I thought she was trying to tell *ME* somethin'," he drawled. "But, you know, anyone can fall prey to its grip after a situation loaded with stress." He thought for long seconds. "Before you were released as a juror, did anyone talk to you about the after affects you might experience post-trial?"

Dorsie nodded. "Judge Howard was very empathetic. He reiterated the pit falls of being sequestered for such a long period. Along with being charged with making a difficult decision about another's life. He encouraged us to attend to our mental and emotional health just as we do with our physical bodies. Really, Dave, I'm fine now." She glanced over at Thor. "Now go, give him his treat and tremendous praise."

Minutes later Harold appeared with his cure-all, chicken noodle soup, a napkin and spoon. He set in on the bedside table. "Maybe this will give your stomach a full feeling and lull you into sleep." He closed the large louvered blind. "Try to sleep Dorsie. You can't keep going like this. I know you like I know myself. Struggling for normalcy, keeping whatever's eating at you bottled up inside. It's not good." He was silent for quite some time. His features creased into a frown as he walked around the bed and began picking up scattered file folders from the floor. "The answers you want aren't in these," he said wielding a manila folder in the air for emphasis. "Eventually you're going to have to talk to someone about it. I'm here if you need me."

"I know." Dorsie shook her head and blew out a long breath. "I feel I'm the cause of all the problems. The store. Rose not being with you." She paused and took a sip of soup. "Maybe you should have Rose come back."

"I'll think about it." He leveled a stern gaze at his sister. "You're not the cause of anything. You did your civic duty. Most think justice is the be-all and end-all for everything. Sometimes due process is the only thing that happens. Tracy Maddox got a fair trial. The jury spoke. That's due process. Justice, well that's something else altogether." He sat on the edge of the bed. "I don't know why you went with a not guilty verdict. Something monumental caught your attention during the trial to convince you. I don't know what it was. Only you know. If people don't like the verdict, fuck 'em."

Dorsie held Harold's gaze with one of her own. "Brandon said almost the same thing. You've all been wondering . . ."

"Does it matter?" Harold said cutting her off. "We don't care about the verdict. We care about you. Your well-being." He got up from the edge of the bed. Before closing the bedroom door he said, "Try to sleep, Dorsie. Your body needs it."

"Harold, when I . . ." she started to say then changed her mind. "Thank you for being here," she said.

"Wouldn't want to be anywhere else, Ole Gal. Try to get some sleep, Dorsie, even if it's only for an hour or two."

She watched his retreating back. How could she tell anyone she was almost afraid to close her eyes? In sweaty, tangled sleep, in the realm of her dreams, Jenna Maddox and the massive German Shepherd hovered like a rainbow hologram. Or, she was in the jury room waging an unwinnable war, one in which she had . . .

Surrendered! Why?

—

In Las Vegas, Security at Bill's Gamblin' Hall and Saloon reached a decision. For some time they'd been observing a young, tall, blond man acting erratically, stopping patrons and trying to engage them in unwanted conversations, losing at roulette, losing at craps and losing at blackjack. With each loss came excessive angry outbursts that startled other patrons around him causing them to move away. Two plain-clothes security officers approached him. They did it quietly, but made certain he understood he was leaving the premises. With subtle force they escorted him out to the sidewalk.

Eric Van Zant turned and yelled at their retreating backs. "Don't you know who I am? I'm The Man who got Hot Bod Mom set free! You know. The one who killed her daughter. Hot Bod Mom is comin' to your city, man. Just to be with me."

Passersby gave him a wide berth but a skinny twenty-something dressed as a Goth aimed her iPhone. She captured a blond, tall man with his arms spread wide, eyes closed, face raised upwards in rapture towards the neon lights above. For the rest of the night she followed him, snapping photo after photo with her iPhone. At the Hard Rock Casino and Hotel she watched him enter an elevator leading to guest rooms. Seconds later she slid a fifty-dollar bill at the night clerk then received a small white note back. She opened it. *Eric Van Zant, Rm 301, NJ.*

Chapter Eleven

Ten Days Post-Trial

Over the next couple of days Harold, Dave, Megan and Brandon continued their late night conference calls to keep each other updated. Dorsie visited her doctor and they agreed if another rapid heartbeat episode occurred, she would come in for further testing. Harold's beloved Rose returned to Blairstown. In NYC, Brandon coped with numerous gossip seekers who came into *Dorsie's Antiques and Design* seeking any non-publicized tidbit about the trial. At one of HLN's infamous cocktail parties, he fended off Lynda Del Myra who tried to coerce him into convincing his mother to do an exclusive interview. In Blairstown, Dave and Thor became familiar figures around town visiting two elementary schools, the regional high school and Blair Academy all as part of Thor's reinforcement training but more so for goodwill and education opportunities to highlight the role of K-9s in law enforcement and the military. On Thursday he left Dorsie in Thor's care while he went over to Montgomeryville Police Department in Pennsylvania to go over details for the upcoming K-9 Trial and Certification Event.

At mid-morning Dorsie sat at the kitchen island sipping coffee. Spread out before her were her To Do lists. She studied the amount of tasks that needed to be done and sighed heavily then stretched to loosen tense muscles. Nagging fatigue engulfed her and overwhelmed whatever energy she thought she had to tackle any item. She pushed the lists aside and picked up the phone and called Maria Sanchez, a very kind and happy woman who, at times, would come and together they would clean the house from top to bottom. The Sanchez's voicemail kicked in and she left a message for Maria to call her on her cell phone, repeating the number twice. She glanced over at Thor. "We need to be outside. I need to be me. You need to be you, a dog." Thor cocked his head in a quizzical manner. "We're going walking. Off leash. Sound Good?"

Woof! Woof!

An hour later, Dorsie spent a few minutes with Harold and Rose at the shop then went on to The Coffee Bin. She sat outside fortifying herself with strong coffee, a mini banquette, a chunk of cheese and imported olives. When finished, she and Thor crossed over State Road 94 heading for the walking trail behind the B&B. It was a beautiful day, blue sky, sunshine, the trees were resplendent in fall color and a distant cornfield showed the light and deep browns of die off from the end of the summer's growing season.

Once on the trail, Dorsie bent and let Thor off leash. He started his sniff, sniff routine wandering off into the bushes. Dorsie took deep breaths, inhaling the scents of fall and felt her body begin to relax under the warmth of the sun. Suddenly, she wished her body was young again. The day was sooo perfect that she wanted to run down the trail with arms spread wide in childlike abandon without a care in the world, soaring in a flow of happiness like the hawk above riding on a thermal current. Childlike abandon, she thought. How wonderful to feel . . .

Without warning her mind's eye brought forth an image of Jenna Maddox dancing in her little pink tutu, smiling and laughing. Off in the bushes Thor whined. She turned towards the sound. Everything swirled in a blur of color as the synapses in her brain fired a signal that jerked her from the here and now. The impulses ignited a memory portion of her brain obliterating the sunny trial behind the B&B. In her mind's eye she was standing in a dark, dank place where overgrown weeds, fallen dead branches, thistle, bittersweet bushes and the rotting vegetation surrounded her. Into a place where the sun didn't penetrate through large old oaks until their leaves fell to the ground in the fall. The crime scene video played in her mind but by some internal memory malfunction she wasn't watching it as a juror in the courtroom, instead, she was an active participant in an interactive X Box crime scene game. She was slowly walking a crime scene grid while a K-9 cadaver dog sniffed and sniffed, nose to ground looking for the scent of tiny, tiny bits of bone belonging to Jenna Maddox. On and on the images played on the screen in her mind. Yellow crime scene tape. Crime scene investigators in white coveralls all busy and focused on taking photos and placing flags indicating where remains were found. Other investigators carrying buckets to a tent where more technicians sifted through dirt and detritus for what remained of the now found Jenna Maddox. She heard no background conversations, generators or law enforcement radios crackling. There was only one sound – Jenna Maddox's sweet, sweet voice singing "Pleez don't take my sunshine away. Pleez don't take my sunshine away. Pleez don't take my sunshine away."

Dorsie's heart pounded. Tha-thump. *Sunshine away.* Tha-thump. *Abandoned.* Tha-thump. *Like Trash.* Tha-thump. *In a bag.* She slumped to the ground on her knees and covered her face with her hands gasping for breath. Her memory recall shifted from the X-Box like screen to a specific video tape released from the Mercer County Correctional Center. A tape of a visit between Tracy and her brother, Tommy Maddox, in which Tommy was diligently questioning Tracy and making a list of places he could search or get information about Jenna Maddox's whereabouts. "Are there any other places I should be looking for Jenna?" Tommy asked. Tracy answered. "Look in places we know. In my heart I know she's close."

Nothing registered in Dorsie's consciousness, not the blue sky, not golden fields or the long open path before her. Over and over again she heard Tracy Maddox say, "Look in places we know."

She told her brother where Jenna was! He just didn't know it!

Dorsie remained on her knees, face buried in her hands sobbing and sobbing and filled with unbearable remorse. A deep, piercing ache engulfed her soul. Her heart was heavy with unmeasurable sorrow. Little Jenna Maddox, an innocent child, did not deserve to be dumped in a place Tracy Maddox and her friends called the Tangle-Wangles.

Thor whined and pawed at Dorsie. Long minutes passed before Thor's whining and the squawks of black crows flying above brought her back to sunny reality. She stared into Thor's bright, alert eyes then sat back on her heels teetering on an emotional razor's edge. "Good boy. Down," she said barely able to get the words out. Thor immediately went into his lay down position. She wiped her nose on the sleeve of her sweater then rubbed her face hard as if to blot out the frightening experience she'd just passed through. *Breathe deep. Exhale. Breathe deep. Exhale.* With each breath she took she felt the semblance of control and normalcy return. She reached out and ruffled Thor's coat, assuring herself she was in touch with the here and now. Burrs pricked at her fingers and she plucked them from his fur. She patted him heavily on his side welcoming the feel of his bulk beneath her hands. "Good boy. Good boy. It's okay. It's okay," she said reassuring herself more than the dog. Slowly she got to her feet. "See I'm fine. Just a bad moment." She tilted her head back and looked upward to the blue sky. A hawk circled and circled, riding a current. Her gaze then took in the fields full of Goldenrod, drying stalks of wildflowers and wild grasses. Satisfied she was in the here and now, on the trail behind the B&B she said, "Up Thor." As they walked heading towards the B&B, she kept looking over her shoulder frightened for her sanity, knowing something within her had come unhinged on that peaceful path.

Acting as if on autopilot, she found the garden hose on the side of the patio of the B&B, opened the faucet and held the hose end towards Thor. She would call Megs, she decided. Tell Megs what had happened even if it meant escalating her daughter's concern over her physical and emotional well-being. Either Megs would reassure her it was a normal stress response or something more serious. But Megs would prod and poke, ask a myriad of questions, keep jabbing away in an irritating way until she'd snap at her daughter with a forceful I-don't-want-to-talk-about it. Dorsie sighed, certain she already knew the answer to what to do about her state of mind. Dorsie turned off the faucet and recoiled the hose. Civic Duty, she thought with distaste. Civic duty had turned her into a coward and a failure. Her civic duty hadn't left her with a sense of pride. It left her with self-loathing. She knelt down on one knee and ruffled Thor's coat. "You're a smart dog. You listen. Never nod your head and never say how-do-you-feel-about-that like a therapist would. You just wag your tail. Maybe I can just talk to you." Thor cocked his head to one side holding Dorsie's gaze with his own. For long seconds he seemed to study her then leaned forward and gave her a big, wet, sloppy lick.

Later, after stopping at the Alpine Deli, Dorsie laid a package of the Alpine's famous beef jerky on the kitchen island for Dave then placed porterhouse steaks and cold cuts in the refrigerator. She glanced at the phone with its blinking message light. She hit the caller ID button then rapidly fast-forwarded through messages until she heard Maria Sanchez's voice. "Ms. Dorsie. I cannot come to clean. I sorry. I cannot clean for someone who . . ." There was a pause. "You not punish the mother! She killed the baby. You not punish. Why? I cannot come no more. Goodbye." Dorsie slumped against the counter and sighed deeply. She glanced over the package of beef jerky from the Alpine Deli. Her hand flew to her cheek as an image of Olga, Herman's stalwart wife, washed over her. Olga had come from behind the counter and for a moment Dorsie thought Olga was going to embrace her in a hug like she usually did. Instead Olga's arm lashed out and her flattened palm connected with her cheek. "Fine lady. You Dorsie Renninger. Ha! No more. You no do right for innocent *bebe*!"

Now, Dorsie shuttered at the thought of what could have happened if Thor had been at her side. Silently, she thanked all the gods in the Universe she'd left him in the car. "I'm a pariah, a persona non grata," she said aloud. She opened a top cabinet, took out a bottle of Johnnie Walker Black Label. She poured the amber liquid into a glass and took a long sip while Diva and Pavarotti rubbed against her ankles mewing, wanting to be fed. Thor watched from his lay-down spot near the garage door.

Later, over dinner Dave tried to cajole Dorsie to participate in the up-coming K-9 Training and Certification Event, telling her he needed another person at the registration table until she agreed. Once dishes were cleared away, Dave left the kitchen while Dorsie pulled another beer from the fridge for him and poured herself another Johnnie Walker. Dave returned with a FedEx box. "Found this propped up against the front door early this morning. Sorry, I was running late and didn't take the time to bring it in," he said, noting the third scotch of the night in his mother-in-law's hand.

"It's nothing urgent. Just something Rick promised to send," she said absently while swirling the amber liquid around in her glass. "This is pretty darn good stuff for taking the edge off. I could get used to this."

"Ya, well don't get too friendly with old Johnnie Walker," Dave drawled. "Old Johnnie has a way of sneakin' up on ya." He pulled a Swiss Army Knife from one of his many cargo pants pockets and slit the tape on the package. "Let's see what we got here."

Dorsie set down her drink and lifted the carton edges then removed an enormous amount of tissue paper. "My, Gawd, no!" Staring up at her from inside the box was a doll, its torso well-worn heavy white cotton. A cloying sweet scent hit her nostrils. A deadly coldness spread in the center of her chest followed by revulsion. "No!" she screamed backing away from the island. "No. No. No!"

In a nano second reaction Dave spat out a command to Thor. Thor scrambled to his feet barking, leaping, and grabbing the edge of a flap on the FedEx box. He gave a forceful shake of his head flinging the FedEx box off the island. Glass broke. Liquid splattered. Packing peanuts sailed through the air. The doll flew out of the box and hit the floor, landing on its side. The FedEx box hit the cats' water and Meow Mix bowls scattering their contents in all directions. Thor zeroed in on the doll, nudging it with his snout, sniffing and sniffing. With his paw he turned the doll until it was face down. Pinned to the doll's back was black construction paper, folded letter style. Thor sniffed and barked, sniffed and barked until Dave grabbed his collar and commanded him down.

Dorsie stood speechless with shock as rapid-fire photo after photo clicked off in her mind. Jenna Maddox hugging her doll. Nick Maddox giving the doll a kiss as Jenna held it up to his face. The doll in the back seat of Tracy Maddox's car next to an empty car seat. A doll Ann Maddox said she sprayed with Febreeze. A doll impregnated with the smell of human decomposition from Tracy Maddox's car.

"What the hell? What is this?" Dave shouted turning towards his mother-in-law. She was shaking, her color ash-white.

"Jenna Maddox's favorite doll," Dorsie choked out.

"The dead little girl's doll?" Dave asked sharply.

Dorsie nodded. "Why would somebody do this? I don't understand."

Dave squatted down and with his knife unfolded the note on the doll's back. Crude letters cut from newspapers and magazines spelled out the message – *Hand Deliver to Jenna. Last Known Address HEAVEN!* He scooted over to the blue, red and white carton laying three feet away. He carefully folded over the carton's edges, looking for a return address, tracking number anything to point in a direction of the sender.

"Don't touch anything," Dave commanded. "I'm calling Farino."

Dorsie stared down at the doll with its grotesque note. Someone had sent this to her HOUSE! What did Hand Deliver mean? Did someone want her to deliver the doll to Jenna on the other side? Did someone want her dead?

Twenty minutes later, Detective Eugene Farino entered Dorsie Renninger's kitchen. His sharp, eagle eyes took in the whole scene. "Did you touch anything?" he asked. He pulled on crime scene latex gloves.

"Dorsie opened the box. Took out the tissue paper," Dave said. "Thor took a chunk out of a flap when he flung the box to the floor. He sniffed and nudged the doll with his paw. Otherwise, no."

"Doubtful there's any meaningful prints on the box." Farino said. "Passes through too many hands. Now, the note, that's a different story," he said, squatting down to view the doll and note at a closer angle. "Might be something there." He stood and faced Dorsie. "I'm not familiar with all the details of the Maddox trial. Tell me the significance of this," he said waving a blue-gloved hand towards the doll.

Dorsie took a deep breath. "This doll looks very much like Jenna Maddox's favorite doll. She was rarely without it. You know how children are when they get attached to something."

"Was the doll recovered?"

"It was never missing. It was in Tracy Maddox's car. In the backseat next to Jenna Maddox's car seat. It was probably taken into evidence. This can't be Jenna's doll. It's an identical looking one."

Detective Farino gave Dorsie a steady gaze. "Someone's going through an awful lot of trouble to frighten you. The vandalism at the store and now this. Then again they could be two different random acts." He picked up the carton and viewed it from several angles. "Dorsie, anything else out-of-the-ordinary happening?"

Dorsie ran her hand across her forehead. "I don't know. I've been . . . I can't think."

"She's still getting hate calls," Dave said. "But we've expected that."

Detective Farino produced a set of gloves from his pocket and tossed them to Dave. "Grab garbage bags and let's put the carton and peanuts in one. The doll and note we'll put in another. That's where anything of significance will be. Chances are this was probably sent from some mail service franchise. We'll see what we can get from the tracking number." He turned to Dorsie. "Got a broom and dust pan?"

Dorsie left the kitchen. When he thought she was out of earshot, Farino said, "Think you can convince her to get out of Dodge for a while?"

Dave nodded. "Got it. We'll make it happen."

"I just don't like what my gut's telling me. This is too specific. Hell, how many people watching the trial would remember the doll? Whoever did this is one sicko. I'll notify Trenton. Something must be up because I get the distinct impression they're keeping tabs on the jurors. Got a call asking me to track down Eric Van Zant, the jury foreperson. Haven't located him yet."

The garage door rumbled open then rumbled shut. Seconds later Harold walked into the kitchen. He took in the mess then glanced towards the door leading from the kitchen into the hallway. Dorsie stood there, broom and dustpan in hand, her face white, eyes wide in shock. He started to move toward her. She handed the broom and dustpan to Dave then held out her hand like a school crossing guard stopping traffic. She turned and left. Seconds later they heard the loud bang of a door being slammed shut.

Chapter Twelve

Day Ten Post-Trial, Late PM

A minute later, Dorsie leaned against her bedroom door for support but her wobbly knees gave out and she sank to the floor. Her stomach threatened to empty its contents and she fought it off by taking deep breaths one after another. Her thoughts zig-zigged from one place to another. The media and people gathered outside her home the day the verdict had been released was difficult. The destruction of *Dorsie's Antiques and Design* was a below-the-belt blow not only for her but a devastating one for Harold. The cold shoulder treatment around town was uncomfortable and showed little signs of a rapid thawing. Marilyn Di Paolo still remained distant. Maria Sanchez did not want to clean for her anymore. Long-time neighbors on Ward avoided her.

Long minutes continue to pass as Dorsie's thoughts kept skipping from one event to another. The vivid dreams. Detective Farino saying he had to get in touch with Eric Van Zant. Images from videos shown during the trial or from ones she'd gotten from Rick flashed by. The doll and its sinister note loomed threatening to engulf her. "Home is supposed to be safe," she cried. But now, it no longer was a safe refuge from outside influences. Her home had been invaded in a cruel, cruel way.

When she felt able to stand without collapsing, she made it to her bed, sat on its edge and waited and waited and waited for her stomach to stop churning, for her hands to stop shaking and for the bombarding thoughts in her head to stop. After long, long minutes she picked up the phone on the bedside table and called Brandon in NY.

"I know, Mom. Dave called," Brandon said before she could say a word. "Are you . . ."

"Brandon. I need to come to New York," she blurted out. Her voice cracked. "Tomorrow. Can you arrange a car for me? Can you get in touch with Deidra Fallon right away?"

Caught off guard, Brandon said, "Deidra Fallon. Wild, wild red hair. The therapist? The one you spent half the night talking to at the charity auction for Safe House?"

"I need help. Her kind of help. Also, I'm going to take Vince Di Paolo up on his offer about his place in Florida. I just need to talk with Deidra before I leave."

"Consider it done." He paused. "You do know Deidra's Del Myra's partner?"

"I don't care. For Gawd sakes, Brandon. The woman's a professional therapist. Bound by patient confidentiality."

"Right. Right." Brandon said in a soothing tone. "This is a good move, Mom. I know how strong you are. But sometimes we can't cope with what's happening to us all on our own. Hang on a sec."

Dorsie waited, hearing a short muffled exchange between Brandon and Rick.

"I know exactly where I can reach Deidra."

Relief flooded through Dorsie. "Have her call me. Tonight. Anytime. If she can."

"If you want to stay in NY instead of going to Florida, our house is yours too."

"I know Brandon. Thank you. But right now, I want to go somewhere where nobody recognizes the name Renninger."

"You could use an alias," Brandon teased.

"Not a bad idea. Color my hair. Appear nothing like what the talking-heads reported as Juror Four, business-like, elderly woman," she retorted in an almost lighthearted way.

"There you go!" Brandon exclaimed with enthusiasm relieved to hear the change in her tone of voice. "Listen, first thing tomorrow, I'm booking a Spa Day for you at that place you like that's just around the corner from the loft. Do you good to have someone pamper you. I hear you're looking pretty, pretty, ragged around the edges."

"Which one of them told you that? Harold or Dave?" she snapped. "They tell Megs too? Gawd! Now I'm being monitored in my own house." She paused and took a deep breath. "Sorry. Sorry, I didn't mean to sound so . . ."

"No problem. I get it. I'll arrange the car for say, three in the afternoon. Get you here before rush hour starts. If anything changes, let me know."

"Thank you. You're a good son, Brandon. See you tomorrow."

Down the hallway, in the kitchen Detective Eugene Farino's cell rang. He flipped it open and listened intently, grabbing a small pad and pen from his inside jacket pocket. "Las Vegas you say. Repeat the number again. Okay. Got it. Thanks."

Harold secured the garbage bags shut then handed them over to Farino. Farino frowned then made a snap-judgment decision. "Las Vegas calling about Eric Van Zant," he said to Harold and Dave. "First Judge Howard's office and now Vegas. I don't like it. Judge Howard's office hasn't called Dorsie have they?"

"Not that I know of," answered Harold.

"Me neither," added Dave. "No messages on the home phone. Her cell, don't know about that."

Farino turned to leave. "Come on, I'll walk you out," Dave said. He motioned for Thor to follow. Once outside Dave said, "Thanks for all your help. I get it that nothing may come of finding out who trashed the shop. But this?"

"Small things make or break a case." Farino reached down and ruffled Thor's coat. "Looks like this guy is ready for a good run. I'll keep you posted."

Thirty minutes later, Detective Farino placed a call to the Las Vegas police and was transferred to Detective Ford Hines. "Thanks for the quick call back. We got a situation here with one of your residents. At least according to his New Jersey license. Eric Van Zant. 2 Park Street. Blairstown. Age 32. 6' Blue Eyes. Blond."

"Repeat the NJ license identification number. What can I do for you?"

"This is official notification that one Eric Van Zant, Blairstown, New Jersey is deceased. We found him 'bout two hours ago in his room at the Hard Rock Hotel. ME's initial call is suicide. But, he'll give final determination after he looks him over. Will forward all necessary paperwork over as soon as we get it signed off. Assume you'll do notification to family. Got nothin' here on that."

"Say again. Suicide! How? Jesus, he was jury foreman on a high profile case out here?"

"Hang job. Yep. It's all in his note. The Maddox case. Although he refers to Maddox as Hot Bod Mom. Poor guy was delusional. Thought she was going to join him here in Vegas 'cause he was The Man who saved her from prison. He wrote some pretty grandiose stuff in the note." There was a pause on the line. "Might want to keep the note For-Your-Eyes-Only. We'll scan it and send to your email. I'd do some digging on Van Zant. Three of the maids said he was roaming around ranting for a few days then locked himself in his room." He paused. "Not to say that's really unusual. We see all kinds of shit out here. High percentage of suicides in this town too."

Still stunned, Farino said, "You're sure it's suicide. We've got another juror here in town being harassed big time. Business vandalized. Received detailed item pertaining to the trial with a threatening note."

"Well, as I said, the ME called it as suicide. Coroner will look him over good based on what you just told me."

"Van Zant's not a long-time local. No family here. He's a Phys Ed instructor at a private school we've got here in town. Those folks keep pretty much to themselves. I'll contact Admin to see who he's listed as emergency contact in his records. As soon as I get it and make notification, I'll call with details."

"Got Van Zant's cell here. Might be somethin' you can use. Got a tech who owes me. I'll get him to do his magic act tonight. Keep checkin' your email."

"Personal effects?"

"The usual. One-way Boarding Pass from Philly to Vegas. Couple of receipts for FedEx Priority Mail in the flight folder. Credit cards. Over 10K in cash. Must be winnings. ATM receipts. Casino chips. Business cards. The kind of junk anyone here sticks in their pockets."

"You say mail receipts. Scan and send those too."

"Will do. Anything else?"

Farino's mind raced weighing the implications of the information he'd just received. "Any chance of keeping a tight lid on this? Van Zant went on national TV after the not guilty verdict. Once the media vultures get a hold of this."

"We can try. Contrary to what they say, all that happens in Vegas doesn't stay in Vegas. Don't know how much Van Zant was runnin' at the mouth. Don't know who listened. Maybe somebody put two and two together. We got TMZers who troll around for celebrities, calling in tips to TMZ's hotline like they were playin' the slots. I'd keep an eye on TMZ's website."

"I hear ya. Appreciate anything you can do. FYI. The case was tried in Trenton, NJ. Gotta' notify the trial Judge's office. For some reason he wanted us to track Van Zant down. No idea why but highly unusual."

"Good Luck," offered the Las Vegas detective. "I'll expedite what I can. Call if you think of anything else you need."

Farino leaned back in his chair staring at the phone trying to connect the dots himself. Late this afternoon he'd talked with Crystal Yates but she didn't know where Van Zant was. But she was worried. Wanted to know how long before a Missing Person Report could be filed. He checked his watch then picked up the phone and called the 911 Communications Center to let them know the disposition of the Vegas call for their records and to see if Crystal was on duty. She wasn't but would be in for the midnight shift. Crystal was a great gal and he'd hate for her to see the inquiry on the Daily Bulletin. He pulled down a black three-ringer binder from the shelf above his desk and located the high-level emergency contact for Blair Academy. He dialed the listed chief-honcho's private number pretty certain the call and his request wouldn't be welcomed at this hour. He placed a call to Trenton leaving a voicemail, asking for a return ASAP then dialed the Warren County Communications Center asking the call-taker to put a high priority on a callback from the detective assigned to Judge Howard's office.

Twenty minutes later, Detective Farino ran up the steps of the Blair Administration Building. All lights were on in the main hallway and he could see a tall male in a jogging suit coming towards the front door.

"Detective Farino, come in," he said, jangling keys nervously. He handed over a manila folder. "Copies of everything we can release, according to our counsel and policy. Van Zant is no longer here at Blair. Has something happened to Eric?"

Farino studied the man's face, noting sincere concern. "Why do you ask?"

He gave a feeble shrug. "Eric wasn't himself towards the end of the last semester. I kind of assumed he was ill. He never said anything but when he didn't come back this year, I just assumed . . ."

"Sorry. Can't disclose. You know. A policy thing." Farino glanced down at the manila folder in his hand. "Thanks for getting this for me so quickly. Really appreciate it."

"Sure. Sure. Hope Eric's okay."

Farino nodded then walked through the door, down the steps and headed for his car. Once inside he flicked on the overhead light and flipped through the papers in the manila folder until he found what he needed. "Awwwh! Shit!" he exclaimed. He rubbed his jawline with its five o'clock shadow while staring at Crystal Yates's name listed as the Emergency Contact for Eric Van Zant. He flicked up the sleeve of his jacket and glanced at his watch. Eleven. "Shit! Shit!" He pounded the steering wheel in frustration. There was no way he could get to Crystal Yates at her home now. The odds were she was already on her way for the mid-night shift. He flipped open his cell and called the Communications Center and asked for the night supervisor for all dispatchers and call takers and asked that Crystal be kept from going on duty immediately. He told the supervision he was already on his way to the Communications Center and needed to talk with Crystal on a high priority police matter. Farino hit his flashers and picked up speed once he was clear of the Blair Academy Campus grounds. He rubbed his now tense jawline. He hated this part of his job – delivering bad, bad news to unsuspecting nice, nice people.

Chapter Thirteen

Day Eleven Post-Trial, Early

Crystal Yates sat in the Communication Center's staff lounge stunned. "Eric's in Las Vegas? What's he doing there?"

Detective Farino waited patiently for Crystal to grasp all the information he'd just given her but when she continued to stare at him shell-shocked he asked, "Is there someone I can call for you? Your family? A friend?"

Crystal blinked rapidly as tears began to fall. "He's dead? Is that what you said? My name listed as Emergency Contact? But I'm just a . . ." She had difficulty finishing the sentence.

"Do you know anyone in his family?" Farino reached across the table and cupped her hands in his. They were ice cold. "We can reach out to his family."

Crystal shook her head. "An old uncle up in New Canaan, Connecticut. That's all he ever said. Never talked about his family much. Didn't like anyone trying to pry." She wiped her tears away with a tissue then blew her nose. "Eric's dead? Why? How?"

For now, Farino decided to spare her the cruelty of the word suicide. "We'll know more when Las Vegas forwards their report and paperwork. Crystal, is there someone I can call for you?"

She stared down at her hands then met Farino's gaze. "I told you this afternoon I didn't know where Eric was. That I was worried. Remember? In another day or so I was going to file a Missing Persons Report, just like you said. Now . . ."

Farino asked again, "Crystal, is there someone I can call for you?"

Crystal looked around the Communication Center's staff lounge as if she were in a strange, unknown place. Her gaze returned to Farino. "Dorsie Renninger. I need to talk to Dorsie. Ask if I can come to her house. I need to talk to her."

Farino's jaw dropped. "Dorsie Renninger. Crystal, isn't there someone else?"

Crystal shook her head. "I've only got a brother left, over in Stroudsburg. He can't help me. I know Dorsie. Please. Dorsie's the kindest person I know. Harold too." She paused. "It's hard to believe. Eric dead."

"I'm sorry, Crystal. Just sit tight here for a minute. Let me see if I can reach someone at Dorsie's." He left the room, closing the door then leaned back against the hallway wall calculating how to handle the situation. "Jesus Christ," he muttered under his breath. Dorsie Renninger of all people. And after what had happened earlier, he had no idea what state Dorsie herself was in. He pulled out his cell and dialed Dorsie Renninger's son-in-law, Dave Broz.

"Broz here."

"Dave, Detective Farino. I really, really got a situation here. Could use your input. Your help."

Dave listened intently as Farino gave all the pertinent details of the events and Crystal Yates's request. When Farino finished he said, "Damn. You know this is going to go viral once the media gets hold of it. Maddox Trial Juror Commits Suicide. They're gonna' have a field day." He paused while running scenarios in his mind to what his mother-in-law's reaction might be to this new development. "You said Dorsie knows this Crystal Yates. Worked with her at the what?"

"Habitat for Humanity," Farino answered. "The girl's in a state of shock. Hell, if I were married, I'd take her home to my wife."

"Dorsie's not in the best of shape either. Though she won't admit it. All I can do is ask," Dave finally said. "Get back to you within fifteen minutes."

Dave clicked off the Jay Leno show and walked down the hallway to Dorsie's bedroom. It was slightly ajar and a light shown from within. He knocked gently. "Dorsie. It's me, Dave. I've got to talk to you."

"I'm awake," Dorsie said. When he came through the door she immediately saw he was concerned about something. "What's wrong? Megs? Megs is okay?"

"Megs is fine." Dave paused searching for some way to lessen the impact of what he was about to say. He dropped his arms at his sides in a helpless gesture. "Hell, there's no way to say this but straight out.

Detective Farino just called. Eric Van Zant committed suicide in Las Vegas. And . . ."

"What!" Dorsie hands flew to her mouth. "What! Suicide!" She threw back the covers, jumped out of bed and began pacing. "Suicide. Oh-my-Gawd. Oh-my-Gawd."

Dave intercepted her and made her stop. He held her by the arms. "Listen! Farino said Crystal Yates was listed as Van Zant's emergency contact. He made notification to her. They're down at the Warren County 911 Communications Center where Crystal works. Farino says she wants to talk to you. Asked him to call to see if she could come over."

"Crystal? Crystal wants to come here? I don't understand. Why would she . . ."

"All I know is Farino says she asked for you. The girl's in shock. He's worried. Doesn't want her to be alone."

For long moments Dorsie stared at Dave in an uncomprehending way. "Eric committed suicide?" She shook free of his grasp and began pacing again, pounding her fist against her thigh. "Damn you Tracy Maddox. Damn you! How many more lives are going to be turned upside down? Changed. Ruined." She stopped pacing and turned to Dave. "I know Crystal. From Habitat. She's a lovely young woman. Always willing to help. But . . ."

Dave walked over and put his arm around his mother-in-law in a comforting gesture. He could feel the slight tremors coming from her body. "You don't have to do anything. You don't have to get involved. I'll tell Farino . . ."

Dorsie sighed deeply and long seconds passed. She ran her hand over her forehead. "Tell him to bring Crystal here. I don't know what I can do to help. But we'll see." She leaned in heavily against her son-in-law. "I've got you here. Harold. Megs. Brandon. Rick. Even Vince Di Paolo. You're my support. Maybe Crystal doesn't have anyone. Let's just see how we can help."

"I'll call Farino. Make some coffee." He walked towards the door. "Anything else you can think of?"

Dorsie shook her head slowly. "What a shock. Suicide," she whispered. "Such desperation. Such a final act. I knew something . . ." she said then stopped.

Dave stood in the doorway studying his mother-in-law. She'd lost weight. Her face showed all the signs of stress – pale, drawn, dark circles beneath the eyes. It seemed as if she'd aged before his eyes, far beyond her sixty-two years. He knew she wasn't sleeping well because he'd hear Thor leave his bedroom in the middle of the night to go and follow Dorsie around the house. Then earlier, there was no mistaking the fear in her eyes after opening the package with the doll. Now, here she was, extending a helping hand to another when she was barely hanging on herself. He knew his mother-in-law was a fiercely independent, secure and strong woman. He just never had an opportunity to see her strength in action, until now. He closed the door slightly and went into the kitchen to call Farino.

Long after midnight Crystal Yates and Detective Farino arrived at the Renninger house. Tears, consoling hugs and intense, emotional discussion followed then a plan established. Harold and Dave would help Crystal go through Eric's belongings stored in her garage with hope of finding information on any family member. Farino would continue to deal with Las Vegas and Judge Howard's office. Dorsie would call Brandon and tell him to cancel the pick-up car. She'd delay going into the city. At two a.m. Dorsie settled Crystal in the guest bedroom.

"Crystal, can I get you anything more?"

Crystal shook her head. "Can we talk for a few minutes?"

Dorsie nodded then sat on the edge of the bed and took Crystal's hand in hers.

"I couldn't get down to Trenton on those family visit days," Crystal said. "My schedule was locked in tight. I couldn't go to my supervisor and say you've got to let me have these days off because these are the only days I can see my boyfriend. Couldn't say he was away. On the sequestered jury for the Tracy Maddox trial. No one was supposed to know who was on the jury. Was Eric okay during those weeks?

Dorsie pulled Crystal close to her in a motherly way. "I didn't talk with Eric much. At the end of each court day I was pretty wiped out. Most of the time I kept a low profile. Sort of lost in my own thoughts about what I'd heard or was hearing in the courtroom. But Eric, he seemed to get on with everyone. Talking sports. They were quite impressed with all the hiking he'd done throughout the U.S. during summer breaks."

"I snooped through some of Eric's stuff," Crystal admitted. "I thought maybe there was something there telling me where he'd gone." She paused then turned to Dorsie, seeking out her gaze. "I found a letter from Blair terminating his contract for this year's semesters. Why wouldn't he tell me something like that? Didn't he love me enough to trust telling me that? Did he ever say anything about going to Las Vegas? He was gone, as far as I can figure, from the day he did the Fox News interview. He never told me about that either. Why?"

"Crystal, this trial was very, very stressful. I suppose each of us is de-stressing in our own way. I know networks don't pay for interviews, but offer other perks. Maybe they arranged a trip to Las Vegas for Eric."

"I suppose I could call and ask," Crystal said wiping tears from her eyes. "You know, where I work I hear a lot. Over these past couple of days I kept imagining the worst when Eric wouldn't answer his cell. Something about Eric changed after he came back from the trial. He just wasn't the same Eric. Before, he was sweet, kind, rarely got angry. But the trial changed him. He'd get annoyed over nothing then swing into what I'd call an Energizer-Bunny-Mode." A deep, deep sob shook her body. "The worst happened! Why? Why did he do that? I thought we were going to be happy living together. I thought we might even get en . . .."

Dorsie gave Crystal another tight squeeze. "You may never know why. What you do know is Eric did decide that living together was a good thing. That both of you were good for each other. Keep remember-ing that, Crystal. If he wasn't happy with you, he would have never wanted to live with you as a couple. Keep remembering that." She took Crystal's hands in hers. "I'm not going to tell you to get some sleep be-cause I know that'd be impossible. But do try to lie down and rest your body. I'll be just across the hall."

At three a.m. Dorsie lay in her own bed, trying to follow her own ad-vice, trying to will her tense body to relax. Eventually she fell into a fretful doze.

At seven-thirty everyone was back around the kitchen island for much needed coffee. Crystal looked fragile and red-eyed. Dave downed a cou-ple of Tylenol for a headache. Dorsie moved about the kitchen as if in a fog. Harold arrived looking somber but well rested.

"I can't thank you enough," Crystal said to Dorsie, choking back tears. "All of you."

Loud banging on the back kitchen door startled them all. Thor jumped to his feet barking. "Di Paolo out here. Collar that brute," he called from outside. Once inside he placed two large brown bags from The Coffee Bin on the kitchen island. The scent of fresh bagels and croissants emerged. "Figured you all were running on empty." He glanced over at Crystal. "Sorry. Hard thing to take."

"You're a life saver, Vince," Dorsie said. "I swear you have some kind of "somebody's in trouble" radar. But why do you insist on always coming through the back?"

He shrugged then winked. "Don't want anyone to see me. Gettin' the wrong idea."

Forty-five minutes later, after eating and consuming enough coffee to kick start them into action, everyone was ready to tackle the day. Crystal, Dave and Harold left to get Crystal's car at the Communications Center. Vince Di Paolo stayed behind with Dorsie.

"You look like hell," Di Paolo said, eyeing Dorsie up and down. "Glad you're gonna' get outta' here. Jesus Christ, wait till the media sinks its teeth into this. It'll be a circus all over again."

Dorsie nodded wearily. "It'll be brutal. Speculation on speculation. None of it good." She paused moving her head back and forth, rolling it side to side, to relieve the stiffness gathering in her muscles. "They'll hound Crystal."

"Hang on," Di Paolo said while opening the kitchen door. He grabbed a briefcase from the deck, set it on the island then snapped it open. "Got this late last night. Maybe if I'd have gotten it sooner. Maybe . . ." He shrugged then handed Dorsie a manila folder tabbed, Van Zant, Eric. "Some of it ain't good."

Dorsie's eyes widened in surprise as she took the folder. "Should I read now or later?"

"Later," Di Paolo said. "Look, there ain't no living relatives for Van Zant. Uncle up in New Canaan died couple of years ago." He paused then rushed on. "Didn't want to spill the beans 'cause I wasn't sure just how much Crystal knows about Van Zant. Give Harold or Dave a call and tell them they're lookin' for trust fund statements, Power of Attorney or anything from a law firm up in Connecticut. Basically, someone's gotta' tell Farino Van Zant's affairs were being handled up in New Canaan. Farino will let Vegas know. Death Certificates, identification of the body, disposition of the body. All that's got to go through the attorney. Crystal is pretty much out of the picture." Di Paolo got up and poured himself another cup of coffee then leaned back against the granite counter top. "Kid was worth a bundle. Old family money." He motioned towards the manila folder. "It's all in there. Just do me a favor, don't go tellin' anyone where the info came from. Let it play out through Farino. Like I said, all he needs is the name and number of the law firm. He knows what to do."

"Thanks Vince. You have my word."

"There's some other stuff in there. Guaranteed to make the hair stand up on the back of your neck. Blockbuster headline maker. Especially since Van Zant was jury foreperson in the Maddox trial. Hell, if any of this info hits the judge's desk down in Trenton he'd be second guessin' himself every time he appointed a jury foreperson. And the State's Attorney General . . . hell, I don't even want to go there."

Dorsie raised an eyebrow in question.

"Read it later." He emptied the dregs of coffee from his mug into the sink, rinsed it out then put it in the top shelf of the dishwasher. "Talked with Gino, Jr. this morning. You're gonna' fly down to Florida in the jet. No arguments. It's settled. Uncle Gino has spoken. I've already called down to The Villages. JB, our guy down there, will be gettin' the house prepped for your arrival."

"I have a few things I need to take care of here, Vince. As soon as I get it all figured out, I'll give you a date. I've got to spend a couple of days in New York."

Di Paolo nodded. "Let me know when you'll be in The City. Uncle Gino wouldn't miss the chance to wine and dine ya. Ah, Dorsie, his eyes light up when anyone mentions your name. How come you never . . ."

"Vince," Dorsie said sternly. "You know better than to go there."

"Yah-yah-yah. I do. Look. Gotta' run. Call Dave and Harold now so they don't waste the whole damn day."

Minutes later, Dorsie found the attorney's information listed on the first page in the manila folder. She flipped open her cell and called Harold.

—

Farino sat as his desk staring at the computer screen. "Unbelievable," he muttered while reading the ten page manifesto found in Van Zant's room. He shouldn't be so surprised, he thought, not after the background Trenton gave him. Dr. Irwin Zucker in Philly made the inquiry directly to Judge Howard. Zucker had recognized Van Zant's profile while watching the interview on his local news channel. Told Judge Howard he'd been trying to reach Van Zant for weeks with urgent medical concerns. Judge Howard won't release any info on Van Zant but immediately ordered his staff to contact Van Zant. Judge Marvin Howard's staff swung into action, uncovering an interesting fact – Zucker was a psychiatrist.

The doc was right to be concerned, Farino thought as he closed the PDF file of the suicide note. Jesus, if the media ever got a hold of the contents. Well, he didn't even want to think about the field day they'd have. Farino opened another file sent by Las Vegas and saw it contained numbers pulled from Van Zant's cell. He noted the number of area 215 calls and the many 908 calls, no doubt Crystal Yates's number and an equal number of Stroudsburg 507 calls. Nothing unusual there, he thought given Blairstown's proximity to Stroudsburg and Philadelphia. He opened another file and studied the scan receipts found among Van Zant's personal belongings. He'd have to check out the mail service receipts and business cards. His cell rang. "Farino."

"Harold Raines, detective. We found some information here. Van Zant's Power of Attorney."

"Bingo! Who's listed?"

"Attorney up in Connecticut. We found all kinds of documents in a small fireproof box stashed in a jumble of camping gear. Dave's on his way now with it. He should be at your office within minutes."

"A nice break. All Crystal has to do now is let Van Zant's lawyer handle all the details. I'll get on it as soon as I've got the info in hand. How's she doing?"

"Much better but still pretty shaken up. In the box is a pretty hefty engagement ring. We kept that out of sight, not knowing . . ."

"Got it. Ask her who her family doctor is. Get her to make an appointment or at least call. I'll drop by later and fill her in on what the lawyer's plans are. That's if he'll divulge. Crystal's lucky you all stepped up to the plate in her time of need."

"I'll get her to call her doctor. Catch up with you later," Harold said then ended the call.

A half-hour later, Farino sorted through the contents in Eric Van Zant's fireproof box. He made notification to Van Zant's attorney of his demise covering all known details he had at his disposal. Pertinent information was exchanged along Detective Hine's number in Las Vegas. Information regarding Crystal Yates was also passed on to the attorney. His next call was to Philadelphia International Airport law enforcement division where he requested a search for Van Zant's Jeep, most likely parked in a lot somewhere. He also called Las Vegas, leaving the New Canaan information for Detective Hines. Satisfied he had covered all his bases, he turned to his computer and Googled TMZ then clicked into the website. "Jesus Christ!" he yelled. "How in the hell . . ." He began reading.

Death Surrounds Tracy Maddox – Juror Commits Suicide.

According to TMZ's unnamed sources in Las Vegas, Nevada, the Jury Foreperson in the Tracy Maddox Trial was found in his hotel room at the Hard Rock late last night of an apparent suicide. Eric Van Zant, a Blairstown, NJ resident, left behind a suicide note but at this time the contents are unknown. Another unnamed source tells us during his stay in Vegas, Van Zant bragged to anyone who would listen as to how he single hand-edly saved Hot Bod Mom from life in prison. Claimed he was responsible for convincing the jury to acquit. Hot Bod Mom is Tracy Maddox who was found not guilty of the murder of her two-year-old daughter, Jenna Maddox, by a sequestered jury in Trenton, New Jersey. What drove him to such a desperate act? Public outcry over the verdict?

Farino flipped open his cell and called Dave Broz, hoping he was on his way back to his mother-in-law's house.

Chapter Fourteen

Day Eleven Post-Trial

Dorsie, Thor and the cats were alone in the house. She sat quietly in the family room holding the manila folder Vince Di Paolo had given her. Part of her was reluctant to open it. She was about to pry into someone's very private life. Whatever was inside she knew it would thorough because the Carapelli family, through lawyers and others, had access to superior resources. She flipped over the initial cover to the main page of the report.

SUMMARY

Eric Van Zant, age 32, is a member of an old New Canaan family. Historical data reveals many family members allegedly suffered from various undiagnosed forms of mental illness. Henrick Van Zant, Eric's father, committed suicide when the boy was nine. Thereafter, he was raised by his mother, Violet Smyth Van Zant, who never remarried. He had no siblings. Violet Van Zant died in her early fifties of breast cancer. She had no living relatives. Eric Van Zant's father had only one older living brother, Fredrick Van Zant, who remained an eccentric bachelor until his death in May, 2007. Eric Van Zant was the last male in the family line and heir to a considerable family trust all managed by a long time law firm in New Canaan. Although privileged, with a high IQ, Van Zant's academic years at St. Luke's School, a private school, were non-stellar. He was an unruly student, prone to periods of hyper activity and periods of withdrawal. He barely achieved passing grades. Even so, afterwards he managed to earn a degree in Physical Education from Western Connecticut State University. Employment records show no long-term employment with the same employer beyond two-year periods as a Physical Education Instructor at private schools in Connecticut, Rhode Island and most recently New Jersey. Each ended with a non-

renewal of contract. No details given as to why contracts were not renewed.

Van Zant has no criminal record. One vehicle is registered in his name, a 2009 Red Jeep Wrangler with New Jersey plates. There is no history of substance abuse. However, at the age of twenty-three, just after his mother's death, Eric Van Zant was admitted to Silver Hill Hospital, a not-for-profit psychiatric facility specializing in psychiatric and addictive disorders. There he was diagnosed with Bipolar Disorder. He was successfully treated with dialectical behavior therapy and drug therapy then released with a medication regimen along with strong recommendations for adjunct psychotherapy. His prognosis stated he had high cognitive functionality to enable him maintain full-time employment as long as the medication treatment regimen was diligently followed. In late June 2007, shortly after his uncle's death, he sought admission again at the same facility remaining there for two weeks. There have been no subsequent admissions.

A financial check showed his credit rating as excellent. Two bank accounts are held in his name in a New Canaan bank and in Blairstown, each carrying balances of over 200k. Credit Card debt is minimal. Socially, he is well liked but associates term him as being "a loner". He has no online social network account but is a member of an online chess club and member/donor of Sierra Club Chapters in Connecticut, Rhode Island, New Jersey and Pennsylvania. He is an avid hiker/camper spending many summer breaks exploring U.S. national parks across the country.

Suddenly, compassion filled Dorsie for Eric. Brandon and Megs had lost their father to a freak accident at around the same age and there had been many dark days and months before the sun shined through the clouds of their grief. But to lose someone to suicide, she couldn't even fathom the emotional turmoil, wondering whether a young Eric Van Zant knew the circumstances of his father's death. She hoped not. Bipolar Disorder, she thought, vaguely familiar with the term but not familiar with the details of the illness.

Dorsie retrieved her laptop from the guest bedroom and over the next several hours Googled and researched site after site providing information on bi-polar disorder. Afterwards, she sat, pondering all the complications associated with having such a mental disorder. She learned someone who was bi-polar had emotions that went on a roller coaster ride without warning. They could become emotionally unstable because a chemical imbalance in the brain caused moods swings from the lows of depression to the highs of mania. A depressive or manic phase, or a combination of both, could be triggered by psychological stress or social circumstances or a life event. Suicidal thoughts were not uncommon. She also learned most people with bi-polar disorder needed to be on medication in an effort to control or alleviate symptoms.

She buried her head in her hands. We were all stressed, she thought. But for Eric, the stress was magnified by his loss of employment, by being sequestered, by the energy draining days in the courtroom. Had Eric been taking his medication all those weeks of the trial? His interpretation of the foreperson's role certainly had been greatly distorted.

Suddenly, Eric's angry outbursts during the hours of deliberation replayed in her mind. "You bitch. You think you can take control from me. YOUR take on the trial is WAY off. SHE IS NOT GUILTY OF ANY MURDER. "You fuckin' bitch. No note is going out of this room! Not from you. Not from anyone. Not if you know what's good for you."

Dorsie brushed her hand along her arm where Eric's grip on her had left bruises and shuddered remembering the automatic fright-flight response coursing through her then. Now, she realized Eric's hostility and physical aggression coupled with excessive irritability, inflated self-esteem and poor judgment were all symptoms. Again, she heard Eric Van Zant's voice sounding like a drill sergeant issuing orders to new recruits. "You WILL have reasonable doubt. It's a done deal. She is Not Guilty. Hear me. Not Guilty. You'll sign off on all major charges as Not Guilty. Don't even think about going against me!"

Eric was manic during deliberations!

"Damn you Dorsie. Why didn't you listen," she cursed herself for not paying attention to her gut. In those final days of the trial she had known there was something terribly wrong with Eric. Why hadn't she found a way to get a message to Judge Howard? But the security guard had told her Eric was fine, stating Eric said that he was just very, very tired. It seemed logical at the time. They were all tired. There was little doubt they'd all been reaching their maximum limit of how many more days of isolation they could endure.

How had Eric even gotten on the jury? She thought back to the jury questionnaire and realized it was primarily one of self-disclosure. Given the stigma associated with mental illness, how many individuals would really disclose their difficulties? Only those who definitely wanted out of jury duty would claim such a thing. Had Eric *wanted* to be on the jury for this trial? Had he had more pre-trial media exposure than he admitted to? Her mind raced back to what she could remember about Eric during the potential juror questioning by the prosecution and defense attorney's as well as Judge Howard, Only bits and pieces came to mind mostly the self-assured tone in which he'd answered questions. He'd passed muster under the eyes of experienced professionals. Most likely even under the scrutiny of the behind-the-scenes jury selection consultants hired to assist Tracy Maddox's attorneys

Dorsie's cell rang. Caller ID displayed Farino. "Detective Farino. I hope you were able to get at least a few hours of sleep."

"I did. Listen Dorsie, I'm the bearer of more bad news. *TMZ*, an online celebrity and sports news website, just made public Van Zant's suicide in Vegas. Given the appetite for the Maddox case, the national networks aren't going to be far behind. Expect a media frenzy again. They only have four juror names. You. Kate Krieger and the alternate juror who also gave an interview. They'll be all over each of you like hyenas." He paused then quietly said. "I read the Van Zant's suicide note. Did you notice anything during all those weeks? Any change in his behavior?

Dorsie paused for long seconds before answering. "We were all pretty stressed in our own way. Coping the best way we could. *TMZ* you said. I'm going to pull up their website right after we hang up. Wait. Was Crystal Yates's name mentioned anywhere?"

Farino noted Dorsie's careful dodge of answering his question about Van Zant. He'd pursued it no further but logged the hesitation in the back of his mind for future reference. "Nothing about Crystal. Not so far as I can tell. When it comes to digging, reporters are just like us detectives. I'd say it's bound to surface sooner or later."

"Should I call Crystal?"

"No. I'll do it," Farino answered. Just be prepared Dorsie. Things are going to get ugly again. I'll check in with you periodically. Don't hesitate to call me about anything."

Dorsie disconnected from the call. Her cell rang again. Caller ID read Rick so she answered.

"Mama D. Leave the house! Come into the city today!" Rick ordered without preamble. "When this breaks nationally, no one is going to be off limits. Attorneys. Jurors. Judge Howard. Anyone who knew or ever had contact with Van Zant will be tracked down. Advocates for mental health issues will be crying bloody murder."

Dorsie sighed heavily. "Jenna Maddox. The real victim was and still is getting lost in the frenzy. Nothing is going to bring her back. Now, nothing is going to bring Eric Van Zant back."

"True. Sad commentary, isn't it?" He paused. "Mama D, it's good you're going to Florida. Brandon already got in touch with Deidra. She's good people. Tell her everything. Look gotta' go. From the activity going on I'd bet the *TMZ*'s report just got top priority. Holy shit! Just got handed the photo *TMZ* posted. Gotta' go. Come into the city today!"

Dorsie closed her cell and sat absolutely still, deep in thought, remembering the affable Eric Van Zant during the early weeks of the trial. He was engaging, talking non-stop, finding common ground with many of the jurors. With Lisa he shared his teaching experiences with young children. Later with Burton, he demonstrated physical therapy exercises to relieve sciatic nerve pain. He seemed to embrace Millie as if she were his own grandmother. And Kate . . . well . . . Kate had her eye on the attractive, tall, blonde, blue-eyed Eric Van Zant. As for herself, for reasons unknown, she kept a polite distance from Eric because her gut had been sending out signals that there was something "off" with him. Her gut had been right. But now, it was too late. Too late to act on what her gut was trying to signal.

You failed him too!

I won't fail Crystal! she silently countered her badgering inner voice.

Dorsie called Harold. "You know what's happened?" When he answered in the affirmative, she said, "Tomorrow when I go into the City, to Brandon's, Crystal should come with me. No one will pay attention to us. We'll get lost in the shuffle."

Harold sighed deeply on the other end of the line. "Dorsie, take care of yourself first. Let Crystal spend another night at the house. Dave's there. Rose and I will take her under our wing." He paused. "I'm over in Stroudsburg now. With Crystal. At her doctor's office. You should follow

Crystal's lead in getting some medical help. Call Dr. Berman. Let him know you're not sleeping at all. At least not enough to constitute restful sleep. He'll call in a prescription for you."

Dorsie sighed on the other end. "I don't like talking any more pills than I have to. I've never taken sleeping pills in my life."

"Do it," Harold admonished. "The strain is showing. Stand next to me and people will think you're my older sister by four years instead of my twin," he teased, hoping he was getting his point across. "You need to sleep. Need to eat more than you are." He paused. "Here comes Crystal. We should be back in Blairstown in about an hour. We'll talk further then. Call Dr. Berman. Now."

"He always looks younger because of his bald head," Dorsie told Thor as if he'd been a part of the conversation. "Gives him a baby-faced look." Thor thumped his tail but not so forcefully as to disturb Diva who was stretched out, full length, against his stomach, taking a blissful catnap.

Ah, the Divine Serenity of a cat, Dorsie thought, on her way to her bedroom. Seconds later she was in the master bath facing the mirror. The woman staring back at her looked extremely ill and uninterested in her appearance. "Is that me?" she asked aloud after being shocked by her reflection. Suddenly, she realized she'd been functioning on autopilot, brushing her teeth, taking a shower, pulling her hair back into an old-fashioned grandma's bun or ponytail then dressing herself without paying attention to what she was putting on. Leaning closer to the mirror for a better look, she examined her face, noting the dark circles, eyebrows in need of plucking and unhealthy, dull skin begging for a good exfoliating facial. Backing away she glanced down at her clothes – old, khaki pants that had seen at least 100 washings and a faded plaid shirt, each appearing as if they were a size too big. She loosened the hair bun. Long, bedraggled silver hair flopped downward lacking the vibrant luster, shine or movement touted in fashion magazine ads and commercials for "must-have" hair products. When was the last time she'd had her hair styled? If she couldn't remember, she told herself, it must have been a long, long time. "You're a mess. Pull yourself together. Take control." she said, shaking a finger and scolding the woman in the mirror.

Minutes later she called Dr. Berman's office, told the nurse what she needed and left the phone number of the local pharmacy. Satisfied she'd accomplished one positive thing for the day she stripped down, took a hot,

hot shower, washed her hair; blow dried it but still pulled it back in an old-fashioned ponytail. Minutes later she stretched out on her bed, pencil and pad in hand ready to begin making lists. Pack. Utility Bills. She wrote nothing further. Instead she set the bedside alarm to go off in an hour. Diva and Pavarotti jumped up on the bed. Thor laid down near the bedside table, putting his head on his paws. Dorsie listened to the quiet of the house, felt the soothing, comforting warmth of the cats against her side. She glanced down at Thor grateful for his presence and ever-watchful eyes. Slowly, she drifted off. For one blessed hour the overwhelming and outside circumstances fate had thrown at her did not intrude.

—

Detective Eugene Farino flipped his cell phone shut and threw his notebook across the desk. He leaned back in his desk chair and groaned with frustration. The tracking number and date on the receipts in Van Zant's possession were for an Overnight Express mailings addressed to his attorney's office weeks before Van Zant become a juror He had nothing to lead him anywhere on finding who had vandalized *Dorsie's Antiques and Design*. He was still awaiting a call back on the tracking number on the box containing the doll sent to Dorsie Renninger. Maybe he'd catch a break there. But from years of experience as a detective in NYC and now in laid-back Blairstown, he knew cases like this rarely got solved. Still, that didn't mean that he should quit trying. He picked up his notebook and the case file, reviewing both again, looking for something he might have missed. Like he'd told Dave Broz, little things can make or break a case. Farino's desk phone rang. "Farino." His eyebrows rose in surprise. "Dave Broz. Out front. Sure. Bring him back."

Dave approached Farino's desk then answered Farino's questioning look. "Pulled into the driveway just as the UPS guy jumped out to deliver," he said. "Took the box from him. Looked it over and got a bad feeling. Thought it better to open it here."

Farino studied the brown carton and its standard shipping labels then turned and pulled latex gloves from his jacket pocket hanging on the back of his chair. He tossed a pair to Dave. Farino lifted the carton to judge its weight then set it down. "Let's see what we got here."

Dave pulled his Swiss Army Knife from his cargo pants pocket and slit the tape.

Farino slowly folded back the carton flaps. Crumpled 8'1/2 x 11 sheets of paper filled the box. He removed the top layer.

"Hold on," Dave said as he unfolded a crumpled sheet. "Jesus!" He handed over a photocopy of a photograph of Jenna Maddox with a superimposed skull with duct tape positioned over the mouth and nose. Quickly they straightened out more sheets of paper. All were the same, photocopies of the same image. Strips of duct tape, theatrically made to look as if it had decomposed, were interspersed between the crumpled papers. On the duct tape was a little girl pink heart sticker."

"This is one sick son-of-a-bitch, going for the psychological jugular," Farino uttered as he sat down in front of his laptop and keyed in a Google search. Up popped sites with information on the Tracy Maddox trial that referenced duct tape, skull and a heart sticker. Dave looked over his shoulder as he clicked, read then clicked to another site then another. Entered into trial's evidence was a gruesome video showing a photo of a smiling Jenna Maddox morphing into a picture with a skull with duct tape superimposed over it. The position of the duct tape over the nose and mouth demonstrated how the tape was used to smother Jenna Maddox. Another site recapped a day's testimony on the significance of the heart sticker found on the duct tape.

Dave took a seat at the side of the desk. "Don't know how Dorsie would have taken this. The strain's already taking its toll. I'm not telling her about this."

Farino nodded in agreement. "Anyone with reasonable technical skills could have pulled this photo off the Internet from any number of sources. One thing's certain. Whoever is doing this followed the trial very, very closely. Was. Is. Obsessed with it."

"Let's hope he's only thinking about sending things."

Farino nodded then added, "He could be a She. The Maddox trial. The verdict. Enraged women. Deep psyche stuff. Primal mother-child hot buttons."

Dave glanced at the carton and the dozens and dozens of photocopied sheets with their gruesome image. He shook his head then stood. "You're good with Dorsie not knowing about this?"

Farino nodded. "I'll work on where this takes me. But . . ." He raised his hands in a futile gesture. "There's not much to work with at this point in time. We got allocation of resources issues. Budget constraints."

"Got it. Thanks."

"I'll keep you posted."

"Appreciate it," Dave said as he grasped the detective's hand in a man-to-man handshake.

Chapter Fifteen

Day 12, 13, and 14 Post-Trial

Within hours Eric Van Zant's name exploded nationally in every media outlet. The next day and the next and the day after television and radio programs aired non-stop expert opinions on every conceivable angle regarding Van Zant's death. Callers into talk shows once again crucified the jury for their not guilty verdict. Bloggers vilified the verdict and jury all over again while opening the gates for dialogues on mental health issues, jury selection processes, legal obligations of fellow jurors, speculations whether New Jersey's Attorney General would call for a retrial. Wannabe legal eagles weighed in with erroneous facts on NJ law. A press conference clip aired from Blair Academy, stating unequivocally that Eric Van Zant was not on the 2011-2012 Staff Roster. They declined to answer any questions on his performance during the previous school term. Video feeds of another press conference held by the New Jersey Court System aired repeatedly. A public relations spokesperson from the New Jersey Courts System read the official statement. "With all jurors involved in trials with emotional and gruesome evidence and testimony, we advise them to seek professional help if they find themselves struggling. The Maddox trial was no exception. May I remind you of Judge Marvin Howard's concern for jurors by ordering a restriction on the release of their names until after the first of the year. During the Jury Voir Dire there was no indication of anything to have excluded Eric Van Zant from serving."

Dorsie arrived at Brandon's and Rick's loft in the late afternoon three days later. Rick called from the HLN studio forewarning them that Lynda Del Myra had secured an interview with Kate Krieger for her program *Consider This . . .* He didn't know the exact airtime because editing was still in progress. As Brandon continued to talk with Rick, Dorsie clicked on the television to cable news channels. The security video obtained by

TMZ of Van Zant being escorted from Bill's Gamblin' Hall and Saloon aired was now being aired on every major news channel. Las Vegas affiliate stations had quickly secured interviews with individuals who came in contact with Van Zant. Short clips appeared one after another – Hard Rock Casino hotel clerks, two men who sat next to him at a Black Jack table and a couple from NYC he nearly knocked over while bumping into them outside Bill's Gamblin' Hall and Saloon. They repeated what they'd heard, his triads about how he and he alone saved Hot Bod Mom.

Brandon quietly took the remote from his mother's hand and clicked off the TV. "Come on, Mom. You've got to eat. I got your favorite from the deli around the corner. Matzo ball soup." He guided her to the breakfast bar and quickly set out plates and silverware.

Dorsie idly arranged and rearrange forks, knives and spoons. "Brandon, I think I need a drink. Can you pour me some scotch?"

Brandon glanced over at his mother. "Yep. But only after you eat. Not good to have booze on an empty stomach."

"Ah! Harold's told you how scotch's becoming my best friend." Dorsie brushed her fingertips across her forehead. "Well, I can assure you I'm not a lush yet."

Brandon placed a steam bowl of soup before his mother and gave her a look. "Mom, come on! No one's accusing you of being a lush."

"Sorry. Sorry. I'm just on edge. Every little thing seems to strike a raw nerve." She lifted the spoon and slurped loudly. "See. I'm eating."

Later, after he arrived home with take out, Rick studied Dorsie as she made an effort to please Brandon and eat some of the Thai food he'd brought from their favorite restaurant. "Mama D, look at me and listen," Rick said. "You're a wretched wreck!" He motioned towards Brandon. "You know what kind of crowd we move in. Sooo, tomorrow you're keeping your spa appointment. We can't take you out in public looking like some refugee straight off the boat from god-knows-where."

"That bad?" Dorsie ran her hand over her hair and down the length of her haphazard ponytail. "You're right. Public? Where is it exactly you think you're going to take me out in public?"

"To dinner at *Del Posto* with Uncle Gino," Brandon answered.

"But before that happens you and I are making a trip over to *Pas De Deux*." Rick interjected then swung into an impersonation of a drag queen. "Our honey of a wardrobe stylist just raved and raved about this little boutique. To die for, she said then crossed her heart. Sooo, dearie. Luv. We just can't have you going out to dinner or down to Florida in rags." He arched an eyebrow with affect connotating distaste. "No matter how comfortable those rags may be." He sashayed towards the coffee table where he picked up a pen and small notebook then went back to Dorsie. "Now, Mama D, stand up," he ordered. He thrusted the pen and notebook at her. "We need a *list*. We must be prepared for those darling little sales associates. With a *list*," he said trying to keep his tone serious. In the background he heard Brandon's smothered laugh. He whipped out a tape measure. "Arms up." Dorsie raised her arms. Rick wrapped a tape measure around her with a tailor's expertise. "Ummm, busty Mama D, aren't we? Write down forty-two on your *list*." Rick wrapped the tape measure around her waist. "Ahhh, we've got middle to late age spread here. Write down . . ."

Dorsie regained her wits and batted away the tape measure from Rick's hand. "I have old-age spread and I'm entitled to wear anything with stretchy waistbands. Even the color purple if I like." Falling into the ridiculousness of the scene they were acting out she wiggled her shoulders in way to emphasize her full bosom. "Ummm. *Pas De Deux* you say. Then they must carry the *Matrone* label. I bet on the rack there'll be a trendy, cleavage showing, stretchy purple shift. I'm writing purple shift on my list."

Rick threw his arms around her in the midst of his, Brandon's and her laughter. "Oh, Mama D. I do love you, so. Tomorrow's spa appointment is no joke. So go!"

The next morning, at nine-forty-five a.m. Dorsie stood at the sign in desk at the Day Spa waiting for the receptionist to finish scanning through times in an appointment book as she spoke with a customer on the phone.

"Good Morning, sorry you had to wait," she said. "Your name?"

"Renninger."

The receptionist's perfectly arched eyebrows shot up. Her perfectly shadowed eyelids glanced downward. "Renninger," she said. She looked up at Dorsie. "OMG! From the Tracy Maddox trial! Look. You're in the paper today." She waved a *National Enquirer* in air then laid it on the Sign-In counter. "See."

Dorsie stiffened as the receptionist tapped her nails against the newsprint. Behind her she heard whispers. She glanced over her shoulder to find faces with expectant expressions. She turned back to the receptionist, ignoring the *National Enquirer*. "I've changed my mind. Please cancel my appointment," she said in a voice icy enough to silence the receptionist. She handed over her American Express card to pay the cancellation fee. As she crossed the waiting area, heading for the exit door, she heard, "How can she live with herself?"

Five minutes later Dorsie stood in front of a popular Tribeca neighborhood news kiosk taking in print headlines – New Jersey Herald – *Maddox Juror #11 Dead – Suicide*; Daily News – *Public Opinion Too Much for Maddox Juror.* The New York Times – *Maddox Jury Foreperson Takes Life.* National Enquirer – *Crazed Maddox Juror Kills Self.* She saw photos of Eric with his arms outstretched, head raised towards neon lights. Her heart skipped a beat and she gasped as she took in the lower second headline with accompanying photos – *Juror #4 Needs K-9 Protection. Shop Vandalized.* She grabbed several copies of the *Enquirer* and handed over a twenty dollar bill to the cashier. "Hey, ain't you?" he asked throwing a meaningful glance at the *National Enquirer* in the rack. Dorsie hurried away without saying a word, without waiting for change. She walked briskly and with every step she was certain every person she passed was staring at her, recognizing her. Her heart rate accelerated. Her chest tightened. She couldn't take deep breaths. No! Not now! she pleaded silently.

Back at the loft she threw the papers on the breakfast bar counter and stared down at the *National Enquirer.* With shaking hands she unfolded it. Eric Van Zant's image stared up at her. She slammed her open palm across the photo as if to obliterate it from sight then lifted her palm away. "No!" she cried aloud, catching sight of her in three photos at the bottom half of the front page. *Juror #4 Gets Protective K-9. Business Vandalized.* There she was with Thor coming out of the Blairstown Diner. The other photo showed her sitting outside The Coffee Bin with Thor at her feet in his lay-down position and next to it, a photo of them exiting *Dorsie's Antiques and Design.* She crumpled the paper in her fist then slumped into a club chair and stared out the floor-to-ceiling window unaware of the view outside. Her cell rang. She ignored it. It rang again. She ignored it. It rang many more times and each time after four rings the calls went automatically into voicemail.

A half hour later Brandon burst through the loft door with Deidra Fallon following behind. He was relieved to see his mother sitting quietly. "Thank God, you're alright. Rick and I've been calling. You didn't answer. I called the Spa, they'd said you'd cancelled and left."

Dorsie raised her hands then helplessly dropped them on the *Enquirer* crumpled in her lap. "I'm sorry. For this mess. I'm sorry. I should have realized Eric was . . ."

Brandon knelt before his mother and took her hands in his. "None of this is your fault. None of it."

"I should have . . ." Dorsie's whole body gave a deep shudder.

Deidra Fallon knelt beside Brandon and placed her hands on top of Brandon's and Dorsie's. "Each juror, each of you were strangers to each other. You couldn't have known Eric Van Zant had serious issues. To know his state of mind was not your responsibility."

Dorsie held Deidra's steady, well-meaning gaze for long seconds. She gave a deep sigh then looked away feeling way too overwhelmed to explain what was churning inside of her. It was bad enough that she failed Jenna Maddox, she thought while emotions of fear, anger, regret and shame raged inside. Now, most likely, she failed Eric Van Zant too. She didn't care what anyone said. She knew she neglected to take the right action as a juror. Why? She wanted to ask Deidra if any kind of rationalization justified neglecting to act? And above all, how did someone atone for not upholding justice for an innocent child?

Dorsie glanced back at Deidra Fallon. In her gaze she found concern and kindness. This woman was a professional, she thought, a quasi guide who tried to help people come to terms with inner turmoil. But, in truth, Deidra did not have any magic power to make it go away. There was no one who could grant her absolution like the absolution she had given to Tracy Maddox. She and she alone would have to find the flaw, confront the weakness within her core that led her to do the unimaginable – sign her name to Not Guilty on the Jury Form outlining all the charges against Tracy Maddox. She alone would struggle with why she hadn't trusted her gut. Maybe if she had, Eric Van Zant would be alive. Until she discovered answers to all her *whys* and *what ifs*, her stomach would continue to churn, her mind would play tricks on her and Jenna and Jury Room dreams would invade her sleep. But what she feared most was that she, Dorsie Raines Renninger, had damaged her soul in an irreparable way.

The doorbell rang and Brandon went to answer. Moments later he returned with a courier envelope in his hand. "From Rick," he said. "Transcript of the Kate Krieger interview scheduled to air tonight. He wanted you to see what was coming." He tore open the envelope then handed one copy to his mother, another to Deidra. He pulled the final copy from the envelope. Quickly he read Rick's note – *She's going the cadaver dog route. Hopes it will publically goad Mama D into an interview.* Brandon glanced over at his mother. Her head was bowed and her hands were clasped in her lap as if she were deep in prayer.

"Well," Dorsie said quietly. "Let's see what more Kate Krieger has to say. Brandon, my reading glasses are in my purse on the breakfast bar. Could you get them for me, please? And could you pour me a scotch, neat."

For twenty minutes, Dorsie, Brandon and Deidra Fallon read through the transcript of Lynda Del Myra's interview with Kate Krieger in silence.

Del Myra: Now as promised, we have Juror Eight in the Tracy Maddox trial. You just saw some of the interview she gave days after the trial ended. Kate, glad to have you on the show. Tell me. What are your thoughts on the recent death of the jury's foreperson, Eric Van Zant?

Krieger: Shocked. I'm in a state of shock.

Del Myra: Given that you've just graduated from nursing school and have had some training in being observant, was there anything during the days of the trial or during deliberations that gave any hint of Eric being troubled?

Krieger: No (head shaking). Eric is, umm, was one of those super smart people you rarely have a chance to meet. We grew close. Talked about all kinds of things. Places he'd hiked. Did you know he was a member of the Sierra Club? But we never talked about what was going on in the courtroom, because we weren't allowed. Not until deliberations.

Del Myra: Did you have contact with Eric after the trial?

Krieger: Yes. (Head bowed then raised. Eyes filled with tears.) We texted. Talked on the phone. We . . . we started talking about living together before getting engaged.

Del Myra: Engaged! You got that close. Even with being sequestered and with restrictions on what you could talk about among yourselves? Did you see him before he left for Las Vegas? From what's been verified by passenger flight records, he left the same day he gave an interview with a local Fox News in Philadelphia.

Krieger: (Slight sob.) Wiping tears from face.) I didn't see Eric before he left but he told me he was meeting with someone interested in doing a book deal. We were going to collaborate. Combine our thoughts and experiences of the trial. But now.. (Lowered voice. Unable to hear comment.)

Del Myra: Let's run the clip of Van Zant's interview and then we'll be right back on the other side.

Dorsie skipped over the word-for-word verbiage of Eric's earlier interview as well as the text for the commercials aired. She glanced at Brandon and Deidra. "My head's spinning. I suspected Kate had her eye on Eric. They were always sitting together. During the rides to and from the courthouse and during breaks. Always sat together at dinner in the private dining room. But engaged. I can't believe it." She shook her head over and over. "Harold did tell me they found a sizable diamond ring in Eric's belongings left at Crystal's house. I assumed it was for Crystal." Her hand flew to her mouth. "Oh! This is going to devastate Crystal even further. I don't suppose there's anyway she's not going to hear about this." Dorsie lowered her head and returned to reading the transcript but overheard Brandon placing a call to Harold back in Blairstown.

Del Myra: Since you mentioned the trial, is there anything you see differently now? Another juror, wishing to remain anonymous, gave his local paper a statement. He stated that if he knew what he knows now after reviewing the trial's public records, he would have said guilty. I'm sure you've had the opportunity to review all that's been said. All that's been reported. Including various things the prosecution could not introduce during the trial because their hands were tied legally. For instance, identity theft.

Krieger: (Interrupting Del Myra. Look of distain on face.) Why would I want to go over any of it? I did my job as a juror. There are lots of us, who are young, party, tell lies to our parents. Some of us may have even been molested. But we don't kill children."

Del Myra: I see in some ways you might have identified with Tracy Maddox. But let me ask you this. We now know one juror had extensive knowledge of cadaver dogs. Mostly, through her son-in-law. A K-9 trainer. In fact, most likely the actual trainer who certified the dog used in the Maddox trial. Did any of this come up during deliberations?

Krieger: No. Just what we learned during the trial. No one added anything more.

Del Myra: You mean this other juror did not offer any insight to the rest of you? Our sources verified this juror has been present at many K-9 training sessions and competitions. Of course, we invite this juror to come on our show so she can share her thoughts and experiences. In fact, we know this juror is now accompanied by a protection K-9 since her business was vandalized a day after the verdict was announced. I find it hard to believe anyone would not offer their insights on how effective law enforcement K-9s are. Especially since cadaver dogs' alerts on human decomposition were hard evidence.

Krieger: (Shrug.) Whatever. What can I say? Eric was the only one who talked about the dogs. Called our attention to how the dogs' training records were not 100% accurate on alerts. They had false alerts too. Eric was super smart. He explained anything any of us didn't understand. He knew we were tired. Some of us confused. So he made everything clear. Even better than Diaz did. There's reasonable doubt in everything in life, he said. If you think about it, you'll see it's true. Eric saved us hours of time. Because of Eric we didn't have to bother looking at anything.

Del Myra: Bother! You're saying it was a bother to review any of the evidence?

Dorsie stood. She threw the transcript barely missing Deidra sitting on the sofa across from her. "That's a lie," she shouted. "She's lying. Why would she do that? I tried to explain how cadaver dogs do not alert on garbage. I tried!" Her hand swept across her forehead. "I don't understand any of this. Why would Kate Krieger lie? Why did Eric Van Zant kill himself? Why would a young mother lie, lie, lie about a missing child? Or throw her in the woods like trash? Not be held accountable? The other jurors . . . they just wanted to . . ." She paced the room. "Why would someone vandalize Harold's shop? Send me a doll identical to Jenna Maddox's? I don't understand. I just don't understand this world we live in anymore." She stopped pacing. "I don't even understand myself anymore!"

Silence filled the loft as Dorsie stood before her son and Deidra Fallon consumed by the chaos assaulting her thoughts and emotions. Brandon started to rise from the sofa but Deidra grabbed his arm, pulling him back down, whispering "don't."

After what seemed like endless minutes, Dorsie regained her composure. She waved her hand in a helpless gesture. "I'm sorry! I'm sorry!" She wiped away the tears streaming down her cheeks. In a strangled whisper she said, "Excuse me. I need to be alone."

After hearing the bedroom door close, Brandon turned to Deidra. "I've never seen my mother throw anything in anger." He rubbed his hands over his face in frustration. "She looks so fragile. So worn out. So beaten down. And there's nothing I can do to help her."

"She's in immense emotional turmoil," Deidra said. "Anger is part of it. Don't be alarmed. It's good she got visibly angry. It's going to take her awhile to work through all the feelings she's having. Not one of those jurors will have immunity from their emotions. There's going to be a lot of, to borrow a military term, collateral damage. Anyone involved in the case, even remotely could get swept up in the havoc. It'll spill over to family, friends, co-workers."

Brandon leaned his head back against the sofa groaning loudly. "I never heard of Tracy Maddox until my mother was selected for the jury. Rick says there was other stuff that could've made a better-aired interview. Lynda cut it. Zeroed in on the K-9 angle. Almost a public way of goading my mother into agreeing to an interview. My mother would never do it. At least I don't think she would. But now . . ." He jumped up and began to pace, a habit identical to his mother's. "Rick and I watched the entire trial on tape. Twice. So did my sister, Megs. We know my mother. We know what she believes. Frankly, I just can't wrap my head around why she would say not guilty."

"Brandon, all of you are doing a wonderful job in supporting your mother. Keep doing what you're doing," Deidra said quietly. "Right now your mother's desperately struggling to understand her own actions." Deidra stood and stopped Brandon's pacing by taking his hands in hers. "Support her in anything she wants to do. Removing herself from this metro area will help."

"But she'll be all alone in Florida!" he countered.

Deidra shook her head. "Physically, yes. Emotionally no. Your mother's smart enough to know she needs some help." She led Brandon back to the sofa and made him sit. "She's agreed to talk with me once a week via Skype. Tomorrow, we're going over to the studio and one of Rick's tech buddies is going to walk her though how it's all done. Trust me. She'll be talking with all of you via Skype every day."

Chapter Sixteen

Late September – The Villages

Dorsie leaned against Thor's solid mass as he stuck his head out of the Town Car window. The car glided up Buena Vista Boulevard making its way to the Village of Virginia Trace. She absentmindedly gazed beyond Thor's snout barely noticing the stunning old oaks draped in Spanish moss lining a section of the boulevard. Parallel to Buena Vista, golf carts, one after another, zipped along a network of paths. Their uniqueness as a mode of transportation barely registered in her consciousness. Within, anxiety churned and a bitter taste filled the back of her throat as if she had acid reflux. She glanced over to the brief case lying on the back seat. It held six months' worth of her medications, information on The Villages' community, pertinent information on Vince's house and Thor's vaccination and certification documents. She gave a deep, deep heavy sigh. Why had Brandon, Dave, Megs and Deidra insisted she take Thor with her? How had Dave delayed Thor's upcoming assignment in D.C?

Now, she was disgusted and ashamed of herself for wallowing in self-pity, insulating herself in New York and not returning to Blairstown. Willingly, no questions asked, she'd turned over all the arrangements needed to get her to Florida to Harold, Brandon, Rick, Dave and Vince Di Paolo. She second-guessed nothing, made no meticulous lists of what needed to be done, just knew Vince Di Paolo handled all transportation and flight arrangements; Rick had packed suitcases full of warm climate clothes and necessities; Harold would close down the Blairstown house and care for Diva and Pavarotti. Gino's private plane had carried her, Dave and Thor South. They landed in North Carolina for a three-hour stopover with just enough time for soothing embraces and loving words from Megs. Dave had given her a final reassuring bear hug before she and Thor boarded the plane again. Now, as the Town Car pulled into a driveway on Duncan Drive, she was deeply grateful to them all.

After opening the front door, Dorsie gave Thor his search command even though she unconsciously knew the house was safe but also had the presence of mind to allow Thor to do the job he was trained for. He returned to the foyer, rushed past her towards the opened door. He went into alert mode filling the air with ear piercing barks. Dorsie turned and found a fit, military crew cut, well-tanned male, about the age of over sixty-something, was standing outside the screen door. She gave Thor his cease barking command. "May I help you?"

"My name's Bowser. House caretaker. Glad to meet you Dorsie Renninger," he said. "Vince let me know your estimated arrival time. Would have been here sooner but the local Publix was jam-packed. Check out at a snail's pace. Got some basic groceries for you. Mind if I come in?" At Dorsie's dubious look, he fished out his wallet from his back pocket and removed his driver's license. "Copy of this is in the house information packet. I'll wait till you check it."

Dorsie opened the screen slightly and took the license. "Excuse me," she said then bent down, opened the briefcase she'd set on the floor and ruffled though folders then papers. Once satisfied Bowser was who he said he was, she stood and handed him back his license.

"Thank you ma'am. Just call me JB. I'll just go and get those supplies now."

Minutes later Dorsie watched as JB efficiently put away everything he'd brought. Not knowing what to do or wanting not to get in the way, she sat at the breakfast table in the kitchen.

"Golf cart is in tip-top running order. Map of paths is on the seat," JB said in a running commentary of need-to-know information. "I'll show you how to charge the batteries later. Mini Cooper's all gassed up too. Registration, etc. etc. in the glove compartment. The neighbors to the left are the Elliots from New York." He glanced at her over his shoulder and saw a shadow of concern wash over her face. "They're never here. Only come down two or three times a year. The neighbors to the right are the Papacheks but they're leaving. Miss the grandchildren so they're going back to Indiana. Moving truck's comin' next week. House's been sold to a couple from Ohio but as I understand it, they're not planning on coming down permanently yet. So, it's gonna' be quiet for you." Again he gave a glance over his shoulder while putting sugar, a box of assorted Bigelow teas and pound of Starbuck's coffee on the cabinet's lower shelf. "You're a Yankee, so make sure you put on lotion when you go outside. Sun's different down here. I put new bottles of different brands of sunscreen in the master bath closet. Get yourself a sun visor or wear some kind of hat. Looks to me like you have tender skin."

Dorsie glanced at her fish white arms. "Guess I am pretty pale. Thanks for the advice. I'll be careful. Will you be coming by often?"

"Once a week, just to check on things. I'll change over the irrigation system run time to winter mode at the end of next month. Only need to water once a week up until late April early May. Landscapers come once or twice a month right now but they wouldn't bother you. But him," he said nodding towards Thor sitting in an attention-like manner next to Dorsie's chair. "He's bound to scare the hell out of them. Vince and your son-in-law gave me a heads up on just exactly what he's capable of. Also understand you've got good control over him."

Thor let out a small whine as if he knew he was the topic of conversations.

"Oh-my-gosh. I'm sorry. JB meet Thor." She paused flustered by her lack of attention in doing what Dave had trained her to do. "Since you'll be coming by and be around the house I've got to let him go through his Meet routine so he knows who you are. Just stand there. He'll really give you a good sniffing once over. If you want, you can extend the palm of your hand out to him, and then say 'Good Boy, Thor.'" Dorsie grabbed Thor's collar lifted him slightly then said, "Meet. Go."

"Glad to oblige," JB said while looking down at Thor who was sniffing at his Eddie Bauer trekking sandals. "He certainly is handsome. Went to Petco and got the list of things your son-in-law said you needed for the dog. Food, rope tug, gnawing bones, 'bout four Kong toys, stuff like that. Also gave Dave the name of a vet down here that takes care of a couple of Seeing Eye Guide Dogs. Vet's card is stapled to the phone book." He held out both of his hands palms up and let Thor's nose nuzzle their centers. "Villages has an on-leash policy. Carry plastic bags with you for cleanup. At your son-in-law's suggestion, I made a temporary duty pit out back in case you don't want to walk him for some reason. In the garage is a trash can designated only for those nasty plastic bags. Garbage pick-up times are posted alongside the light switch near the door leading from the garage into the kitchen."

Thor returned to Dorsie's side. She shook her head in amazement. "Dog toys. Duty Pit. You did all that?"

He shrugged as if to say it was nothing then gave her a hard, levelled look. "Just so you know, me and the Carapelli family go way back. Don't hesitate to call me for anything." He reached in his pocket then walked to Thor, bent down and offered Thor a treat. "Good Boy. Fella, if you want when I come over every week we'll have ourselves a tug-of-war session. Cause I suspect you'd drag Miz Dorsie here right to the ground." Thor lifted his paw. JB took it in his hand and gave Thor a human handshake. "Fella' you've got yourself a deal!" He stood and faced Dorsie. "I've scouted out some places where you can take him for a good run. Tomorrow morning I'll come by and we'll get you started off on golf cart basics. You'll drive the golf cart paths down to the Town Square then over to a nice little stretch I found running along the The Villages High School football field." He paused then asked, "'Course if that's okay with you?"

"Of course, of course," Dorsie answered caught off guard by all the things she'd need to know while staying. "Is eight ok?"

"On the button, early man myself. Now, Dorsie, let's get down to the basics of this fine house." For forty-five minutes he showed and instructed on how to operate the house thermostat for air conditioning and heat, garage door openers, fuse box, water shut off valve. He showed her the golf cart and mini Cooper keys and laid out the resident gate cards, guest pass and current copy of the Recreation News and The Villages phone book on the island countertop. "All kind of activities here," he said, pointing to the Recreation News. "In there you'll also find locations of all the Rec Centers, pools, opening and closing times, etc., etc. Look it over when you have a chance. Now, anything else I can do right now?"

Dorsie shrugged. "Not that I know of. Thank you very, very much. What do I owe you for all the things you've bought?"

"Not a penny. All goes on the house account Vince has set up."

"Oh," she said, genuinely surprised before becoming overwhelmed by being in a strange place, faced with a whirlwind of things to know and how Dave and Vince Di Paolo had thoroughly prepped JB for her and Thor's arrival. "I . . .this was so unexpected. Unplanned. I just didn't think . . ."

"No need to explain. Got briefed by Gino on the circumstances. The Villages is a safe place. Just settle into it." Sensing Dorsie's unease, he said, "It'll be getting dark in 'bout an hour or so. Before I go, want me to walk with you to give Thor some exercise? People know me here. So if we happen to meet any of the neighbors, I'll introduce you."

"Thank you," Dorsie said. "Thor draws a lot of attention. Right now, I'm not sure I'm up for a lot of social chit-chat."

"Fully understand," said JB.

Later, after feeding Thor, Dorsie took a long, hot shower, put on a fluffy spa bathrobe she found hanging on a peg, blow dried her hair quickly then caught it up in a loose nape-of-the-neck ponytail. She stepped into the master bedroom and opened one of the suitcases Rick had packed. She laughed aloud as a riot of colors jumped out at her – electric blues, lime greens, corals, and pastels to deep pinks, crisp nautical navy, reds, khaki and whites. She fingered through age appropriate shorts and capris. In another suitcase she found lightweight nightshirts, two pairs of memory foam padded slippers, underwear on the far side of white cotton grandma panties but not exactly Victoria Secret style either. She checked the label on four bras finding them to be her brand and size. Over a dozen sport socks lined the inner sides of the suitcase. She removed and shook out one of three hoodies with matching long pants and felt the soft texture of good quality knit cotton jersey. Like a child opening presents, she unzipped the third bag and lifted the lid. Packed neatly were three bathing suits in a tropical floral pattern, two cover-ups, a collapsible sun hat, two sun visors, two pairs of chic beach sandals, one pair of Sketcher Walkers, a pair of sturdy Columbia sandals and two pairs of straightforward flip-flops. There were bottles of top of the line suntan lotions ranging from SP30 to SP8, Bare Minerals foundation, blusher, eye shadow, Bobbie Brown mascara, eyebrow and eyeliner pencils and protective lip-glosses in various shades. All were neatly protected from accidental travel spillage in plastic zip-lock bags. Small colorful jewelry cases held extremely casual, yet extremely tasteful earrings, bracelets and necklaces with beads of hammered silver and copper as well as sea-glass beads in every conceivable color. She stood back viewing the open cases and cried. Whether the tears were of joy, exhaustion or from being just plain overwhelmed, she didn't know. But there was one thing she was certain of – in her guilt-ridden soul there was still room for deep, intense gratitude. She reached for her cell and pressed Brandon's number.

"I'm here safe and sound," she said when he answered. "You'll let everyone know?"

"Will do, Mom. How is it?"

"Oh Brandon, before I go into that is Rick there? Can I speak to him?"

"Sure," He handed his cell over to Rick.

"Mama D, safe and sound?"

"Yes. Yes. But Rick, how did you manage. All those clothes. Right sizes down to the bras. Everything. I'm dumbfounded."

"HLN hires very resourceful people. But, it was a little bit of help here, a little bit of help there. Remember I did take your measurements," he said with a chuckle. "One of the HLN stylists owes me big time, so I cashed in. She's used to doing this all the time. Packs for the bigwig anchors when they need to be somewhere pronto. Also, and I hope you're not going to freak out, but I had Harold take Rose over to the house and take a look-see at some things. Somehow I couldn't ask Harold to go through your underwear drawer. Hope you're not mad."

"No, I'm just so ashamed of myself. Locking myself up in the bedroom there. Not paying attention to anything, anyone but my sorry self. I'm just so grateful Rick. There's still room in my ugly soul to appreciate true loving and giving."

"Hush, Mama D. There's nothing ugly about any part of you. Don't worry about any of that stuff. If it doesn't fit, send it off to some charity shelter down there."

"But the cost of it all. Have Brandon write a check."

"Nope, it's all buried somewhere in HLN's tabs. Also, Jezza gets deep, deep discounts just by flashing the HLN credit card. I told you I was owed a big, big favor. We hope we got the style right. And, oh. You won't find any purple shift in there. Nothing purple in fact."

Dorsie could almost see the twinkle in his eyes but a sudden unkind, suspicious thought popped into to her head. "Rick, I'm not obligated in any way to HLN, am I? This isn't some perk to sway me into an interview?"

"God! No! No way! I'd *never* do something like that to you, Mama D."

"Sorry. Sorry." Dorsie said with a crack in her voice. "Rick, I didn't mean. It's just that . . ." She paused then continued on, "I'm always apologizing for something now. I seem to see or sense some ulterior motive in everything now. This is not like me, Rick. You know that. So sorry to say such a thing after all you've done."

"Mama D. It's okay. Don't go getting yourself in a tizzy. We all get it. There's nothing enviable about the situation you find yourself in. Don't go worrying your head about Deidra Fallon either just because she's Del Myra's partner. Ethics are everything to Deidra. Love you. Now, here's Brandon."

"What was that all about?" Brandon asked. "Everything ok?"

"Just a lapse in my muddled judgment," Dorsie answered. "Brandon, I'm so grateful to all of you. How much you'll never know. Why, the house caretaker here went out and bought toys for Thor! He even put a Duty Pit in the back. Vince's house is lovely. It feels very comfortable. Tomorrow, I'll get outside, take a better look around."

Brandon laughed. "A Duty Pit. I can just hear Dave giving the care-taker exact measurements as if an inch or two would make a difference. That brother-in-law of mine has two loves in life. First Megs then his K-9s. Too bad babies are out of the picture for them. Won't mind being an uncle."

Dorsie sighed. "Megs mothers those tiny, tiny helpless babies. It was good to see Megs if only for a short time. For Thanksgiving, they'll either come down here to The Villages or maybe I'll just drive up there and spend a week or two with them."

"Sounds like a good plan. When everything's definite, let me know. Rick and I will fly down. Maybe Uncle Harold and Rose will too. We'll have ourselves a Southern Thanksgiving. Start looking up recipes for collard greens, pecan and sweet potato pie." He chuckled. "Bet Dave can help you out there, being the Southern boy he is."

"That he is, Brandon. You'll take care of calling everyone, letting them know I'm here and okay?"

"Yes, Mom," Brandon said in his most dutiful son voice. "Now, I know you must be exhausted. Eat something. Take Thor out to the Duty Pit. Have a drink. Get yourself to bed. We'll talk more tomorrow. Love you."

"Don't forget to call everyone. I already said that, didn't I? Love to all of you. Bye."

Dorsie sat on the edge of the bed staring at the cell phone in her hand. I'm so lucky, she thought. I don't know what I'd do without everyone's support. Her hand flew to her forehead. Oh. Oh. Crystal Yates. She'd forgotten about Crystal in the days of her self-pitying state. Who was supporting Crystal? How was Crystal coping? How selfish of her to be concerned only about herself when there was such a kind hearted, lovely girl who was in the midst of numbing grief. She glanced at her watch. Too late to call now, she thought not knowing what shift Crystal might be working. Was she working? Tomorrow, she'd call Harold and find out. She let out a sigh of relief remembering Harold and Rose promised to take Crystal under their wings. That engagement ring Harold found in the fireproof box, surely it had been for Crystal, not Kate Krieger. What a ridiculous thing for Kate Krieger to say in that interview.

"Stop. Stop. Do something!" she muttered aloud in an effort to block her thoughts, to bring them to a halting stop before they could go round and round and round in endless *what ifs.*

She quickly changed into the hoodie and long pants lying on the bed then unpacked filling empty drawers and hangers in the master closet which was almost a room unto itself. When finished, she flipped on all the lights in the main interior room. Slowly she walked about with Thor following her every step. Her decorator's instincts appreciated the comfortable feel of the large, great room. It was neither overly feminine nor overly masculine. She studied a large piece of artwork on the focal wall, a wonderful piece featuring an elegant, crimson-capped Sandhill Crane standing in a wetland. She brushed her fingertips across the canvas feeling the bits of Venetian plaster, acrylics and glazes the artist used. The color palette – pale slate greys, creams, muted browns and greens and splashes of red and black – were used throughout the room. When she opened the doors to the three guest bedrooms and turned on the lights, she found the same color story flowing nicely from the main area to those rooms as well.

She ended her tour in the kitchen where she opened the fridge. There she found a pre-made salad and two rotisserie chicken breasts as well as various chunks of cheeses and bottles of white and red wine. She removed the salad, one chicken breast and a bottle of Acrobat Pinot Gris to the counter. She found a corkscrew then opened it. With a no-fuss movement she sliced the chicken, tossed the salad, poured the wine then sat on a barstool and ate at the countertop. With the same efficient movements she cleaned up, refilled her wine glass, grabbed a plastic bag then went and opened the door to the lanai.

Warm, balmy air filled her senses. A hint of some flower fragrance she couldn't identify drifted on a slight breeze. Jasmine? she wondered. Did Jasmine flower all year in a warm climate? The space beyond the lanai was filled with bright moonlight casting a silvery glow on the fronds of palm trees and low-lying bushes. More lush bushes lined a low fence and beyond the dark sky was filled with the twinkle of stars. She stood there lost in the quiet, serene loveliness of it all. Somewhere far off in the distance the echoing sound of a train whistle carried across the night air. Suddenly, she felt lonely. Far away from those she loved but mostly cut off from her former self. A confident self not one filled with anxiety. A self who made more right decisions than wrong ones. A self who was at peace in her soul not one who now had a soul stained and riddled with guilt.

The loveliness of her surroundings and being-in-the-moment faded. She took a gulp of her wine and motioned for Thor, taking him out to the Duty Pit hidden behind newly planted shrubs. Minutes later, back inside, Dorsie refilled her wine glass, made the rounds of making sure doors were locked, all the lights were turned off then went into the master bath to begin the nightly get-ready-for-bed ritual. She rummaged through the zip lock bag that held her prescriptions until she found the one with the newly prescribed sleeping pills. She shook out one, stared at it then washed it down with a gulp of wine. Not a good idea to do that, she silently told her image in the mirror as she brushed her teeth.

Minutes later, she lay in the strange bed, listening to unfamiliar sounds then dangled her hand over the side to feel Thor's mass as he settled himself. Reassured by his now familiar presence, she closed her eyes, took deep breaths to help her body relax and waited for the sleeping pill to kick in. Please, please, she silently asked some unseen yet believed in power. Just let me sleep the sleep of the dead. He eyes flew open in alarm. Why did I say that? Sleep of the dead. On-my-Gawd. Jenna. Eric Van Zant. When the drug finally circulated through her blood stream and seeped into the command center of her central nervous system, she fell into darkness. But all through the night she shifted from one sleep cycle to the next getting stuck in REM periods where Jenna Maddox's clear sweet, sweet voice sang "Pleez don't take my sunshine away." The scene would abruptly shift. Someone on the border of being recognizable would be grabbing her arm in a vice-like grip. The movie in her mind would again segue. An old-fashioned flipbook appeared showing verdict forms and headlines flying by in rapid, animated motion.

Chapter Seventeen

Early October

In the following weeks Dorsie and Thor came to know the streets within the Village of Virginia Trace and anyone out and about in their yard waved a friendly hello then went back to what they were doing. They ventured down to the Town Square passing by various shops, restaurants and the movie theater. As instructed by Dave, Dorsie had Thor wear his blue K-9 training bib which gained him access and attention anywhere they went. The attention Dorsie came to realize was a blessing in disguise. Answering questions about Thor deflected interest in her and since she never offered her last name to anyone she never saw a glimmer of recognition in anyone's' eyes. In spite of the The Villages being billed as the "Friendliest Hometown", no one, much to her relief, ventured down the lets-do-lunch, let's-get-to-know-each-other path. Daily, she and Thor walked the boardwalk along Lake Sumter to the Waterfront Inn then in reverse back to the Lighthouse Point Bar and Grill's parking lot.

Some days were pleasant especially when Thor encountered other dogs on leashes and they stopped for some doggie socialization and idle chitchat with the dog's owners. Other days were oppressive because the nagging voice within taunted her, leaving her oblivious to sunny blue skies, passersby and swaying palm trees. On such a day, she watched Thor lap up water from the supply she kept in the golf cart then glanced over her shoulder at Lighthouse Point. I need a drink too, she thought, knowing a nice Johnnie Walker Black would soften up her thoughts. Thoughts that sparred and jabbed, backing her into a corner where she struggled to deflect guilt packed punches. After securing Thor's bowl back in the golf cart, she straightened his bib then ran her hand over her hair, pushing back wisps hanging loose from her haphazardly tied ponytail. "Come on Thor. Let's check this place out."

Minutes later, Lighthouse Point's door swung open. The bartender gave the new, unfamiliar customer coming through the door an intense once-over. "Dudes!" he exclaimed to all sitting at the bar. "Look at this awesomeness comin' in." All heads turned towards Dorsie and Thor. "Cool. *That* my friends is show-dog quality." He quickly altered his statement. "The dog. Not the lady. Damn, that didn't sound right either," he said. He walked toward the end of the bar where Dorsie was settling herself into a seat. He extended his hand across the glossy, nautical blue bar top, "Put my foot in my mouth didn't I? Sorry. Skeeter Brooks, ma'am," he said. "Seen ya walkin' the boards every day. Never could get out before you disappeared. Got two chocolate Labs and some purebred Bloodhounds myself. The Labs do agility competition with my sister. Me and the Bloodhounds do the man trailing circuit." He swiped a cloth over the nautical blue bar top. "What can I get ya?"

"Johnnie Walker Black, on the rocks," Dorsie answered. She gave Thor his lay-down command. She glanced down the bar. Seats were filled with what looked to be golfers fresh off the course. Most of the tables in the restaurant area were empty. Three were seated with ladies in picture perfect golf attire picking away at large bowls of salad and sipping from mason jar glasses filled with what she assumed was iced tea.

"What's the deal with him?" Skeeter asked, nodding his head towards Thor. He set down two Johnnie Walker Black's in front of Dorsie. She raised her eyebrows in question. "Happy Hour. Two for one. Two to five Monday thru Friday," he answered. "Man. That dog is just soo cool. K-9 law enforcement? Service dog? You the trainer?"

Dorsie took a sip of her drink taking note of how many at the bar were glancing her way, waiting to hear her response. "Neither," she said. "K-9 Protection. My son-in-law's the trainer." She glanced down at Thor and gave him a ruffled nudge between his ears. "You could say I act as sort of a Grandma. Dave's charges are like his children." She took another long sip of her drink. "Right now I'm Thor's transition person. Weaning him away from his attachment to my son-in-law and my daughter. Dave flew to Germany to pick him up when he was six weeks old. But now, Thor's ready to do the job he's been trained for. Soon he'll be going to D.C. Assigned to a foreign diplomat with young children."

"Wow! Thor, Norse god of thunder. Suits him. Top breeders. Top pedigrees in Germany. He must've been one expensive puppy. I'd say now that he's trained he's well worth over 30k." Skeeter turned to all the other occupants at the bar. "Hear that. Protection. Now you dudes know you ain't gonna' be messin' with this lady here. So forget about runnin' home for your supply of Viagra."

Moans and good-natured hand waves followed. "Skeeter, we ain't dead yet," someone piped in. "But you better watch out, I hear Boy Toys aren't that uncommon. Anyone sporting a 30K dog as a fashion accessory just might be able to afford you."

Skeeter flipped his bar towel towards the speaker. "Hey, you think I can live on what you geezers tip? Go back to pontificating on politics and rehashing your golf games," he said jokingly. He turned back to Dorsie. "All regulars. Kinda' like having a family of old uncles."

After that, Dorsie became a regular in what she called "Happy Hour Bliss" sipping away at the two for one Johnnie Walker Blacks Skeeter placed before her. Skeeter also would set down a fresh bowl of water for Thor then whisper, "I'm going to get Grandma to agree to a play date. You'll have fun Hershey, Rocky Road and Buster" Every day, rain or shine, with or without Thor, Dorsie treated herself to "Happy Hour Bliss". She'd sip her Johnnie Walker Blacks and listen to Skeeter's good natured rallying back and forth with his family of uncles. The banter and the Johnnie Walker Blacks made any anxiety or guilt tainting her well-being on any given day fade into negligible background noise.

Early mornings were devoted to talking with Brandon, Harold, Megs and Dave via Skype assuring them she was fine and that Thor was fine getting his exercise, play and thunderbolt runs. Halfheartedly, but faithfully, she kept her bi weekly sessions with Deidra Fallon and made an attempt to do what she labeled as "Deidra's Homework" – writing about her emotions; using techniques to stop negative thoughts and talking, talking, talking about how she felt about having her and her family's privacy invaded. How she felt about being recognized as one of the jurors on the Tracy Maddox trial. How unrealistic it was to take on the responsibility of the shop being trashed almost as if she had gone in and wrecked the place herself. How symptoms of anxiety and panic over being recognized all fit within the parameters of acute stress disorder. Even though Deidra probed for signs of flashbacks and nightmares, Dorsie never disclosed her recurring dreams of Jenna Maddox and the magnificent German Shepherd. She refrained from mentioning "Happy

Hour Bliss" when asked about her activities. Nor did she tell Deidra of her continued obsession with visiting legal websites, social media blogs and forums where Joe Public rehashed and reanalyzed every aspect of the trial. She also didn't divulge her continued need to Google for new information about Tracy Maddox, Alberto Diaz, and Greg Ashcroft.

She kept another secret. No one knew that "Happy Hour Bliss" had continued on into many evenings. Evenings in which she sat out on the lanai letting the hours slip by while a half-empty glass of Johnnie Walker Black dangled from her fingertips. One evening, a glass of Johnnie Walker slipped from her fingers and shattered on the floor. As she stared at the mess, an aha! moment gripped and shook her to the core. She was heading down a dangerous path with Johnnie Walker. And, she was also a reluctant, non-participant in her own counseling sessions. Therefore, they were of no value. When the moment passed she added her newly revealed flaws to the list of Self-Loathing Attributes.

Now, she felt ashamed as she sat before her laptop waiting for Skype to connect with Deidra. She was about to summon up a false front and go back on an agreement she'd made with the bright, lively and lovely young woman.

"Hello Deidra," she said when her image appeared on the screen. "Still sloshing through buckets of rain?"

Deidra laughed. "I want to be where you are! You're getting tanner but it isn't hiding the dark circles beneath your eyes. Still not sleeping well? Dorsie, such a serious expression you have today. What's that all about?"

Dorsie hands flew to her face, covering it as she lowered her head for a moment then looked up, straightened her shoulders, and faced the laptop camera eye square on. "I've come to a decision, Deidra. I don't want to continue on with our sessions," she said.

"Oh!"

"I value your expertise and the time you've given to me. But Deidra, you and I both know I'm the only person on this planet who can really change anything about me. This includes my thoughts too. You've given me tools to work with. I think I can take it from here."

"Dorsie, do you think that's wise? I just want you to think about it over the next week. If you still feel the same, I'll have to respect your decision." She paused for long seconds. When Dorsie offered nothing further she said, "Dorsie, you were thrust into situations beyond your control. They've disrupted your life in monumental ways. Shaken your emotional equilibrium. You're still nailing yourself to the cross for things you had no control over. Even though you haven't said it, I strongly suspect you're still avoiding any kind of meaningful contact with people."

"Deidra, intellectually I know that and I own it. It's just that . . . well, I just think I need to work on this alone. You'll have to agree, I'm certainly old enough to know what works for me and what doesn't work. I'm a sort-it-out-myself kind of person."

"I'll give you that Dorsie. You have a wealth of life experiences to guide you. Maybe, and I'm not certain, but just maybe, life experience will serve you better than all my clinical training. Also, from what you've told me about yourself, it's evident you're resilient."

"I appreciate you saying that."

"As a professional Dorsie, all that I can say is – trust what you know to be the basic truths about yourself. They've been with you for over sixty plus years. Re-accept them and you'll be fine. Sounds like a cliché but it's a Universal Truth. Your tombstone isn't going to read – Here lies Dorsie Renninger, a Tracy Maddox Trial Juror." She gave Dorsie a genuine smile. "So will you think about this decision for a week then call me? But now, go enjoy all that sunshine and the wonderful place you now find yourself in. I hear it's like a landlocked cruise ship, having everything you may want to do from A-Z. Go play. Don't isolate yourself even though I know you're sticking to exercising Thor. How's that Exposure List going? The one you told me Dave gave you listing all sorts of activities Thor needs to continuously encounter."

Dorsie smiled knowing exactly where Deidra was going with her questions because Dave's list was designed to force her to take Thor beyond the confines of the house. "Oh, we've done quite a few of them. We go down to Town Square to listen to the music. We especially like "Rocky and the Rollers". Once I even let Thor add quite a few loud barks to the applause. Lots of people oohed and aahed over Thor after that. He's even been to the Virginia Trace pool. Couldn't tell if he minded not seeing any hot bikini-clad bodies."

"Ah! Your sense of humor's coming back. Good. Good," Deidra said. "Keep at it. See if you can check off all the items on the list. You'll call me, then? About your decision?"

Dorsie reached her fingertips towards the screen as if to brush them across Deidra's cheek. "I will. Thank you. When I get back, I'll come see you. I'd like to help in any way I can with your work at the Safe House."

"I'll hold you to that," Deidra said. She waved her fingers in a gesture of goodbye before the screen went blank.

Dorsie closed the laptop then laid her head on the kitchen island. Inside she was flooded with relief that she'd been able to hold herself together while speaking with Deidra. "Play!" she said aloud, startling herself with the vehemence in her voice. "I have to LIVE with what I did in that jury room." she shouted out to empty air. "For Gawd sakes, I'm hiding here. Not playing. Not gadding about. Hiding just like Tracy Maddox is going to hide. In that respect I'm no better than she is."

Next to the laptop lay a stack of books, piles of papers full of information gleaned from Internet searches on NJ law, depression, PTSD, dreams and their meanings, expert opinions on jury selection processes and jury dynamics. She picked a book up from a stack a book collaborated by seven of the jurors who served on the Scott Peterson murder trial. She studied the front cover then flipped through the books pages and noted how many portions she'd highlighted. She set it aside then picked up another book which was co-authored by several members on the O.J. Simpson trial. She set it back down. Her gaze fell on a paperback, *Dream Power, #1 Self-Awareness Book of the Decade.* She'd found it at a used book store she'd discovered in Colony Plaza. She lifted it from the stack and held it to her nose, smelling the musty odor that seemed to flow out of all old books. She'd slogged through the well-researched theories the author cited on the work done by the pioneers in dream research – Jung, Hall, and gestalt master Frederick Perls. She fanned the book's pages while reviewing how she'd given cursory attention to study statistics included within it pages. But, she'd intently studied each and every example that described how a dream could be analyzed. She cast the book aside feeling no closer to understanding her Jenna Maddox-German Shepherd dream.

She sat back and surveyed all the material she'd collected. She'd searched every piece of it looking for reasonable answers as to how she, Dorsie Renninger, a person in possession of good communication skills, could fail? How she, a businesswoman who had stood her ground while negotiating with tough union tradesmen, could not make any inroads with an average group of people? She was also someone who had more than average experience in bringing compromise to couples who were at war over what to buy and what to spend on home improvement projects. How could she have failed in what was probably one of the biggest, ethical, moral tests in her life – persuading eleven other people to stop, take a deep breath and not make a hasty decision? She had failed miserably in getting the other eleven jurors to examine evidence with an open mind. And now, because she had failed, Tracy Maddox walked away free. Walked away unpunished for taking her daughter's life then tossing her away in a trash bag as if she were nothing but garbage.

But YOU did let her walk away! YOU could have changed Not Guilty to Hung Jury! You did wrong!

"She still would have walked! It would have been a mistrial. No guarantee of a retrial!" Dorsie argued back aloud.

You still did wrong! Van Zant. An alternate may have . . .

In anger Dorsie stood and forcefully brushed everything from the counter top, sending it all flying through the air. It all crashed to the floor making a loud racket. The bar stool she'd been sitting on toppled over on its side with a bang. Thor came charging into the kitchen filling the air with ear piercing barks. She froze in panic, afraid to move, as Thor continued to bark and bark and bark. Slowly, she realized it was her own actions that had created the disturbance sending Thor into alert mode. She gave him his stop bark command and when he sat quietly with total focus on her, she gave him reassuring pats. She glanced over to the digital microwave clock and took note of the time. "Oh hell. Come on! Golf Cart, Thor." His tail waged in anticipation. "Off we go. First we walk. When we finish a cold drink of water for you and for me, Happy Hour Bliss!"

Chapter Eighteen

Mid October

At Lighthouse Point, Skeeter Brooks glanced out the bank of windows facing the end of Lake Sumter's boardwalk. There he saw Thor walking briskly side-by-side with the lady he took to calling Grandma because she never said her name. Odd, he thought, but then again he knew everyone on the planet was odd because asking "what's your pleasure" and serving it up was the equivalent to being a shrink without a degree. Every heavy drinker had a story to tell and wanted an audience. Just about every lush harbored heartaches of some kind and wanted to spill his guts out to someone. Others, well a good percentage of them had enough wires crossed inside their heads to make them certifiable nut jobs. Grandma didn't fit any of those profiles, didn't have the vibe of someone who got her fix through booze. If he had to take an educated guess, he'd say her Johnnie Walker Blacks were newbies on her scene and whatever edge they were numbing had happened recently.

"Grandma and the awesome Thor," Skeeter called out when Dorsie and Thor entered. He scooted around the bar to remove bar towels from the end seat. By stacking towels there he saved the seat for them mainly because next to the bar stool Thor had plenty of room to be comfortable as he took a snooze while Grandma enjoyed her Johnnie Walker Blacks. He quickly filled a stainless steel bowl full of water and placed it on the floor. When Dorsie took the seat, he arched an eyebrow, "Same?" When Dorsie nodded, he poured out her Johnnie Walker Blacks and set them before her. "You guys were really truckin' it out there today. But man, Grandma, you look like you're gonna' bite someone's head off."

"I miss my cats. They're back home with my brother," Dorsie said before she could stop the words from spilling out of her mouth.

"Cats? Thor doesn't get on with them? Where's back home?" Skeeter asked. "Everyone down here is from someplace else. You never did say and, honestly, I'd like to quit calling you Grandma."

Dorsie eyed Skeeter as he spread his hands silently asking "your name?" She took a deep breath to gain control over the uneasy feeling gathering her in chest. "Dorsie," she said purposefully omitting her last name. "Home is in New Jersey. But I'm not a snowbird or a permanent resident. Just here for a couple of months." She paused and glanced down at Thor. "He gets on with Diva and Pavarotti but they don't travel well. So they're with my brother."

"Jersey! Me too! Hey what's wrong? He was quick to catch the wild look of panic that skirted across Dorsie's face. "Something wrong with Jersey boys?"

Dorsie took a gulp of her drink then shook her head while twisting her drink round and round. "Of course not. Somehow I just didn't take you for someone from the Northeast."

"Born and bred at the Shore. Ocean City. From sixteen all through my college years I did the lifeguard thing."

"I know Ocean City well. My son Brandon was an O.C. lifeguard too, but you wouldn't know him. Brandon's quite a bit older than you," she added quickly not wanting Skeeter to ask for a last name. She lifted her drink as if to study its amber color and gazed over the rim of the glass at Skeeter. "How'd you end up bartending in a retirement community?"

"Easy. Grandpa needed help. Couldn't figure out what I wanted to do after college. So down I came to help Grandpa with the hounds."

Dorsie raised her eyebrows in question. "Hounds?"

"Ah, forgot to say Grandpa was a top breeder of Bloodhounds. After he passed, I couldn't find a reason to leave. My older brother was already down here. A veterinary surgeon with a solid practice up in Ocala. You know its big thoroughbred country up there, don't you?" He didn't wait for an answer and continued on with his explanations. "So between us we've kept the champion hound bloodline going that Grandpa started. ' 'Bout ninety percent of our pups end up in law enforcement or search and rescue. My sister wants to start breeding Labs. Right now she works down at the Southeastern Guide Dog Campus where they have an excellent breeding program."

"Ah, that explains your admiration of Thor."

"Hang on a sec," Skeeter said. He glanced down the bar and saw a new customer settling himself in a seat. "Be right back."

Dorsie finished her first round of two for one drinks. Feeling smug she silently addressed an imagined Deidra Fallon. *There you go, Deidra. I am getting better. Took a risk. Told someone where I was from. Talked about my family.* She glanced over at Skeeter serving a frosty mug of beer to one of the regular uncles then sighed. Big risk, she thought. What interest would a single, thirty something guy have in the Tracy Maddox trial? He may have seen the photos of Tracy and Jenna Maddox. National coverage had been flashing photos almost non-stop during the entire trial and during the reporting of Van Zant's death. But would Skeeter be one of those people who had a heavy interest in the verdict? In the jury? She doubted it. The Lighthouse's big screen TVs were constantly tuned to sports and financial news channels. So what risk had she really taken? None, she concluded.

Short minutes later Skeeter returned setting down two more glasses of scotch. "Got a proposition for you" he said. "Sunday we're having a Doggie Social at our place up in Pedro. Like to invite you and Thor. Don't worry. It's an elite gang. There's no worry about Thor mixin' with a scruffy crowd."

"Oh, I'm not sure. I pretty much stick to The Villages. Don't know my way beyond that."

"My sister's holding a get together for guide dog puppy raisers," Skeeter said talking over any further objection to follow. "A.J., the handler for Lady Lake's K-9, is gonna' be there. Irwin from Orlando's airport detail will come up with his German Shepherd. Annie and Meredith, Bloodhound handlers from Tampa and Sweetwater, are also coming. They each have a male from the same litter. Come on. Give Thor a break. He's gotta' have some social time of his own. Plenty of room to run. Tug-of-war matches with guys his size. Also, my sister makes the best potato salad you'd ever want to taste. My smokin' ribs aren't bad either."

Dorsie glanced down at Thor resting at her feet then back up at Skeeter. She had to admit, Skeeter's enthusiasm was catchy and Thor did deserve a more rigorous workout than she could give him. She took a deep, deep breath and said, "Ok. Where? What time? And what can I bring?"

"Yes!" Skeeter exclaimed. He gave an arm pumping motion of victory. "Just yourself and Thor. Pedro is about thirty-five minutes from The Villages. I can call The Judge and have him pick you up. He's been out to Pedro before so you won't have to worry about finding the place. The Judge is over in Sabal Chase and he's got a van so there's room for both Gabby and Thor." He slid a napkin and pen towards Dorsie along with a business card. "Give me your number and I'll have him call you to set up a time."

Dorsie stared at the blank white napkin and business card. There was a slight shake to her hand as she picked up the pen then realized she didn't know the house number and she wasn't about to give out her cell one. "I . . . um . . . don't know the number. Wait. I think I put it in Notes on my cell." She removed her cell from her pants pocket then busied herself with finding the house phone number. She wrote it down and slid the napkin back towards Skeeter. She wiggled her cell in the air. "The beauty of technology. The Judge? A real judge?"

Skeeter folded the napkin and slipped it into his pants pocket. "Yep. Retired. The Honorable Joseph Kelly. Super guy. You'll like him. He's on his third puppy he hopes will go on to Guide Dog College. His previous two made it through."

"My Gawd, "elite gang" is an understatement," Dorsie said. Inside she felt a spark of genuine interest sitrring. "All pros. Don't think I can add anything to the mix except Thor."

"That's good enough. Look, I know how finicky trainers can be about lettin' their dogs mix with unknowns. So if you want, I'll give your son-in-law a call." He mugged an embarrassed face and pointed towards Thor. "Actually, I'd just like to talk to him about this awesome, cool dude. Got his number handy?" he asked. He tapped her cell phone lying on the bar.

Dorsie glanced down at Skeeter's business card, fighting the urge to end the conversation and leave. "How 'bout I have him call you?"

"No problemo," Skeeter answered. "He's not in the vicinity, is he? Cause I'd sure like for him to join us too."

Dorsie shook her head. "North Carolina. Too far to drive for one day."

"Ah, thought as much." He glanced down the bar. "Gotta' go. Uncles need their refills."

Much, much later at three in the morning unable to sleep Dorsie threw back the covers and got out of bed. "Thor. Stay," she said as she left the bedroom. In an obsessive way she paced and paced through the house, out to the lanai then back through the house again convinced one minute she was going to give some excuse to Skeeter Brooks on why she couldn't attend the Doggie Social. The next minute she convinced herself to go reminding herself that Dorsie Renninger had never shied away from meeting interesting people. She wasn't socially inept but pretty good at drawing out people and good at getting them to talk about their interests and what excited them. Granted it was all done with the goal of being able to identify what they wanted their homes to look and feel like, but even so, it still was something she did all the time – listening more than talking. She'd ride with The Honorable Joseph Kelly to Skeeter's place in Pedro and on the way she'd ask all kinds of questions about what it took to be a guide dog puppy raiser. She glanced at the digital clock on the microwave. At a more reasonable hour, she thought, she'd call Dave, give him Skeeter's number and confirm what Thor should or shouldn't participate in during the Doggie Social. Also, before Sunday, she'd go back and review all of Dave's talking points and take Thor to the Polo Grounds There they'd go through all leash, hand and voice commands. She'd also put him through thunderbolt runs. While he was running with wild abandon, burning off energy, she'd hide some Kong toys in the bushes and maybe throw one up into the bleachers. After a cool down period, she'd have him search for every one of his Kong toys. She could do this, she told herself. At the Doggie Social, it was doubtful anyone would recognize her or ask about the trial. They all would be showing off their dogs and proudly talking about them just like mothers who shared stories about their high-energy toddlers while keeping an eye on them at the playground. That's exactly what Thor needed – to expend large amounts of energy. Even though she exercised him and JB played tug-of-war with him she was almost positive Thor had much, much more energy in his muscular body than he was letting out.

Feeling better and more certain of saying yes to Skeeter's invitation, she sat at the small breakfast table and flipped open her laptop. In the browser bar she typed in Skeeter's web address and when it popped up she read through the entire website's content. A click on the *Photos-*

Testimonials tab brought up pictures of law enforcement officers in crisp uniforms posing with their Bloodhounds.

Click. Click. Click. Like a camera taking rapid shots, images flashed through her mind and blurred the photos on the screen. Suddenly, she was transported back into the courtroom.

Click. Click. Click. The camera's lens stopped and like looking through the viewfinder Dorsie saw Sgt. Meryl Haggerty, the handler of the second K-9 brought into the investigation of the death of Jenna Maddox.

"Sgt. Haggerty, could you please tell us what's happening in the video with your K-9?" Greg Ashcroft asked. "Could we have the lights?"

Another crime scene investigation video filled the large screen in the courtroom.

"You see Jessie here go into her search and sniff mode," Sgt. Haggerty said.

Silence filled the courtroom.

"Now, she's in her alert mode at the back of the vehicle. The same place Sgt. Gussard's K-9 alerted. Now, you see me giving her the command to enter the vehicle through the opened hatchback. She immediately goes into the search and sniff mode. There she halts then alerts with a bark and since the roof is too low for her to be in a sit alert position, she goes into a lay-down position while continuing to bark until I give her the stop bark command. She's alerting at the exact spot where Sgt. Gussard's K-9 alerted."

"Lights, please," said Greg Ashcroft. "Sgt. Haggerty, how many false alerts has your dog had since you've been her handler. For seven years now?"

"Yes sir, that's correct. Jessie and I have been together for seven years. In that time during certifications, competitive trials and mandatory training she's only had one false alert.'

"One false alert in seven years. That's got to be a record. Is it a record?"

"No, sir," said Sgt. Haggerty. "It's impressive. But when certification judges review her previous records, they always make it a point to tell me Jesse's one of the top hundred dogs in the U.S. with only one false alert."

"Does Jesse ever get deployed anywhere else other than in New Jersey?"

"Yes sir. When a call goes out for a K-9 such as Jesse, our department tries very, very hard to respond. Jesse's worked in many states on Search and Rescues and Amber Alerts."

"Thank you Sgt. Haggerty. No further questions, Your Honor."

Now, Dorsie shivered remembering at the grilling Alberto Diaz gave Sgt. Haggerty. He harshly pointed out that Jesse was nearing retirement age. Was it possible she was just getting older, a little slower, more likely to make a mistake just like aging senior citizens find themselves doing? Now, she recalled how Sgt. Haggerty responded in a controlled voice, "No sir."

Dorsie ran her hand over her bedraggled ponytail envisioning Sgt. Haggerty's crisp uniform. Not a wrinkle in spite of the time she'd been sitting in the witness box. Dorsie refocused on the photos on the website now fully understanding what had triggered the flashback – uniforms. "Gawd," she sighed loudly. Was she doomed to reacting this way anytime she saw someone in a uniform? Anxiety filled her as she frantically wondered whether anyone at the Doggie Social would be in uniform. *Stop!* Dorsie commanded using a technique Deidra Fallon had suggested to halt and redirect thoughts. Stop. Don't be such as doddering old fool. Whoever's going to be there will be there because they're off-duty. No uniforms.

Annoyed with herself, she pushed away from the laptop then paced around the kitchen aimlessly back and forth, back and forth for long, long minutes then raised a glass to her lips and took a gulp of scotch. Jolted by the taste on her tongue, she stopped and stared down at the glass in her hand. *Did I pour this! When?*

She stood at the sink with the glass in hand, deeply unsettled. In the last few days, while going over and over what she should have done, could have done in the jury room, to her horror she realized she couldn't remember certain details. Couldn't remember what happened after she entered the courthouse on Verdict Day. She only could remember picking up the pen and signing her name to the official verdict forms. She only had a vague sense that she'd walked through the courthouse hallway alongside Eric Van Zant. After that, black emptiness. Only from reading national news accounts of the timeline of that day did she know they had

been in the jury room for only one hour before Judge Howard was notified that they'd reached a verdict. What transpired before the signing of
the verdict forms, she had no idea. She did remember the night before,
pacing and pacing in the dimly lit hotel room, remembered coming to a
decision to get a note to Judge Howard one way or another and then
going in search of one of the deputies assigned to their floor. Still holding
the glass, still standing at the sink, she squeezed her eyes shut. Like
watching a scene in a movie she saw the deputy walking towards her as
she rushed towards him.

"Can I help you ma'am?"

"Yes," she said. "I need to get a note to Judge Marvin Howard. I need
to talk with him right away."

"Ma'am, are you sure there's nothing I can help you with?"

"No! No! I need to talk to Judge Howard! Can you have him call me?
Now? Juror 1389. My room number is 406. I'll go back and wait. It's
very, very urgent."

"Ma'am are you ill? Do you need medical assistance?"

"For Gawd sakes! No I am not ill! I do not need medical attention.
You can see I'm fine," she said sweeping her hand in a downward motion
like someone using a wand to do a body scan. "What I need is to get a
note to Judge Howard. I must speak with him. Tonight! Now! Before the
court day begins tomorrow."

The deputy shifted his stance and glanced over her shoulder to see if
other jurors were opening their doors to investigate what was going on.
"Ma'am, please keep your voice down," he said. "Ma'am it's three a.m.
We have protocols and they say we can inform the judge at any time of a
medical emergency with any juror. Again, are you in need of assistance?"

"Yes! I need assistance. Your assistance. I need to get a note to Judge
Howard." She balled up her fists tightly and frantically fought to gain
control of herself. "I have something urgent I need to tell Judge Howard," she said more calmly. "It's extremely important I talk with him
before we go into the Jury Room tomorrow."

"Ma'am. You do understand you are in the middle of deliberations."

"Yes. Yes. I'm not senile. I know that!"

"Please, go back to your room and check your jury instructions. You'll
see the outlined procedure for getting a note to Judge Howard. All communications from any member of the jury during deliberations must come

from the Jury Foreperson." He took Dorsie gently by the arm and turned her back towards her opened door. "Let me walk you to your room. Are you sure you are not in need of medical assistance?"

"The hell with protocol. Bureaucracy. I don't care if you lose your job. *I need to talk with Judge Howard!*"

"Yes, Ma'am. I understand. But my hands are tied. Now, ma'am. Each one of you is under a great deal of stress right now. Try to get some rest. Things may look differently in the morning."

But now, standing at the sink, glass still in hand she couldn't remember parts of the next morning. Now, in retrospect, she surmised that if she'd gotten to speak with Judge Howard what would she have said? Eric Van Zant is acting erratic. Something's wrong with him. What would Judge Howard have done? Ask *her* if she needed medical attention because of being too stressed? Spoken privately with the other jurors? But now, there was no doubt in her mind the other eleven jurors would have said they felt everything was fine. They would have given Judge Howard no reason to impose any delay. They'd made it clear. They had made their decisions. Short of a last minute plea deal or a confession from Tracy Maddox no one and no piece of credible evidence was going to change their minds. Is that what had happened to her? Like the others, was she just so exhausted and worn down that she just gave in? From Deidra and her own research on acute stress disorder, she'd discovered it wasn't unusual for someone to have bouts of dissociative amnesia regarding a traumatic event. Did the act of signing her name to something that forevermore could not be changed qualify as trauma? Is that why she had lost chunks of time?

Dorsie emptied the half-full glass of scotch into the sink then went back to the laptop. She knew she had to focus on something, anything other than her disturbing thoughts. Her hands were shaking as she typed "U.S. police canine associations" in the browser bar. Multiple sites popped up and she spent the next two hours drilling down through them. She stayed focused and reviewed all the terminology used by handlers along with all the commands a handler and K-9 were required to perform to gain certification. When she finished, she felt she could hold her own in conversations at the Doggie Social.

She ran her hands over her face then through her hair. Every muscle in her body ached with fatigue. My Gawd Ole Gal, she silently told herself. Pull yourself together before Sunday. Get a massage. Get your hair styled. Unconsciously she wiggled her toes. Get a pedi. Bright red polish. Make Rick proud. Be stylish. Not a frump. She laughed aloud. K-9s, Bloodhounds and whatever breed of dog at the Doggie Social wouldn't care one iota about fancy toenail polish.

At six thirty a.m. she made coffee, took Thor out to the Duty Pit, cleaned up then sat in a comfortable lounge chair out on the lanai and tried to sort through her emotions. Unable to come to terms with the missing time in the last hour of deliberations, she vowed to set her full will to pulling out of her unconscious whatever was buried there. She didn't care whether it was good or bad because whatever was there was the key to why she'd checked not guilty and signed her name to all those official forms.

She took sips of the strong, black coffee from the mug in her hands. Beyond the lanai a mockingbird landed on the low fence catching her attention. The bird fluffed its wings then seemed to adopt a performer's stance. Seconds later she heard the mockingbird thrill out the first aria in its repertoire. Dorsie closed her eyes and concentrated on the complexity of the notes resounding in the morning air. She took one deep breath after another. *I find joy in small things,* she mentally whispered. She took another deep breath. *Joy in small things.* Another deep breath. *Joy in small things*

On the fence the mockingbird continued his operatic performance. Dorsie sighed. Within, the nagging, badgering voice stayed silent, honoring the bird's pure, glorious songs.

Chapter Nineteen

Mid October – Blairstown

At the Blairstown Diner, Vince Di Paolo and Harold Raines waited for Bud Eckley. Even though it was Eckley's second day off-shift, he'd agreed to an early morning meeting. Minutes later he slid into the booth while Shelly, the waitress, followed right behind with the coffee pot. She filled his mug, topped off Harold's and Di Paolo's then left without saying a word.

"You do something to Shelly?" Di Paolo asked. "Ain't like to her say nothin'."

Eckley waved his hand at Di Paolo in annoyance then turned to Harold. "Before we get started, how's Dorsie doing down there in Florida?"

Harold poured more sugar in his coffee mug. "'Bout the same. She's looking better." He glanced over at Di Paolo. "Sunshine's given her a nice tan. But . . ."

"But what? Someone botherin' her?" Di Paolo snapped.

"No." Harold ran his hand over his bald head. "I'm just worried some old stuff may have resurfaced for her. Old stressor remnants from getting mugged."

"Mugged! When?" Di Paolo and Eckley exclaimed in unison.

"Years ago. When she was in her thirties. In New York. She was just getting back on her feet after Steve, her husband, was killed in a freak construction accident at one of the sites we were renovating. Then out of the blue, she gets mugged. Badly beaten. In the hospital for two weeks. Never would talk about it for a long, long time. Still not sure if she's ever told me the full story. Dorsie can keep a tight lid on things. Even now, she doesn't like to be touched by anybody she doesn't know. She hides it pretty well. But sometimes. Well it's just a hell of a thing to see. Years and years after the mugging we were coming out of a restaurant in New York. Big guy, in a big, big hurry crashed into her knocking her up against the restaurant's foyer wall. In reaction the guy grabbed onto her to keep her from hitting the floor. She froze like a deer in headlights. Started shaking like it was below zero. Wouldn't say a word for hours after that. She went into a deep tailspin that lasted for weeks. Drank more. Wouldn't leave the house. I had to go with her when she had to meet with clients. When I pushed her to talk she'd just look sad and say "bad memories". That's when I figured it out. Big guy. Knocked off her feet." He paused and shook his head slightly. "Mugging memories."

"Uncle Gino ever know about this mugging?" Di Paolo asked.

Harold lowered his head and said quietly, "Oh yes. Gino knew. How he found out, I don't know. Arranged for a private room. Best doctors. Was at the hospital every single day. After that or at least it seemed to me, Gino was always there just on the outer edges of our lives." Again he glanced over at Vince Di Paolo and said, "Still is. After Dorsie recovered, she was in demand. Clients calling her left and right. Business sky rocketed." Harold paused then locked eyes with Vince. "Dorsie got mugged not more than two hundred paces from the entrance of the building where Gino had the top loft. She was in and out of that building every day at all hours. We were doing a rennovation on the second floor."

"Jesus fuckin' Christ," Di Paolo uttered connecting the dots. Someone thought Dorsie was Gino's goomatta. Decided to send a message through her." He wiped his hand across his mouth as if to get rid of something distasteful. "Explains a lot about the old man and Dorsie."

"Dorsie was never Gino's side woman!" Harold said, glaring at Di Paolo. "Anyways, about that night. Don't know what Dorsie suspected. Don't know what Gino said. Don't know what she told him. Like I said, Dorsie can keep things very, very tight to the chest."

All three of them sat in silence for long, long minutes lost in their own thoughts about what Harold had just revealed. Breaking the spell, Eckley said, "Well let's hope Crystal Yates stays out of harm's way. Harold, I checked around just like you asked. Crystal wasn't being paranoid about being followed." He fished a notebook from his windbreaker pocket and flipped it open. "Talked to both desk clerks at the B&B. They probably thought we were still investigating what happened at your place, Harold. Turns out there's been a squirrely kind of photographer stayin' there quite a few times. He was there the day the verdict was announced. Stayed a week, left then came back right after the news hit about Van Zant. Been back and forth on weekends since. Ran his plate number."

Vince Di Paolo raised his eyebrows in question.

"We got ourselves one John Pritcher from Elizabeth, NJ. Called up there. Nothing on him but they know him. Freelancer. Ambulance chaser. Sleaze bag. A wanna-be big time paparazzi. Crystal was right. Someone was taking pictures of her down at the reserve. Not just of the wolves."

"Think he's the one who took the pics of Dorsie?" Di Paolo asked.

"Yep. Shelly said he'd been hangin' around askin' all kinds of, as she put it, "intrusive questions". But, as luck would have it, I just happened to be in the lobby when this skinny, stringy-haired guy came in. Thought all the camera equipment dangling from his scrawny neck made him look like a big shot. Had a word with him, kinda' friendly like cause I'm respectful of civil rights and free speech, yada, yada, yada. Stupid guy blurted out how he was even gonna' make more money off this small hick town. Couldn't keep his trap shut. Bozo said he knew a lot about Crystal Yates, her brother and Van Zant."

Harold shook his head in disgust. "Think we're going to be seeing pictures of Crystal in the *Enquirer*?"

Eckley nodded his head up and down. "Real possibility. Or in some other rag. My gut tells me he's onto something but what I don't know. Called Farino to see if Bobby Yates was on his radar for any reason. He had nothin' except a few calls from Van Zant to his number. Not unusual since he's Crystal's brother."

Harold sat back in the booth. "Well I suspect I know what it is."

"Spill it," Di Paolo snapped.

"A week ago Crystal asked if I would go with her up to Connecticut. Van Zant's lawyers wanted to meet with her. Apparently, somewhere about mid-April Van Zant made out a new will essentially putting Crystal's name on everything connected to the Van Zant name. The ring Dave and I found in his fireproof box was meant for Crystal no matter what that Krieger woman said. The old lawyer confirmed it. Van Zant was going to propose and marry Crystal before the end of the year. Don't know the full details of anything else because I was asked to leave the room. As I understand it from Crystal, it's all bound up in confidentiality relative to trust funds. With Van Zant's death, everything connected to them passes to her with lots of legal constraints, conditions and responsibilities. One of them being the administration of said trusts remain with the old law firm up there."

"Holy shit," said Di Paolo. "The kid was worth a bundle."

"There's more," Harold said. "Crystal's pregnant. Finally a Van Zant progeny. An illegitimate heir not that it matters to Crystal." Harold shook his head sadly. "What a shame. Van Zant had no idea his family's DNA was going to continue on."

"Old money. Two women. One professing love on national TV. One in the dark. Suicide. Illegitimate child. Yep . . . the bozo photo guy has a nose for what the rags want." He glanced at Harold. "Better prep Crystal on what might be comin' down the line. Also, tell her she needs a lawyer of her own to check every detail out. I'll give Gino, Jr. a call. Get a referral for a top-notch attorney who handles trusts and estates. Will also get somebody to nose around more on the Pritcher guy." He paused for a few seconds then said, "Harold, do I need to say me and Eckley's lips are sealed?"

Harold shook his head in resignation. "No Vince. I know how you and the Carapelli family operate." He locked eyes with Di Paolo. "Crystal's a very, very nice young woman."

"Got it. Belongs to my town. Gotta' watch out for her," Vince Di Paolo said then rapped his knuckles on the tabletop. "Move that fat ass of yours," he told Eckley sitting next to him. "Let me out. Gotta' go. Got things to do."

Minutes later, in the parking lot, Harold called Farino's private cell number. He was in his office at the Blairstown Police Station across the highway from the diner. Harold opted to walk over instead of driving his car such a short, short distance. While waiting for a chance to cross Route 94, he wondered if he'd said too much to Vince and Eckley then discarded the thought. When Vince said his lips were sealed, they were. Bobby Yates. Why had his name been tossed out? He'd met Bobby. Seemed like a nice young fella. Going to college over in Stroudsburg, working on a Physical Education degree. A little scruffy around the edges but what college kid wasn't. Van Zant and Bobby Yates must have had a lot in common besides Crystal. He'd have to ask Crystal how Bobby and Van Zant got along. He'd also have to ask Crystal if he could tell Dorsie the positive news about the ring, the outcome of the meeting with Van Zant's lawyers and of course, the news that Crystal was expecting. He and Rose already had Crystal under their wings but he also knew once Dorsie got back she'd be taking Crystal into New York for a shopping spree of all things Baby. His sister was like that. A good, good woman down to her toes. He didn't give a rat's ass that she'd voted not guilty. She was his twin sister, a part of him like no other person on the earth could be.

Harold took his chance in the lull of traffic and crossed the highway. Once inside Farino's office, he gave him a brief summary of what he'd learned in Connecticut.

"Whoa!" Farino exclaimed. "Based on what happened in Vegas and the note Van Zant left, think any challenges are in the making? Maybe by the old family law firm? 'Cause they've had a tight rein and some control over the trusts?"

Harold shrugged. "Di Paolo's going to get a top-notch lawyer's name who handles trusts." In response to Farino's frown he said, "I know you don't care much for Vince. But when it comes to Blairstown and its citizens, Vince's heart is in the right place."

"Yep, that's true. It's his methods that cause me to lose sleep," Farino said. "Eckley gave me a heads up on Bobby Yates's name being tossed out by the photographer hanging around town. Don't see anything there. Interviewed him and Crystal together 'bout the calls Las Vegas' tech geek pulled off of Van Zant's phone in his possession at the time. Seemed like routine stuff."

Harold rose from his seat. "Well, just thought I'd fill you in. At least one detail is closed. We know that the ring really was intended for Crystal. I'm suspecting the old attorney up there didn't include it in Van Zant's estate assets. When he placed the ring in the palm of Crystal's hand, crocodile tears were running down his cheeks."

Farino started walking with Harold towards the front entrance to the station. "How's Dorsie doing down there in Florida? All quiet? Anyone recognize her?"

"Nope. She's lookin' better 'cause she's getting lots of sunshine. But I know my sister. All is not well. Yet. Think the town will ever forgive her?"

Farino clapped his hand on Harold's shoulder. "Yep. I do. They'll remember who Dorsie really is. Hell, Olga over at the Alpine confessed to me she slapped Dorsie in anger over the verdict. Wants to apologize to her, but . . ." Farino did his best to mimic Olga's strong guttural German accent, ". . . Dorsie not here no more. Where she go? She not bad. Is me done bad thing."

Harold couldn't help smiling. "Hey, that's pretty good. Sounds just like our Olga."

As Harold crossed over the highway back to the diner's parking lot and his car, he thought about what a good place Blairstown was and he hoped his sister would come home soon. He also hoped Crystal Yates wouldn't be fodder for any small town gossip or criticism over being an unwed mother.

Back at the Police Station, Detective Eugene Farino sat at his desk staring into space feeling the tingle of a hunch nudging at his brain. He picked up his desk phone and placed a call to the Westin Hotel in Princeton, New Jersey, now known to be the place where jurors were sequestered during the Tracy Maddox trial.

Chapter Twenty

Late October–The Villages

On Sunday, the retired Honorable Judge Joseph Kelly arrived promptly at nine a.m. and rang the doorbell at the house on Duncan Drive. Coming from the other side of the closed door he heard ear-piercing barks, the kind meant to make someone freeze in their tracks. Gabby, his guide-dog-in-training, started to back away, and pulled hard on the leash. Judge gave Gabby a correction tug. "Sit," he commanded. Seconds later, the barking stopped and the door opened. Behind the screen door stood a very attractive woman with stunning long silver hair that just brushed the nape of her neck.

"Dorsie, I'm assuming. I'm Joe Kelley. Most people call me Judge. Or to use Skeeter's moniker – "The Judge.""

"Thor, Stay," Dorsie said then opened the screen and stepped outside. "Oh my Gawd, Judge! You sound exactly like James Earl Jones! I would hate to be a witness in your courtroom. I'd be thinking the wrath of Darth Vader was going to come down on me any minute."

"Well, I wasn't a trial judge and was spared the intense visibility that comes with that. I didn't have to worry about people pulling up the image of Darth Vader. But my colleagues never let me forget who I sound like. They still send me some new Darth Vader memorabilia they've come across in their travels."

Dorsie glanced down at the black Lab sitting patiently next to him. "This is Gabby?"

"Yes. Not a she. A he. Names are given by those who sponsor a dog and when a new litter is born whatever names are on the list next get assigned no matter what the gender of the dog. Most certainly the name Gabby belonged to someone who was dearly loved."

"Do I need to let Gabby smell me first?"

"You can give him a pat if you want. He's quite socialized. Used to other dogs," Judge said, and then added, "although I have to say when he heard Thor's bark he started to back away."

"It's a problem? Maybe we shouldn't . . ."

"No. Just means he was very cautious. Which he should be. Thor has a mighty, mighty fearsome bark. But being a protection K-9 that's what he should have. Gabby, being he's a candidate for Guide Dog College, he should not be timid. He'd need to warn a blind person but he should never put his tail between his legs like a whimp. He didn't do that. Just tugged hard on the leash and took a few steps back. Being cautious." He gave Dorsie a reassuring look. "It's going to go just fine. Get Thor."

Dorsie brought Thor out and he sat at her side tight against her calf."

"It'll be fine," said Judge noting the look of concern on Dorsie's face. "They both know how to navigate around each other."

Dorsie pulled gently on Thor's collar and said "Thor. Meet."

Seconds later, the two dogs went about their sniff, sniff, let-me-see-what-you're-about behavior. Thor circled Gabby several times then lowered his head, gave a small whine, stretched out his paws, bowing to Gabby signaling in doggie behavior a come-let's play invitation. In response Gabby sat then abruptly dropped to the ground, rolled over and showed his stomach.

"Ah," Judge said. "Gabby's granting dominance to Thor. But who wouldn't. I can see why Skeeter couldn't stop talking about him. He is one fine specimen. But, I'm going to have to check with the certified guide dog trainer whether Gabby's behavior in doing this in play is acceptable."

For fifteen minutes or so Judge and Dorsie let the dogs tussle in friendly play while they chatted about inconsequential things then went about getting Gabby and Thor settled in the van. Five minutes into the drive Judge glanced over at Dorsie taking note that at some point she'd swept up her hair in a simple ponytail. Nice profile, he thought then concluded she didn't look as elderly as reported in the news accounts of jurors. He reached over and touched Dorsie's forearm lightly. "I knew who you were before Skeeter gave me a call," he said. Surprised at the uneasy look settling on Dorsie's face he quickly added, "I shoot pool with JB Bowser, the house caretaker. He's been going on non-stop about Thor just like Skeeter."

Dorsie glanced over her shoulder to the back of the van. The two dogs lay quietly next to each other and she felt a sense of relief that Thor was the main subject of interest "Yes, Thor does attract attention. I'm sure Gabby does too."

"You never mentioned your last name, but might it be Renninger?" Judge asked.

Dorsie's heart skipped a beat. The very thing she feared most, being recognized, was happening. She sank into the van's seat then a second later using sheer willpower sat up straighter then turned slightly toward Judge. "Yes, it is Renninger. How did you know?"

"We judges, even when retired, take note of unusual trials. You've had quite a time of it haven't you, Dorsie Renninger?" He took his eyes off the road and glanced at her. She looked uncomfortable but he still felt he had to be forthcoming with what he knew. "My son is a V.P. at Bristol-Myers Squibb at the Plainsboro Campus. He, his wife and my grandson live in West Windsor off of Old Trenton Road not more than eight miles from where Jenna Maddox was found." He glanced over at Dorsie again and saw she was sitting rigid in the seat while listening. "Based on that alone and the fact that Melanie is a criminal attorney, we were interested in each other's perspective and analysis of major portions of the trial. She's taken a sabbatical from practice to stay home with my grandson, Jamie, for his first year. Thus, she had time to keep abreast of all the details."

"I see," Dorsie said in a very cool tone.

"Please, don't let my knowing spoil your day. Just thought I had to be upfront with you. As far as anyone else you meet today, I'd venture to say it's highly unlikely they'd know who you are."

Dorsie took a deep breath. "I hope so. Most people who followed the trial aren't feeling very kindly towards me."

"Well, that's not the case with me. I have a high respect for the men and women who serve on juries. Sometimes it's easy. Other times, depending on the case, it can alter one's perspective on our justice system and how we go about applying it."

"You mentioned you were not a trial judge," Dorsie said her tone softening slightly. "What kind of judge were you?"

"Appellate Judge, State of Maryland. Served on the bench for over twenty-five years. Mandatory retirement is at age seventy but I retired a few years earlier."

"I'm not sure I know what an appellate judge does. Those long ago social study lessons must be in there somewhere in my long term memory, but . . ."

"Amazing what age does to memory, isn't it?" Judge said with a deep good-natured laugh. "Okay, since you asked, I'll give you a quick refresher course on those social study lessons. You'll see why having a sound-like-Darth-Vader voice presented no problem. But," he said glancing over at her, "I'm passionate about law and if my verbal dissertation on it gets too boring just shout out "enough". I won't be offended."

For the rest of the drive to Skeeter's place in Pedro, Judge explained how appellate judges read, read, read and then did more reading on the facts of a case, and the preponderance of precedents in State, Statutory and Constitutional law. Much research was done by law clerks but much was also done by a judge himself. He gave an example of one case brought before the Court and detailed his approach to rendering a decision. He summed up by stating appellate judges look for clear error, misapplied fact on the law or abuse of discretion by another judge on any case brought before the Court of Appeals. To do that, a judge had to be meticulous and objective in analysis. He ended by emphasizing that all judges possessed certain key qualities – common sense, scholarship, the never-ending study of human behavior and a deep-seated drive to apply the law fairly to everyman no matter where they came from or what their circumstances happened to be.

"So," he said while pulling on the emergency brake after parking the van among cars, jeeps and four by fours already parked on Skeeter's property. "Having this recognizable voice wasn't a hindrance because most of what appellate judges do is solitary." Again, he gave a deep, good-natured laugh. "In Maryland it helped a great deal that appellate judges wore red robes when seated. At least then, lawyers presenting arguments before the panel or when I probed arguments, they weren't conjuring up an image of Darth Vader in his black flowing cape." He unbuckled his seat belt then turned to her. "Are we ready? Let's get these guys out of the back." He gave Dorsie a wide, encouraging smile. "Today is a day to have fun."

For six hours, Dorsie lost herself in the day, in the continuous activity of dogs running, jumping, navigating agility course obstacles and handlers comparing notes on performances. A.J., the Lady Lake Police K-9 handler, took Thor and Dorsie under his command, pairing them with himself and his dog, Ace. All together they drilled through basic obedience commands – heel position, finish position, obedience recall and walking control. A.J. profusely praised Dorsie and Thor on their execution of hand and voice commands. And when he learned how just how long she and Thor had been paired together, he gave her the handle of "silver alpha". He then took Thor and put him through more advanced agility commands involving hurdle jumping, catwalks and crawling. When A.J. returned Thor to Dorsie, they, with dogs at their sides, went to find cool drinks and a shady spot for a rest period. A.J. offered to put Thor some reinforcement training if she'd bring him over to the Lady Lake station. He'd don protective gear and put Dorsie and Thor through all the attack commands needed to keep Thor's skills sharp. Dorsie said she'd consider his offer but would have to check with Dave before she could commit. She took A.J.'s number with a promise to get back to him within a few days.

In a lull in all the activities, Dorsie scanned the area looking for Judge and Gabby and found them among a group of puppy raisers sitting in a circle giving their charges some sort of massages. Before the day ended, Skeeter and his sister took her down to the kennels where she fell hopelessly in love with a four-week-old litter of adorable Bloodhounds.

Much later, while unloading Thor from Judge's van she agreed to meet him the next day for lunch at the Mallory Hill Country Club. The following week she went with him to the Polo Grounds to let Thor race and play with Gabby. After that they continued to exercise the dogs together every Monday and Thursday then headed to Lighthouse Point for a late afternoon snack and for Dorsie's "Happy Hour Bliss", sharing the two for one Johnnie Walker Blacks Skeeter placed before them.

On a beautiful late October afternoon, with the temperature hovering just below eighty, they sat at an outside table on Lighthouse Point's deck taking in a panoramic view of Lake Sumter and the Arnold Palmer golf course on the opposite side of the lake. Dorsie glanced over at Gabby peacefully snoozing beside Judge's chair. "Will you be sad when you have to turn Gabby back over?" she asked.

"Sad, yes," he answered. "But it's sort of like watching your child go off to college. But with Gabby, I know he might be going on to perform an invaluable service. He'll be helping a non-sighted person. Or if he doesn't get through the seeing guide dog training, he'll be in the Paws for Patriots program. He'll be paired up with a veteran warrior who needs help. The other two puppies I raised went on to be fully trained guide dogs. When they're turned over to their forever person, it's quite an emotional ceremony." He paused and reached down to give Gabby an affectionate stroke on the head. "We hand over our dog's "Puppy to Now" book. It has all the photos we've taken while the dog went from puppyhood to young adult. This way the person taking ownership of his or her dog knows how much they were loved and how they were brought up. I always feel a great sense of pride that I'd been a part of giving a non-sighted person the ability to go out into the world in the safe care of a dog I'd helped raise."

"I know what you mean about feeling proud," Dorsie said. "I feel the same way when we finish a Habitat Humanity House and place the keys in the hands of someone deserving of a big, big boost in life. We turn over a photo book too. One that shows all the phases of construction and photos of the people who took on the task of performing them."

"Just think, now you and Thor are in pictures in Gabby's book. If he makes it through Guide Dog College to where he's ready for a forever person, will you come to the ceremony?" Judge asked then added quietly, "I'd like that very much."

Dorsie studied the man sitting across from her and thought how she'd only known him a short time but yet it felt like she'd known him forever. They had in common certain life experiences – losing spouses early, never remarrying, and a desire to give back in a meaningful way. Perhaps, she thought, it was also because his gentle and caring ways were much like Harold's. And, much to her surprise, she found she waited and loved to hear his deep, good-natured laugh. She felt uplifted by his laugh. Felt released, at least for a short period of time, from her own relentless thoughts which contained very little joy in them. No matter what he was saying or talking about, his voice could lull her into believing she was her old self, a woman who had been at peace with who she was and where she found herself in life, not someone whose life had been drastically interrupted and changed by a young woman named Tracy Maddox.

"Dorsie, are you there? Drifting again, are you?"

"Sorry," she said, pulled back to the moment. "Of course I'll come. Just say the word and I'll fly down. I was just thinking about my brother, Harold. Did I ever tell you I was a twin? I'm a couple of minutes older. He calls me "Ole Gal" all the time."

Judge smiled. "No, you've never told me. I'd venture to say there's quite a lot you haven't told me because you have an uncanny ability to get me talking about myself. So much so that I forget to ask you about what it is you like, where you've been, what you've done."

"Comes with the occupation," she said. "If you can't listen to the way people move in life, as a decorator, it would be very difficult to help them achieve something they could feel good about. Comfortable in. Living with it day-in-day-out."

He reached across the table and gave her hand a pat. "Are you missing home?"

"Very much. It's beautiful here in The Villages. I feel as if I'm now living in a resort. But I do miss my own house. My own things." She sighed wistfully. "My cats. I just hope everyone in Blairstown forgives me. They couldn't believe one of their own would . . ." She stopped to glance over at Judge took a deep breath and finished the sentence. "Would vote not guilty."

"Does the not guilty verdict bother you?"

Within, Dorsie felt the tight bind of restraint loosen for an instant. "Yes. Yes it does." She turned in her chair to face Judge wanting to say more but the restraint gripped and tightened again causing her to feel as if she couldn't breathe. "It's very difficult to ..." she said then stopped.

"I *do* understand, Dorsie," Judge said. He reached across the table to give her hand a comforting pat. "But if you ever feel like you could talk about anything to do with the trial or jury responsibilities, I'm well qualified to listen. My years on the bench have exposed me to many, many kinds of human frailties, debaucheries and depravities." He gave her a kind, understanding gaze. "I realize your civic duty has caused you harm and great emotional distress. I'm willing to listen if you're willing to trust. When you're ready, and if you'd like me to listen, I will. Perhaps my judgeship can offer you insights no one else can."

"You're a kind man, Your Honor. Thank you. But . . . I just can't . . ."

"Shhh. Shhh," he said. "I'm not pressing, just offering." A breeze blew up and dark clouds passed over the sun hanging low in the sky. "We'd better go," he said glancing at his watch. "Our Villages weatherman, Neil Kaster, is on target again with his forecast – expect a thunderstorm to roll in at about five o'clock."

Later, after making herself a quick dinner, Dorsie made her round of daily phone calls. She talked with Brandon and Rick. Harold wasn't answering and her call went straight to voicemail. Dave and Megs were on speaker together and from them she learned they would be adding a new puppy to their daily routines. Dave was flying over to Germany at the end of the week to pick her up. The breeder had a thing for Norse gods and named this female German Shepherd after the Goddess of the Sea in Norse mythology. Her name was Ran.

"Dave, my new friend, Judge, is about to turn over Gabby back to the Guide Dog School. What about Thor?" Dorsie asked. "When is he going to the family in D.C.?"

"Well," Dave drawled. "There's been a change in plans for Thor."

"Oh, he's going somewhere else?"

"Well. Ah. 'Bout that . . ." Dave said. He paused. "He's not going anywhere. Thor is staying with you."

"What? Who decided that? You?"

"No. Gino Carapelli did. He bought the dog. Did it the day your picture appeared in the *Enquirer*. My partner and I had heated words with Uncle Gino. But in the end we all know Uncle Gino gets what he wants. What Uncle Gino wanted most was protection for you. Believe me, price wasn't the obstacle. He had a few choice words when we told him that Thor was slated for a foreign diplomat down in D.C. He asked whether Thor was paid for yet. We told him no." Dave paused for a breath then continued on. "To Uncle Gino it was simple. No money. No contract. Give the diplomat from Belarus another dog. He was transferring funds to us within the hour. Didn't matter how much. He also had us estimate the cost of all Thor's needs throughout his life. I'm holdin' a sizeable amount of money for you to plunk into an account to cover Thor's food. Vet bills. Collars. Leashes. Everything and anything he'd need."

There was silence on the other end of the line. "Dorsie, are you there. Did I lose connection?"

"No, Dave. I'm just stunned. I should have realized something was not in keeping with how you handle your dogs. There's no such thing as a transition person for a dog like Thor. Is there, Dave?"

"Not as a matter of routine."

"Why didn't you tell me then?"

Megs jumped into the conversation. "Mom, you were so fragile and Uncle Gino asked us not to tell you just then. Why we don't know. But what we did know is that Thor would keep you from shutting yourself in. His needs forced you to go out. It worked! Skeeter. The Judge. Gabby. The other puppy raisers. And of course, A.J. and Ace."

"Thor deserves to do the job he was trained for," Dorsie said finding herself getting angry. "He needs to protect a family. He's wasted on me. Dave, can't you do something about this?"

"'Fraid not. Ownership belongs to you." Dave paused and cleared his throat. "Dorsie, whatever it is about this protection thing, my gut tells me it's deep seated with Uncle Gino. Harold and Brandon tried to talk him out of purchasing the dog outright. Tried to cajole him by saying you only liked cats. Maybe you wouldn't want a dog. Especially a dog like Thor. He was having no part of it. He just decreed and I'm quoting, 'Dorsie will keep the dog because it is a gift from me. She will understand.'"

Megs joined in again. "Mom, I sure hope someday you're going to tell us all why Uncle Gino is so tied to us. Brandon and I have wondered for years and years. It's like there's some big, dark mystery there. We've asked Uncle Harold many times. He just says Uncle Gino and you have a bond that won't be broken until one of you is no longer here. As if that solves the mystery for us. Like did you and Uncle Gino have an affair somewhere along the line?"

"Gawd, no! Ah, Megs, by now you've learned life is complicated. The bond Harold talks about is complicated." Her next words were meant for Dave hoping he'd rescue her from the direction Meg's conversation was taking. "Sort of like the bond combat soldiers develop for each other. And Megs, maybe very much like the bond you develop with those tiny, tiny babies and their moms and dads." She paused, then redirected the conversation by saying, "Anyway, I'm still looking forward to Thanksgiving. And now, meeting Ran. Megs, you think maybe we could include Crystal Yates and Judge into our family dinner? That's if they don't have other plans."

"No problem Mom. The more the merrier. Uncle Harold and Rose are growing very fond of Crystal. The Judge, my goodness, are you really bringing someone for us to meet? You know, meeting family signals something serious."

Dorsie laughed. "Megs, you're way ahead of yourself. You're so in love with that handsome husband of yours that you want everyone to be in love no matter how old they are. Now, gotta' go. Love you both."

Later, deep into the wee hours of the morning, Dorsie tossed and thrashed in her sleep, murmuring, then pleading with some unseen force, then struggling as if she were fighting off the very same force. Thor sat beside the bed watching, cocking his head to the side as if contemplating what he should do. When she screamed, he whined, placed a paw on her chest and licked her face in an effort to wake her.

Seconds later Dorsie sat at the edge of the bed sweating, wiping her face with the edge of the sheet. She laid her hand on her chest and waited for long, long minutes for her thumping heartbeat to settle into a resting rhythm. She gazed down at Thor. "Good boy. Thor. Good boy," she said and patted him on the head. "It's okay. I'm okay," she said more to reassure herself than the dog. Thor gave a small whine and laid his massive head in her lap. She looked down at him again, studied his long, dark muzzle, his pointed ears and his bright almond shaped eyes now watching her with intense alertness. By now she knew each black and little tan marking he had and the feel of his lean yet muscular body from the daily brushings she gave his shorthaired coat. Thor was noble, commanding in presence and would be loyal and protective. She knew beyond a shadow of a doubt Thor would remain with her. He was Gino Carapelli's final gift of protection.

She sat on the edge of the bed for a long, long time still shaken. An old nightmare full of things she managed to keep suppressed for years and years had sprung up again, letting her know she could never fully forget what had happened. It was a nightmare full of fear. A nightmare that replayed the dark ugly sounds and smells that had left her helpless. Thugs. Garlic and cigarette breath. A rough calloused hand covering her mouth, cutting off air and the ability to scream. Hard palm strikes against the face and head. Fists in the stomach and ribs. Clothes being torn off and the hand still cutting off all air. Harsh guttural laughter. Menacing Italian words she didn't understand. Words she did understand. Bitch. Bitch. And ugly movements that violated every sense in her being.

She mindlessly patted Thor's head more to comfort herself than him. She knew why Gino Carapelli had bullied his way to purchasing Thor. She understood his reaction to her safety being threatened. She would not insult Gino by turning away his gift. Never, until the day she died, would she ever make light of anything Gino Carapelli did to atone for the indecent acts committed upon her outside his building while he was safe inside unaware. All happening because someone mistakenly thought she belonged to him.

Dorsie bent down and placed a light kiss on the top of Thor's head. Thor was Gino's final act to protect – the protection he swore he would make happen in whatever form it was needed until the day he died. That time was close, too close because Gino was doing battle with deadly cancer. What bonded her and Gino together throughout the years was his need to atone for being responsible for what happened on that night so long ago. Now, she deeply felt for and more than ever fully understood his anguish over not being able to right a dreadful wrong. Now, she too would have to take ownership of an unchangeable wrong and atone for it. She had failed the young, sweet, sweet Jenna Maddox who came into her dreams and danced in her pink tutu singing "Pleez don't take my sunshine away." Atone. She thought deeply about all meanings of the word then looked down at Thor and asked, "How do you atone for justice not being done?"

Chapter Twenty-One

November – December

Plans are always subject to change, Dorsie thought as she looked over one of her all-important lists. She had three, each one listing Things-To-Do for the upcoming visit of Brandon, Rick, Harold, Rose, Dave, Megs, the new puppy Ran, and the mom-to-be Crystal Yates. Collectively they all decided to forego celebrating Thanksgiving on its assigned calendar day. They'd celebrate a week earlier based on Megs' and Rick's schedules and with consideration to Mother Nature who always seemed to present the Northeast with a weather event causing travel delays at airports and bad driving conditions leaving travelers stranded, unhappy and unable to get to their holiday destination.

"Well, Thor," she said using him as a non-replying sounding board while holding up her Entertainment List. "We are going to be busy, busy, busy. Tickets for Blue Man Group at Universal Studios for Brandon, Rick, Dave, Megs and Crystal." She looked down at Thor and asked him in a serious tone, "But do you think that's a good idea for Crystal. All that noise. Babies in the womb hear things. You know that don't you?" Thor gave a small, small whine. "I thought so. Now, here are tickets for all of us for Cirque Du Soleil's *La NouBa*. We have to find time for me to take Harold and Rose to the Carriage Museum. They'll like all those old antique buggies." She set the list down and picked up another list and presented it to Thor. "This is a loaded one. Groceries. My Gawd, with all the things we want to do, who's going to have time to cook? You?" She laughed when Thor gave a loud bark as if to say yes.

Dorsie went on checking over items, making side comments to Thor because she felt happy, a feeling she hadn't had for what seemed like a long, long time. Nightmares and dreams still inhabited her sleep causing her distress. But now, on this day, no images of Darth Vader in a red robe floated into her thoughts. Or images of Thor, who stood on his hind legs, showing off the pink tutu he wore around his middle. Or images of Thor and Gino Carapelli dancing together as Gino sang, Please Don't Take My Sunshine Away. The chaotic flip, flip, flip of photos of Tracy Maddox, Ann Maddox and Eric Van Zant were stilled. Dorsie was happy. She was going to see all the people she loved and cared about.

They all came. They did the Entertainment List. They went to the Town Square and tried to learn line dancing by watching those who'd taken lessons at a class listed in The Villages Recreation News. They did "Happy Hour Bliss" at Lighthouse Point on a day when Skeeter Brooks was working. Rick oohed and aahed over her trim fit figure and golden tan but tenderly tried to remove the dark bluish smudges from beneath her eyes while flashing a what's-this-all-about look. Harold shot pool with Judge and JB. Dave went over to the Lady Lake Police station to meet with A.J. and Ace face-to-face. Crystal, Megs, Rick and Rose went to the pool to "get some color". The golf cart was in and out, charged and recharged. They ate. They drank. They laughed. Dorsie wept when Harold told her Gino Carapelli had put himself in hospice care while remaining in his home in Westchester. She smiled when Rose told her Maria Sanchez had come to the shop looking for her, saying she was sorry for not coming to help Dorsie. Harold told of Olga's confession to Detective Farino that she had slapped the good Dorsie Renninger in anger. Blairstown was back to normal. Maybe it was time to come home Harold said the day before they were scheduled to leave.

Dorsie watched as luggage was loaded into The Villages Airport Van and everyone checked to make sure they had their cell phones, wallets and purses. Hugs, hugs, kiss, kisses where passed among each of them including Thor, Gabby and the puppy Ran. "Oh, she said, clasping her hands together in front of her chest. " This is what I needed." She turned and linked her arm through the Judge's. "Aren't they all just wonderful?" He nodded then left her side to give Harold a final handshake and spoke quietly telling Harold he would help Dorsie in any way he could. Dorsie waved and waved until the van made the right-hand turn at the end of Kline onto Canal Street then disappeared from sight.

Four weeks later, Dorsie, sitting in another Villages Airport Van, made the same turn onto Canal Street. She glanced out the window and saw all the golf carts parked at the Virginia Trace pool. Once again, they failed to cause any reaction. Her heart was heavy. She was on her way to Orlando to board a plane for New York. On the following day she, Brandon and Harold would drive up to Westchester, stay overnight then at mid-morning attend Gino Carapelli's memorial service.

The service was somber with only family and the closest of friends in attendance. Afterward, a tasteful, catered reception was held at Gino and Sofia's grand home. Black Town Cars came and went. Friends, acquaintances, and associates circulated offering condolences to the family then gathered in groups to reminisce over old times and the good old days. These groups of men were small in number. Not many were left from the good old days when the mere mention of Carapelli brought instant respect within certain areas of the city and across the river in Jersey. They'd glance over their shoulders towards Gino Jr. and wonder what lay on the horizon for the Carapelli name.

Dorsie sat quietly in a comfortable wing back chair nursing a scotch. She followed Sofia's stop and chat movement among those gathered noting how gracious she was under such circumstances. A giggly inappropriate laugh caught her attention and she scanned the large room to see where it had come from. To her horror, Angie, Gino Jr.'s wife, was motioning to several other women for them to follow her. They all stopped before Dorsie's chair.

"This is the decorator who did my house that you all *sooo* love," Angie said. "And, do you know who else she is?" She waved a claw-like hand in the air at Dorsie, wiggling long, fingernails painted black. "A juror on the Tracy Maddox case." The others turned toward each other, raised eyebrows then turned back to stare at Dorsie while Angie grabbed Dorsie by the hand pulling her from the wing back chair. "Come . . . come . . . let's find a quiet place to sit. Then you can tell us *everything*. Do you think Tracy and Alberto Diaz had a thing going on? It sure as the hell looked like it from where I was sitting."

"Angie, I don't think now's the time." Dorsie frantically scanned the room for Harold, Brandon, Vince Di Paolo or anyone who could come to her rescue. Her eyes locked with Sofia.

Sofia excused herself from the small group she was standing with and rushed towards them. She grasped Angie by the arm and whispered through clenched teeth. "You disgrace Gino *on this day*! He ordered you to never ask Dorsie anything about the trial. From his deathbed! You forget I was standing there." She turned and motioned for Gino Jr. "Take this wife of yours who disgraces your father somewhere else," she told him. She turned back to Angie. "Have you no shame? A woman of your age should know better!"

After Gino Jr. led his wife away and the women abruptly turned away with noticeable smiles of amusement, Sofia locked her arm through Dorsie's. "Let's go to the study." Once inside Sofia slumped down into the soft leather sofa. "That girl. No class. No manners. Black nail polish at her age. Probably thought she was making a fashion statement. One in keeping with the day. Gino would have been rummaging in my closet for remover or acetone if he were here." She glanced up at Dorsie then patted the space beside her and said, "Sit."

Dorsie sat down next to Sofia and reached for her hand. "It's a difficult day."

"Yes it is. We can thank Angie for that. Maybe even Marilyn. They're close you know. Love. Love. Love to gossip." She paused and glanced at Dorsie. "I overheard Marilyn telling Angie how she slammed the door in your face. I spoke with her. Gino lectured her on why we don't disrespect those we consider family. Did Marilyn make amends today?"

"She did. I believe she meant it, Sofia. Put it out of your mind. Concentrate on taking care of yourself right now."

Sofia faced Dorsie. "It's been a long road. We knew what the prognosis was. We did our grieving together." She waved her hand toward the closed study door. "This is just the formality. Mostly for the others. Gino went in peace. Made peace with the life he led. He wanted me to tell you that you too should make peace with yourself." Sofia squeezed Dorsie's hand. "I was insanely jealous of you when I was a young bride. You never knew that did you? Was convinced you were his . . ." she paused then said, "Well you know what the Italian word is for woman on the side. But, one night after I threw dishes at him he told me why he had a . . . I don't recall the Italian word he used. But got that it meant obligation. After that I never doubted Gino's friendship with you." She sighed heavily. "We're getting old, Dorsie. Do what Gino says. Honor his wish. Find peace over this Maddox business. Honor yourself. At our age anguish is not a good thing."

Outside, grey December light filtered through the windows of the study. Sofia and Dorsie sat together in quiet comfortable silence, holding hands, each lost in her own private thoughts of Gino Carapelli and what role he had in their lives.

In the following days, in NYC, accompanied by Rick, Dorsie tried to do some last minute Christmas shopping. The holiday spirit in all the hustle and bustle filling the air on 59th Street and Lexington or at Herald Square or Rockefeller Center could not ignite a spark of enthusiasm in her. Rick chalked it up to sadness over Gino's death. But Brandon had other thoughts. He'd overhead several conversations at the reception following Gino's funeral. He'd caught the words, Maddox, juror, "that's her" being whispered while one person or another glanced over at his mother. Had she heard them too? From Uncle Harold via Vince Di Paolo he'd also heard about Gino Jr.'s wife's faux pas. Now, it seemed to him his mother was quickly slipping back into silent brooding when weeks earlier, during their visit to Florida, she seemed like her old self. Now, she wanted to fly back to Florida instead of staying with him and Rick for Christmas holidays. She nixed the idea of spending the time with Harold and Rose. He called Megs hoping to get some advice. Megs called Uncle Harold after talking it over with Dave. Harold, after conferring with Rose, placed the most important call of them all. He phoned the retired Honorable Joseph Kelly.

—

In Princeton, New Jersey, Detective Eugene Farino strode into the lobby of the Westin Hotel located in the Forrestal Village. He asked for Tobias Bradley at the reception desk then after glancing at the clerk's nametag realized he was speaking to him directly.

"Detective Farino," he said. He discreetly and quickly flashed his badge. "Do you have a minute?"

"Yes, sir. Let me get someone to cover for me."

Minutes later, Farino removed an envelope from his inside jacket pocket and started to open it.

"Not in any trouble am I?" Tobias Bradley asked. "All I did was make a phone call for a very large tip. Didn't know it was a big deal. Just called a number. Said a name. Said the number next to the name. Remembered it 'cause it sounded lucky. Played it straight – 1389. It hit a couple days later."

"Relax. Like I told you over the phone, I'm just tying up some loose ends related to an investigation I'm working on. All I need from you is to tell me if this is the person who gave you that very large tip?" He removed a photo of Eric Van Zant from the envelope in his hand and slid it across the top of the table toward Tobias Bradley.

"Yep. That's him. The guy who offed himself in Vegas. Honest, I didn't know those people were jurors. Thought they had something to do with Princeton U. Or maybe they were attending some training gig at one of the big corporate offices. We get a lot of groups like that stayin' here."

"I'm sure you do," Farino said. "Do you remember the name of the person who answered the phone?"

"Ya. Ya. I do. Rhymes with pitcher. Pritcher. Ya, that's it Pritcher."

"Thank you Tobias. That's all I need. Have a good day." Farino stood and turned to go then remembered another question he had. "Did you check with the other clerks about ever seeing a skinny, stringy-haired photographer around?"

"Ya. He was here with another dude. No one liked the looks of him. Big guy with sleeve tats and muscle. Didn't look like someone who'd be flashin' press creds. Both were askin' like, did anyone know if any jurors were stayin' here. Like, did the manager know or the accounting office. Stuff like that."

"Okay then. I'm done. But a word of advice. Be careful of what you say to anyone from now on about those jurors and the phone call you made. Somebody may offer you money. It may seem like easy money. It's not. Dirty money has a way of coming back to bite ya."

Minutes later, out in the parking lot, Farino flipped open his cell and called Judge Howard's office and asked for an appointment. He told the staff member it was an urgent matter regarding Maddox trial jurors. He was gratified that Judge Howard's right-hand assistant had the intelligence to garner the importance and told him to be at the judge's chambers no later than five thirty. Farino started the ignition and drove out of the Westin parking lot onto Route One heading for Trenton. Hate to be in the judge's shoes, he thought. Without a doubt Judge Marvin Howard was going to be appalled by the fact that the person he selected as jury foreperson was the very one who gave Dorsie Renninger's name to the media. He did it right in front of deputies' noses that were charged with keeping a watchful eye on all the jurors. Did it before boarding the bus for Trenton. Did it in the morning of the day the verdict was announced. Yep, he thought, Judge Howard was going' be calling quite a few folks on the carpet.

As he drove towards Trenton and the Capitol Building he thought about Eric Van Zant and how the chemical imbalance going on in his mind had caused him to take his own life. It's everywhere, Farino thought, remembering his days in NYC where the mentally ill and homeless were on every street corner. Everywhere and anywhere well maintained individuals, with the help of legit drugs, were a dime a dozen functioning as waiters, waitresses, stock traders, retail clerks, cab drivers, bus drivers, teachers, priests, actors, symphony caliber musicians. The list was endless and no city or small town had a census devoid of anyone suffering from any form of mental illness. People just didn't talk about it because even now, as much as was known about depression, bi-polar disorder and all those classifications listed in the DSM, there still was a stigma attached to all of them.

Celebrities may have made it seem that some form of emotional disturbance was fashionable. But in everyday life, for everyday people, the stigma was deeply seated. Often it led them to unconsciously shun, ostracize and discriminate. If the question about seeking mental health guidance or treatment was honestly answered with a yes and explanation, another candidate would get the job. Another student would gain admission to the same college. He once heard a well-known psychiatrist on NPR radio flatly advising anyone who ever had therapy or counselling sessions with a mental health care provider to keep it to themselves. He advised never to reveal it on any application or questionnaire. No wonder why individuals lied on applications for jobs, college, insurance, licenses, and jury forms or withheld the true state of their mental status from spouses.

Eric Van Zant had withheld such information from Crystal Yates. Farino doubted very much whether Van Zant would have told her before their never-to-be marriage. She would have found out just as she had – when Van Zant deteriorated. Farino found himself grasping for a reason or answer to why Eric Van Zant had gone off his meds. But he knew the answer. There was no reasonable answer.

Yep, he thought, Judge Marvin Howard would be making many phone calls to other justices seeking guidance and gathering knowledge and wisdom. Law clerks were going to be busy searching for any precedents in case law for any binding ruling governing such a situation. Farino mulled it over in his mind. Most probably none, he speculated, since Van Zant was now deceased and the verdict was not guilty. Now, if the verdict had been guilty, that was another ballgame. Alberto Diaz would waste no time filing appeals. But that wasn't the case. Would the verdict have been different if Van Zant had been functioning as a rational person? How *was* he functioning? Farino made a mental note to talk with Dorsie Renninger. With some luck, he thought, she would be able to offer some insight. He also hoped luck would drop a lead in his lap. Something that would give him a lead to follow to who had trashed *Dorsie's Antiques and Design* or who had sent the identical-to-Jenna's-doll to the Renninger house.

God Bless the woman, he thought with genuine goodwill. Dorsie had a lot on her plate as a result of being a juror. Hopefully soon, she'd be back in Blairstown. He knew of at least three people who were going to welcome Dorsie Renninger back with sincere apologies. He also knew, after talking with Judge Howard, he'd call her and tell her who gave her name to the media. Would this new twist in the Maddox trial cause another media frenzy? He won't be playing the odds on it. Hadn't Eckley told him Pritcher blabbed he knew a lot about Crystal Yates and Van Zant? Said he was going to make more money off of Blairstown? Maybe Pritcher wasn't referring to the Van Zant trust angle. Pritcher knew from the get-go who slipped an envelope to Tobias Bradley with a wad of cash, a note, name, number and instructions. Farino walked down the hallway towards judges' chambers mentally running scenarios in his mind of how Pritcher was connected to Van Zant. He made a mental note to dig deeper into Pritcher.

Minutes later, Detective Farino walked into chambers and shook hands with The Honorable Marvin Howard.

Chapter Twenty-Two

Late December – JFK

Jet Blue Flight 281 from JFK to MCO (Orlando) was showing a three-hour delay on the Flight Departure/Arrival Board. Outside, freezing, pelting rain fell from the Northeast's dull grey skies blanketing roads, bridges and planes with slick ice. At Gate 8 Dorsie sat in a seat directly facing a floor to ceiling window while gazing at the wall of oppressive gray outside. With tremendous effort she tried to shut out all the noise around her. Luckily she'd found two empty end seats and placed her carry-on on the seat next to her giving the impression that it was taken. Gate 8 was full of boys and girls of various ages bubbling over with excitement that could barely be contained because they were on their way to the wondrous realms of Disney World, Universal Studios or Sea World. Now, with the flight delay, parents were having a tough time reigning in their children's pent up energies. High-pitched voices whined for snacks, trips to the rest room, yammering complaints that they were bored and then asking over and over "Can we leave yet?"

"Is this seat taken?"

Dorsie turned. Before her stood a middle-aged man who could have easily been a stand-in for Indiana Jones in any one of the movie's trilogies. He pointed to her carry-on. "Looks like it might be the only seat. That's if it isn't your husband's who's just off to get a coffee."

Dorsie removed her carry-on. "It's empty now," she said. "I just needed a little space. I love children but . . ."

"Know what you mean," he said. He removed his vintage overcoat and beat-up Fedora, draped them over a battered carry-on then sat down. "Bet you're not going to any of the fantasy lands." He gave her a quick once over. "I'd say you're headed home. Probably to The Villages."

A surprised sound escaped from Dorsie's lips followed by a laugh. "I am going to The Villages. You have good people reading-skills."

"I just fly this route a lot. Hate it more than the red-eye to LA. I like kids too but . . ." He reached into his pocket and pulled out a business card and handed it to Dorsie.

"RockMan," she asked with a questioning look. "Is that the name of a band?"

"Naw. So you thought I was an aging rocker? Although I am an artist. Just not the musician kind. I paint all kinds of materials and mediums. Make things look like real rocks."

"Now, this is a first for me," Dorsie said. "In all my years in the renovation and interior design business I've never met anyone who did just rocks. It certainly takes an artist's eye and skill to get the right appearance of texture, shadow, blending of color. Rocks are beautiful things. I've used them in interior design work as accent pieces. Small ones, that is. How'd you ever get interested in rocks?"

"In my early teens I wanted to do comics then my mother and I went to see the Grand Canyon. That did it. I was hooked on rocks. Officially, by geology degree I'm a petrologist. But I'd always had natural abilities in art, so I took some courses then tromped all over the world to look at boulders, cliffs, caves, rock formations by the sea and volcanic rock. Studied how ancients used them. How modern man uses them. Then one day in our old neighborhood down in Philly, I took it upon myself to do a mural on an old warehouse building. Guy from a museum saw it, tracked me down then contracted me to do background for an exhibit. That set the course. Earned me the moniker of RockMan and led to projects with museums, photo shoots, movie sets, ad campaigns. Ever go to Disney or Universal?"

Dorsie shook her head. "Not the parks just to see *Blue Man Group* and *La NouBa*." He bent down, unzipped a compartment of his carry-on then handed a bright card to her. "Lifetime VIP Pass. On me. Perks of being Disney and Universal's RockMan. Go and stand before some of my work. Do the Zen or Tao thing. Contemplate. Get into the moment. One of my rocks just might . . ." He formed quotation marks in the air, chuckled then said, "Speak to you. Sound Department's forte. Not mine. You in First Class?" Dorsie nodded. "Good. No kids kicking at the back of your seat."

He bent down again and removed a Barnes & Noble bag from another compartment in his carry-on. "Bought this for my mother. Has a house in The Villages. Loves it there. Better read it so I can at least follow what the hell she's talking about."

Dorsie glanced over at the book. She stiffened when she saw the book's title – *Broken Trust, Prosecuting Tracy Maddox* by Greg Ashcroft.

"Already on the NY Times Best Seller List. Selling like hotcakes from what I understand," RockMan said. He wiggled the book slightly in the air. "You know anything about the case?"

Dorsie swallowed hard. "A little."

"My mother and a group of her biddies are obsessed with it. Me, I know squat. My mother swears she's passed that juror . . ." He snapped his fingers in the air in a memory recall gesture. "Dorsie Renn . . . something. Remember Dorsie because it's so unusual. Mom swears this Dorsie person is in The Villages. Claims she spotted her walking with the K-9 that was in the picture in the *Enquirer*. By the way, my real name is John Magon. What's yours?"

Dorsie's mind raced frantically. She quickly said the first name that popped into her head. "Rose."

"Well, Rose. Nice to meet you. I've chewed your ear enough," he said. He put on a pair of reading glasses and shifted in his seat to get more comfortable. "Better get started on this." He examined the front and back cover of *Broken Trust*. "Beautiful child," he said quietly. He leaned towards Dorsie and offered her a view of the sweet photo of Jenna Maddox on the back cover.

Dorsie glanced at it then nodded. She let out her breath when Rock-Man opened the book to read the inside cover flap and said nothing further. She turned and stared at the bleak weather outside. Her shoulders gave an involuntary shrug as the harsh chords of Twilight Zone's theme song filled her head. What a freak coincidence, she thought. Her cell phone vibrated in her inside coat pocket. She retrieved it and glanced at the incoming call's ID – Farino.

"Detective Farino," she said while rising from her seat and moving closer to the floor to ceiling window in an effort not to be overheard.

"Dorsie, you have a minute?"

"Actually no," she answered. "I'm at JFK. It's quite noisy here."

"Well, I'll make it quick. I wanted you to know right away in case something hits the media. Wanted you to get it directly from me."

"I'm getting nervous. More bad news?"

"Yes. Brace yourself. Van Zant gave your name to the press. You probably have questions. Call me back when you're in a place where you can talk freely."

Dorsie felt her knees wobble and she went back to her seat. "You've taken my breath away. Do you think there's any chance of . . ." She glanced at RockMan sitting next to her engrossed in his book then asked in a hushed voice, "Chance of it going to media?"

"Don't know. Judge Marvin Howard's office hasn't released any statement. I think they'd like to keep this quiet. Need your opinion. What about Crystal Yates?"

"Oh my," Dorsie quietly exclaimed. Her thoughts raced frantically seeking the right answer "Call Harold. He and Rose are keeping a close eye on Crystal. Right now, he's in a better position to judge her state of mind than I am. I'll call you when I can talk."

"Will do. Have a good flight back to Florida."

Dorsie closed her cell phone and sat facing the oppressive weather on the other side of the window. Inside the airport was quite warm. Even so she felt the weather's cold, damp, grayness seeping into her bones. Her cell phone vibrated in her hand. She glanced at caller ID – Rick HLN. She sighed deeply then let the call go into voicemail. *He's calling to warn me,* she thought. *He never uses his HLN desk phone to call any of us.* She sighed heavily. Right now, and probably forever. She just didn't want to hear anything vaguely connected to Tracy Maddox or Eric Van Zant.

At eight p.m. Dorsie crossed from Concourse B to A at Orlando International. She stopped briefly to view a TV screen with CNN coverage. She gasped. The names Van Zant, Maddox and Renninger were crawling along the red news banner at the lower bottom of the screen. Quickly she turned away not wanting to know what spin, what opinion or what analysis the CNN anchor was going to put on those names. Rapidly she walked towards the escalator leading down to Ground Transportation and The Villages Airport Van's parking slot. When she got there two couples and RockMan were waiting for their bags to be loaded into the van. She quietly gave her name to the driver so he could check it off his passenger manifest.

"Gottcha' right here Dorsie Renninger, Village of Vir . . ."

"Are we waiting for anyone else?" Dorsie said loudly cutting him off. She made a big show of checking her watch in concern over the time.

"No ma'am. You're the last."

RockMan turned to face her and exclaimed, "Renninger! You're not Rose. You're Dorsie. The juror whose name got leaked! Just saw your name running on the CNN news banner. The biddies are . . ."

Dorsie didn't hear the rest because she was acutely aware of the other passengers staring at her with avid curiosity or looking over their shoulders at her at they boarded the van. Dorsie pulled the driver aside, palmed a substantial tip into his hand and asked to be the last person to be dropped off and could he please not say her address out loud.

"Were you really a juror on that awful trial?" someone asked from the front of the van as Dorsie took the only empty seat next to RockMan.

Dorsie scanned her fellow passenger's faces then took a deep breath. "Yes I was. But right now, I'm going to ask for your kindness and understanding. Please don't ask any questions because I won't answer them."

Awkward silence filled the van. It was broken by the driver announcing the first stop he'd make would be the Village of Caroline then the villages of Mallory Hill and Hemingway. He left off the Village of Virginia Trace.

Minutes later, when the van entered the Florida Turnpike using the Sun Pass lane, RockMan quietly but profusely apologized for acting somewhat overzealous when he realized who she was. Long, long minutes into the ride to The Villages, he removed *Broken Trust* from the Barnes & Noble plastic bag and handed it to Dorsie. He reached to the inside pocket of his jacket and withdrew a pen offering it to her. "Page 200. Ashcroft's juror descriptions. Juror Four is on that page. Would you sign it?"

Dorsie gave him a shocked look.

He spread his hands in a pleading apologetic gesture. "Means nothing to me. But my "good son" rating will go off the charts if you do. I swear. She'll never know you're in The Villages. Far as I'm concerned. Saw you at the Barnes & Noble at the airport. Recognized you and asked you to sign."

Dorsie thought for a long moment recalling how freely RockMan had handed over an expensive VIP pass to her, a total stranger. She thought about Brandon and how often she'd told him he was a good son during the last months. She turned to RockMan. "Could you flip your cell open? If you do that I'll have some light to see the page numbers."

He did and she signed.

For the rest of the ride Dorsie sat next to RockMan knowing there was no guarantee that he wouldn't tell his mother the truth. There was no guarantee that the van driver wouldn't casually mention to someone that Dorsie Renninger was in The Villages on Duncan Drive in the Village of Virginia Trace. With painful acceptance she now knew that no matter where she went, while interest remained high in the Tracy Maddox saga, the names Renninger, Van Zant, Diaz, Ashcroft and Judge Marvin Howard, and many others, would be linked to Maddox in one way or another. Their names would become synonymous with Maddox just as Marcia Clark's and Johnnie Cochran's were with O. J. Simpson's or George Parnham's with Andrea Yates. There was no way to predict how or when the flow of the universe would cause a random encounter with a complete stranger who would recognize her or her name. Just like the receptionist at the spa and newsstand cashier in Tribeca and RockMan, someone who just happened to sit next to her in a major, crowded airport. Would she come face-to-face with RockMan's mother somewhere in The Villages? She didn't know. What she did know was that she had to face down the fear of being recognized and learn to temper her emotional reactions when it did occur.

She sighed deeply, contemplating all the hidden metaphysical meanings behind thought provoking phrase – *Nothing is by Chance.* Meaning that in all the random flux in the Universe, certain events are meant to occur. When the van turned off of Canal Street onto Kline then turned again on to Duncan, she made a decision. She would take Judge up on his offer to listen. She would tell him everything, hold back nothing. In the telling, coupled with his insights and wisdom, maybe she would be able to understand and accept her actions as a juror. Maybe then she could take the first steps towards making peace with herself.

Chapter Twenty-Three

Back In The Villages

The van came to a stop in front of Vince Di Paolo's house on Duncan Drive. The Judge's van was parked in the driveway and lights were on in the house. Before the van driver could unload Dorsie's carry-on from the back, Judge was at her side. He tipped the driver, grabbed the handle of the bag and took Dorsie by the arm. "Harold called me. Then I called JB. Between the three of us, we figured you wouldn't mind if JB unlocked the house for me. Let's get you inside. You look exhausted."

"I am. The flight delay turned a simple trip into a very long, long day."

Dorsie stepped into the foyer of the house. Thor came running, sat down, whined excitedly while wagging his tail as if it were a metronome set to keep a fast beat. "Thor. Come," Dorsie said. In excitement Thor stood on his hind legs and over zealously placed his paws on Dorsie's shoulders causing her to stumble backwards from the force of his weight. "Thor. Down. Have you forgotten your manners?" Thor whined. She sat down on the foyer floor. He nuzzled her neck and gave her wet, sloppy licks all over her face. "You didn't give Judge any problems, did you?"

"Not a one," Judge answered. "Thor and Gabby were a sight to see when I walked them. Looked like a drill team in perfect step with each other. Followed every command given to them almost in unison. I left Gabby home. Figured the excitement of one dog was enough for you to handle right now," he said. He while extended his hand to help her up from the floor.

"Thank you for being here. Have you seen any of the news?"

"Yes. Come on. Let's have a drink first before I make any comment." He took Dorsie by the arm again and led her into the large center room.

185

Thor followed alongside Dorsie with his muscular body pressed tight against her leg. She sank into a deep, comfortable chair and removed her shoes.

The Judge handed Dorsie her drink. "I would say Judge Marvin Howard is extremely upset right now. Bizarre twist. That's how the media's playing it. Another Bizarre Twist in the Maddox Trial.' Photos of Van Zant are being shown again. Of course Tracy Maddox's too. And Jenna's. There have been some shots of *Dorsie's Antiques and Design* as well. Your photo from the Habitat brochure aired on some of the less responsible networks. JB went and got the *Enquirer*. Nothing there yet. We also pulled up the *TMZ* website and they're all over it."

Dorsie raised her glass in the gesture of a toast. "Here's to the Word-of-the-Day, Bizarre," she said. "In keeping with the word, let me tell you what happened at the airport. A perfect stranger . . ." For the next several minutes she described her encounter with RockMan. "In the van he asked me to sign the page where Greg Ashcroft gave his impressions of the jurors. In all of this craziness someone wanted my autograph," she said laughing. The sarcastic laughter turned into tears. She set down her drink and buried her face in her hands. "How bizarre is that?" she asked through quiet muffled sobs. "I'm sorry. Don't mean to be such a crybaby. It's just that . . ."

Judge rose from his seat then knelt before her taking her tear-stained hands in his. "You're exhausted," he said. "Probably feeling pretty rumpled. Probably hungry. JB went down to Bob Evans and got a quart of that chicken noodle soup you rave about. I'll heat it. Maybe take a shower first?" he asked raising his eyebrows in question. "Once you're refreshed and fortified by some food you'll feel better. Now, go on. Trust me. That's what you need right now."

Thirty-five minutes later Dorsie sat at the small breakfast table wrapped in the fluffy spa robe she'd taken to wearing for comfort. Her hair was down, only given a quick blow dry and her face was scrubbed clean of make-up. The Judge place a bowl of soup, salad and bread sticks before her along with a tall, tall glass of water with lemon slices in it. "Now eat. I'm taking Thor out for a quick walk. All that better be gone when we get back."

Dorsie was in the large center room, back in the comfortable chair with her legs drawn beneath her when Judge and Thor came in from outside. Thor made a beeline for her and placed his head in her lap. She ruffled him between the ears. "Good boy. Thor. I missed you too."

Judge poured himself another scotch and sat in the chair directly across from her. He made note that the TV was off. "Good. I'm glad you're foregoing the rerun of Anderson Cooper's show earlier and any other of the talking heads."

"In what you've heard, was there any mention of Crystal Yates?" Judge shook his head. "Well, that's a relief. Did Harold tell you some photographer was sort of stalking her around Blairstown?" The judge shook his head again. "Apparently took some photos of her. We're holding our breath that they don't turn up in one of those rags with some sensationalizing headline." She paused then gazed over at the Judge. "Oh, I'm sorry. You don't know the whole story of Crystal Yates. Crystal and Van Zant were living together before the trial started. Then . . . his . . ." She paused unable to say the word suicide. "Such an awful thing added to the fact Eric was going to ask Crystal to marry him. That juror, Krieger, she was way, way wrong about what she thought her relationship was with Van Zant." Dorsie sighed deeply. "We have no doubts about it because weeks before being selected as a juror he, Eric made a new will putting Crystal's name on everything and anything to do with the Van Zant family trusts." Dorsie took a long swallow from the glass of water. "That's what we thought this photo guy was on to." Dorsie looked off into space for long seconds then sighed deeply again. "So sad. So tragic. Crystal's pregnant. Eric never knew he was about to become a father. Crystal was about to tell him but she said he was under such stress when he came back from being sequestered, she decided to wait a week or two." Dorsie brushed her hand across her forehead. "Oh, this is just so complicated. All these twists and turns. Sounds like a daytime soap opera. Only it's real."

"I'm hoping someone's advised Crystal to get a good attorney to scrutinize the will and all the details related to the trusts," Judge commented.

"It's being taken care of. She has a top of the line attorney so I believe she's in good hands. On the night she found out about Eric, she wanted to talk with me. What could I say? No? She'd just suffered a terrible blow. Did I tell you I've worked with Crystal at the Habitat? That she was a regular visitor to Harold's shop. Harold was teaching her how to recognize quality antiques."

Judge shook his head and sat quietly hoping Dorsie would continue to talk freely not as if she were censoring her thoughts before she spoke.

"I have a confession to make. Please don't think ill of me but I had to know. I had suspicions."

"I'm here to listen, Dorsie. That's what I promised to do. So go on."

"After Van Zant's suicide I asked Vince Di Paolo, who's related to the Carapelli's, to do some checking on Eric. I have a substantial private investigator's report. Some of what's in it may cross patient privacy rights."

"JB told me just a little about Gino Carapelli after you left for New York," said Judge. "In fact, he raised quite a few toasts to Carapelli then reminisced about the good old days in spite of the fact that he knew I was a man of law. He told me the Raines and Renningers were considered family. That he'd had . . . I'm not going to say orders." He spread his hands in a helpless gesture. "He was told to keep a close eye on you. To make sure you were comfortable and not being bothered by anyone."

Dorsie nodded. "I know. I figured out as much when JB told me he and Gino went way back. If JB told you enough, then you probably already know just how thorough Carapelli's people can be."

Judge nodded but remained silent letting the silence force Dorsie to fill it with additional information.

"Eric Van Zant was bi-polar on a strict regimen of drug therapy. Hospitalized twice. He lied on the jury questionnaire."

"Many people do, Dorsie. The only ones who are forthcoming about any type of mental illness are the ones who want to get out of jury duty. Many lie about that too, and then pay off some health care professional to give them a note to send to the court." He gave a small smile at her shocked expression. "Not everyone takes civic duty as seriously as you did. People are excused from jury duty for all sorts of minor inconveniences. Any time I hear of some corporate executive pulling the job excuse it burns me up. If they can be out on the golf course or whatever else they do for entertainment, they sure and the heck can take the time to do their civic duty." He stopped talking suddenly after seeing Dorsie smother a yawn. Judge then realized he was about to launch into an elaborate analysis of one of his pet peeves. "Sorry. It's something that just sticks in my craw." He glanced at his watch. "You're tired. I'll take Thor out for one last duty call. Then you'll both be settled in for the night."

"Sorry about the yawn. You weren't being boring. These last couple of days have been draining."

Judge rose from his chair and motioned for Thor to come. Thor looked at Judge then at Dorsie. "Thor. Go." Dorsie said while getting up out of her chair. Thor got up from his lay-down position and walked over to Judge. He sat down in front of him then looked over his shoulder at Dorsie.

"Thor. I'm not going anywhere. Go do duty. I'll be here when you come in."

"Come. Thor," Judge said then headed for the door with Thor following behind.

Dorsie followed the Judge's retreating back feeling more convinced than ever that her decision to talk with him was the right one. If I have to be judged, she told herself silently, then let it be by someone who has a full understanding of the law. Let it be by someone who still has the ability to have empathy for the whys of people's behaviors. Deidra Fallon was an undeniable professional, she thought. A now familiar feeling fluttered in her stomach. Guilt now corroded her decision to terminate her sessions with Deidra. But Deidra was young, lacking in the wisdom and experience the Judge had by virtue of age and years on the bench. Yes, she thought, reassuring herself, she had made the right decision.

Judge and Thor returned. "He's all set. I'll be going now. I'll call you in the morning."

Dorsie rose and walked with him to the door. She linked her arm though his. "Thank you for everything. For being here."

Judge turned to say goodnight and Dorsie took his hands in hers. "I'm going to take a leap of faith. If your offer still stands to listen then I'm ready to honestly and openly talk about this whole Maddox mess."

"We'll take it slow. It doesn't have to be a marathon. Now go. Sleep like a log. Call me when you're up and about."

Dorsie watched Judge's van pull out of the driveway, closed and locked the door then went to bed.

At five a.m. Dorsie cycled into her last period of REM sleep as her brain's cortex tried to interpret random signals coming from fragmented brain activity. Strong, vivid images leaped into view. In REM sleep, Dorsie sighed deeply and smiled at Jenna dressed in her soft luminescent pink tutu. She followed Jenna's every step as she did her circle dance moving closer and closer to the magnificent dog sitting patiently inside an imaginary circle. Step. Twirl. Step. Step. Twirl. Step. Fast-fast twirl. Jenna threw out her hand as she stumbled, losing balance. From outside the perimeter of Jenna's imaginary circle a man's hand reached in and grasped hers. She pulled the man beside her and smiled up at him then continued to hold his hand while she skipped along her circular path until it tightened and ended at the magnificent German Shepherd. In unison Jenna and the man knelt. Jenna put her arm around the dog. The man put his arm around Jenna then leaned inward to whisper in her ear. Dorsie cried out, "Jenna . . . Jenna. What's he saying?" All three. The dog. Jenna Maddox. And Eric Van Zant looked up as if they'd heard a sound off in the distance. All three continued to peer outward to somewhere beyond where Dorsie's dreamland couldn't take her.

Dorsie came awake abruptly while the images in her dream remained fixed for long seconds embedding themselves into her now awake consciousness. She laid staring at the barely visible overhead ceiling fan's rotations as her thought jumped from one thing to another in a desperate attempt to understand the new element in her recurring dream of Jenna Maddox. What did Eric Van Zant's appearance mean?

Minutes later, she gave up trying to assign a plausible explanation for his appearance then threw back the covers and got out of bed. She felt sluggish, as if she'd flown from one time zone to another and was filled with a deep, deep weariness. For the rest of the early morning hours she slowly went about making coffee. She let Thor off leash and unattended while he did his duty call but stood at the lanai door to make sure he didn't have a streak of wild energy and decide to take a thunderbolt run. "Thor. Come," she called after what seemed like enough time for him to finish his duty and have a sniff, sniff at the bushes. He dutifully came back inside the lanai. Beyond, the sky was growing lighter, turning into various shades of grey blue and orange pink as dawn came into full bloom. A mockingbird settled on the low fence as Dorsie settled into a chair and set her mug of coffee on the side table. She waited for the mockingbird to begin the performance he gave for her every morning. She only half-listened. The mockingbird's notes soared then trilled as Dorsie's mind churned and churned trying to fit together the fragmented pieces of her dream, the ones that lingered, refusing to fade away so they could be forgotten.

Later, between nine-thirty and ten-thirty, a flurry of phones calls were answered and placed. Satisfied she'd assured Harold, Brandon, Megs and Rick that she was fine and that she hadn't watched any news she returned Detective Farino's call. He detailed how he discovered Van Zant was the one, who through a third party, gave her name to the press. Afterwards, she placed a call to Crystal. For a long thirty minutes, they openly talked about Eric Van Zant. Next, she called Judge.

"I'm up and about," she said when he answered. "Again thank you for being here last night."

"No thank yous are necessary, Dorsie. Glad to do it."

Immediately Dorsie felt something was wrong. The Judge's voice sounded extremely tired. His Darth Vader voice was a little deeper and seemed to hold in it held back resignation. "Are you alright? You just don't sound like yourself." She heard his long, long sigh over the line. "What is it? Anything I can help with?"

On the other end of the line Judge sighed deeply. "Nooo," he said. "The dreaded call came this morning. They're recalling Gabby. I've known it could come any day now. I've got to take him down to Guide Dog Campus in Palmetto on the day after Christmas."

"Oh, Judge I'm soo sorry. You must be feeling terrible. Like you're best friend has been ordered to deploy."

"That's a good way of putting it, Dorsie. Yes. Deploy." He paused to clear his throat. "Would you be interested in coming with me? I already cleared it with the coordinator in the off chance that you would. Thor will be welcomed. As they say, the more the merrier, and the more exposure the better the dog."

"Of course I'll come. Thor will be on his best behavior."

"How do you think he is with puppies? There's an upside to leaving Gabby so he can go into intense training. I'm getting another puppy to raise. Rudy. He's only six weeks."

"How wonderful! A day-late Christmas present. A bundle of puppy smells, wiggles and licks. I know you're never going to forget Gabby, but my, a puppy. That's like having a baby in the house."

Judge laughed. "Yes it is. I'm in for some nights of interrupted sleep. That's until he's over missing his mother. So you'll go. Thank you. I don't like making this last trip alone. Took JB with me last time.

He cried more than I did. Suppose this time he'll shed a couple of tears too when he gives Gabby a last pat."

"I'm going to call Dave afterwards and tell him where Thor's going to go. Like you, anything unusual one of his dogs does, he puffs out his chest like a proud papa."

"Dorsie, it's about a two hour drive, so we'll have time to talk. It'll keep my mind occupied with something other than the heavy separation thoughts I get when I drop off one of my charges. You'll be doing me a favor." He paused. "I hate to ask this. But have you watched any news?"

"No and I'm not going to. All those talking heads will put their own spin on it all. Don't need to hear it. I've lived it. Am living with the after-shocks. So no, I'm not watching any of it."

"Good attitude, Ole Gal," he said. "You don't mind my calling you that, do you?"

"Not at all. I am an ole gal. Now, this evening why don't you bring Gabby's "Puppy to Now" album over and show and tell me where every picture was taken and what the two of you were doing. I'd enjoy that."

"Gabby and I will be knocking on your door at seven with pizza in hand."

Dorsie sat for long minutes after ending her call with Judge feeling satisfied she was able to do something for him in return for all he'd done for her. She glanced down and realized she was still in the fluffy spa bathrobe and rose to go and shower. The doorbell chimed. Thor rushed to the door letting loose his fearsome bark. "Thor. Stop," Dorsie said, "That's probably JB." She opened the door. "Dorsie Renninger?" asked a dark haired woman with a mike in her hand. "Orlando, WESH 2 News. We'd like your comments on the recent . . ."

"I have no comment," Dorsie said coolly. "Now, if you'll please leave."

The cameraman behind the woman stepped around her to get closer to the door. Thor gave a low, guttural threatening growl. The reporter thrust the mike closer. Again, Thor gave a threatening growl. "How has your life changed since . . ." the reporter said trying another tack edging even closer until the mike was touching the screen door.

"Thor. Bark," Dorsie whispered. Thor responded as trained. Over his loud scare-the-hell-out-of-you barks, Dorsie said, "You're invading my privacy. I don't think you want to mess with him. Now please leave." She closed the door and didn't give Thor his cease command until she saw the WESH 2 News van drive away. Vince Di Paolo's house phone rang. Its Screen Calls Function was set to On and Dorsie listened. "This is Susan Paige from The Villages Daily Sun. I'm trying to reach Dorsie Renninger. I understand she's staying at this address. Please have her call me at . . ." Dorsie ignored the rest, leaving the voice talking to empty air. Minutes later she was in the shower, letting the RockMan encounter, WESH 2 News and Daily Sun reporter roll off her like the droplets of water hitting her body from the showerhead above. For a few seconds she looked down at the shower's tile floor and the water flowing over it then closed her eyes. She imaged the previous day's events and WESH 2 News flowing straight into the drain. *How's that for a creative visualization and a way to dispose of negative stuff. Down the drain it goes!* She gave a small smile. If Deidra Fallon knew how she was handling these incidents, Deidra would applaud her.

Chapter Twenty-Four

The Talk Begins

For Dorsie, Christmas Day was very different from how she celebrated the holiday in a northern climate. Skeeter Brooks and his sister hosted a Pedro Ho-Ho-Ho Social for K-9 handlers, and puppy raisers. Anyone, friends and friends of friends, who didn't have other holiday plans, were welcomed with shouts of "Merry Christmas!" In all, thirty people sat at makeshift plywood tables covered in red checkerboard cloths. Plates of turkey, smoked ham, pork barbeque, down-home Southern Boil of shrimp, sausage, corn, potatoes, were handed from one smiling person to another. Side dishes of candied sweet potatoes, stuffing, gravy, creamy mashed potatoes roasted corn, collard greens, tangy coleslaw followed. Holiday cookies of every variety could be had. Pumpkin, apple and sweet potato pies sat on another table. A sign – Made from Blue Ribbon Recipes – promised mouth-watering dessert. An old barn door served as a bar. Ice-filled tubs kept beer, soda and mason jars filled with lemonade and Southern Sweet cool. A sunny blue sky with puffy white clouds and a seventy-degree temperature made for a stellar day. Labs, German Shepherds, Bloodhounds and Golden Retrievers tolerated Santa hats and fake reindeer antlers on their heads while they posed with their handlers for photos. No one went home hungry or feeling as if they hadn't celebrated Christmas Day in the most wonderful way.

The next morning, Judge and Gabby arrived at Dorsie's promptly at eight a.m. For thirty minutes Dorsie and Judge sat over coffee reviewing the events of Christmas Day marveling at Skeeter and his sister's resourcefulness and ability to organize and manage so many people and dogs without it turning into a fiasco.

"It's a community at work," said Judge. "Everyone there shares in a special interest beyond just being an animal lover. All of us raisers, handlers and dogs belong to a special breed. We believe in community service and giving back." He glanced at his watch. "We'd better get going."

Twenty minutes later, after last duty calls for the dogs and bathroom visits for people, they were off heading for the Guide Dog Campus in Palmetto. Once on I-75 S towards Tampa, Judge said, "I'm sorry my daughter-in-law, Melanie, can't be part of this. It's a rare, rare opportunity to be able to pick a juror's brain on what happened in such a high profile case." He glanced over at Dorsie. "That's what I'm going to do. Pick your brain. In spite of all the jury consultants out there and all the research done on group dynamics, picking a jury is still a crapshoot. Anyone who claims they can predict an outcome is an idiot. That's in my humble judgeship opinion. There are also specific areas in this trial I'd like to gain an inside view. Specifically on how the jury perceived and reacted to some key forensic evidence."

Dorsie took a deep breath, "I don't know where to start. I'm liable to ramble all over the place. Sort of spitting it out as it comes into my mind."

"No problem. I'm very accustomed to putting pieces together. Even the smallest details about the people on a jury give insight. Why don't you just start with telling me how you answered the voir dire questions?"

Dorsie focused her thoughts and told him what she was able to recall.

"I can see why the defense and prosecution would want you," Judge said. "Your statement on design theory being fluid not fixed told both sides you most likely would not to be judgmental but mostly likely more willing to consider all sides of an issue. Also, based on your reading habits, specifically *National Geographic* and *Discovery,* indicated to them you were not in the last century of what's happening in the sciences. How did you find Judge Howard?"

"I liked him very much. He had a sense of humor and tired very hard to make things as comfortable as they could be for us." Dorsie paused for a moment. "Some of the other jurors had issues with him in spite of that. They thought Gregg Ashcroft and Judge Howard were ganging up on Alberto Diaz. Every time we had to leave the courtroom one or another juror would make a comment to the effect of 'what's Judge Howard calling Diaz on the carpet for now?' It wasn't hard to surmise that some of those breaks had to do with something Diaz did or hadn't done. As the days wore on, I suspect they viewed Diaz as an underdog in comparison to the prosecution attorney's courtroom experience and professionalism. In the end, I think they were unconsciously rooting for Diaz because they saw him as the underdog. They wanted him to do good. At least by some of what they said when we were finally able to talk to each other. They complained about Judge Howard constantly telling him to rephrase the question. I think someone was keeping count because I heard the guys laughing after one of them said, 'Ashcroft 27. Diaz 201.'"

"Interesting. Someone keeping score as if it were a sporting event," Judge mused. "Tell me about the other jurors. You have excellent people skills so tell me your impressions."

"We were strangers. We knew nothing about each other, what sort of lives we were living. In the beginning it was uncomfortable. Well, I'm not so sure about my people skills after spending time with them," Dorsie said. "I started feeling inept. Finding common ground was difficult. In the initial getting-to-know-each other period, everyone related what they did, married, unmarried, children, grandchildren, etc. Right off the bat I got labeled. Sara, retired, long-time smoker voice, now working part-time as hair salon receptionist, actually said to me 'So you're one of those hoity-toity people who are in and out of the city all the time.'" Dorsie paused and shook her head. "I sort of got the cold shoulder from her after that. She was the juror during the short deliberation time that went on and on about Nick Maddox having an affair.' How you couldn't trust anything a man like that said under oath?' she kept repeating it over and over." Dorsie paused again for long moments collecting her thoughts. "If I had to sum it up, I'd say we were a group of strangers who were forced to step outside of the normal scope of our daily lives. It was difficult."

"There were a total of five women, including you. What about them?"

"Oh, Millie was a nice grandma type about to go on a 50th anniversary cruise. All the scientific evidence was beyond her. She readily admitted that. Her religious beliefs came into play. She said God told her Tracy Maddox did not kill her child. Lisa, a young woman in emotional years, had one school age child. The boy was having the time of his life at Grandma's and Pop Pop's house with sleepovers at Aunt Suzie's with all his cousins. Lisa had a habit of asking the most naive questions, the kind that come from someone who's had very limited exposure beyond family and a circle of friends who lived in the same town for generations. Her life centered on her child and her husband who was her high school sweetheart. But Eric Van Zant talked with her a lot. Her boy, who was going into 1st grade, was giving her some trouble. Fighting with his cousins and play buddies. Talking back. That sort of thing. Eric gave her some pointers and explained why little boys act the way they do."

Dorsie paused to take a breath.

"Take your time," Judge said. "I'm following it all. If I need further explanation I'll stop you and ask for it."

"Okay," Dorsie said. She took another deep breath. "Kate Krieger doted on Millie, treating her like the grandma she was. Kate had what I'd call an attitude. Let it clearly show toward Sara, the hair salon receptionist. Gave me the impression she thought anyone over fifty didn't have abilities to be in what she called "the real world". I found it interesting that although Tony was in her age bracket, she seemed to treat him as if he were beneath her. Since she'd just graduated from nursing school, I thought maybe she felt she'd moved up in the world. Blue-collar to professional. From day one, it seemed she subtly pursued Eric Van Zant. Sometimes I felt she didn't grasp the seriousness of our responsibility or just didn't care. Kate and Eric sat together in the vans. They also sat next to each other at lunch and dinner."

Dorsie reached over for her water bottle and took a long sip then glanced at Judge. "You said you had a high interest in certain parts of the trial. Care to share?"

"If I get long winded, stop me," he said. "This was a circumstantial case in spite of solid forensics, a well-executed investigation and a defendant who demonstrated she was incapable of telling the truth. Because there was no definitive cause of death, the case demanded, required, a seated jury that was willing and motivated to work hard. To work at piecing together facts into a cohesive whole and applying common sense in evaluating how normal people behave under a specific set of circumstances. We commend people for stepping up to do their civic duty but it doesn't guarantee they'll be individuals who are capable or willing to exert intricate mental thought processes. That's what this case required." He paused then continued, "Having said that, for any jury, maternal filicide is the most difficult crime of all. Just too horrible to comprehend that a mother would kill her own child in the absence of not being mentally ill. Did any of the jurors ever mention Jenna Maddox by actual name?"

"To my recollection, Jenna Maddox's name was never mentioned by anyone but me. I remember pounding my fist on the table, probably shouting, 'Jenna Maddox is dead. Jenna was an innocent child. She is dead!' All I got in return was Diaz's explanation – she drowned in the swimming pool. It was an accident. Nick Maddox covered it up. End of story. We want out of here."

The Judge simply nodded. "I was also interested in the scientific portions. Specifically the odor mortis. Smell of death. The 30 molecules the forensic anthropologist from Tennessee has isolated. I agreed with Judge Howard's ruling that the new science had a firm foundation in established science." The Judge paused and glanced over at Dorsie. "I'm going to give you an interesting little sidebar irrelevant to the case or trial. You may be interested or not, but this will help you to understand why there was so much emphasis put on the scientific part of the smell of death."

"So the label of junk science is inappropriate?"

Judge nodded. "The average person wouldn't know or even have an interest in knowing that Ashcroft was among the first prosecutors to successfully introduce DNA evidence in the courtroom. In 1987, in the Tommy Lee Andrews trial." Judge reined himself in stopping himself from going into a full, detailed explanation of how Ashcroft went about introducing DNA evidence. "What's interesting to me is that here he was again bringing cutting edge science into the courtroom. Ashcroft's challenge was to present it in a way the jury would actually understand it.

Dorsie gave a small huff of disgust. "Well my fellow jurors wanted no part of it. Some admitted they didn't understand it. Didn't even *want* to try to understand it. I had a tough go of it at times but got the final outcome of it all. You *can* analyze the smell of death by chemical composition with that machine that nobody could pronounce. I could once, but don't ask me now."

"GC-MS Gas chromatography–mass spectrometer," rolled effortlessly off Judge's lips in his deep Darth Vader voice.

Dorsie laughed. "Say it again. Real fast."

Judge repeated it with perfect diction.

"Well, for me that machine, the doctor from the Oak Ridge National Laboratory and the cadaver dog's nose convinced me a decomposing body was in the trunk of Tracy Maddox's car. There was never ANY. And I mean *ANY* discussion at all other than the 'I didn't-understand-it, so it means nothing' attitude of the others. They bought Diaz's junk science label." Dorsie thought for a moment then added, "Rodney, the Gulf War veteran.

Very quiet man. Unmarried, but did have nieces and nephews. Took the older nephews camping. Was teaching them how to survive in the woods. I do recall him saying 'Once you smell it. You never forget the smell.' But he said it so quietly I doubt the others paid attention. At first I thought I had an ally in him believing the cadaver dog's nose." Dorsie thought for another long minute. "Eric Van Zant talked with Rodney a lot too. Eric was a hiker. So, I guess woods, camping, and hiking. That stuff gave them common ground. Rodney and I had common ground in the fact he found all things in nature beautiful. I think he had a very artistic eye. When we talked, his descriptions of Persian Gulf, desert and desert sky, were given with sophisticated knowledge of the color spectrum."

Dorsie continued on in a matter-of-fact manner outlining her impression of the remaining male jurors. Only one of them was currently married and had children and worked with his brother and father running a small, yet elite family bakery. They'd had many conversations on the ups and downs of being business owners, specifically family business owners. Two others were retired-early-had-enough-years-in from government service jobs. One took applications for WIC programs. The other retired from issuing drivers' licenses. They too seemed to be avid sports fans but between them had a good time reviewing their likes and dislikes of many science fiction action movies. Sometimes, Tony, thirty-four, unmarried, a Verizon lineman, out on disability because of hand injury, joined them and added his take on certain movies as did Eric Van Zant. Tony had a live-in girlfriend, wasn't keen on getting married just yet and couldn't wait to get back to work. Tony had two Bengal cats and he and Dorsie were able to develop a rapport over being owners of such an energetic and beautiful breed of cat. He'd shown her picture after picture on his cell of the intricate catwalks he'd built to keep his cats from getting bored. Tony offered to build some for Dorsie if she wanted.

"That leaves one more male juror," Judged commented.

"Burton. Poor Burton. He was suffering from very bad sciatic nerve pain caused by all the sitting we were doing. He had a passion for model trains and through the years visited many train museums. But now, with his mother having a stroke, he said his get-up-and-just-go jaunts were limited. He too admitted the science stuff baffled him, but did give weight to the cadaver dog's nose. But it wasn't enough for him. Wasn't going to send a pretty, young woman to prison for life based on a dog's nose. He actually said, 'Prison is no place for a pretty young thing like her.'"

Dorsie shook her head and said quietly, "After the trial ended, I felt as if Jenna Maddox's death was just an aside to her mother's behavior. Jenna didn't seem important. What seemed more important was for us to understand her mother's deep, dark shadow. If we understood that, then whatever Tracy Maddox lied about was supposed to be viewed as okay. To be excused and not viewed as lying to cover up."

"How many of the juror's smoked?" asked Judge. "Surprising question, I know. But smokers band together while taking their breaks. Sometimes even the deputies assigned to monitor get lax while their having their own nicotine fix."

"Ummm, I really need to think about this. I didn't pay much attention to who left with the deputy." They drove along for a few minutes. "I'm drawing a blank."

"Who had the smell of smoke on their cloths? Think about who you sat next to in the van, at dinner or near when you were in the jury room waiting for the sidebars to conclude," Judge prompted.

"I remember now. Rodney, the two government service retirees, the baker, cigarette voice Sara and Eric Van Zant. Burton usually went with them for the smoking breaks. Not to smoke but just to be able to move and walk around. Oh, something else I forgot to tell you. Burton's back problem. Eric had Burton doing stretching exercises. Asked the deputy to get some tennis balls for Burton. When he got them, he showed Burton how to do pressure point releases. Convinced Burton not to ask Judge Howard to release him as a juror because of medical reasons. Burton saw it through to the end but you could see the stress of pain on his face."

The Judge went on to ask more questions. Who were the most dominant males? The most dominant women? Did Dorsie think the others might have stayed in touch, excluding Van Zant and Krieger? Who actually convinced the others to eat dinner at a particular restaurant they wanted to go to when Judge Howard's staff presented them with their options? Was anyone reading a book? Have a Kindle? How much time was spent in trying to dissuade initial guilty votes? Who did most of the talking during deliberations? By the time Dorsie answered them all to the best of her ability, they arrived at the Guide Dog Campus.

From then on it was a flurry of activity. The Judge went on to take care of all the necessary details required for the return of Gabby and those needed for him to take possession of the new puppy. Dorsie, with Thor at her side, was given a more in-depth and behind-the-scenes tour of the facility and grounds. She marveled at how the campus included rail crossings, bus stops, and sidewalks of varying textures, construction areas, and curbs of various heights, a playground, and an old school bus. She watched as dogs boarded then exited the bus with their trainers. They passed a mini petting zoo full of animals. As they toured the grounds, several certified guide dog trainers asked her to demonstrate her command over Thor. All asked her to give Thor his bark command. When the fearsome barks filled the air, the trainers took the opportunity to work with their Labs or Golden Retrievers to refine their dogs' skills on how to attend to the danger while in working mode with a blind individual. From those responsible for the breeding program she learned German Shepherds are not ideal candidates for guide dogs. German Shepherds had the trait of being extremely loyal to their owner. The instinct to protect was highly developed. As a result, this strong protective instinct caused aggression. One trainer gave the example of how, if a stranger reached out and grabbed a blind person by the arm to stop him from doing something unsafe, a German Shepherd's protective instinct might cause him to attack. Labs and Golden Retrievers were just as loyal to their owners but had the trait of being friendly even to strangers.

At two in the afternoon, Judge found Dorsie and Thor in the kennel. Dorsie was sitting on the floor surrounded by energetic puppies. He paused in the doorway, pleased to see she was smiling and talking baby talk to all the puppies that were scampering around, crawling in her lap and giving little yips of come-play-with-me. He doubted she noticed the puppy cam or realized the pupply activity was streaming live on the Southeastern Guide Dog website. He walked through the door slowly making allowances for Rudy, his new puppy. Rudy was trying to play with the leash while walking. Judge tapped Dorsie on the shoulder lightly to let her know he was there. "You look like you need to be rescued."

"Heavens no! Oh, they're all sooo adorable."

"Dorsie, meet Rudy," Judge said. He bent down and scooped Rudy into his arms. Rudy immediately started giving him puppy licks on the chin. Judge handed Rudy to Dorsie. Rudy immediately dispensed more puppy licks.

Dorsie set Rudy in front of Thor. "Rudy, meet Thor. You're going to be buddies."

The foursome left the kennels and made their way to the park area and stood near an oversized picnic table. Minutes later a delivery boy appeared on the walkway. The Judge waved his hand. "Over here."

They sat at the picnic table eating, saying little, comfortable with each other's silence. Thor patiently stayed in his lay-down position even though Rudy was making a pest of himself, climbing over his back, licking his snout and tugging on his ears.

Fifteen minutes later, Dorsie said, "Would you look at that, Rudy finally wore himself out." She pointed to Thor. Rudy was curled up against Thor's side, snuggled against him taking a puppy snooze. Suddenly, Thor perked up his ears in attention. He gave a small whine. His tail swished back and forth vigorously against the grass.

Judge turned and looked in the direction of Thor's alert gaze. Gabby and his new trainer were coming down the walkway headed towards them. "Ah, Gabby's intense training begins. Watch this."

Judge stood and walked over to meet the trainer. He glanced down at Gabby for a second then returned his attention to the man's face. Gabby remained close in to his new trainer's side. He did not exhibit any excited behavior at seeing the Judge or move in any way to approach the Judge. Only his tail signaled his acknowledgement of the Judge. It was wagging back and forth, back and forth rapidly as he sat still with his gaze turned upward towards the Judge. Next, the Judge shook hands with the trainer then carried on a two-minute conversation. Gabby sat obediently at the new trainer's side. When the Judge reached down to pat Gabby, Gabby remained calm and steady exhibiting no overly excited behaviors. The new trainer gave a tug on Gabby's leash and they walked off.

Dorsie and Judge watched them go. "Ahhh," they both said in unison when Gabby looked back over his shoulder for a quick second. He gave a small bark then resumed his working dog pace with his body pressed tight against his new trainer's calf.

"All that in just two hours with the certified trainer," Judge said. "Gabby did me proud. Yes, he did me proud. He's going to make it all the way through." He put his arm around Dorsie and pulled her close to his side. "The next thing you know, you'll be back down here for his turnover ceremony to his forever person."

Chapter Twenty-Five

The Talk – More Revelations

Thirty-five minutes later, they were on I-75 N heading towards Tampa. In the back of the van, Thor made playful dog sounds at Rudy who was climbing all over him, licking his ears then giving little puppy yelps. Dorsie glanced over her shoulder to make sure everything was alright. "Oh you're in for it, Judge. He looks like a feisty one," she said.

For over twenty minutes both Dorsie and Judge were lost in their own thoughts until Dorsie broke the silence. "There's something bothering me about your question on who smoked. About Eric Van Zant smoking. It's there in my brain but I just can't get a grasp on it."

Judge glanced over at her. "You up to talking about Eric Van Zant? From all you've told me so far, it seems as if he was quite affable. At ease with mixing with the others."

"He was," Dorsie said. "Before I forget this. I don't think he smoked in those early weeks. At least I don't recall smelling cigarette breath or smoke on his clothes when I first met him. We did the general chitchat when we discovered we both were from Blairstown. Blair Academy is a prestigious prep school so I'd have to say I was impressed that he was on the faculty there. He never mentioned Crystal Yates and neither did I. Although in general conversations with others I might have told any one of the other jurors I volunteered at Habitat for Humanity. He may not have heard that. Also for family visits, there were two rooms. He was always in the other. I don't recall seeing Crystal. If I had, I would have mentioned it."

"Can you pinpoint when Van Zant's behavior started to change?"

Dorsie felt herself getting anxious. "Talking about Eric is hard. Bear with me."

"Dorsie, I'm quite comfortable with how it's going. Quit worrying about it. Just continue on," Judge said.

"I can't say when his behavior started to change. As the days went on, I was mentally and emotionally exhausted at the end of each day. I think we all were, so someone eating dinner in their room wasn't something out of the ordinary. Eric got quiet except with Kate. One night I asked the guard to check on him because I was concerned. Over what I'm not sure, just concerned. The guard relayed back to me that Van Zant was just tired. I did notice he started to pace when we were in the jury room after being excused from the courtroom for one reason or another. I began to notice that one day he would be quiet then the next he'd be like a rapid-fire machine gun conversationalist. He sat behind me in the jury box, so how he appeared throughout the trial, I don't know."

For long, long minutes the only sound in the van came from outside tire to pavement interaction. Dorsie glanced over her shoulder again back at the dogs. They were both asleep. She faced forward and took a deep breath. "After we were instructed on deliberations and back in the jury room, Eric was very, very different. Agitated. Authoritarian. He made it clear he was in charge. What he said was what we were going to do. I don't know how the others reacted. I only know I went into challenge mode. Read the jury instructions on the foreperson's responsibilities. When I said I wanted to send a note to Judge Howard, he leaped from his chair and grabbed my arm with such force I had bruise marks for weeks afterwards."

"What did the other male jurors do?"

"Rodney backed Eric away from me. Tony came to stand at my side. In those moments it seemed as if the entire room was filled with a menacing presence. I felt that flight or fight reaction. The room went deadly quiet until the deputy banged on the door and Burton gave him a plausible excuse for the racket he'd heard moments earlier."

Dorsie fell silent again, lost in her thoughts until the Judge asked if she wanted to stop. She shook her head. "No. It's just that something is really, really bothering me about Eric smoking."

She shrugged, closed her eyes and focused her thoughts then in a steady voice void of any kind of emphasis on words, phrases or sentences, she told Judge every detail she could recall on what happened next, who said what, the results of the second vote, how she was the only one who stuck to guilty. She related other jurors' comments of just wanting every-thing to be over, just wanting to go home, just wanting to get out of the jury room. She turned to Judge and asked," What would have happened if I'd have gotten a note through to Judge Howard telling him Van Zant was acting erratic?"

"Before I answer that, give me your best gut feeling on whether the others were upset over Van Zant's outburst."

"Lisa, the young mother cried. Millie gripped her by the hand and shushed her. Kate immediately rushed to Eric's side and began soothing him, whispering to him, holding his hands in hers. Tony switched his seat with one of the early retirees to be beside me. Eric was at the head of the table. I was the first person to his left. They were extremely stunned. I glanced at Rodney. He was watching Eric like a hawk. Now, that I see it in my mind's eye again, Rodney had both hands balled up in fists."

"About a note to Judge Howard," Judge said getting back on point. "Howard most probably would have halted deliberations for the day and sent all others back to the hotel. He would have called you into chambers and given you wide latitude to express your issues. Most certainly he would have adopted a soft, concerned approach in questioning you. Asked if you needed any medical assistance. Would have asked you to rate your stress and anxiety levels. He would have let you talk and talk until you ran out of steam. Sort of got it off your chest. Then he would have asked you if you could continue or wanted to be excused. Following this he would enter into more conversation with you gently bringing your stress level down through the use of empathy. His main goal would have been to guide you to a decision to remain on the jury. This was a very high profile case. He was doing everything in his power to make sure it stood up to an Appeals Court if it ever came to that. Releasing a juror at that late stage would have sent Diaz to the moon if the verdict came back guilty. However, if Howard sensed in any way that you were unable to continue, he would have dismissed you.

He paused for long moments thinking then took a sip of water and cleared his throat. "Depending on State law, if a juror is released during deliberations the Judge would confer with the defendant and his attorney. If the defendant agrees, then deliberations would continue with only eleven jurors. But I can guarantee you Judge Howard would have used everything he knew about human behavior and emotions to guide you to a point where you felt you could continue. Not coerced you. Guide you to where you could make a free-will decision."

Judge paused and took a sip from his water bottle, looked into the rearview mirror to get a glimpse of the dogs in the back. Satisfied all was well back there he continued. "Bear in mind criminal trial judges in their time on the bench have had encounters with distraught jurors faltering under stressful circumstances. You would have been the only one coming to him with concerns. It would only be your interpretation of the arm grabbing aspect and to him would have been signaling evidence of someone in extreme stress. Not only in you but also in his appointed foreperson." He paused again gathering his thoughts, his accumulated experience and knowledge. "Would he have spoken to the other jurors? Doubtful. Not at that late stage. Judges know things can get pretty heated in a jury room with conflicting opinions and discussions on guilty–not guilty. Tempers flare. Shouting matches happen. Some buckle down and refuse to talk to anyone. People cry. It all happens until they find a way to work it out."

"I would have been the one exhibiting erratic, perhaps irrational behavior."

Judge nodded. "I'm quite aware that I only have your point of view but experience tells me the majority of your fellow jurors had their minds made up before deliberations even began. Could they have been swayed? Maybe. Van Zant's behavior prevented that. They closed down. From being sequestered for a long period. From exhaustion. From stress. The explosive nature of Van Zant's behavior was the key that locked away motivation to have an open mind. I say this because no one was willing to stand with you. Had all eleven of you pushed aside Van Zant's authoritarian stance and collectively opened the door to talk with the deputy things would have been different."

"After we broke for the night I approached a deputy and tried again to get a note to Judge Howard. He kept asking me if I needed medical assistance. That was the only way he was going to contact Judge Howard. I didn't sleep all night. I was determined to put forth my best arguments the next morning."

"The deputy followed protocol. Like all judges and those responsible for jurors he'd probably seen his share of upset, stressed-out jurors. He was giving you an out by asking if you needed medical attention. If you had said yes he would have acted according to the rulebook for such a situation. Judge Howard would have been notified that EMS was on its way."

Dorsie remained silent for long minutes mulling over how she missed the subtle out the deputy was signaling by continuing to ask her if she needed medical assistance. It was another error on her part. "There's something else. I'm just going to say it. I can't remember anything from the time I entered the courthouse to picking up the pen and signing the verdict forms." She couldn't control the rising pitch in her voice. "It's blank. Lost time. I don't know what happened during that lost time. I would have held out. Made it a hung jury. I would not have said not guilty. Something happened to me. I just don't know what."

Judge reached over and patted Dorsie on the knee. "Let's stop. I can feel the tension building in your body way over here. I'm not diminishing what you've just told me. I'm not putting it on the back burner. I just want your frustration level to lower a couple of notches. We'll figure it out together. I promise."

Dorsie heaved a heavy resigned sigh. "I sure could use a drink right now."

"Me too. We'll be in The Villages in about twenty minutes. I asked JB to go down to Fresh Market and stock a rotisserie chicken and salad in the fridge. He's probably still there waiting patiently for us. He's like a grandpa waiting to get a glimpse of a new grandchild. That being Rudy back there. I've been trying to talk JB into being a puppy raiser. He's not budging."

Dorsie gave a small laugh. "Ah, Mr. spit and polish, get-everything-done-perfectly has a big, old soft spot. Good for him. We all need soft spots in our hearts."

Once back in The Villages, the next three hours were taken up with attending to dogs' needs, watching Rudy explore his new surroundings and fortifying their bodies with food, drinks and one too many cups of coffee. JB went down memory lane, recalling his days with young Gino Carapelli but never specifically said what his role was with Gino. Almost in round robin fashion JB, the Judge and Dorsie gave a multitude of reasons why they never remarried again, thus reaching this stage of their lives more or less alone. They all agreed they had no regrets for choosing to fill their lives with family, work and a select circle of friends and concluded equally that they'd never felt lonely. JB left at eleven after giving Rudy very many belly rubs then placing him in his doggie cage in the Judge's bedroom. Thor stretched himself alongside and Rudy made body contact with him in spite of the wire.

"You want me to leave Thor here tonight?" Dorsie asked Judge while they filled the dishwasher. "It's been such a long day. With Thor here, Rudy will settle more easily for the first night."

"Sounds like a plan. I'll bring him over in the morning. You tired?"

"Not anymore. I really shouldn't have had those two large cups of coffee. Too much caffeine. I feel wired."

"Me too. Want to continue where we left off? I said we didn't have to do a marathon but looks like it's turning into one."

They walked into the large center room now dimly lit with very masculine lamps sitting on tables next to soft leather chairs and a soft, supple leather sofa. One wall had floor to ceiling built-in bookshelves filled to full capacity with books. Many of the books looked as if they'd been read and handled many times. Dorsie settled herself on the sofa and Judge settled into a comfortable recliner."

"Let me recap my thoughts so far," he said. "There have been many, many cases where juries convicted people of murder based on less evidence. Cases where the cause of death was unknown. However, as I said before, maternal filicide is difficult for any jury. If you had caused a hung jury, Judge Howard would have instructed all of you to deliberate more. In the end, if it still remained hung, a mistrial would have been declared. A retrial after a mistrial does not constitute double jeopardy. Regarding a juror behaving erratically, he might have removed the juror and as a worst case scenario declared a mistrial." Judge rose from his seat and started to pace as he spoke. "What I'm going to tell you next is going to be upsetting. Never-the-less it's how things work."

For the next ten minutes he went into great detail explaining the complex political ramifications and state funding implications for a State prosecuting attorney to reach a decision to retry a case. He gave examples, citing how a deadlocked jury of 11-1 for conviction most likely would be retried. If a deadlocked jury was 11-1 for acquittal, then it was less likely to be retried. Eric Van Zant's state of mind, mental illness – judges were reluctant to throw out a verdict even if was discovered a juror suffered from mental illness based on the 11-1 scenarios.

"Given all these factors, its unlikely that a mistrial would have been declared in the Maddox case. Diaz tried every angle he could will the trial was in progress. The jury rendered the verdict of Not Guilty. Maddox can never be brought to trial again because the U.S. Constitution prohibits someone from being prosecuted twice for the same offense."

Dorsie felt her stomach convulse in knots. "So what you're saying is no matter what I did, no matter how hard I tried, the outcome would have been the same. Even if I had stuck to my conviction of guilty, Tracy Maddox would have walked no matter what."

"Pretty much. Its unfortunate that the individuals on this jury were not suited or motivated enough to *really* act in an ethical, responsible manner." Judge sat down again.

Dorsie rose then took over pacing the central room just as Judge had minutes earlier. After two turns around the room she left to peek in on the dogs in the Judge's master bedroom. She came back to the center room and stood before Judge. "There's one thing I forgot to mention about jury voir dire. It will sound crazy. But, with regard to Diaz. I heard my inner voice whisper *Con Man* twice. I trust my intuition. When Diaz came out with all the molestation stuff during his opening statement, I heard that same voice again. He conned the jury. Knew how to hit hot buttons. My Gawd, mention a daughter being molested by her father and judgments are formed immediately. It's so repulsive that it never occurs to anyone that the daughter in question might be lying."

"Diaz certainly knew his jury when he came out with that. Any con man will tell you the real skill in crafting a great lie is finding what the mark wants to believe and giving it to him. In this case, I refer back to maternal filicide. How no one wants to believe a mother would kill her child. Diaz gave his marks, the jurors, what they wanted to believe. An accident. She drowned in the pool. All the lies and odd behavior. Oh-by-the-way, she was molested. This was the cause of all her lies and party-girl behavior. She was still acting out from the trauma or acting out because repressed memories had surfaced."

Judge paused and watched Dorsie begin her pacing again. "Psychologist will bear this out. When we can't make sense of an act, we will grasp at something in order to try to make sense of it. Diaz gave the jury something to hang on to. The Con, as you call it. I'll give Diaz kudos for knowing his jury. He's got street smarts and it carried the day for him. I'd deem him unethical in some areas. I suppose he was hoping he'd get away with certain issues. But, Judge Howard was sharp. He only let a few things slide. Unimportant things."

Dorsie plopped back down on the sofa. "This makes me sick."

"Ashcroft may have made an unconscious critical error. He assumed. And I emphasize assumed, or more probably hoped, the individuals on this jury had good common sense. From what you've told me there was a lack of psychological insight to piece together how B, C, and D were related to A. He also assumed his presentation of forensic science was at an intellectual level they could understand and get behind. So you're right. They were conned by Diaz. Believed the lies. The result – justice for Jenna Maddox became the collateral damage."

"I'm still sick," Dorsie said. "Everyone lied. Tracy. Ann Maddox. The whole family lied to themselves for a long, long time that Tracy didn't have problems." She sighed heavily. "My fellow jurors lied when they voted for not guilty on all counts because maybe they really believed it was okay to lie about a missing child. Maybe buried deep inside of each of them they had lies they couldn't or wouldn't face. So they thought it was okay to lie to police officers and in a court of law. I wonder if any one of them is lying to themselves now? Hiding behind 'the jury did their job'."

Judge went and sat next to Dorsie on the sofa and put his arm around her in a comforting manner. "Dorsie, you can't continue to think you carry the sole responsibility for what happened. Perhaps you feel this way because you've always had sole responsibility. For young children. For being a cornerstone in your family's business. You're used to having control over things. Bending them to your will. This time you couldn't. It was all way beyond what influences you could bring to bear upon it." He felt her shudder then tense trying to keep from crying. He pulled her even closer as a means of comfort. "There, there, Dorsie. Don't spend the rest of this short life in anguish and guilt."

"I dream of Jenna Maddox all the time. It started just after the trial began. I always wake up feeling as if she's trying to tell me something. Now, Eric Van Zant has entered into the dream. It's as if they both want to tell me something."

"Well my advice is simple. Doesn't come from years on the bench. Just ask them, Dorsie. Ask them in sort of a gestalt way. Or, you've told me you meditate. Ask the question there. You'll get an answer."

"That still doesn't help me with my lost time issue. I still have to know what happened. What made me sign my name to not guilty? I really do have to know if I'm going to be able to let this go. Any advice on how to do that?"

Judge gave her a gentle squeeze. "I have to think about it. But I have a suggestion. I'm really tired now. You're tired. Thor and Rudy are asleep. Stay here tonight. Stay in the guest room. I've got lots of tee shirts and boxers. Even a brand new bathrobe I've never used. There's bound to be a new toothbrush in the guest bathroom. Melanie stocked it for me. I think you'll find all the necessities there."

Dorsie pulled away from the Judge and studied his face. It was washed with fatigue and she really didn't have the heart to ask him to drive her home. She glanced toward the hallway that led to the guest bedrooms and saw the convenient pocket door used to close off all the guest bedrooms from the rest of the house. "You don't sleep walk do you? In case you do, I'll barricade myself behind the pocket and bedroom doors. If anything gets dicey, I yell for Thor," she said in a joking manner."

"Ole Gal, what the hell are you thinking? I'm an honorable man," Judge exclaimed pretending to be offended. "But thanks for the compliment. It's been a long time since any female suspected me of taking advantage of her. Now go. Take any guest bedroom. I'm going to lock up."

In spite of being exhausted, caffeine kept Dorsie from slipping into restful sleep. All night long segments of the day's conversations repeated themselves in dreamlike bursts. At other times during light sleep, cigarette packs of various brands flashed through the air landing on jury room table in front of Eric Van Zant. The dream world scenes swirled, faded then reappeared again until Dorsie finally sensed the light of dawn coming through the half-closed vertical blind. For a long, long time she thought deeply about all Judge had discussed the previous day. Sadly, she came to the realization that, since the trial, there were times she was so wrapped up in herself that she failed to recognize others' concerns and worries including those of her own family. They were giving her much needed and appreciated support. By now, they also must be feeling the strain and wondering when she was going to snap out of it, come home and be her normal self again. Today is the day, she vowed silently. I'm going to take the first steps to snap out of it. Today, tomorrow and however long it takes, I am going to ask Jenna why she and the magnificent German Shepherd visit me. For Gawd sakes, she told scolded, you're no stranger to meditation. Use it!

Thor found his way to the guest bedroom and gave a small whine. She got up then quietly opened cabinets in the kitchen until she found plastic bags stored under the sink. She took Thor out for his duty call. When she returned, Judge was out back in the yard waiting for Rudy to do his busy work in a pit similar to the one JB had built for Thor. They laughed aloud at the sight of each other in their almost look-alike attire, boxer shorts, large tee shirt, lightweight hoodie and sandals.

Chapter Twenty-Six

Absolution

On New Year's Eve evening Judge and JB cajoled Dorsie into accompanying them down to the Town Square telling her she just had to see how The Villages celebrated. JB drove the golf cart, dropped them off near Lighthouse Point and went in search of a parking place. Golf cart after golf cart filled every parking space. Those parked directly around the old-fashioned square served as people watching posts for their drivers and passengers as men, women and children from ages five to eighty-five filled sidewalks and crosswalks. Kids visiting grandparents raced around the gazebo bandstand while parents chased after them. Various line dancers formed groups and showed off their moves. Young and old couples danced in the traditional twosome form. Grandsons danced with grandmas. Small granddaughters stood on grandpas' feet while they danced the waltz box step style. Restaurants and bistros were filled. Haagen Daz Ice Cream was doing a booming business as were the Two for One bar shacks. The weather accommodated all by hovering at sixty-five degrees. Light jackets sufficed. Those visiting from the northern climates wore sunburned faces and shorts. The atmosphere was festive and a crowd had gathered to listen to the The Red Garter Band playing on the corner of the Old Mill Playhouse. They swayed and clapped in time with the beat of New Orleans jazz standards. JB found Judge and Dorsie there. In his usual no muss no fuss manner, he poured three neat scotches in plastic tumblers he retrieved from a small cooler slung over his shoulder. The three of them raised the tumblers and toasted the night. When the The Red Garter Band finished their sets, the threesome moved on making their way through the crush of people heading for Lighthouse Point to wish Skeeter a Happy New Year. The Judge and JB shouldered their way maneuvering through the crowd unaware that they'd lost Dorsie.

Dorsie stepped out of the flow of pedestrians near the ATM machine when she lost sight of Judge and JB and waited to see if they'd turn back when they realized she was not following. She decided to stay put in one spot so if they did come looking, she'd be able to spot them before they did her. She watched people pass by then took note of three handsome young men with football physiques coming towards where she stood. They all had dark, curly hair, Mediterranean coloring and wide, bright smiles mostly likely the result of expensive orthodontists. She smiled after noting their similar features surmising they were related in some way to each other. Good naturedly they jostled against each other laughing and joking. Dorsie looked away, raised herself up on tiptoes and scanned the crowd again for any sign of Judge and JB. As the hulking young men passed in front of Dorsie, the one closest to her received a little too forceful shove from his cousin. He lost his balance and lurched sideways, his bulk connecting with Dorsie's body.

"Oh," Dorsie cried as she felt herself being slammed against the wall. The back of her head hit the bricks and she crumpled to the sidewalk knocked senseless.

"Ma'am. I'm sorry. Are you okay?" the hulking young man said hovering above her as his cousins squatted down to her level. Three pairs of large hands reached towards her. "Let's get you up."

Dorsie stared at them blankly while memory synapses short-circuited beneath her hard hit skull. She wasn't seeing three young clean cut-men. In her disoriented state, she saw ugly men with harsh guttural voices and laughs. She smelled the stench of cigarette breath. Felt pairs of hands grabbing and punching her body. "No. No. No," she screamed, lashing out with her arms, kicking out her feet towards the stunned young men. "NO! HELP! HELP!"

Passersby stopped. The young man reached for her again.

"No! No!" she yelled kicking forcefully at him as if he were an attacker. He stepped back unsure of what to do.

"Call 911," someone in the crowd said. "Call 911."

Cell phones flipped open but before anyone could punch in the numbers, JB was kneeling in front of Dorsie. Over his shoulder he called out "No 911. She's okay. I'll take care of her." He turned back to Dorsie and patted her face gently. "Dorsie. Dorsie. It's me. JB. You're safe. You're safe."

JB's voice penetrated. Dorsie's eyes refocused to the present. She locked eyes with JB. A nanosecond memory from the past flashed then disappeared. "What happened? What am I doing on the ground?" she asked. She glanced upward at the burly young men.

"Ma'am. I'm so sorry. Sorry," he said. He glanced at his cousin "We didn't mean to scare you."

With JB's help Dorsie stood. She ran her hand over her forehead then to the back of her head feeling the stickiness of blood and matted hair. She tried to smile. "I know. An accident. Too many people. Not enough room."

The Judge shouldered his way thru the onlookers. He took Dorsie's hand in his and noticed the blood on her fingers. He placed his own hand at the back of her head and felt the wetness pooling there in her hair. Quickly, he pulled a handkerchief from his jacket pocket and placed it at the back of her head and told her to hold it there. With purpose he strode over to the first parked four-seater golf cart he saw with occupants. "I'm Judge Joseph Kelly," he said in his most commanding Darth Vader voice. "Take us over to the Urgent Care Center next to Sweetbay. You can get us there faster. EMS is going to have a tough time getting through all this," he said. He swung his arm towards the crowded square.

A half-hour later, Dorsie sat in an exam where a doctor checked her reactions, shined a light into her pupils, examined her head wound, cleaned it and applied a butterfly bandage

The Judge settled Dorsie into a chair when she returned to the waiting room clutching Patient Head Wound Instructions. He was unnerved by the extreme paleness of her face. "Hell, we didn't mean for you to bang in the New Year with your head," he said. "JB went to get the golf cart. You'll be home soon. Let's have a look at those instructions." He made a show of reading the first page. "Dorsie, say something. Are you sure the doctor said you were okay?""

"Accidents happen," she said. She waited in silence staring straight ahead as if she was unaware of anything.

The Judge went to the reception window and asked to speak with the doctor who had just treated Dorsie. Several minutes of consultation with him assured the Judge Dorsie was still reacting to events. Once she was home in a safe environment, she'd feel more comfortable.

JB and Judge bundled Dorsie into the golf cart. JB ignored the *No Golf Carts Beyond This Point* sign. Instead of taking the golf cart path, he zipped through the Stillwater roundabout. He bypassed the security gate by entering Canal Street in the oncoming traffic lane. Short minutes later they were at the house on Duncan Drive. Once inside, JB took charge of Thor and Rudy, taking them back to the Duty Pit. Judge kept assessing Dorsie, unnerved by her drawn, white complexion and silence. "Do you want me to call someone?" he asked.

She shook her head then lifted her arm, her hand feeling the back of her head.

"I can stay. Maybe I should stay," he said. "You shouldn't be alone."

She made a face that silently said no and shook her head.

JB returned with Thor and Rudy. He gave Dorsie a once over and saw the same paleness and the distant dead-eyed look as Judge did. He took Judge aside. "You'd better go. I'll drive you and Rudy home then come back." The Judge looked at him taken aback by his sudden, yet deliberate take-charge demeanor. "Judge, ya gotta' trust me on this one. Let me take you home. It's the best thing you can do right now. I've got this covered. I will call Harold, if you're worried about her not letting anyone know. She'll be fine in the few minutes it'll take me to get you and Rudy home. Don't worry. It's something other than a concussion. Please, just trust me on this."

Perplexed, Judge let JB take Rudy and him home.

When JB let himself back into the house on Duncan Drive, Dorsie was pacing the large center room. She stopped when he entered the room and faced him. "It was *you*!"

JB motioned for her to sit. "I figured as much when you didn't recognize me the first day. Remember I did tell you Gino and I went way back. I was the one who found you that night outside of Gino's building. Rode with you in the ambulance. You went into cardiac arrest. Broken rib punctured your lung. I threw Gino's number at the nurses. They called Gino. He called Harold. Afterwards, when the police, Harold and Gino made it to the E.R., I just stepped into the background, as was my place at the time."

Dorsie shook her head in amazement.

"Gino had me sitting outside your private room the whole time you were in the hospital. I don't think you ever noticed. Days later, when Brandon and Megan came to see you, I've never forgotten their scared faces when they saw you all bruised and, bandaged with an IV stuck in your arm. But, why am I repeating this? You know all the medical facts."

Unconsciously Dorsie ran her fingertip over the two-inch scar at her hairline above her forehead. "Did Harold, Brandon or Megs recognize you when they were visiting?"

JB shook his head. "Not Brandon and Megs. Harold did. I can understand him not telling you. Why stir up bad memories?"

"This is much, much too late," Dorsie stood before JB taking his hands in hers. "Thank you. Thank you. You saved my life that night. At first I didn't remember much for a long, long, time. But the flashbacks came and when they did they were bad. I buried everything deep. I don't go there. Funny though, about a week ago I had a hellish nightmare. Relived it again in my dream. That dream comes when I get under a lot of stress."

"Understandable," JB said very quietly. "Floored me when Vince Di Paolo called and told me who to get the house ready for." He hung his head and stared at his clasped hands. "When I saw you on the ground tonight, it took me back." He paused then said quietly, "You were very, very important to Gino. He never forgot the price you paid."

"Those big, burly young men. That hard bodily contact. I got bounced back to that night too. There was another time, almost twenty years after that night. I was at a NY restaurant when this big guy accidently pushed me into a wall. Like tonight I ended up on the ground. When the man tried to help me up . . ." She paused and thought back to her reaction. "It was like I was reliving that night in Tribeca all over again. Same thing happened this time. Only now, I've been spared the long lasting state of shock and memory loss. It was days before I could remember what happened even though Harold told me several times. The whole affair sent me into a not so good tailspin."

Dorsie froze. Once again her synapses fired erratically.

Flash. Eric Van Zant walking beside her. *Flash.* Hard shove. *Flash.* Hit wall. Down on floor. *Flash.* Van Zant's face close. *Flash.* Cigarette breath. *Flash.* Not Guilty. Bitch. *Flash.* Do it! *Flash, flash, flash.* Deputy helping her. *Fast Forward.* Van Zant silently mouthing *Bitch* when he handed her Juror 1389's packet of verdict forms.

"Oh-my-Gawd. Oh-my-Gawd," Dorsie cried. She slumped into a chair and buried her face in her hands. She sobbed uncontrollably as she realized the enormity of what had just been shaken loose from her memory. An ugly, ugly memory imprint had turned into a real-time flashback.

A long buried psychological weakness forced itself upward like hot volcanic lava obliterating her capacity to function rationally. During the final ninety minutes of deliberations she had turned into a frightened, not-thinking-straight woman, a woman who was unable to pull herself together. Unable to stand-up and fight for justice for Jenna Maddox. Her ability to think clearly had been altered by fear. That dark, ugly night in Tribeca still had the power to fill her with paralyzing fear.

JB put his hand on her shoulder. "Dorsie. I don't know what to do. You're crying so hard. Should I call Judge? Should I call Harold? What? You shouldn't be alone. You hit your head hard. Someone needs to keep an eye on you. Check on you through the night."

Dorsie marshalled her emotions. She rubbed her face hard then stood and gathered JB to her in the most heartfelt of human-to-human embraces. "Thank you. Thank you so much for what you did so long ago," she said. For long seconds they stood, holding on to each other like two people who had gone through a horrendous event together then reconnecting with each other again years and years later. Dorsie finally pulled away. "You're right. According to the Patient Care notes, I shouldn't be alone. I'm going to call Judge. See if he'll take me and Thor in for the night. It's too much to ask him to come here. He's got his hands full with Rudy. And Rudy needs to be in his own house getting used to routines."

JB's heartwarming laugh filled the room. "That Rudy. He's quite a fella. Judge isn't sleeping much."

"You'll drive me and Thor over?"

"Yes Ma'am, would be my pleasure to escort a lady on New Year's Eve. Even if she is going to another man's house. But I do believe it's now New Year's Day."

As an afterthought Dorsie asked, "Does Judge know you knew me before I came to The Villages?"

JB shook his head. "No. I never thought that after all these years I'd still be following Gino Carapelli's orders to keep my mouth shut about anything to do with Raines or Renninger."

At twelve-thirty a.m., the Judge opened the door and welcomed Dorsie with open arms. After getting her settled in the guest bedroom, he closed down the house and tried to get some sleep. Rudy whimpered off and on in his sleeping cage and every two hours Judge rose and went to check on Dorsie. He knew she wasn't sleeping soundly either because when he stood in the doorway she'd murmur "I'm alright. Go back to bed." He rose early. Took Thor and Rudy out to the Duty Pit. When Dorsie still wasn't up at ten thirty, he got very concerned. He quietly walked into the guest bedroom and shook her shoulder lightly. He was relieved when she opened her eyes and said, "What?"

Later, over a light brunch, Dorsie and the Judge sat in his sunny kitchen while Rudy scampered about doing puppy things. Thor watched quietly from a comfortable spot he'd found in a band of sunshine streaming through the window. Dorsie set down her glass of orange juice then studied the Judge's face. She saw no signs of fatigue even though she knew he had been up every two hours during the entire night. "I owe you some explanations," she said. "About last night."

The Judge pushed his chair further back from the table. "I was very worried. Quite taken aback by JB taking command of the situation. But I know JB well enough to trust him when he said he knew what was wrong and get it under control.

"He was right," Dorsie said. "As is my habit I'm just going to say it all as it comes."

For a long, long two hours she told the Judge how JB had saved her life. How she'd been unaware of the part he played on a night in Tribeca when he'd found her after being brutally beaten and raped. As unemotionally as she could, she described the physical, emotional and psychological trauma she'd suffered. Recounted some of the struggles she'd had in the long, hard road to recovery. Admitted how elements of the entire trauma could be resurrected by certain triggers in the form of flashbacks. It didn't happen often, she told him. But, when it did, it would plunge her into a state where she was unable to function normally or even remember the trigger event itself.

She then went on to explain what she believed happened on Verdict Day in the Tracy Maddox trial. How Eric Van Zant's purposeful shove caused her to hit the wall and collapse to the floor. How his insincere effort to help her had acted as a trigger. A trigger that snapped open the lock on a cage where she kept an almost unbearable fear imprisoned for life. Imprisoned to keep it from consuming her *life!* She told Judge everything, the smallest details she'd kept hidden deep down. Explaining that she'd kept it buried for one reason only – self-preservation.

Long silence followed as the Judge digested what he'd just heard. He studied Dorsie's face. It was pale and drawn, her shoulders sagged and he knew what she had just confided had left her in a tremendous state of vulnerability. He rose from his chair, went to Dorsie and pulled her out of her chair. He faced her head-on and placed his hands on both of her upper arms to square her stance. He locked his eyes with hers. Within himself, The Honorable Joseph P. Kelly, retired Appellate Court Judge, summoned up all the wisdom he'd gained. He filled his James Earl Jones sound-alike voice with authority that could not be challenged. He articulated his findings.

"Dorsie Raines Renninger. This Court finds you to be a remarkable woman with deep beliefs in fair justice as ruled by law but also by a Higher Power beyond the scope of our justice system. After hearing all mitigating factors and relying on reviews of legal precedents deemed law by all Courts, I have given grave consideration to them all. It is this Appellate Court's decision that in the case of the State of New Jersey vs. Tracy Ann Maddox you acted in keeping with the responsibilities charged to an ethical and moral juror. You are a human being. No Court in the land expects perfection in any human. No one can turn himself into a robot devoid of all human conditions of emotions, values, biases, life experiences and deeply held spiritual beliefs. This Court on this first day of the New Year rules and finds *you*, Dorsie Raines Renninger, Not Guilty. This Court reverses the verdict of Guilt imposed upon you solely by your deeply held convictions that you failed in being just. It is the opinion of this Court that the appointed jury foreperson was under extreme mental aberration and as a result unethically and unlawfully intimidated another juror. If he were alive, I would consider a charge of perjury for lying about his mental status in Jury Voir Dire. I would also charge him with jury tampering. However, the verdict in the State of New Jersey vs Tracy Ann Maddox Criminal Court Case will stand." He paused and tightened his grasp on Dorsie's arms in an effort to make sure she paid close attention to his next words. "Go in peace Dorsie Raines Renninger. From the Highest Court of Angels Jenna Maddox looks down upon you. She knows how hard you tried."

Dorsie stood before Judge unable to speak. Humility and gratitude flooded her soul and rushed into the self-loathing cracks and gullies that had altered the terrain of her self-image. The walls in her ravine of guilt began to soften. She knew in time they would finally come crumbling down. Through tear-filled eyes she held Judge's gaze feeling her battered and bruised self-esteem enter into the first phase of restoration.

Judge opened his arms and Dorsie walked into them. She found comfort in his very presence. She felt as if he and she had finally come together again after journeying apart in other times and in other places. She said a small grateful prayer to the Universe for placing Judge in her direct path. To be there. To be kind. To be gentle. To use his wisdom to show her she was still a part of humanity who knew the difference between right and wrong. To acknowledge that she was someone who saw through a pathological liar's wall of lies. To validate that she was someone who recognized a street-smart defense attorney's construction of the almost perfect con. Judge was someone who, in spite of her signature on verdict forms, confirmed that she, was worthy of self-respect.

"Thank you." Dorsie whispered.

The voice within added.

You've met the wise man along the way.

Chapter Twenty-Seven

New Plans

Later, after returning to Vince Di Paolo's house on Duncan Drive Dorsie connected with her family via Skype wishing them a Happy New Year. Dave and Megs held up Ran to show her how he'd grown. Thor stood on his hind legs, paws on counter and yelped at Dave and Megs's images on the screen. Harold and Rose convinced Crystal to stand sideways so Dorsie could see her baby bump. Brandon and Rick proposed she make a New Year's Resolution to come home within three months, reinforcing how Crystal really wanted her to be there for the baby's birth. Rick gleefully held up adorable unisex infant outfits one after another for her inspection. Much later, she called Harold and went over every detail of her discussions with the Judge. She explained how a simple accident and a hard knock on the head had led to the recognition of JB Bowser but more importantly the recall of what had happened on the last day of deliberations.

"Ole Gal, you've been put through the wringer again," Harold said. "But I can hear it in your voice that you've made it over the bump in the road. Are you going to tell Brandon and Megs the full story?"

"I don't know. But if I did, it would finally put to rest their questions about Gino Carapelli's relationship with me. With us. Gawd, Megs asked if Gino and I ever had an affair."

"Oh," Harold gave a small chuckle. "Megs already asked me that a long time ago. Brandon asked me why I thought you never married again. Or never had any interest in having a long-time partner. Think of them as understanding adults, Ole Gal. Not your children. That night long ago impacted the present. I fully understand why and how. They will too."

"I'll give it serious thought. But I'm not promising anything."

"Fair enough," Harold said then added, "One last thing for you to think about. When will you come home?"

"Soon, Harold. Soon," Dorsie answered.

Feeling lighter in spirit and less fearful of being recognized, Dorsie struck out to explore more of The Villages and its touted lifestyle activities. She went beyond the Village of Virginia Trace and visited many of the recreation centers marveling at the excellent, interesting and well thought out décor of each. As a curious bystander she, with Thor at her side, watched pickle ball, bocce and shuffleboard games. After discovering the Kite Flying Cloud Chasers, she bought a shocking neon lime green and fuchsia Quantum stunt kite and went to the Polo Grounds every Tuesday to learn how to do simple stunts. On two occasions she went to the Civil Discourse meeting at the Mulberry Recreation Center and listened to vigorous discussions and opinions voiced on the selected subject of the night. She and Judge learned how to do the Carolina Shag and then went to the weekly dances held by the Shag Club. On Monday evenings, she became a regular with JB at Bunco at the Lake Miona Recreation Center.

One Monday evening after introducing themselves by first name only, a chatty woman exclaimed, "I know you. You're that juror. I've seen you with the German Shepherd." In a puffed-up manner she informed the other players at the table, "You autographed that book the lawyer wrote – *Broken Trust* – on the page describing Juror Four. You met my son at the airport."

"You must be mistaken. This is my sister-in-law, Dorsie Bowser," JB said. "She's escaped from brutal Wisconsin winters." He winked at the chatty lady. "You're not the first one to think she's that juror because of her name."

Dorsie covered her mouth to hide the smile that formed there at JB's outright white lie and silently applauded him for his quick thinking.

In between her busy, want-to-see-it all excursions, she still kept to a schedule of taking Thor to the Polo Grounds for heavy exercise. Only now, the Judge's puppy, Rudy, scampered about while Thor did his thunderbolt runs to burn off energy. She still stopped by Lighthouse Point for "Happy Hour Bliss" to have Skeeter pour the two-for-one Johnnie Walker Blacks. Only now, it was once a week not every day.

In mid-February, Dorsie and Judge watched the Nightly News together with Brian Williams reporting on the severe Northeaster dumping over twelve inches or more of snow in various parts of New Jersey, New York and Connecticut.

"Ugh. I'd be shoveling that awful stuff if I was home and I'm getting too old to do that," Dorsie said in a rare admission. "It's so easy being here in the lovely, mild weather. Maybe I should become a Snowbird."

"I think that's an excellent idea," said Judge with great enthusiasm. "I've got those three spare guestrooms. Want to rent them? You could redecorate and turn one into a sitting room just for yourself. There is that pocket door, you know," he joked. "Or tomorrow we could call JB and he'd put you together with a good realtor."

"Oh my! Not so fast! I've never given any thought to retiring or moving for that matter," Dorsie said. "I'm flattered at the offer to . . ." She made quotation marks in the air. "Sort of" live with you. I admit there have been times when the hard fact hits me that my house is just too big now. Requires a lot of energy for upkeep. Megs and Brandon rarely come home anymore. I'm always going to their places."

"It's something to think about. The Villages is a wonderful place. It has some drawbacks but overall there's nothing like it out there. Me. I'm a Frog." When he saw Dorsie's eyebrows raise in question, he said. "Snowbirds come for the winter months. Frogs. They stay till they croak!"

Dorsie burst out in a fit of laughter so hard she had to hold her sides.

"Here's another one for you," Judge said. "I have it on good authority that this is the true sentiment of many single women here. About the men in The Villages. They say, and I am quoting because I heard it firsthand, 'The men either want your purse or they want you to nurse.'"

"Nooo," cried Dorsie still laughing uncontrollably.

"Dorsie, as you can see, I don't need a nurse. I certainly don't want your purse. Please give serious consideration to coming here, even if it is to be a Snowbird behind a pocket door." He paused to gauge her reaction. She'd stopped laughing and was looking at him in surprise. "You and I, just like JB, we're committed loners. But still, we could have a nice, easy companionship. At my age, I've finally realized life is too short not to enjoy and share it with someone of like mind. Don't you find yourself feeling the same way? Mind you, I'm not lonely. But I like having you here. I like going out and about with you very much."

"I don't know what to say," Dorsie said. "I've been alone so long that I just never . . ."

"Think about it, Dorsie. That's all I'm asking right now. Also, I sense you're mulling over when to return home. I have a suggestion. I need to visit my son and his family. See how big that grandson of mine has grown. Why don't we make plans to drive north together? We could take our time. Stop where we want along the way. Maybe spend a day or two in Charlestown, Savannah or Annapolis. Or how about the Biltmore Estate? We could also pay a visit to your Megs and Dave. Sound like something you'd consider?"

"It's a good suggestion," Dorsie said. "I admit I have been thinking about going home. Harold, Brandon and Rick are putting slight pressure on me to get back before Crystal's baby is due in late March. Let me think about it further."

"Good enough. Now, let's pack up Thor and Rudy in the car. Go down to Kilwin's before they close. In addition to ice cream, I'll even spring for some of that fudge you've gotten addicted to."

—

Two weeks went by before Dorsie settled it in her mind that she would return to Blairstown by mid-March. In her phone call to Dave and Megs, Dave immediately launched into a checklist planning mode of what needed to be done to have Thor onboard any airline as a service dog, telling her once she made the airline reservation he'd take care of everything else. Dorsie stopped him in his mid-planning thought processes.

"Dave, Megs, I'm not flying, The Judge and I are going to drive north together." Meg's soft whisper to Dave of I-told-you-so was easily picked up by the speaker function on Dave's cell. "I'd like to stop on our way and spend a day or two with both of you. If that would be okay?"

"Aww shucks, Dorsie," Dave drawled. "Why are ya even askin'? Right Megs? Come one. Come all. The Judge. The new guy on the block too. Rudy's his name if I'm recallin' correctly."

Megs chimed in. "Give me dates when you get them finalized. I'll see if I can arrange to be off. Way-to-go Mom. The Judge. His voice alone makes me want to swoon in the old-fashioned way."

"Megs, dear. Don't go getting way ahead of yourself. This is just a mutual convenience. Sharing driving. Things like that." Their muffled giggles and exclamations of "yeah right" were picked up by the speaker.

Plans fell quickly into place. Dorsie and Judge planned the route together and the dates of when they would be where. They split travel-planning tasks. Dorsie would handle all arrangements for their stop in Asheville, NC and the Biltmore Estate. Judge would make all arrangements for Savannah and Charleston. In Annapolis, they would wing it since Judge would be in familiar territory. What to do about Rudy was a dilemma since he was still an unruly puppy. After checking with travel assistance at Biltmore Estate, she'd been reassured Rudy would be given access because of his status as a guide dog in training. But, it became apparent Rudy would not do well on the tour of all the rooms. The Biltmore maintained a private kennel and if she'd fax proof of K-9 certification and vaccinations they'd make arrangements for Thor to be housed with the estate's own K-9 unit. Thor was free to walk the grounds with them if he was on leash. Judge made the decision to leave Rudy at home in the good care of JB, who by now was very familiar in the practices, commands and procedures in the raising of guide dog puppies. In the coming weeks JB and Judge would put Rudy through his paces together while Southeastern Guide Dog Association did the necessary background check on JB.

With all plans and details almost completed, Dorsie went back to her see-it-all-excursions zipping here and there in the golf cart with Thor riding as co-pilot. She'd discovered a lovely winding botanical walking path near Sumter Landing. She and Thor would meander along slowly. Sometimes they'd stop at a bench and sit and enjoy blue skies and sunshine. Often she found herself thinking more and more about putting the Blairstown house on the market and retiring fully. She liked the ease of living in a warmer climate. She liked the laid-back casualness of going to restaurants and events in capris and sandals. She started to lean towards thinking that if she missed the diversity and culture she was accustomed to finding in NYC, it was only a plane ride away. Brandon and Rick would always welcome her with open arms. Then there was Harold in Blairstown. He would always have room for her. In a startling admission, she confessed to herself that she liked Judge very, very much, was drawn to him more than any other man she'd met in the long years of being a widow, nearly half of her lifetime.

So engrossed was she in her thinking that she didn't notice the dark clouds coming in from the West. Suddenly, she and Thor were caught in a drenching downpour. They ran for the pavilion not far from where they were sitting and waited for it to blow over. Twenty-five minutes later, back at the house, Dorsie brought Thor around to the back to begin giving his coat a good drying rubdown. She stopped in mid-stride as she rounded the corner. A glorious, double rainbow arched over the golf course. Against the now clear blue sky, the bright, vivid colors of red, orange, yellow, green, blue, indigo and violet were breath taking. The second rainbow was slightly dimmer with inverted colors. With her eyes still fixed on the sky, she bent down on one knee and mindlessly started to rub Thor's coat dry. The scene before her was in perfect balance. Large, grand, old oaks and Queen and Washingtonian palm crowns were silhouetted against the blue sky and drew the eye upward to the wide, wide arch of the two rainbows. Never, in all her life had she seen such a natural phenomenon. Her hands stopped toweling Thor. Her left arm remained draped across Thor's broad muscular shoulder blades. The exquisite perfection in nature became overwhelming. She knew she was in an exquisite present moment and it was sublime. Tears ran down her cheeks. As she brushed them away, she realized they were tears of joy not tears of shame, frustration, anguish or sadness, not the ones she'd been shedding since Verdict Day.

She bent her head and brushed her cheek against Thor's massive head. Suddenly, the memory of the Jenna Maddox dream came forward – bright vivid colors of the rainbow. The magnificent German Shepherd with Jenna's small arm draped around his neck. In an instant she recognized that now, in real-time, her own posture was identical to Jenna's posture in her dreams. As the second rainbow faded from the sky, she knew what she had to do. But more importantly, she knew *how* she was going to do it. Like Judge suggested, she would ask Jenna Maddox what it was she wanted to say. A rainbow meditation exercise she'd learned long, long ago would be the vehicle. It would be the guide to help her reach a place where Jenna and the magnificent German Shepherd would be waiting. There, the soul essence of Jenna Maddox would speak to the essence of her own soul.

Chapter Twenty-Eight

The Rainbow

The next day Dorsie devoted the entire morning to research. She Googled Rainbow Meditation and clicked into all kinds of websites, some very good, some not so good. She watched YouTube videos and listened to free sample downloads of voice directed meditations. Quickly she discarded the notion of using the voice directed material because she found none of the voices appealing or soothing. In her heart of hearts she knew what voice she wanted – the sound-alike James Earl Jones voice. In a large closet hallway, a wireless printer was stored along with other electronics and techno gadgets. The website reference pages she'd sent to the printer were scattered on the floor. After gathering them up and scanning all the gadgets, an idea came to her and she went back to the laptop and started another Google search typing in *Create Own CD* in the browser. She ploughed through computer and techno websites and *How Stuff Works* while taking notes for later reference.

Thor whined and she took him outside to the Duty Pit. Back inside she made and ate a slapped together sandwich and returned to the laptop. An hour later she gave up searching, sat back in the chair and started reviewing what she'd printed out for reference. All were different in approach but all held the same basic elements. She chose to use the Buddhist Primary Rainbow Meditation and would modify it only slightly. She got up and poured herself a diet Coke then went out to the lanai, sat down, got up again then went inside to retrieve her cell. First she considered calling Rick at his HLN studio number then changed her mind. Rick was too far away. On speed dial, she hit JB's number. JB was the one person she knew in The Villages who was extremely resourceful with lots and lots of contacts for various services.

"JB, I've got a little project I'm working on but I'm stuck," she said then went on to explain what she wanted to do. How she wanted the

Judge to record a CD for her. She didn't tell him of the subject matter or why and he didn't ask. Quickly she reviewed what she learned by her Internet search.

"Ahh-uh, music making software," JB said. "I know just where to go. There's a flamenco guitarist here who burns his own CDs. Has a top-of-the-line set-up in his house. I'll give Eduardo a call, see if he's here in The Villages not off down in Miami doing a gig. Get back to you later."

"JB, you're one in a million," Dorsie said. "Thank you."

Next she called Judge and outlined her plan.

"Brilliant!" he exclaimed. "Bring the script over as soon as you can. I'll practice. Stand in front of the mirror and pretend I'm James Earl Jones delivering a soliloquy from a Broadway stage. Ole Gal, I do love the way your mind works."

Five days later, a courtly Eduardo Emmanuel Guttierrez took it upon himself to deliver the CD to Dorsie.

"Most pleasurable work," he said. "The Judge and I were inspired. We took little creative liberties. Not to the script. Something other. You will see when you listen." He handed over the CD along with a brightly colored gift card. "For you and the Judge. You will come and enjoy flamenco dance. Yes?"

After thanking him profusely, Dorsie took the CD and popped it into the Bose Wave player. A single haunting note from what could only be a classical guitar filled the room. A simple, peaceful composition followed, repeating itself in various chords and rhythms then fell into silence. The single haunting note returned and as it faded, the deep, baritone voice of the Judge began to deliver the script of the Rainbow Meditation. When the CD ended Dorsie sat back and clasped her hands to her mouth. "On-my-Gawd. It's beautiful," she exclaimed aloud. Not only had Judge delivered the script with elegant elocution but Eduardo Emmanuel Guttierrez had played his classical guitar softly in the background. She guessed it to be an original composition. The entire result was a work of art, a CD which could, if released, gain commercial success under the category of meditation. She listened to it again finding more and more intricate subtleties in Eduardo Emmanuel Guttierrez's artistic skill. When she shared this CD with Rick, she knew he would swear it was the voice work of James Earl Jones. She retracted the CD and examined the label. – *EL ARCOIRIS, The Rainbow* – Joseph P. Kelly with Eduardo Emmanuel Guttierrez.

Next, she turned her attention to the gift card and found it was for two complementary dinners that included the Flamenco Dance Show at the Columbia Restaurant in Ybor City. She put aside the CD and added get directions – Columbia Restaurant – on her Places to Go list then left with Thor to run some of the errands on her weekly Must Do list: Gifts – Skeeter/sister/JB, gas in Mini, groceries, dog food, Rudy (new toy).

Two days passed before Dorsie felt ready to use *EL ARCOIRIS* for its intended purpose. She decided morning would be the best time, a time when she was fully rested and not distracted by anything. After feeding Thor and taking him for an early morning walk, she placed him out on the lanai. "I have something important to do. Be quiet," she told him. He gave a small whine and immediately assumed his lay-down position, placed his head on his outstretched paws and gave Dorsie a forlorn look.

Dorsie closed the lanai door and partially closed the blinds. She made a trip to the bathroom then placed a box of tissues next to the chair she found to be most comfortable. She inserted *EL ARCOIRIS* into the Bose system and picked up its remote control. In an effort to settle her anticipation she paced the center room twice and removed the band holding her ponytail in place and shook it loose. For long minutes she stood before the large piece of artwork featuring a single Sandhill Crane standing in wetlands and traced her fingertips over the artist's brushwork then turned and sat down in the chair. She took a deep, deep breath and pressed play on the remote.

A single haunting note plucked on a guitar string filled the room. She took another deep breath. Another note followed. She exhaled then repeated the same sequence with the next eight notes until Judge's deep resonating voice began.

"Feel your body becoming lighter and lighter. Before you is a rainbow. Let your gaze follow its arc from end to end. Reach out and touch the rainbow." Seconds passed with only the sound of soft tranquil notes "Slowly, step into the rainbow. Step into the color red. Your whole body is being absorbed by the color red. Feel yourself receiving energy and strength."

Dorsie followed the deep lulling voice's instructions through the colors of orange, yellow and green. She floated into blue. As instructed, she rested in the color blue becoming one with it. Peace and tranquility filled her whole being. Almost at the top of the rainbow she paused for long, long seconds in the color indigo. There she felt released from the tether that kept her bound to the earth. She felt true inner knowledge along with an understanding that went beyond words and feeling. Next she rose to the color violet. There in its saturated color she felt awe and reverence.

"You, in this moment, ARE the rainbow," the voice told her. "Remember this feeling. Now, you are moving towards the source that creates the rainbow. Step onto a beam of sunlight. Its energy is pulling you upward. Upward. Going higher. Higher beyond the earth's atmosphere."

Dorsie imagined herself floating out into the deep reaches of space.

"Higher still. Now, moving through star fields. You feel the Universe's energy all around you."

Complete silence filled Dorsie's consciousness. She no longer heard the gentle, soft notes and rhythms of the guitar. She peacefully floated on a stream of energy."

"You are now in the never ending Universe. A part of all that is. Breathe deeply. Exhale. All concerns and worries are leaving you, released into the vastness of space never to return. Before you is the everlasting white light. Flow into to it. Merge with it. Be one with it."

Very, very long minutes passed before she heard the deep baritone voice again.

"You are one with all there is."

In Dorsie's mind she saw herself standing calmly in the center of a far-reaching white light. It was warm, comforting and she felt protected within its center. She called out, "Jenna."

The white light surrounding her turned to mist and through the gossamer veil came small, innocent Jenna Maddox dressed in her little girl pink tutu. The magnificent German Shepherd followed then sat down. His massive body pressed against Jenna's.

"Jenna, I'm Dorsie. You've been visiting me in my dreams. Is there something you want to tell me?"

Jenna's soft little girl lips pursed as she nodded. "Uh-huh." Her arm reached for the German Shepherd as if she was seeking protection.

"Are you afraid?"

Jenna shook her head. "Not now. I was. Mommy was mad. We drove and drove all over the place. I was hungry. I was crying. Crying. I was hugging my doll," Jenna gave a loud sniff as if holding back tears. "Mommy yelled. ' Shut the fuck up. Just shut the fuck up!' She called Steve, her new boyfriend on her cell phone." Jenna stopped and shook her head then scrunched up her face in fierce look of distaste. "Steve didn't like me. He really liked Mommy. Not me. I was in the way. Steve only wanted to use Mommy for sex." Jenna looked at the magnificent German Shepherd for seconds then turned her gaze back towards Dorsie. "After Mommy talked with Steve, she was happy. She called Grandma over and over then got mad again. She wanted to drop me off at Grandma's work. Grandma said no. Grandma told Mommy to go home. To get dinner ready. She wasn't supposed to be out late because she had responsibilities – me. I was afraid and cried harder and harder. Mommy was hitting the steering wheel. She was yelling 'You'll pay this time. If you won't watch her tonight, you'll never see your little angel again. Never!' I was crying hard because I was real scared. When Mommy got out of the car she looked crazy. She went to the trunk then came back with a white washcloth and opened the back door. She wiped away my tears. Made me blow my nose hard in the white washcloth. Told me to close my mouth and breathe hard through my nose. I don't know what happened next. But when I woke up I *WAS* an angel!"

Jenna paused and reached out almost touching Dorsie's face. "Don't cry. I still love my Mommy because she made me an angel."

Dorsie wiped away the tears streaming down her cheeks. "Jenna, why did you visit me in my dreams?" Dorsie waited and waited for what seemed like eons for Jenna to answer. She saw Jenna's small body heave a deep sigh. Her little face assumed an expression of a wise man's look of deep sadness.

"Mommy lied to everyone about me. Mommy always lied. Lying is bad. Mommy had hate in her heart for Grandma. Hate makes you do bad things. I wasn't *supposed* to be an angel. When you're bad you get punished. I wanted you to know Mommy was bad." She gave the magnificent German Shepherd a pat. "He smelled me. But you already knew that."

"Jenna, I'm sorry. I'm sorry you became an angel so early. I tried . . ."

"Miz Dorsie. Your heart is good. I know what happened." She turned to look over her shoulder. From behind, Eric Van Zant came into view. He knelt down beside Jenna and put his arm around her. "Eric wants to tell you something," Jenna said. "Will you listen?"

Dorsie nodded.

"I'm healthy now," Eric Van Zant said with a broad smile. "I'm sorry. I'm sorry for the difficulties caused by my actions. I was wrong. You were right. If I had been healthy I would have worked with you towards a guilty verdict. I'm asking for your understanding. I'm asking for your forgiveness." He paused. "Thank you. Thank Harold, Rose and your family for embracing Crystal. I love her. Tell her. Never let her doubt that I loved her. The baby boy. His DNA has the Van Zant gene for high IQ but not the faulty one causing mental illness. Reassure Crystal." He paused and gave Dorsie a penetrating look. "My son will do many good things that will atone for my actions. You'll live long enough to see some come to fruition." He tightened his grasp on Jenna, pulled her toward him and placed a tender kiss on her cheek. "Jenna has forgiven me. Can you find it within you to forgive me? Please."

Dorsie had many, many questions she wanted to ask but before she could Jenna, Eric Van Zant and the German Shepherd stood and turned away. Together they walked back through the white, shimmering gossamer veil then disappeared from sight.

Forgive me. Please. Forgive me resonated as Dorsie became aware of the deep, baritone voice again.

"Now, it's time for you to leave the white light. You're floating through star fields into the Milky Way where you find our sun. You are sunlight travelling down to the earth plane to form a rainbow." The voice fell silent for a long stretch of time before returning again. "Step into the top color of the rainbow. Move downward through each color."

Now, she could easily hear the soft notes and altering rhythms of the classical guitar as she slowly moved from one color to the next.

"You are feeling your body getting heavier and heavier in the color red. Your spirit remains light. At peace. The knowledge you gained will be remembered. Whatever it may have been it is to be used to do good. Now, step out of the rainbow to a wakeful state. Three. Two. One. Awake."

Dorsie's eyelids fluttered open. She felt wet tears on her cheeks and reached for tissues to wipe them away. The CD played on for several minutes filling the room with the softest of softest tranquil notes.

Dorsie sat quietly assessing her reactions. She knew she had a certain degree of skepticism that had served her well throughout her life. But she also knew from her long, long years of using meditation that the very practice itself opened paths to deeper and profound knowing.

Spirituality was important to her and to her life. But not the kind found within the strict tenets and confines of the Christian faiths. She'd explored Judaism, Buddhism, Zen, Hindu and Tao's belief principles as well as the many spillovers into New Age thinking. Many, many hours had been spent in reading, comparing and thinking until she reached a conclusion, one only meant for her. The foundation building blocks of all religions were true for their time and the environs in which they were conceived.

Carl Sagan, Stephen Hawking, both anchored in science, and Joseph Campbell, scholar of ancient myths, contributed the formation of her spiritual worldview. For her, in the modern world, the doctrines and dogmas of organized religions were in conflict with the findings of modern astrophysics. Except for hydrogen, all the atoms that make up our human bodies came from thousands of light years away in space, billions and billions of years ago. Before life on earth, before time was known, before homo sapiens evolved into man with the intelligence to conceive and put forth the edicts found in organized religions. However, she respected those who had faith. And, she also believed in the recurring theme of forgiveness found in all religions and in universal mythic motifs.

But now, in the first few minutes of probing her reactions, she knew she would never voice or claim she'd been given *the truth* from the lips of those who'd passed over. She also questioned whether her deep-seated conviction that Tracy Maddox was guilty manifested itself into a story fantasy directed and produced by her own imagination. She sat in stillness knowing she would examine and ponder where *EL ARCOIRIS* had taken her for the rest of her life. Had she stood at the doorstep of the invisible plane?

Right now, in the seat of her soul, she believed she had. There was a palpable sacredness to her journey into *EL ARCOIRIS*. It was her private journey, It was a gift. A healing gift perhaps created from her need. Or a gift from the unfathomable, inexhaustible love in all gods – Jesus, Buddha, Yehovah, Brahman, Allah, Jehovah, Elohim, Huwa, Confucius, Yin and Yang and on and on. Whichever it was, it was her gift, unique only to her, to keep or not keep; to share or not share; to believe or not believe.

Chapter Twenty-Nine

Going Home

The Judge surprised Dorsie with his latest taking-care-of-trip details by parking a brand new white Honda Odyssey in the driveway. "Ole Gal, we're going in style," he said. He walked around the van opening doors then motioned for her to take the passenger seat then proceeded to point out all the features on the van's dashboard. He turned sideways in his seat to face Dorsie. "More important than all these bells and whistles is that this Honda is one of the safest mini vans. And . . ." he said raising a finger in the air to make an important point. "Excellent reliability. The other van was getting iffy. So, now, we're good to go."

"I can't believe you did this! You never said a word," Dorsie exclaimed.

"Wanted it to be a surprise," Judge said. "Really, we're good to go now. JB is now officially a puppy raiser so all's taken care of with Rudy. Start wrapping things up here, Ole Gal."

Three days later on the first of March they left The Villages. While travelling a stretch of U.S 301 N, the first leg of the routes towards Savannah, Dorsie did a quick check of all her important lists to make sure nothing was forgotten or overlooked. "Don't worry, Ole Gal," Judge advised. "JB will take care of what we didn't. Settle in. Enjoy the ride. Did you make a list of topics we should talk about?" he teased.

"As a matter of fact I did," Dorsie retorted. "It's called *Dorsie's Questions*. There are 200 of them. Now, that should keep us from getting road boredom. I'll ask one. You answer then I'll tell you my answer." She paused then touched the Judge's arm lightly. "My way of letting you know I'm not taking a laissez-faire approach to this relationship you're proposing." She made a show of flipping through her bulging organizer, found a page then then randomly pointed to an item.

"Ummm, interesting," she mused while reading. "First question. When did you last sing to yourself? To someone else?"

Judge gave her a startled glance. "You want me to sing? Sing to you? Lord, thank you for Sirius Satellite Radio. But to answer the question truthfully I sing in the shower. I've got a question for you. Did you read *Broken Trust* yet?"

"I did. Right after I used *EL ARCOIRIS* for its intended purpose. Not ready to talk about it yet. But we've got hours and hours to fill. It'll be amazing if you're not sick of my quirky *Dorsie's Questions* by the time we hit the New Jersey border."

He reached over and patted her knee. "Not a chance, Ole Gal. Not a chance."

The trip went as planned. Judge used maps then compared his routes with GPS directions. In Savannah they waited patiently in line to experience the fare at Paula Deen's, The Lady and Sons. They howled at each other in laughter with their first instructions on how to navigate the Biltmore grounds on Segways. They reached Dave and Megs's place in good spirits, had many pictures on their cell phones to show and interesting little stories to tell of their stops to enjoy the views while navigating up the Blue Ridge Parkway. Thor wrestled Dave to the ground and covered him with happy, sloppy licks. Megs just beamed and beamed at her mother because she was so happy to see her mother happy.

During the three-day visit, Dorsie found an opportunity to talk with her daughter privately. In a no nonsense, matter-of-fact way she told Megs about the night in Tribeca. She told her how Eric Van Zant had bullied the jury, how he had grabbed her arm during deliberations and on verdict day how he had shoved her against a wall making it seem like an accident. She may have checked Not Guilty on verdict forms, but that had not been her true intent. That long ago night in Tribeca and Van Zant's shove had set off a trigger, releasing fear, rendering her almost helpless during the final hour of deliberations.

Megs gathered her mother in her arms and silently wept trying to imagine the emotional chaos her mother had gone through after that night in Tribeca. She gazed at her mother and lovingly ran her fingertips over every feature of her mother's face. "We love you, Mom. We all knew *something* must have happened," Megs said. "We know how you think. How you break things down then put the pieces together. We know how adamant and stubborn you can be when you feel you're right. It all just didn't make sense how you could say not guilty. But now, after what you've told me . . ."

"I know. But now you *do* have the full explanation," Dorsie said. She brushed some of Megs unruly hair away from her eyes just as she had when Megs was little. "I have a request I hope you'll honor." She locked her gaze on Megs. "What I told you about the night in Tribeca. That's between you and me. As women. Please don't tell that part to Dave or to your brother. Just say I got mugged. Harold knows the full story. But there's no need for Dave, Brandon as well as Rick to have the ugly details. I don't need to see shock or sadness in their eyes just like the sadness that's in your eyes now. I don't want them to look at me differently, even at my age."

"I won't," Megs said. "Cross my heart and hope to die." Her hand made the universal sign over her heart just like it did when she made promises when she was a little girl.

Two days later, Dave and Megs begged Dorsie and Judge to stay longer but they insisted they needed to continue on. Dorsie's cell rang just as she was about to climb into the van. She glanced at the incoming caller ID – Carapelli, G. For a moment she was disoriented then realized it must be Gino Jr. "Gino, how are you doing?" she said. "Everything ok with Sofia?"

"She's coping. We're coping. Listen, Vince told me you're on your way back to Jersey. As executor I'm carrying out my father's final wishes. It's all complicated how my father did things. Bringing his affairs in order is keeping the family attorneys' and me pretty busy. Anyway, my father made some last minute changes in his will the weeks before he died and one of them concerns you."

"Oh. Is it about Thor? You know about the dog, don't you?"

"Yah. Nothing to do with the dog. It's about the house you were staying at. The deed has always been in my dad's name, not Marilyn's or Vince's. There's a couple of properties down there. Vince just handles the rental end of it." Gino paused. "The house on Duncan Drive goes to you. The attorneys will take care of all the legal work associated with it. You can either come into the city to sign or all the docs can be sent FedEx. Whatever. There'll be no hassle on your part other than signing your name. There's also a house account handled by J.B. Bowser. It'll be transferred over to you. It'll take care of the taxes for quite some time."

"Gino . . . I can't take . . . what about you? What about Sofia and the others?"

"No problem. Mom told me she knew why he wanted you to have the house. Just like she knew why one of the other properties was going to JB. But she wasn't sharing. Told me it was a very, very private matter."

"I'm stunned. I don't know what to say."

"Dorsie, you're always going to be part of the family. Nothing's changed. I intend to take care of all of us just like my father did. You can count on me for anything. So when you get to Jersey, let me know how you want to handle all of this. Mom would like to see you again. Maybe we can all get together for dinner in the City or come out to Westchester and spend some time with Mom. I know she'd like that."

"I'll call. Tell Sofia I've been thinking about her. Thank you Gino. Also thank you for getting Crystal Yates into the right legal hands."

After ending the call Dorsie turned to Megs, Dave and Judge. "The most extraordinary thing has happened. The house I was staying in Florida. Uncle Gino left it to me in his will." Flustered, she ran her hand over her forehead. "I need to sit down. Have a stiff drink. Gawd! Thor was a shock. I would have never imagined this!"

Later than expected Judge, Dorsie and Thor continued on their drive north backtracking to Asheville to get on the Blue Ridge Parkway again then continue on up Skyline Drive. Onward they went on their long drive north. *Dorsie's Questions* became an inside joke to them and at any time one of them would call out "I've-got-a-question." Sometimes neither felt the need to fill long stretches of silence while Judge concentrated on driving and Dorsie gazed out the window at the passing view. If they were tired, they stopped to stretch their legs and exercise Thor. If something caught their attention or interest, they stopped. They winged it for accommodations in Annapolis. They had dinner in two grand homes of colleagues of the Judge. During both visits not one sentence in the conversations contained the name Maddox. After Annapolis, Judge made the decision to stop in Washington D.C. and take their chances of finding a hotel since it was the first day of the 2012 Centennial of the Gift of Trees. Luck and a last minute cancellation landed them in a luxury room for four days at the Mandarin Oriental on SW Maryland Avenue. After producing Thor's K-9 and service dog credentials, no one on staff raised an eyebrow as Thor went about with Dorsie and Judge. On the days they left Thor in the room, they posted a sign on the door – Dog Inside. Stay Out. Upon their return they would find a plastic bag with a chew bone for Thor lying in front of the door. They never figured out who had left them there.

On the third day of their stay, they commandeered a bench near the Capitol Reflecting Pool to take a break from festival activities, crowds and constant walking. They pulled bottles of water from the backpack the Judge wore and gave Thor a much-needed drink of water. They sipped their water and sat quietly enjoying the view before them.

Dorsie turned to Judge. "I've enjoyed every minute of this," she said. She patted his knee. "I know I've been silent on *EL ARCOIRIS* and my thoughts on *Broken Trust*. All I will tell you about *EL ARCOIRIS* is my conviction in Guilty forever stands firm. In many ways it was a healing experience. That's all I'll ever say about it. Now, as to *Broken Trust* by Gregg Ashcroft, I learned things I didn't know even though I'd been through all the material Rick had the HLN researchers assemble. My Google obsession was pretty comprehensive and there were things in Ashcroft's book that weren't anywhere on the Internet." She took a pause, took a deep breath while gathering her thoughts. "What has stuck in my mind the most is exactly what you told me. Greg Ashcroft cared. He fought. He did his best. But just as you said, through many years of being a trial lawyer, he'd learned the dangers of taking on a mantle of guilt. I placed the mantle of guilt on myself. Ashcroft has regrets. The verdict won't haunt him but Jenna Maddox, the victim, will be locked in his memory. Like many, like me, he believes the wrong decision was made. Even though he served up politically correct statements regarding the jury, his dislike of us, the jury, crept in here and there. And that includes me."

Long seconds passed filled with silence. She took the Judge's hand in hers. "But he's like you. He believes in the law. In our justice system in spite of how the Maddox trial exposed flaws that exist in it. I liked what he said at the end, that justice isn't always decided in the courtroom. I'm going to keep that in the forefront of my mind if I find myself slipping backwards towards . . ."

She squeezed the Judge's hand. "We're done with talking about the Maddox trial. But I will say this. More or less my final thoughts. Eric Van Zant was a force in that jury room, an unstable, frightening one. On that final day his physical actions put me in his grasp by setting off the emotion of fear in me. It's not an excuse but a statement of fact." Again she paused, organizing her thoughts. "It's hard to make guesses about the future. If you believe in Karma, Karma will impose it's punishment upon Tracy Maddox. Somewhere along the line Karma will place a task before me to complete which will be directly related to my actions as a juror. But on a less metaphysical level. A more down to earth one. I think I'd be safe in saying Tracy Maddox's future will be complex because she's complex. Where she goes. Whenever or wherever she surfaces she'll always be fodder for tabloid trash. A horrendous way of having your life on display. That's my point of view. What goes on in the mind of a pathological liar, member of the cult of self-gratification or borderline psychopath, I don't know. And now, I don't want to know."

Dorsie sat quietly afterwards recalling her recent conversation with Sofia Carapelli. Sofia had gone to lengths to reassure her she was in accord with Gino's wishes regarding the house in Florida. Why he did it just weeks before he died, Sofia explained to Dorsie a little known fact about her husband. In spite of a tough and sometimes uncaring exterior, beneath it laid a very tender, sensual romantic. In his process of saying goodbyes to JB he'd learned about Dorsie and Judge. He was happy and had hope for Dorsie. Sofia further confided that Gino always believed the night in Tribeca had kept Dorsie from letting any open, trustworthy relationship break through the wall she'd built to protect herself. She told Dorsie Gino had never liked hearing from anyone about Dorsie's casual flings and how Gino always wanted Dorsie to find someone to trust and love. So he decided Dorsie would have a reason to go to Florida often. He made a last minute change to his will. The house, not far from the Judge's, would pass to her.

Again, Dorsie turned to Judge and took his hand in hers. "So much has happened since we met. I've told you things I've never told anyone else, with maybe the exception of Harold and some not even to him. Given to you a level of trust that I haven't given to many. For me, I find that amazing. So out of character for me."

The Judge squeezed her hand. "You're not going to go down the Soul Mate route are you?" he asked his voice full of dramatic, yet teasing, displeasure.

"No. I was thinking about my conversation with Sofia Carapelli. I always admired her for her grace in a marriage that must have had many trials and tribulations. Marveled at the unbreakable bond she and Gino had. You and I, we don't have the luxury of decades to be together. But we do have our health. Our passions." She brushed her fingertips across his cheek. "Our good looks are intact. We're the young old, not limping yet. We can make a stab at living life to the hilt just because it *is* life. We can either be feisty or serene. I think I'm safe in saying we have no impossible expectations of each other. We should at least try to see where being together takes us. Because it feels like the right thing to do."

Judge put his arm across Dorsie's shoulders and pulled her close.

"My turn for a question. Snowbird or Frog?"

"Undecided."

Judge burst into laughter. "Hell, after that speech I'd thought you'd made a decision."

Chapter Thirty

Home

On March 27th Dorsie stepped into her house on Ward Road ending her self-imposed exile. She took deep, deep breaths and gave Thor his Search command because she never wanted to get lax and turn Thor into a pet. He was too well trained and noble for that to happen. As Thor went about his sniff, sniff routine, she was surprised the house smelled fresh, clean, aired out with no trace staleness of a house closed and unlived in for six months. She opened the garage door for Judge then turned to view her kitchen. It was Spic and Span clean with Windexed windows letting in bright sunlight. She stood at the sink gazing out the window at her dormant garden and saw small, small signs that it was about to spring to life again. A deep sense of peace flooded through her. She was home. She turned away from the window then noticed a white envelope propped up against the coffee maker and opened it. Inside was a photo card with a field of bright, happy yellow sunflowers. Inside was a simple handwritten message – *Welcome home Señora. All is clean. All is right. – Maria Sanchez.*

The Judge tromped through the garage door with the cooler from the van. He opened the fridge expecting it to be empty. "Whoa, look at this."

Dorsie looked over his shoulder. The fridge was completely restocked. More than fifteen meat market packages with the logo Alpine Deli sat on the middle shelf with a white envelope lying on top of them. Inside, on butcher block paper, three simple words were scrawled in heavy, black magic marker. *Welcome home. Olga.* Dorsie brushed her hand across her cheek recalling Olga's hard slap then smiled.

After half unpacking the van and a tour of the house, Dorsie and Judge sat in the kitchen, relaxing and being fortified by strong cups of coffee. Bang. Bang. Bang. Thor raced to the door leading to the back deck and barked his ferocious bark. "Corral that brute!" yelled Vince Di Paolo from the other side. Dorsie gave Thor the stop command and opened the door. "Bout time you decided to come home," Vince Di Paolo exclaimed. His wife, Marilyn, stood beside him. "We brought ya Marilyn's famous lasagna." He held up two bottles of Johnnie Walker Black. "I brought these." He glanced over her shoulder while his face took on a glaring scowl. "So, that there's The Honorable Judge Joseph Kelly you've been . . ." He stopped talking as his wife's elbow came in contact with his ribs. He maneuvered past Dorsie and Thor and stood before Judge giving him a once over then stuck out his hand for a handshake. "Vince Di Paolo. Just how honorable were you?"

"Joseph Kelly. Friends call me Judge. Others call me The Judge" he said matching Vince Di Paolo's macho handgrip.

"Hello . . . Hello. Dorsie's home!" sounded from the opened garage door. Rose entered the kitchen, followed by a very pregnant Crystal Yates then Harold. Judge gave Harold an acceptable manly hug and kissed Rose on the cheek. He turned his attention to Crystal. "Good to see you, too." He linked his arm through Crystal's. "Come. Sit down. It's my understanding your baby's due at any time." Crystal nodded her head then took a seat in the family room, propping her feet up on a hassock Dorsie pulled over for her.

A shout came from the garage door over Thor's loud barks. "Dorsie Renninger, are you here? If you are, come and call off the dog."

Dorsie left the family room and gave Thor his stop command. Detective Eugene Farino started to offer her an official handshake then opted for a quick hug. "Glad to see you back in town." He held her at arm's length. "Some issues we were able to resolve. Those still open . . ." He gave a shrug then said, ". . . may never be resolved because there were no viable leads. I've got hunches but they're not solid enough to open inquiries. But I'm not giving up."

"I understand," said Dorsie. She took him by the arm and led him into the family room.

Farino took the drink offered to him by Vince Di Paolo then glanced around the room. "Ahh. No Brandon. No Dave Broz. But still . . ." He lifted his glass in the air. "A good Welcome Home party."

Three hours later, after every bite of Marilyn's lasagna was consumed and everyone was sitting around drinking coffee, the whoop, whoop of a police cruiser sounded from outside. Dorsie opened the garage door. Bud Eckley stood at the end of the driveway. "Welcome back."

"Come have some coffee," Dorsie said.

"Can't. On duty. The regulars at the diner are anxious to meet the new man you're sportin' on your arm." He gave Dorsie a wave, climbed into the cruiser and whooped, whooped the siren all the way down Ward Road.

Back in the family room, Dorsie found Marilyn and Rose hovering over Crystal with concern. In all the excitement of catching up on town happenings, gossip and listening to Dorsie and the Judge's little travel stories no one, except Thor, took notice that Crystal began to look more uncomfortable. Every time she went to the bathroom he waited at the door. If she sat, he sat. If she walked to the kitchen for a glass of water, he was at her side. When she stopped and hunched over, he raced to Rose and pawed at her lap, whined. When she placated him with a pat on the head he let out ear piercing barks and raced to the kitchen to sit in front of Crystal."

But now, Rose glanced over to Dorsie standing in the doorway of the family room. "We're going to have a baby very, very soon," she said beaming from ear to ear. "Harold, call Crystal's OB. Speed dial 3 on my cell." She turned back to Crystal and in an assuring labor coach voice said, "Breathe deep, honey. Just like we practiced. In . . . Out . . ."

Eugene Farino jumped to his feet. "I'll take you to the hospital. Flashing lights and all. Just tell me where."

"Pocono Medical Center," Rose said. She helped Crystal to her feet. "We just need to stop at the house for Crystal's bag. We have time."

With that, Farino and Harold got Crystal settled in Farino's SUV. Rose climbed in and sat next to her, murmuring reassurance to the new about-to-be-mother. The back window slid down and Rose yelled to everyone standing in Dorsie's driveway. "I'll call with updates."

Ten hours later, at 7:05 a.m. on March 28th, baby boy Van Zant came into the world.

A week after Crystal settled in with Baby Boy back in her own cozy renovated cottage, she phoned Rick in NY to ask for his help. She wanted a celebration. A Naming Day. Could she please have it at the loft in NY? Rick needed nothing more and swung into action, tapping into his network of resources. Invitations went out from a list drawn up by Crystal.

He went on a spree, hiring a photographer, party decorator, florist, caterer with bartender and wait staff, chose a menu, wrote a script for Crystal. He was so excited he couldn't contain himself. He scoured the city with Jezza, the HLN wardrobe specialist, until he found the "right" outfit for Baby Boy Van Zant. He had three dresses sent to Crystal for her to choose from to wear on the day she'd announce her baby's name.

In the following days and weeks, Dorsie, Harold, Judge, Brandon, Megs, Dave and half the town of Blairstown had a hard time understanding why Crystal hadn't settled on a name for Baby Boy. So they waited. Judge and Dorsie left Blairstown for a few days to go and visit the Judge's family. While there, Melanie, his daughter-in-law approached Dorsie asking if she might ask her some questions about the Maddox trial. Melanie's request set off no alarms in her body and even though she'd told Judge she wouldn't speak about the trial anymore, she gave grave consideration to all Judge had done for her so she agreed to talk with Melanie. For over two hours she answered all of Melanie's questions in a matter-of-fact manner only saying that Eric Van Zant had frightened her terribly after purposely and forcefully shoving her, knocking her to the ground then threatening her quietly before deputies rushed to her assistance.

"Fear is the most paralyzing of emotions," Melanie said. "How awful it must have been for you. Would you ever want to serve on a jury again?"

"I want to say no," Dorsie said. "But I believe our justice system needs people like me on juries for all the reasons I've explained. Even though I failed to bring consensus to the Maddox jury. That doesn't mean I wouldn't be able to do it with another group of people. So, I'd have to truthfully say, yes, I'd serve again."

Back in Blairstown, Dorsie was welcomed back in the "regulars" crowd at the Blairstown Diner. She and Judge assumed Dorsie's habit of having breakfast there at least four times a week. The most dominating topic of discussion, other than politics, centered on Crystal and why was she waiting so long to give Baby Boy a name. A betting pool sprung up as to whether the baby's last name would be Yates or Van Zant.

On April 24th over twenty people gathered at Brandon and Rick's loft in Tribeca. Present were Crystal's attorney as well as the attorneys from the old law firm in New Canaan. Crystal was radiant showing no signs of sleep loss that came with having an infant to care for single handedly.

Harold, Rose and Dorsie beamed as if they were grandparents. Bobby Yates, Crystal's brother had cleaned himself up nicely for the day, shedding his laid-back college student scruffiness. At two p.m. Rick called for silence and for all to form a circle around Crystal.

"Thank you all for coming," Crystal said, holding Baby Boy in her arms. "I know many of you have been patiently waiting for me to give this little guy an official name. I've always known what his name would be. I just wanted it to be announced in a special and celebratory way." She paused then sought out Rick with Brandon standing next to him. "Brandon and Rick, please stand beside me." They flanked her. Her gaze travelled over the faces in the room. "I name Brandon Raines and Rick Cardona supporting adults to be guides, teachers, friends and someone who will be there for this little guy if anything should happen to me before he reaches the age of twenty-one." She paused. "I've chosen the age twenty-one because he'll have to take on many heavy responsibilities tied to the family Van Zant trusts. He'll need someone other than attorneys to guide him and advise him. For this reason, I assign legal guardianship to Brandon Raines and Rick Cardona in the event anything should happen to me."

Crystal paused again and sought out Dorsie and Harold. "Harold, Dorsie, please join us here." Seconds later she continued. "I'm so grateful to both of you. You've embraced me as part of your family when I desperately needed caring and loving people around me." She looked out into the faces again. "This includes you Rose. Please come and join us." Baby Boy let out a whimper and squirmed in his mother's arms and she automatically swayed back and forth, like all mothers do when soothing a babe in arms. "Now, that you're all beside me and here with me, I, Crystal Marie Yates, name . . ." She handed Baby Boy to Harold. "Name him E. Raines Van Zant. E. for Eric, his father." The loft was filled with reverent silence as they watched as tears welled up in Crystal's eyes. The diamond ring on her left hand caught the light in the room and emitted a sparkle as she wiped her tears away. Crystal cleared her throat. "Raines for Harold Raines. Raines for Dorsie Raines Renninger."

Dorsie glanced up at her twin brother's face. Tears ran down his cheeks as he gazed down at the small bundle in his arms. He held him for long, long minutes before handing him over to his older, by minutes, twin sister, Dorsie Raines Renninger.

Applause and good wishes erupted from all gathered at the loft for the naming of E. Raines Van Zant. Later, Dorsie sat off by herself with Raines cuddled in her arms. She held his little hand in hers and opened his little fist to examine each of his tiny, delicate fingers She then studied his palm as if she were a palm reader deciphering the future in the tiny, tiny lines just barely visible in the pinkness of precious infant flesh. She studied Raines' facial features intently and found his father in his pale coloring and the downy tuff of blond, almost white hair on his head. His nose, now just a small adorable button, she imagined forming into a more Nordic feature one carried in Van Zant's DNA not the larger noses found in Crystal's Slavic genes. She stared at the innocent she was holding in her arms and marveled at the miracle of birth and life itself. She smiled, hearing E. Raines Van Zant's father's voice echoing in her mind – *"He will be very bright. No mental illness. Do good things."* She smiled then bent down and placed a tender kiss on the baby's forehead. "Raines. You will do good things in your lifetime. Your father told me so."

Epilogue

No human can predict the future. No one present on Naming Day in 2012 could have foreseen Crystal Yates losing a battle with ovarian cancer before Raines' seventh birthday. Or that Brandon and Rick would be called upon to fulfill the responsibilities Crystal bestowed upon them on that day of celebration. No one would have imagined Harold Raines outliving his dearly beloved Rose. Or that Dorsie Raines Renninger would only have Judge, Thor and her beloved cats by her side for less than twelve years. No crystal ball would reveal how Harold, Dorsie, Brandon, Rick, Dave and Megs would follow Raines' accelerated path to graduation from high school at fifteen and acceptance into Princeton University at sixteen.

Raines Van Zant was well aware of all the career paths available to individuals with extremely high intelligence. Early on, his mother, Dorsie Harold, Brandon, Rick and Judge left no stone unturned to find and place him in schools with programs to challenge his mind. As a child he spent many summers with Dave and Megs. There at the K-9 training kennels he learned to use his body by helping maintain the kennels, exercising the dogs and participating in the daily regimen necessary to turn a German Shepherd into a certified K-9. Dave Broz instilled in him the need for balance of mind and body by taking him hiking, camping, fishing and introducing him to martial arts. Imprinted in his maturing psyche were his visits to the NICU with Megan Broz. There he saw first-hand how fragile life can be and how helpless infants needed people like Megs to will life into them through intensive medical intervention and gentle, healing touch. During other summers, at college universities with programs for gifted youths, he interacted with others poised on the path to make serious contributions to society in physics, technological fields, mathematics, medicine and music. But he had no internal driving force pushing him towards any specific discipline. He was interested in everything.

Before entering Princeton, he returned to his old home in Blairstown with Brandon and Rick at his side. His mother's renovated cottage was finally going to be placed on the market even though Brandon, Rick and trust attorneys advised him he had the financial means to maintain ownership. He told them "no" because there was too much of his mother there and he wouldn't keep her memory alive in a house full of things. He told them he had her forever in his heart and he didn't need anything further.

Still spry at seventy-nine, Harold and Dorsie were there to meet Raines, Brandon and Rick with their sleeves rolled up ready to work, ready to prep the cottage for showing and to help Raines sort through personal items all according to Dorsie's lists. Rick was assigned to closets. Raines and Brandon were responsible for the attic.

Left alone in the attic Raines discovered a box containing an old scrapbook full of coverage clippings of a trial – the State of New Jersey vs Tracy Ann Maddox. There he discovered his father's and Dorsie's names in news clippings and Internet print-out pages reporting the aftermath of the trial as well as news, Internet and Blog clips with the reporting of his father's death in Las Vegas. Also included were articles by legal experts analyzing and debating the jury selection system in all courts in the United States. Along with Greg Ashcroft's book, *Broken Trust*, he found other books authored by expert psychiatrists on the Maddox family's dysfunctional dynamics. Other experts opined and outlined multiple factors that placed Tracy Maddox in the categories of social psychopath and narcissistic personality disorder. He gathered up everything and marked the box RAINES TAKE HOME.

Later in the evening, while they were relaxing in the family room at Harold's, he brought out the scrapbook and asked Dorsie to tell him everything she could remember about the trial. So once again, and for a final time, Dorsie Raines Renninger talked about her experience of being Juror 1389 in the trial of Tracy Ann Maddox and all the events that happened afterwards. She omitted nothing. She told Raines of the private investigator's report she had in her possession. Gently and carefully, she explained the nature of bi-polar disorder and how it had affected his father during jury sequestration.

Days later, back at the loft in Tribeca, Raines used his considerable intellectual talents to do in-depth research on bi-polar disorder. He used the NY Library system and CUNY's Law Library retrieving everything available on the trial. Dorsie had kept all the material Rick's HLN research staff had organized for her in a fireproof box which he now had in his possession. He viewed CDs, DVDs, retrieved material from thumb drives, read and re-read *Broken Trust* and the other books on Tracy Maddox. Afterwards, he thought long and hard for days then came to a decision. After Princeton he would seek acceptance into Yale Law School and become a criminal attorney.

Once again, no human can foretell the future. But history has shown throughout all of time, human behavior repeats itself over and over and over again. Humans, in every era continue to commit infidelity, suffer from mental disorders, cheat, steal, lie, harm, attack, and murder. No one could have predicted that five short years after receiving his degree and passing the Bar in Connecticut and New York, E. Raines Van Zant would be part of a prosecution team assigned a case for a crime that shocked New Canaan, Connecticut to its core. And that it would grab the attention of national and international news media and go viral on social media. Once again an attractive young mother, from an affluent, good family, was charged with the homicide of her young daughter. She did not report her adorable two-year-old toddler missing for weeks then gave a litany of lies as to where her child was. Law enforcement and many good, honest people went on a futile search for her missing child who was already dead. Months and months later the toddler's skeletal remains were uncovered by a bulldozer operator clearing property for the expansion of a town playground.

No one could foresee a decision made by the State's Attorney to replace the lead counsel, who suffered a fatal heart attack during trial preparation, with E. Raines Van Zant. Experienced legal commentators were stunned. Controversy raged throughout traditional media outlets as well as on social media. How would a young untested attorney fare against a seasoned defense attorney known for his pit bull style? The irony of the prosecution's attorney's name, Raines Van Zant, was not lost on a new generation of media anchors and reporters after uncovering the names of Raines and Van Zant as vilified jurors in the Tracy Maddox case. They resurrected the saga of Tracy Ann Maddox's pre and post-trial years along with the sensationalized reporting of her unsolved homicide in Brazil. There, it was reported, she'd scammed a quasi-older lover who was part of the country's society's elite class. Over and over again available photos of Eric Van Zant were placed next to E. Raines Van Zant's. Endless comparisons were made between both trials. Once again through widespread media attention the entire country developed an insatiable fascination with every detail of both cases.

Raines Van Zant ignored it all. He dug in and prepared the State's case using his brilliant mind. However, he never let the prosecution team forget how iffy juries could be and constantly placed random Post-It-Notes in his distinctive handwriting on trial prep work documents. Each and every one read – *Juries Are a Crapshoot*.

The trial lasted eight weeks with cable channels and network news programs covering it extensively. Brandon, Rick, Megs and Dave were in court to hear Raines's expertly crafted closing argument delivered with somber grace. Headlines read *Pit Bull Antics vs Quiet Reason*. Brandon, Rick, Megs and Dave accompanied him to the courthouse when the call came that a verdict had been reached. Guilty. Guilty. Guilty. Guilty. The jury found the defendant Guilty on all charges.

Outside the Fairfield County Courthouse media from across the U.S and Europe waited. Later, when Raines Van Zant and the prosecuting team walked through the courthouse doors, the media thrust microphones in front of him while cameras rolled. He positioned his co-counsel in the area designated for a press statement then stood behind her. With the focus on her he inched his way into those gathered behind then left before the news media realized he was gone. He walked to the first police cruiser he saw parked at the curb in front of the courthouse, produced his Court ID and asked to be driven to the Franciscan Monastery not far from the courthouse.

There he was welcomed by Brother Thomas who escorted him to the monastery's small chapel He sat alone not moving for a long twenty minutes. Suddenly, his sobs filled the silent chapel with the grief he'd held at bay for three months during the exhaustive hard push before the scheduled trial date. During that intense time Harold and Dorsie had died within weeks of each other. He'd forced his disciplined mind to shunt aside his emotions and stay on task – preparing for the trial. Now, his thoughts lingered on Dorsie whom he adored since his earliest memories. Never once had he ever heard her utter a single unkind word against his father; and she, along with his mother, formed his pride in the name

Van Zant, a name respected in many philanthropic echelons. He sat there alone, flooded with relief, flooded with immense sadness and over-whelmed with emotions he was unable to define in words. Long ago his father had intimidated a jury into a grossly wrong verdict forevermore placing the trial in the annuals of *Infamous Trials throughout the Decades*.

Now, he, E. Raines Van Zant, had just won a conviction for the same crime of maternal filicide committed by another beautiful, young mother. He'd been a part of a larger vehicle that *had* delivered perfect justice. The law, his extraordinary abilities and the jury had been synchronized. To-day, this jury had reached the right verdict. He leaned forward and buried his face in his hands. His shoulders shook from the deep emotions finding their way to release.

Minutes later he got up from the pew and stood before the simple al-tar. In his own way he said a prayer for his mother who always told him to stand tall and be proud when his name was called. He offered a prayer of gratitude for *his* family – Harold, Dorsie, Brandon and Rick. They'd set a course for him that had prepared him for the responsibilities of being heir to old-moneyed Van Zant trusts and foundations. Raines was another name he was proud to bear. He put his hand on his heart and brought up in his mind the faces of Harold and Dorsie. "Forever here," he whispered in the silence of the chapel. He stood for a long, long time before the altar as if in a trance lost in another time, in the details of another trial.

A long time passed before he knelt on one knee then rose again and walked down the aisle of the simple chapel. Before leaving, he turned to look up at the small window above the altar and became mesmerized by all the colors of the rainbow infused into the stained glass. His gaze trav-eled from red to orange to yellow, green, blue, indigo and violet. Pure grace flooded though him. Humbled, he turned away and closed the heavy chapel door. Outside he straightened his shoulders and walked away knowing that he, in his father's stead, had atoned for an imperfect justice that happened a long time ago to a sweet, innocent, little girl named Jenna Maddox.

Acknowledgements

My hand is over my heart for my *1389* project team. My first reader, Bonnie Aitoro, was with me every step of the way. To Karen Ilaria, Jude Corbin and Patti Maury, thank you for your insights on what a reader wants from a story. A sigh and groan, along with sincere thanks, to Carolyn "," Pandelaky Hawks. You made sure I adhered to comma rules. Neva Kanteman read with an editor's mindset. Your comments quelled my doubts. To William T. Loppnow, I give a big smile for your willingness to do an author photo shoot. Harry Ilaria, without you putting the Kindle bug in my ear, I wouldn't have pursued Indie Author route.

There are those who don't know they helped with *Juror 1389*. I thank you here – Ron Landbeck, puppy raiser, Southeastern Guide Dogs. The visit to the Southeastern Campus left an ever-lasting impression. Jack N. Shorr, O.D., Mid-Florida Eye, your care plan helped to push *Juror 1389* over the finish line. Without it, I wouldn't have been able to spend extended hours focusing on a laptop screen. To a chance meeting with a stranger – Dora Ricca, who gave a thumbs-up or thumbs-down on what looked good.

And, lastly, *Juror 1389* owes its listing in *Books in Print* to my son. He initiated CPR on a dying dream. Thank you, J-Bird. You threw down the challenge. Challenge met – published novel by G.T. Trickle.

www.gttrickle.com

51297933R00142

Made in the USA
Charleston, SC
20 January 2016